with Best wishes

Tracy Elner

Blue E

Copyright © Tracy Elner 2008
US Library of Congress 2011
ISBN 978-1-84914-429-2
First Edition 2013
Published by CompletelyNovel.com

Joint Winner of the OBBL Book Awards 2014.

https://www.youtube.com - Tracy Elner Blue Eye

Feb 17th 2015

Dear Javier

Happy Birthday!

For Graham: 'Dream the myth on.'

'When the right man has the wrong means, the wrong
means work in the right way.'
The Secret of the Golden Flower: 8th century Taoist
canon of meditation.

`

'Science may set limits to knowledge, but should not set
limits to imagination.'
Bertrand Russell: British philosopher, mathematician &
author.

Now you have the 'hard' copy!

A Worldshift Genre

Tracy

iii

Prologue

Winter 1991: Irkutsk, Siberia. Five time zones east of Moscow.

Dawn had already broken the vast skyline over the Angara River as the ageing academic emerged into the raw chill. Shivering, he checked his watch with the station's clock. It was 8:35.

Good, I'm on schedule, he confirmed as he wrestled his greatcoat collar against a flurry of snow, the bizarre phone conversation of earlier that morning still firm in his mind.

'9 o'clock. And be punctual.'

'But that's in two hours. Is it urgent?'

'We have important visitors. They've asked for you.'

'Really? Who are they?'

'Officials from Moscow. I've been told nothing.'

'Are you sure it's me they want to speak with?'

'Please, Ivan Yegorovich, just be there on time.'

His Director's instruction had been direct but cryptic.

Why the secrecy, though? He quickened his pace across the glassy pathway. *Could it be related to the deaths?* Two of his team had drowned during a fishing excursion, only days before. *Just a tragic accident,* he reminded himself as his focus quickly switched to the icy steps that led up to a building he rarely visited.

'*Zdravstvuitie,* Ivan Yegorovich!' The young receptionist greeted him.

'*Zdravstvuitie,*' he replied, passing her his coat, thankful for the room's warmth.

'And your *ushanka?*' She smiled shyly.

'Ah, yes!' Embarrassed by his absentmindedness, he removed the traditional rabbit-fur hat as his wife's distant reprimand rang back. *Sable is far too extravagant!* She preferred spending the little remaining from his monthly salary on luxury food or some popular English language novels for their teenage granddaughter.

'*Chai?*' The girl offered tea.

'Yes, please. Are the guests here?'

She nodded, coyly and turned away to fill a cup from the ornate samovar.

He reached into his jacket for a comb. 'Do you know who they are?' he probed, running its metal teeth through his tousled hair and slicking down the stray strands with his other hand.

'No,' she uttered blankly.

Has she been instructed to keep quiet?

He held her gaze for a second longer than comfortable then took the steaming drink and stepped away across the stained terrazzo floor, wrestling with the scant information.

These officials probably just want to discuss the funding, he speculated, stopping outside the Director's office to sit and sip the sweet tea while straining at the muffled voices coming from inside. Cuts were inevitable, a result of the command economy's recent collapse but he felt bolstered in the knowledge that he still had a full programme of research to complete, authorised from the very top. *And if there had been any serious changes to that, I would have been summoned to Moscow.*

Shortly, the Director's drawn face appeared and the academic politely stood.

'Ivan Yegorovich! Sorry for the wait. We will not be long now,' he announced with a cursory smile before swinging his gaze to the girl.

'Irina, please bring in more tea!'

The solid oak door slammed shut.

He seems tense. A pang of doubt surfaced again. Ivan Yegorovich had been ordered to omit certain crucial details from his reports. *But he can't possibly be aware of that.* His worry, though, evaporated with the girl's loud expletive. Tray-laden, she was struggling against the inertia of the huge door causing him to smile uneasily at the metaphor – the need to diminish the individual for the sake of the State.

For Ivan Yegorovich Isotov, the State had been his life. Growing up in poverty in another country or regime, he might have become a desperate individual, but not in the Soviet Union. It had fed and educated him and excelling in his studies at the polytechnic had earned him a place at *Akademgorodok* – its centre of excellence – among its finest minds.

His eyes shone, glancing up at a faded portrait of the once glorious leader, still hanging against the flaking walls, and reliving the collective sacrifices made to ensure that Russia's fledging nuclear programme would change the course of history forever. But then the liver spot on his brow creased, prompted by discordant memories – the incredible phenomena he had stumbled across had caused instant alienation from his peers and interrogation by his masters in Moscow. Then, there followed humiliation at having to publicly refute his claims, stating that he had made fundamental errors in his observations. It ultimately led to his *relocation* – exile by another term – to an unknown institute. There was little consideration for his wife's senior position in local government or his children's elite schooling. All those privileges had been lost along with his hope of developing a technology that could have given his Soviet Union, peaceful superiority in the world.

Was it all worth it? His pride rose momentarily: *Russia could become great, once again.* But then his head dipped and he stared vacantly at the floor. *Unlikely; too much has changed.*

'We're ready for you now!' A sharp call snapped him back to the moment.

He rose and automatically dusted off his shoulders before striding the few steps to grasp the Director's outstretched hand.

3

'How are you, Alexander Vladislavovich?' he asked politely but the cold, moist palm provided the answer.

'Come in, please. These gentlemen from the Ministry wish to discuss some things with you.'

What Ministry? I don't report to any Ministry!

The receptionist quietly slipped out past them, masking her unease as he was invited to sit. There were no handshakes.

'Ivan Yegorovich, do you know why we are here?' the sour-faced stranger asked.

'Not at all,' he replied, smoothing out a striped polyester tie while clocking the obnoxious casualness of the man's gum-chewing colleague.

Kretin! These new apparatchiki lack any respect for my generation.

'We want to discuss your research work with you,' the visitor continued, fingering his collar away from a roll of fat.

'I see. What aspects, if I may ask?'

'All of it.'

'All of it?'

'Yes, you are instructed to halt it.'

'On whose authority?'

'The funding is to be stopped.'

'But the programme is scheduled to run for another two years,' he said, registering a cruel harshness in the man's bulging eyes. 'I'll need to have clearance from my superiors before there can be a cessation of my research.'

'That is not necessary. This is the only instruction you will need!' He tossed a letter across the desk.

Isotov smouldered, eying him for a fraction before picking it up and noting the ministerial stamps that confirmed its legitimacy. Reading it slowly, it became clear that his former chain of command had been usurped.

Stunned, he lingered a stare at his Director in a desperate bid for support – to buy more time – but it was met with impotence.

'So you see, Ivan Yegorovich, your programme is to be closed with immediate effect.'

'That's impossible! The technology is still undergoing important tests.'

'It will be decommissioned and removed.'

'On whose authority?'

'Mine! From today you will report to me.'

'And *Sphinx*...the Institute?'

'It will continue with its other lines of research.'

'So there's still funding for that?'

'That's the responsibility of another ministry. Just make sure that you comply then you can retire quietly with your pension.'

'What!' He flung down the letter and stood up. 'That's it? My entire life's work finished because of some bogus instructions.'

Flushed, the stranger glared back, unfamiliar with defiance.

'Then I have nothing further to discuss with you!' He turned and stormed out of the room.

'Ivan Yegorovich!' the crumpled Director called out, fearful that his fate had been sealed by the scientist's rash behaviour. But Isotov was already across the lobby and snatching his things from the startled young woman.

How could they have found out about the machine? He shook with suppressed rage. *It's classified to the highest echelons within the Kremlin. These Neanderthals couldn't possibly have had access to that!*

Outside, brilliant sunlight had pierced the veil of low cloud, transforming tiny snowflakes into a shimmering mist that hung in the air around him, stinging his cheeks. Oblivious, he looked about to see if he had been followed into the station. It was impossible to tell from the ubiquitous crowd milling about the platform, stamping its feet in a discordant cacophony to keep warm. Within minutes, though, he was sucked into the wake of huddled bodies, surging to meet the train's arrival and escape from the frigid conditions.

The regular sway of the carriage and its oppressive heat only seemed to intensify a looming sense of desperation. A pensioner, sitting opposite, attempted a smile as she juggled several small jars of pickled cabbage on her lap but her young grandson was scrutinising Isotov with an expression that seemed to comprehend his plight.

The academic looked away, out into the dense pine canopy, squinting against the sun's strobing rays. Then a crushing revelation descended upon him. *That's inconceivable!* Yet he understood it was the only possible explanation. A caricature of his own terror stared back at him from the window's reflection. *There hadn't been any accident.* His hapless colleagues had been murdered.

Strategic assets of the State's military-industrial complex were being blithely expropriated by a new breed of *biznismen*, greedy for untold wealth.

Those bastards will exploit my technology and then discover its real function. He shuddered convulsively. *I pray that they haven't got to Lubimov yet.*

The boy's eyes met his again as he considered the possible options. A small window of time now remained in which to reach *Sphinx* and his close friend. Together they could destroy their crucial files before disappearing, perhaps to the West.

The journey dragged but as the train slowed, Isotov was already leaping from the opened carriage door onto the platform.

A dirt-splashed Lada screeched into the station's car park and jumped to the head of the taxi rank. Honked horns of disapproval soon stopped as a shaven head emerged into the biting wind and its bulky owner held out a palm to the approaching academic.

What the..? Isotov's heart raced, instantly recognising the intent behind the jaundiced face. His earlier refusal to step down gracefully had meant that he too faced a fate similar to his friends. *Their deaths must not be for nothing.* He resolved, sinking his posture in feigned submission and fingering the Nagant M1895 pistol in his pocket.

A single gunshot sounded and fleetingly, Isotov believed he was simply a witness to the act. But as the crowd's screams rushed violently into his ears and the wounded man staggered towards him, he let out a suspended gasp and ran.

His legs tired in the snow, slowing his escape and then a piercing pain shattered his shoulder. He slumped down, panting and watching the red polka dots of his blood diffuse into the thick snow.

It can't end like this. A kaleidoscope of images ran before his eyes then, in a show of defiance he turned his trembling pistol back towards the injured man. But another shot had already rung out.

His friend, Lubimov, would now have to face the thugs alone.

One

Sunday 19th June, 2005 - Fourteen years later. Almaty airport, Kazakhstan.

Flickering strip lights irritated Scott Carty's tired eyes as the mild stench of lamb's fat confirmed his arrival in a totally foreign land. Lena, though, was fresh and alert, even at that early hour.

'Can I have your passport please, Scott?' she asked, pushing him into the semi-formed queue.

'Why?' he asked nervously, catching her glancing down at the briefcase for just a fraction longer than she should have.

I wonder if she knows what's in it.

'I need your details to complete this declaration form.' She flashed the piece of paper in his face.

'Ah yes, of course.' He fingered his passport before reluctantly handing it to her. 'How long will all this take?'

'Not long,' she said. 'Now, what money are you carrying with you?'

He did a double take, frowning back at her.

'It's one of the questions you need to answer.' She drew close, her expensive perfume filling his nostrils. 'How much foreign currency do you have? It doesn't need to be exact.'

'About £1,000, some of it in travellers cheques.'

'Travellers cheques!' she repeated, coyly tilting her head as she noted down the amount. 'Please sign here and make sure it's stamped by the customs official.'

Shortly, an official ushered her over to a customs booth, and Carty tracked her lithe figure as she purposefully approached the desk. He then scanned the other booths, noticing that they were mainly populated with women officials wearing expressions of drudgery, masked only by shades of bright makeup that clashed with their drab uniforms.

One of them beckoned him forward.

'Passport!' she ordered, automatically glancing up into the angled mirror above his head – a remnant from the Soviet days, to check what he had at his feet. His grip on the case's handle was sweaty and he self-consciously looked elsewhere, avoiding eye contact. But the woman unashamedly stared through him, holding the passport up several times, to compare its photograph with his features and then enter data into a screen. It took an uncomfortable few minutes before she stamped his visa and apathetically waved him through.

Ahead of him, Lena had already picked up her hand luggage from the scanner, so he hurriedly placed the case and suit carrier through, only to notice a copper-faced official gesturing at him to step out of the line. He had been singled out for a pat-down and was momentarily distracted, but as he turned to retrieve his things he found another uniformed man fiddling with the locks to the case. A shot of adrenalin spiked his system.

'Hey, what are you doing!' he instinctively yelled, surging forward. The official shot out an arm, stopping him in his tracks.

'*Shto eta?*' The colleague barked, locking stares with the Englishman and holding up a zipped document wallet from the case.

'Scott!' Lena shouted, trotting back as fast as her sling backs would allow, 'he's asking what it contains.'

'Confidential contracts,' Carty uttered, his body language now defiant.

She translated in a calm, soft voice and apparently satisfied, the man crudely tossed it back down. Carty moved in to retrieve the case but the Kazakh angrily grunted something else.

Lena grabbed at Carty's forearm. 'He wants to know what's in the other envelopes.'

What other envelopes?

Perspiration now beaded conspicuously over his brow as two bulky manila packages were placed in front of him.

'The same, I think,' he bluffed, turning his palms skyward, 'documents.'

Lena translated but unconvinced, the man tore one of them open with a force that spilled its contents across the desk.

'*Shto eta?*' he bellowed again, slowly shaking his head at the greenbacks now sprawled between them.

'Scott, why...?'

Carty turned to her, his face now frozen with panic. 'I haven't got a clue, Lena. Just get me out of this mess!'

'How can I?' Her voice faltered as the two grizzled guards, barely contained by their uniforms, parted to allow another official through.

'*Documenti!*' the new man demanded coldly, delighted at the fear registering in Lena's eyes as the customs officials obeyed. Tall and wiry with a sharp Slavic bone structure and shorn blonde hair, he sneered as he scanned the Englishman's passport.

'*Meester* Carty?'

'Yes.'

'Please go with my men.'

The guards moved in on Carty.

'Where are you taking me?' he asked, trying to resist, but a sharp push sent him stumbling forwards, his knee taking the impact.

'Shit head!' he screamed.

Lena mimed a protest but Blondie's raised hand blanked her.

'Scott, just go along with them!' she urged, as they hauled him back up. He turned to snatch a glimpse of her sapphire eyes and for an ephemeral moment it seemed that this was all just a dream. But then reality snapped back as he felt his wrists being locked in the guard's tight grip.

They quickly marched him away, towards a battered door on the far side of the concourse.

Inside, Carty gazed around the grimy walls of the airless room. Its atmosphere yelled of fatigue and the terror of countless interrogations.

Why has D'albo deliberately lied to me?

A retching sensation forced him to bend forwards, cupping his trembling hands over his closed lids, attempting to rationalise what had made him bring the case in the first place.

It all began with that dream, he acknowledged, poring over the very odd sequence of events in that past week that had led him up to this moment.

Two

Six days earlier.

Mark Boyd barged into the office, interrupting the team's strategy meeting.

'What do you think you're doing?' Carty barked.

'Come with me!' Boyd insisted, offering out a hand.

Inexplicably, he felt compelled to take it and was led out onto the trading floor, past desks of smirking traders.

Boyd stopped at the floor-to-ceiling windows, overlooking the Thames.

'Scott, do you know what's out there?'

'No? What?'

Boyd didn't answer but simply turned and walked straight through the plate glass as if it were liquid.

'Mark!' Carty called out, incredulous, as the background transformed into a vast pine forest. But the man had gone and in his place stood a golden-haired maiden, the outline of her figure prominent as the sun streamed through her diaphanous dress.

'Follow me; your life depends on it!' she said, smiling before turning away into the foliage.

Carty jolted awake. He was on the Underground, several stops from his destination with the dream's images still playing across his mind's eye as if wanting to reinforce a message.

They continued to do so for the rest of the journey but quickly evaporated as soon he strode onto Albion's huge trading floor, past young men screaming orders between the numerous screens scaffolded around their desks. The place seemed to hold an odd gravity of its own, an irresistible maelstrom of chaos and seething greed that somehow swamped any individual's integrity. Ordinarily, he had revelled in this sphere, but today he paused outside the glazed compound he called his office, breathing in the stale air and staring at the frenzied kaleidoscope of flashing phone lights.

Is this where I really belong? he wondered, for the briefest of moments.

'Morning, Scott!' Davina greeted him. She was tending to her peace lilies and orchids in an attempt to maintain some aspect of femininity in this place.

'Morning, Davina!' he said, ignoring the grunts from some of the team, still glued to their screens.

'D'albo's already called three times. He wants the strategy paper.'

'Yes, I know. Would you do me a favour?'

'What?'

'If he calls again, don't disturb me.'

She rolled her eyes.

He sat and logged on to his PC, opening a file document to review the draft paper.

Cashing-in on Carbon: Emission-linked options.
Dr Scott.T.Carty – Head of Derivatives.
Albion Gas, Light and Power Plc.
June 2005.

This is the pinnacle of everything I've been working on for all these years, he mentally gloated remembering how he had stumbled into the world of commodities at a business conference ten years before. Intrigued by the impressive lines of the key note speaker, Mr Arthur D'albo, Carty introduced himself during the coffee break and immediately felt an uncommon resonance with the older man who inveigled him. Carty's analytical abilities were the *must-have* skill-set in a brave new world of investment products, soaking up huge sums of cheap cash generated by a booming global economy.

Discarding his former ambitions to move into research, he took up D'albo's offer: a seat among Brightwell Carter's team of *quants* – quantitative analysts, an eclectic group of maths whizz-kids – with a brief to develop new and exotic derivatives products. He settled in quickly and was soon exceeding expectations.

But it was all too good to last. By 2000, Brightwell Carter had collapsed due to irregular trading activities and Carty was a casualty without a job. He consulted for a number of months before D'albo called him with the position at Albion. He accepted it unequivocally. A naive reverence for his former mentor and an unquenchable thirst to be back in the markets, overrode a gut instinct to reconsider the offer.

Now, five years on, Carty had a new team and a fresh calling – the carbon market. The Kyoto Protocol had been recently ratified by the United Nations as a result of Russia's signing-up and thereby pushing the critical number of qualifying member States over the line.

Politicians and environmentalists saw it as a catalyst for genuine CO_2 reductions, but the trading world understood it meant something far less utopian. A gold rush ensued as financial institutions and privately managed wealth-funds stumbled over each other in a frenzied melee to secure the Third World's emissions credits: African landfill sites, Chinese coal-mine methane and Indian fluorocarbon plants were just a few of the *low-hanging fruit* in a fledgling market that had not been tested.

Carty's exuberance, though, had positioned himself one step ahead of the game. Having already gambled on Kyoto being a done deal, he had not wasted time and money on sourcing projects. What the market really needed was the forward price security his carbon derivative products would provide.

Smiling, he rechecked the projections then printed off a copy.

Profiting from saving the planet. D'albo's going to love it! The thought raced as he leapt up the stairs two at a time. Suddenly, he slipped, crashing onto his knee. The searing pain suspended a sharp in-breath for an instant before his unrestrained yelp echoed down the stairwell. There he sat, doubled-up, massaging the joint in muted anger at his clumsiness.

After some minutes he finally pulled himself up and limped into the executive reception.

'Mr D'albo is on a conference call overseas. I'll let you know when he's finished!' Cynthia, the executive PA, announced unsympathetically. She had few friends in the company.

Carty slid onto a chair and hid behind *The Financial Times*, staring vacantly through the pages, still out of sorts.

'Mr D'albo will see you now,' the woman uttered perfunctorily after a short while, but he was deaf to her. The dream's recurrent imagery had loomed again as an all-consuming daydream.

'Mr D'albo is ready. You can go in now!' Her raised voice shook him and he stood to shuffle past an array of sports trophies and framed photographs littering a lacquered walnut cabinet. D'albo was in all of them, tanned and smiling with an arm around his wife and sons, or shaking hands with mandarins of the business world and the odd rock star. A Rhodes Scholar, he was a surrogate Englishman, able to tap influence on both sides of the pond.

'Ah, Scott! What's up with the leg? Are you getting old?' D'albo jibed, flicking his lank, silver hair back from an unconventional centre-parting.

'No, Arthur, it's just an old war wound that I've aggravated again.'

'Well, just remember one thing. Only the fittest survive at Albion.'

Carty flinched as he stared back into the unusual green eyes. The comment was out of context and smacked of insincerity. The man registered it.

'Close the door and sit down!' he instructed, walking around his desk and using his tall physique to subtly threaten. 'You've been ignoring my calls this morning.'

Carty looked self-conscious. 'I had a lot on my plate.'

'Have you finished the paper?'

'Yes. Here's the final draft.'

'Good, so no more amendments?'

'That's right.'

'And does it differ greatly from the copy you left with Cynthia recently?' He fanned the document across his lips.

'No. Just the figures.'

'The figures, eh?'

'Yes. I've erred on the conservative side.'

'I see,' D'albo screwed up his face in an expression of mock pain, 'and you think the Committee will rubber stamp the trading of emissions derivatives?'

'I don't see why not. The projections are promising.'

'That's a bit too vague, don't you think?'

'Why?'

'I don't think *promising* is going to cut it in this market.'

The impact of the comment was immediate and Carty's posture sank. 'Shouldn't we at least let the Committee review the paper first before dismissing it out of turn?'

'No, Scott,' he rebuffed. 'It's not going to happen!'

'But I've spent more than six months testing the sector. It's ripe for the taking, Art, and the quants...they've been modelling like crazy!'

'Tough!' D'albo was irritated. 'Things are changing around here. We want *vanilla* products that will sell in volume and, besides, I've decided that you need help in disciplining those *anoraks* of yours!' D'albo considered the quants a necessary evil, grossly overpaid and ill-disciplined. Carty knew otherwise. His team was essential to maintaining Albion's edge.

'What kind of help?'

'Scott,' D'albo uttered in a mock filial tone. 'You've always been the innovator at Albion but recently, you seem to have dropped the ball.'

'I'm not sure I understand what you mean, Arthur?'

'Well, let me spell it out for you. You've lost focus on the short-term returns that pay our bonuses.' D'albo paused, almost unable to hide a cruel grin. 'So I've asked Mark Boyd to join the team.'

'Boyd?' Carty stammered in near shock. 'But he's out of the business.'

'That doesn't mean he's lost his edge.'

'I can't believe this!' Carty's pitch moved up a gear in defiance. 'You're going to let Mark Boyd into my department. You do remember what he did, don't you?'

'Of course I do.' He eyed Carty coolly, in a brief moment of self-doubt.

Carty flushed. 'I don't think the FSA would agree with your decision to employ a criminal, Arthur.'

D'albo flourished his large palms. 'Don't worry. He won't be let loose on the trading desk or be allowed to speak to clients. The FSA won't permit it, but it's useful to have a poacher-turned-gamekeeper on the team to spot the tricks others may be tempted to play.'

'Are you implying that my team isn't loyal to me?'

'Never underestimate anybody, Scott.'

'Not even Mark Boyd?'

D'albo shrugged at the comment. 'Now, if that's all?' He picked up a phone's receiver, indicating the end of the conversation.

'Then I guess you've made up your mind?' Carty stood, pressing the man but was waved away.

Disguising his fuming annoyance, he turned to make his way out, trying to ignore the shooting pain in his knee.

'Oh, I almost forgot!' D'albo called after him.

'Yes?' Carty stopped in mid-stride, hopeful.

'I'm having lunch with the Russians today. I need you there, and wear a tie. That casual dress-down approach you're promoting is sloppy!' He shook his head, reinforcing his disapproval.

Carty nodded and wheeled around, a mix of fury and helplessness churned inside him. Something strange was happening in his world, something he had no control over.

'Scott's the man who's spearheaded the energy derivatives business at Albion.' D'albo grinned at the two young Russians facing him across the lunch table as a young woman seamlessly translated his words. One of the foreigners smiled reservedly and casually shook out a cuff-linked sleeve to ruffle his Tintin flicked fringe, a subterfuge to snatch a glance at his oversized watch. He then looked sideways to his partner, an overdressed man whose bulldozed crop and sullen, pock-marked face belonged in a very different world. D'albo clocked their body language and continued.

'Without him we wouldn't be the market leader that we are,' he bragged, turning to Carty who was awkwardly nodding in feigned solidarity, only to find himself the object of the woman's absent gaze. *She's cute,* he thought, taken by the picture of her sky-blue mascara at odds with her golden hair. She skittishly looked away.

'Scott, there's a power and energy conference in Almaty at the weekend,' D'albo added.

'Almaty?'

'Yes, in Kazakhstan,' he stated loudly. 'Our friends, here, from CentralniySib are co-hosting. It will be an ideal platform for one of your presentations.'

'Really? On what?' Carty uttered, confused by the suggestion.

'How about the emissions derivatives you've been working on for so long!'

The sarcasm bit. *What the hell is he playing at?*

He looked across at the expectant faces. 'I think that can be managed, Arthur, but perhaps we should invite our guests to an in-house presentation instead.'

'Nonsense! This is an opportunity to demonstrate Albion's market presence to a much wider audience.'

'In Kazakhstan?'

'Why not?' he said as he stood to briefly excuse himself.

Carty attempted to make small talk with the Russian men, but found them already absorbed in a closed conversation, allowing him a moment to analyse the bizarre motive behind this lunch. He understood that the relationship with CentralniySib Energo, a gargantuan energy producer controlling assets throughout Siberia had become too important for Albion to lose.

But these two men couldn't possibly be its decision makers, he surmised, *so why's D'albo playing to them?*

He knew his mentor too well: the man always had an agenda.

Emerging from his thoughts, he glimpsed a hint of a smile creasing the corners of the translator's glossed lips as she purposefully twirled the ends of a braided ponytail, draped theatrically over her breasts. She too had been excluded from her colleagues' conversation.

'Have you ever been to Russia?' she asked quietly.

He was momentarily taken off guard by her warm tone. It was unlike the typical high-pitched Moscow accents he had heard before and it softened her corporate persona. He downed a glass of wine, his third.

'No, no, I haven't,' he responded. 'I'm sorry. We weren't properly introduced. I'm Scott Carty.' He passed her a business card.

'I know.' She broke into a grin revealing a slight gap between her front teeth which for Carty, threw up fond memories of Beatrice Dalle's in the 80s French art-house film, *Betty Blue.*

She pulled her own card from an haute couture handbag and handed it to him. His smile slipped as he struggled with the Cyrillic writing.

'Turn it over,' she said.

He did, noting it was in English.

'Ah! Elena Isotova – Energy Markets Analyst,' he mouthed. 'So you're not a translator?'

'Not really, and you may call me Lena. It's easier.' Her rolled pronunciation charmed him. 'It will be my pleasure to escort you at the conference as my famous guest.'

'Thanks!' he said, flushing a little.

'I have already organised a letter of invitation to assist with your visa application. If you need any assistance, please do call me.'

'That's kind of you,' he said, camouflaging his confusion.

How on earth could she have known about the conference? D'albo has only just suggested it.

D'albo had already ambled back to the table, having concluded a highly visible conversation with a business group across the restaurant.

'Shall we go, Scott?' He smiled hollowly. A veiled instruction, his question cut across the men's conversation.

Carty nodded. He shook hands with the reluctant Russians then turned to take hers. 'Well, Lena, I suppose we will see each other at the conference?'

Her tapered eyebrows arched. 'I hope so,' she uttered.

'You impressed them,' D'albo conveyed as they paced back to the office.

'I'm not so sure, Arthur. Those two Russians seemed indifferent to anything you were suggesting.'

'Don't worry about them. It's the big picture you should be focusing on. CentralniySib's board is seeking an IPO listing on the London Stock market later this year.'

'Yes, I did hear rumblings about that.'

'We need to make sure that Albion is involved in wrapping up some of the risk. There will be big fees to be made from it and it's why I suggested the conference presentation, to help smooth the relationship.'

'I understand, Art, but why didn't you tell me that before the lunch.'

'Because I only heard about it myself this morning.'

A lump hit Carty's stomach. Lena told him that her invitation letter had already been arranged, possibly days before.

If she knew about it, then he must have known too.

'Are you still struggling with that leg?' D'albo switched subjects. 'You better have it checked over before you leave, to be on the safe side!' His concern seemed genuine.

'I'd rather talk about Mark Boyd.'

'You're not still smarting, are you?'

'No. I just can't see your reasoning,' Carty edged. 'For God's sake, Art, Boyd committed fraud and there's no escaping that fact. If it leaks into the market that he's back, it will undermine my credibility and damage Albion's reputation.' He broke off momentarily, to consider his next statement. 'If that happens, I will have to rethink my position.'

D'albo's eyes narrowed. 'Don't threaten me, Scott. I'm trying to give you some space to grow, and Mark needs a second chance. You can't begrudge him that, surely?'

Carty shrugged. 'When does he start?'

'Tomorrow.'

'And the bad news is that the Executive Committee hasn't decided on the strategy paper yet,' Carty casually announced in the afternoon team meeting. It was received with an audible groan.

'But the good news is that I am going to present the thrust of it at a conference in Kazakhstan at the weekend. Davina, we should be receiving a letter of invitation from CentralniySib.'

'Here it is,' she interjected, handing him a fax page. 'It arrived yesterday evening after we had closed.'

Strange! He scanned its contents, suspiciously.

'Tell me, have you ever sent my passport details to CentralniySib before?'

'No.'

'So how did they end up in this letter?'

'No idea but I guess it was Cynthia,' she fired back.

'So they must have been sent last week then?'

'Yes, probably,' she shrugged. 'Do you want me to check with her?'

'No.'

Why is D'albo lying and why is this damn conference so important to him?

He closed the meeting, having avoided any mention of Boyd's imminent arrival.

Sitting back at his desk, he then Googled Kazakhstan. Bordering China in the east and the steppe of Russia to the north, it was the biggest of the Central Asian *Stans* and the ninth largest country in the world, formed by the break-up of the Soviet Union in the early 1990s. The information, though, didn't do much to excite him about the trip and he ventured out onto the trading floor to mix it up with the dealers and AEs – the account executives. Business was particularly active and an almost forgotten surge of adrenalin pulsed, urging him to take an empty seat. Picking up calls and giving quotes were rare for him nowadays but this was the *coal face* where his derivatives were traded, and he still loved it.

Sergei, one of CentralniySib's executives, called in from its rep-office in the British Virgin Islands, the Caribbean tax haven. Carty struggled with the Russian's heavy accent for some minutes as he was quizzed on the sentiments driving crude oil prices. Then the Russian blurted out an instruction.

'Close out all of the WTI *calls* for July!'

'What was that?' Carty was taken aback and hastily pulled up CentralniySib's positions on screen, noting that most of its July WTI crude oil *calls*, options to buy, were profitable.

Carty's trading instincts were pricked. *Crude prices are rising. He should wait until these options expire in a few weeks' time, he'll make more profit.*

'Okay, Sergei, so you want to close out all of your July calls at the current market, correct?' he reconfirmed. It was a habit of old, leaving the client no chance to contest the instruction at a later date, even though all conversations were taped.

There was no reply.

'Hello...Sergei? Are you still there?'

'Who am I speaking to?' The Russian asked coldly.

'Scott Carty.'

A silence yawned.

'Does the instruction still stand?' Carty pressed.

'No,' the Russian hesitated. 'No, I am cancelling that order!' He abruptly hung up.

Did I piss him off? Carty had encountered difficult clients before but never one who had pulled such a big order without reason. A worry churned. Upsetting D'albo's main client now, before the trip, was not good timing.

The desk was chaotic and Carty had one of the dealers call the Russian back.

'Sergei's left for the day!' The response was shouted back minutes later.

'What? He's only just hung up on me!'

'He probably mistook you for Watts...Duncan Watts,' the AE smirked. 'Sergei only ever leaves orders with him.'

'And just where is Watts today?'

'Dunno, but you're sitting at his desk!'

From the muffled obscenities, Carty clearly understood that Watts was not liked.

Who is he anyway? Carty had never heard of him and ordinarily wouldn't care, but now he was questioning who was handling one of Albion's biggest clients.

Rechecking CentralniySib's book positions again, he was struck by the large number that had been closed out the past few days. *That's interesting.* He decided that he would speak with one of the trading directors to arrange for Watts to be questioned as soon as he returned.

He sauntered back into his office and picked up his jacket, noting an unfamiliar document sitting on his desk with a yellow Post-It stuck to it on which Davina had written a question.

Scott, where should I file this?

He skimmed through its several pages, confused by the Russian text, but he caught the footnote she had highlighted. It was a reference to an English publication.

xii. Spent Nuclear Reactor Waste; Strategic disposal scenarios in Europe.

What's it doing here? He wondered. Albion had no nuclear power stations or waste processing facilities in its portfolio, especially not in Russia.

Puzzled, he tossed it into his out-tray.

Davina caught his eye. 'Is everything all right, Scott?'

'No, not really.' He winked in mock resignation. 'I'm probably going to need surgery on my knee sometime soon, D'albo's insisting I give a presentation in some god-forsaken place and Mark Boyd is about to ruin my career all over again!'

'Who's Mark Boyd?' she frowned.

'Ah, yes, sorry. I forgot to mention it earlier. He's an ex-colleague whom D'albo has seen fit to land us with.'

'I see. And when are we going to meet him?'

'Tomorrow. I'll see you then.' He was about to walk away but a sudden thought stalled him.

'By the way, Davina.'

'Yes?'

'Duncan Watts. Do you know who he is?'

'No, I don't. Is he a friend of Mark Boyd's?' she grinned.

He chuckled quietly as he strode out.

A niggling anxiety bothered him the whole journey home as he acted out in his head various scenarios of how Mark Boyd might ruin his empire once again.

Wandering into the study, he poured a cognac and slumped down next to the fire. It was now late and unusually chilly for the time of year and tossing a log into the flames, he marvelled as they flared in sympathy with the lightning of an approaching storm.

'What's wrong?' Diane said, habitually kissing his cheek.

He smiled back. 'Nothing, particularly.'

'Are you sure?' She gathered back her bobbed, dark hair with both hands to reveal tell-tale stress lines across her otherwise youthful complexion.

'It's the end of James' school term next week and I thought we could go away for a few days.'

'Where to?'

'Dorset?'

'That's a long drive and I'm not sure I can get the time off,' he said, coldly.

'Why not? You've been working too hard lately. Arthur can at least give you a few days holiday. You are allowed one, you know!'

Carty lowered his head. 'We have a new guy joining the team and Arthur's insisting that I go to a conference at the weekend.'

'Where?'

'Kazakhstan. I only just found out today.'

'Really? We can't go on like this, Scott. It has to change. There's always something more important. It's as if James and I are just appendages to your career.'

He was silent, taken by her odd stare.

James ran into the darkened room in his pyjamas, altering the dynamic as he jumped onto Carty's knees.

'Goodnight Daddy!'

'G'night, James!' He folded his arms around his young son and gently ruffled his sandy hair, touched by the honesty of childhood.

'Come on!' Diane said, still frustrated and pulling James' arm to lead him away to bed.

Carty watched her shapely form climb the stairs then poured another brandy. The need for alcohol had slowly crept back after a forced abstinence.

One or two won't do any harm though.

He emptied the glass in one gulp, stopping to stare through the bottom of the crystal tumbler, his calm disturbed by the feeling of a presence behind him.

'Diane, is that you?' he called out. There was no reply but he noticed that the front door was ajar. Tense with a mixture of fear and curiosity, he rose and moved to pull it open.

A small girl stood there in front of him, motionless, her eyes shining with a beatific innocence that he could not ignore.

'Why are you here?' he asked, in disbelief.

Silently, she leant out a freezing hand and took his.

Outside, a damp mist now hung along the line of the house, smothering the entrance to a set of stone steps which dropped away before them.

'Strange, these don't exist!' he said, half-expecting her response, but her grip only grew tighter. It was clear where she was taking him and, reluctantly, he felt an overwhelming urge to protect her as they descended into a dank cellar.

The girl then looked up at him briefly before moving on alone, through an arched vault. His eyes adjusting to the scant light, he watched her slowly dissolve away into the blackness.

'What now?' he asked himself, fearful of something he could not quite fathom.

Then, seconds later, her silhouette suddenly reappeared, back-lit by the reflection from a candle's flame against the aged brickwork.

'None of this makes any sense!' he uttered, shaking his head.

'Does everything have to make sense?' a deep voice resonated back.

Carty staggered back onto the steps, his shocked gasp condensing around him in the freezing air. From out of the darkness, a hooded figure had emerged and was now looming towards him.

The tumbler shattered on the hearth.

'Shit! Another damn dream,' he muttered, shaken and attempting to dismiss the vision as the irksome beep of an SMS text drew his attention away. It was Sally, a marketing executive he had been seeing casually for more than a year. Lust had kept him chasing her, arrogantly convinced that she was just a play thing he could drop at any time. Disorientated, he dialled her.

'Hi, it's me. Where are you?' He attempted a whisper.

Her tipsy voice was drowned out by the background music of a club.

'Where are you?' he repeated but it was useless; she couldn't hear him.

'I'll call you tomorrow.' He said and hung up.

He dowsed the fire then wandered upstairs, catching sight of his wife slipping into the bedroom.

'Diane!' he called out, fearful that she might have overheard the call. 'I must have dozed off and the glass slipped out of my hand. I'll clear it up tomorrow,' he said, following her.

'Ah, that's what it was. I thought I heard you speaking to someone.'

'No, I was just cursing myself.'

She eyed him coldly for a second. 'Can you sleep in the attic room? I don't want to be disturbed when you leave in the morning.'

Unhappy with the suggestion, he raised his hands in acceptance and climbed the flight of stairs.

As he lay awake, milling over the day's strange events and the prospect of Mark Boyd entering his life once again, the hooded revenant's words resurfaced: *"Does everything have to make sense?"*

Three

The doctor's comments rumbled over and over in Carty's head as he made his way back to the office, mid-morning. The knee would require keyhole surgery to repair cartilage damage, sometime soon. The question was when? If he could avoid strenuous sport, he might get away with another three months, possibly six.

Don, one of his quants, met him in the corridor.

'D'albo's waiting for you and there's some guy called Boyd asking too many questions. Who is he?'

'Arthur's new boy.'

'Really!' A wry smile creased Don's lips. 'Do the others know?'

'No, keep it to yourself for the moment.'

'What's he here for?'

'Not sure yet, but let's just say Boyd and I have a past.'

'Scott, where the hell have you been?' D'albo yelled as he postured from the centre of the office. Behind him a bloated Mark Boyd grinned, hardly recognisable to Carty from memory.

'Here we go then!' Carty muttered to Don, forcing a smile as he stepped forward.

'Sorry I'm late, Arthur. I'm still struggling with my knee.'

D'albo shook his head. 'It's not good? Mark's been here for two hours already. And what about the conference presentation? Is it finished yet?'

'Almost,' he retorted nervously.

'Almost?' D'albo flushed. 'Mark, you may as well get started with the team. That should free up Scott a bit!'

Carty eyed Boyd as he reached out to shake his hand. The man reciprocated, feigning camaraderie. Davina shot a nervous glance at her boss, noting the tension between the men but not knowing the reasons why.

Carty's academic talent had led him to his current position but Boyd was a self-taught trader with a rudimentary understanding of Carty's complex derivatives. That, though, had not detracted from his uncanny nose for the markets, a God-given ability that had made him a small fortune and, until the fraud, a legend at Brightwell Carter.

'Okay, Mark, come into my office, would you?' Carty glared, slipping his hand from the clammy grip and ushering him in. He slammed the door shut behind them.

'Nice place you've got here, Scott. Looks as if D'albo's still carrying you.'

'I suggest you cut the sarcasm, Mark,' he said, struggling to slap down Boyd's arrogance.

He smirked. 'Your *anoraks* seem to like it.'

'Maybe, but they know where their loyalties lie.'

'To their pay cheques?' Boyd stabbed.

Davina entered without knocking, blanking the new man.

'Scott, the visa and tickets for Kazakhstan will be ready tomorrow and someone called Lena Isotova is holding for you. Do want to take her call?'

A thrill gripped him as he recalled the quirky gap-toothed smile of the woman he had briefly flirted with.

'Yes, put her through, please,' he answered. 'Sorry, Mark, our conversation will have to wait.'

Boyd shrugged, grinning slyly as he sidled out after Davina.

'Hi, Lena, how are you?'

'Mr Carty, I am very well.' Her accent sang, lifting his mood. 'Do you have your visa yet?'

'Apparently I do, thanks to you.'

'Good,' she hesitated, 'and do you have time to meet for lunch?'

'When?'

'Today.'

'Umm...I think so,' he replied coolly. 'Is there any urgency?'

'I would like to run over the details of the conference with you before I leave.'

What is there to run over? He pondered, intrigued by the hastiness in her voice.

He agreed a time and place and, hanging up the phone, reclined in his chair, quietly excited at the prospect of the impromptu meeting. His focus, though, was quickly drawn beyond the glass wall, to where Boyd was now soaping up the team, reminding him again of the dream.

It couldn't have any meaning? he mused, unable to completely shrug off the bizarre coincidence of Boyd's reappearance.

An intuition then galvanised him into action.

'Now everybody, I need to speak with you at the double!' he ordered. The team jumped up and filed in, some sniggering at Boyd's muttered shibboleths.

'Are you all here?' One by one, Carty nonchalantly scanned their faces as he perched on the corner of the desk, clearly still the master of his universe. 'Good, then you're probably wondering why Mark has joined us.'

They stared back expectantly.

'Well, as I said yesterday, it seems that the Executive Committee doesn't believe that our emissions derivatives are that important to its bottom line. Nevertheless, I'm going to present the reasons why they are at the conference, to get some real market feedback.' He smoothly fed the story, smiling to allay the unspoken doubts some still had. 'Arthur has suggested that I do a round of client visits over the next month or so, to boost our

31

product sales. Mark will be standing in for me while I am away so I'm asking for your full support in showing him the ropes.'

It was a shrewd move, laying the ground rules while indirectly disarming Boyd.

'Any questions?'

'Yes!' Don raised his hand, smirking. 'Is there any chance you can bring back a stick of rock from Kazakhstan?'

Hoots of laughter broke out.

'I'll try!' he bantered. 'Right, let's soft-launch the systems. Don, take Mark through the basics, would you? I don't want any screw-ups while I'm away.'

Lunch time found Carty nervously sipping a Bellini at the agreed venue, a small fusion restaurant in the City. He had been answering emails on his Blackberry while taking snatched glances at his reflection in the bar's long mirror to finger his hair.

It's thinning. He smiled uncomfortably to himself but beneath the blue eyes, the folds of skin seemed darker than ever. His good looks were fading and his waist, thickening. Late night runs across the heath were not going to cut it anymore, not with his knee playing up.

What the hell am I doing here, waiting for this woman? He asked himself, suddenly self-conscious that he was sitting alone, rapping his nails impatiently.

I hope she's not going to stand me up. She was almost 40 minutes late and he was about to call when he noticed several heads straining towards the entrance. And then she materialised, her taller than average balletic frame weaving between the tables in a black tailored jacket with red border stitching. All the while she maintained a soft focus on Carty causing a nervous excitement to stir, like a teenager expectant of his first kiss. He stumbled forward, off the stall, catching his image again in the mirror.

'Mr Carty, it's nice to see you again,' she announced through burnt-red painted lips. A beauty mole sat on her cheek, which he could not recall seeing there the day before.

'Scott. Please call me Scott.' He responded as she slipped her toned backside onto a bar stall.

'I'm sorry to have kept you waiting.'

'Don't mention it, although, if it's all right with you, we will have to eat at the bar. This is a popular place and they couldn't hold the table booking.'

'That's fine.'

'So, were you stuck translating for your bosses?' he asked, grinning, aware that he had the most of restaurant's male attention.

She frowned. 'No, I was late because I had a visit from the police.'

'The police?'

'Yes, my apartment was broken into last night.'

'I'm sorry to hear that.'

'They are suggesting that it was a mistake.'

'Why?'

'Because nothing was taken.'

'That does seem strange.'

'It is,' she said, 'and I want to forget about it a quickly as possible.'

He nodded and picked up the menu to order.

'So, Scott, how did you become the leader in your field?'

'Leader?' He blushed. 'I'm flattered, but, actually, I prefer to think of myself as an innovator developing new products with my team of quants.'

'Quants?'

'Quantitative analysts,' he said patronisingly, as he toyed with a drenched salad.

'Ah, and they analyse all the data?'

'Yes, something like that.' He scanned her milky, fresh complexion, guessing that she was probably in her late 20s. She was naturally beautiful yet her manner was parochial and somehow restricted by the regime she had grown up in, leaving him with a feeling of impatience for her.

'What about you, Lena, tell me about your background?'

She hesitated, staring straight back at him, uneasily picking at the tapas with her manicured fingers.

'I come from Irkutsk, a city in Eastern Siberia.'

'And your education?'

Her voice lowered. 'I graduated from the Institute with a diploma in power transmission engineering.'

'That's interesting. It's rare to meet a woman in that field.'

'What do you mean?' she said bluntly, her coyness evaporating.

'Sorry, I was being complimentary – I'm impressed.' He smiled openly back at her and she calmed.

'What's unusual is that I have the opportunity to discuss my background with a man who can appreciate it, intellectually.'

'Really? Why's that?'

'Men typically have other interests in me,' she murmured as her sapphire eyes scanned his left hand and the wedding ring.

'Can I ask about the subject of your presentation?'

He frowned, puzzled by her sudden switch in conversation. 'Yes, it deals with the trading of complex derivatives in the emissions and energy sectors.'

'And are you proposing that CentralniySib Energo should be trading these as well?'

'That's the idea. They're essential in managing revenue streams and will be useful if CentralniySib plans to become an international energy player.'

'I see, and will the presentation include anything about nuclear power?'

Why is she asking that? The question resonated uncomfortably with him.

'No, not at all, why should it?'

'No reason. Could I see a copy of it before the conference?'

'Yes, that shouldn't be a problem,' he said, masking irritation at her manner. 'I'll send you a draft before I leave. Now, why don't you tell me more about the speakers and the delegates?'

She began toying with the ends of her plait while explaining that experts in the Kazakh power sector and a mixture of Russian and European energy companies would be attending.

Then, she leant forward and deftly moved her hand toward his face. Surprised, he instinctively pulled away, his pulse racing as his eyes locked onto hers.

'This has been annoying me all through lunch,' she said as she innocuously snatched a piece of cotton from his lapel and held it up momentarily before casting it adrift. 'And this suit's colour matches your eyes. Did your wife choose it for you?'

'I can't remember.' He shrugged nervously.

'Are you from London?'

'Yes, from North London.' The words instantly transferred him back to the middle-class semi in Finchley. 1930s built and pebble-dashed with a small square-dug bed in the front garden full of overgrown rose bushes and a shared tarmac driveway leading to prefab garages. It was a sad home to a lonely boy and his mother, an unloved wife. Occasionally, in vacant moments, he wished he could change it for the better.

'And I read that you studied Physics at Cambridge.'

'That's right, a PhD, I'm afraid.'

A quizzical look raced across her face. She hadn't understood.

'A doctor of philosophy,' he confirmed.

'Ah.' She grinned exposing her gap teeth once more.

'Do you mind if we skip dessert? I'll have to start making my way back shortly.' Captivating as her presence was, the threat of Boyd running loose with his team bore a greater priority.

She shook her head.

As he casually ordered two coffees with the bill, an intuition prompted him to ask a question that had been lurking from the day before.

'Tell me. Are you familiar with Sergei from your BVI office?'

'No, should I be?'

'I'm not sure. It appears that he manages the option book for CentralniySib.'

She tilted her head. 'I don't have any involvement in the trading business.'

But Carty noticed that her cheeks had slightly flushed.

'Thank you for lunch,' she said, standing. 'I look forward to seeing you in Almaty.'

'Me too.' He was off his stall again and gently shaking her hand. *I'm sure I will!* He thought, grinning as he watched her glide elegantly away.

'And when will you arrive?' he shouted after her.

'Saturday.'

Saturday! I wonder if she'll be on the same flight.

His knee prevented him from trotting back to the office, forcing him to walk and contemplate the woman and their conversation.

Why had she wanted to meet me for lunch? We could have discussed everything over the phone.

But he dismissed the nagging doubt. She had imperceptibly got under his skin.

A routine meeting to review the clients' trading positions had been scheduled that afternoon, to introduce Boyd to two of the directors handling Albion's risk positions. In reality, though, with the implementation of the quants' super-programmes, their role had become relegated to monitoring *margin calls*: the cash deposit required from clients as security against volatile commodity price swings.

Focusing on the trade summary, Carty was surprised to see that CentraniySib had closed out all of its July options that morning.

So, Sergei must have given the order after all! His frowned stare drew Boyd's attention. The new man had been sitting for 20 minutes or so listening quietly, his body language bristling, waiting to lay down his marker.

'Scott, these gimmicky exotic options of yours...they're just ripe for manipulation.'

'What do you mean, Mark?'

'Fraud!'

The other men smiled economically. Boyd loved the melodramatic and knew exactly the impact that his statement would have, playing on the worries some senior market analysts had voiced in the media. Derivatives had become, in the space of a few short years, the investment instrument of choice and their total traded value was hard to quantify exactly. Some estimated it to be nearing a quadrillion dollars – a figure several times the world's combined gross domestic product – and a sudden economic sneeze would set the whole thing collapsing like a house of cards.

'That's unlikely, Mark, but now you're among us, I'm sure you will prevent it from ever occurring,' Carty said, narrowly resisting the temptation to remind him of his background, fearing it would get back to D'albo.

'Right, gentlemen, shall we leave it there? I have a deadline to meet for Arthur.' He was referring to the conference presentation.

'Yes, and he has to pack his bags in good time!' Boyd churlishly added.

The comment sealed the meeting but also stirred a mad thought as Carty returned to his desk. *Does Boyd have something on D'albo?* The vague suspicion had surfaced years before, while at Brightwell Carter. *It could explain why he's suddenly employed him again.*

It was 4:55 pm when he dropped a draft of the presentation on Davina's desk for proof-reading after emailing it to D'albo.

Don had strolled over. 'Some of the lads like Boyd. They find him witty,' he said.

Carty glanced around, wary of being in earshot before sternly fixing the quant's gaze.

'Don, you all need to be careful. Boyd is not your friend.'

'I can see that, Scott, but what's happened? Don't you have any say in all this?'

'I do, but D'albo wants him around,' he said, toying again with the temptation of outing Boyd's tainted history.

'Well, if it means anything to you, I can't stomach him. I would have an easier time discussing our structures with my pet parakeet!'

Carty chuckled. 'So where is Boyd? Has he left for the day?'

'D'albo called him an hour so ago. We haven't seen him since.'

'Really?' His expression momentarily exposed his latent anxiety, but just then his mobile chirped into life. It was Nick Hall.

'Hey, Nick!' Carty's joy in hearing his best friend's voice was obvious as he wrestled one arm through his jacket's sleeve and juggled the phone against the other shoulder.

'Why don't you come over tonight? Diane and James would love to see you. We can order in pizza and have a chat.'

'Thanks, but I don't touch the stuff,' Nick fired back. 'There's something I must show you, though. Why don't you come here instead?'

At that moment Boyd moved noticeably into his line of sight. 'D'albo wants to see us,' he mouthed.

'I see,' Carty frowned. 'Nick, I'm about to go into a meeting but I'll come over later.'

'Sit down, guys,' D'albo pointed, his mood seemed buoyant.

As they did, Carty caught the hint of something in Boyd's expression.

What does he know that I don't?

'Great presentation, Scott!' D'albo boomed. 'It will certainly give the conference a bit of edge.'

'That's what I'm aiming at!'

'Good. Then you'll also be pleased to know that the Executive Committee has accepted your paper.'

'Huh? What's changed in a day?'

'Don't be sarcastic. It took a lot of persuasion to sell the long-term value of your strategy. I've already instructed Mark to get your team onto it while you're in Kazakhstan.'

That's why Boyd's acting so smug.

'They're already onto it, Art!' Carty responded curtly. 'I am just interested to know why you shared it with Mark first.'

'There's a very good reason why.' He lent forward, extending his large hand. 'You've been promoted. Congratulations, you're now formally Albion's Director of Risk.'

Carty's mouth hung open, barely able to believe what he had just heard.

'Congratulations, Scott,' Boyd added hollowly.

'Mark, why don't you leave us for a while?' D'albo winked. 'I'll speak with you later.'

The older man slid back his chair. 'Still worried about your position now?' he uttered as he shook the cigar box at Carty.

'I suppose not.'

'That's what I thought you might say.' A grin had broken through his inscrutability. 'This promotion will give you the chance to do the one thing you've always wanted, to take your expertise global.'

Carty quietly observed his mentor, recognising what it was, that had originally endeared the man to him: his relentless drive towards success. Something, though, refused to allow the news to excite him as much as it should have done.

'Cynthia will give you the details of the remuneration package, share options and use of the company's facilities. It's a major step up the ladder, Scott.'

'Thanks, Art, I didn't expect this.'

'Don't mention it. Now let's get down to business!' He laid an executive case casually on the desk and stared at Carty while clearing his throat.

'This is for Kosechenko. I want you to give it to him in Kazakhstan.' His voice was hesitant.

'Kosechenko, the General Director of CentralniySib?' Carty clarified.

'Yes.'

'What's in it?'

'Documents.'

'What type?'

'Gas supply contracts.'

'Wouldn't it be easier to courier them directly to him?'

'You can't trust couriers, not in Russia and these documents are too sensitive. They might fall into the wrong hands,' he uttered, sliding the case across to Carty. 'Besides, Kosechenko already knows you're going to deliver them personally. Only he and I have the combination codes,' he added. 'It shouldn't be too difficult a task for you, should it?'

What in God's name is he up to? Carty caught a look that chilled and his instincts told him to refuse.

'Ordinarily it wouldn't, but unfortunately, Art, it looks as if I may have to miss the conference altogether,' he bluffed.

'What!'

'The doctor recommended that I shouldn't travel, not with my knee having a problem.'

'What are you talking about?' D'albo bellowed. 'I haven't seen you limping around today. You're fine, the problem is with your mind!' He lightly tapped the side of his temple to emphasise the point. 'And you're taking your eyes off the prize.'

'The prize?'

'CentralniySib's IPO. Kosechenko calls the shots and must be courted if Albion is to win that pot of gold.'

Carty stared quizzically back. 'Is that the reason why the Committee approved the strategy paper?'

'Partly, and if the IPO goes ahead, then I will be recommending you have a non-executive Board position. So you see how important it is that you're involved from day one. Give this case to Kosechenko and call me if there are any problems.'

Carty nodded benignly and then made for the door.

'And Scott...'

'Yes?'

'Make the presentation one of your best!' he said, flourishing a lighter at the Cuban.

Scott Carty sat in his office, nervously studying the locked case.

Is this promotion just a charade to get me out of the office and allow Boyd to take over? And why are these gas supply contracts so confidential that they can't be couriered?

His mentor's reasons smelled wrong.

What if the case contains something else? Albion's intellectual property perhaps.

Passing it on would constitute a breach of his duties. Ignorance was no excuse. He pored over the consequences and then quickly subdued them. *D'albo has no possible reason to be involved in something underhand that could put me at risk. It would ruin his career.*

He grabbed at the case's smooth handle with a plan to get out for some fresh air. Davina stopped him mid-pace, beaming.

'Congratulations, Scott.'

'What have you heard?'

'Your promotion! Boyd told us.'

He was unprepared for her approbation and the team's impromptu celebrations. They swarmed around him slapping his back and breaking open two bottles of Bollinger.

'What's in the case, your bonus?' Don asked jokingly, thrusting a filled champagne flute into his hand.

'If only I knew, Don!' he muttered. 'Where's Boyd?'

'He left a little while ago.'

Carty swung back to the others. 'Thanks, everyone, this is as much your success as it is mine,' he said with attempted nonchalance, but Davina clocked the anxiety hidden behind his raised glass.

He downed it in one. 'Now, if you'll excuse me, I need to get going!'

'What's the hurry? You're not flying until Saturday?' Davina cried.

'It's all right, Scott. Mark will take care of us now that you've joined the *gods*!' Don joked.

Carty shrugged as he slipped away from the laughter, wishing he could share their levity.

Four

Nick Hall lived a short drive north of London, beyond the suburbs, on farming land belonging to his parents. Carty relished Nick's ease with life, alone with his dogs and his workshop, and the friendship – one of only a few – made for a psychological bolt hole where Carty could be himself.

'Hi, mate, how's it going?' Nick shouted, peeking over the edge of a car's raised bonnet as Carty's open-top pulled to a stop on the uneven lane behind his rambling garden.

'All's fine,' Carty hollered back, hauling himself out and squinting against the evening's sunshine. Nick's silky Ridgebacks immediately leapt up at him with their muddy paws. Carty didn't like dogs, didn't trust them, but tolerated Nick's. He pushed them down. 'How's the project?' he uttered jokingly.

The project was the unfinished house. It was meant to be *passive* – consuming minimum energy but hadn't quite got there due to a lack of funds. Carty didn't doubt that Nick would complete it one day and had even suggested developing property on adjacent land to provide the finance. Nick always declined, leaving Carty stumped by his friend's apparent lack of business acumen. This was the fundamental difference in their philosophies; otherwise the camaraderie was solid, nurtured through healthy competition during their school years. Carty loved athletics, particularly long-distance running, while Nick favoured martial arts. The different disciplines showed in their physiques. Carty's was taller and leaner with a lighter bone structure, Nick's of medium height with a stockier frame. They often joked about which exercise was the better and had agreed to differ, although Carty was becoming painfully aware that his fitness was ebbing while that of his friend's appeared to be improving. Nick swore that it was down to his early morning routine of *T'ai Chi Ch'uan,* a system of fluid movements developed over thousands of years by Taoist monks. Its efficacy was so successful that the Chinese Communist Party had adopted it as a means to ensure the nation's fitness.

'How's Diane?' Nick enquired, ignoring the question and continuing to wipe engine oil from his hands.

'She's well.'

Nick sensed a tension. 'And James?'

'Yeah, he's a great kid and growing up so quickly!' Carty's smile lingered. 'I love him to pieces.'

'So what's up then, Scott?' Perhaps it was Nick's ability to be uncluttered in his life that allowed him to see into his friend's problems.

Carty shrugged. 'Nothing really...' he dipped his head and kicked around a stone.

'What?'

'I'm embarrassed to say...I've been having some really weird dreams lately.'

'Dreams, eh!' Nick chuckled. 'I thought it was going to be something far worse than that!'

'I'm not joking Nick. These were quite disturbing and seemed almost real.'

'Perhaps they might have been!'

'Huh! I don't think so somehow.'

'Well, you can consider yourself lucky. The ancients considered dreams to be messages from the gods.'

Carty stared vacantly back.

'Anyway,' Nick winked, 'let me divert your attention for a moment to the real world and this hybrid car.'

'A hybrid car?' Carty shook his head worriedly, understanding that Nick Hall had spent his early life in industry working on technologies the Official Secrets Act prohibited him from discussing.

'Yes, I've cannibalised it, replacing the petrol engine with a diesel one.'

'Should I be impressed by that?' Carty goaded, rubbing his light stubble.

'It may not seem very sophisticated to you, but I have my reasons.'

'Which are?'

'Do you know what Rudolf Diesel's original engine ran on?'

'Diesel?'

'Nope, peanut oil!'

Carty grinned cynically. 'Ah, biodiesel!' he boomed, rolling his eyes skyward. He was familiar with the fact that processed vegetable oils were being blended with regular diesel to meet new emissions regulations in Europe and the USA.

'That's the modern name for it,' Nick quipped. 'But when Diesel demonstrated his prototype at the World's Fair in 1900, vegetable oils were the fuel of choice. It's said that Henry Ford had apparently planned to run his cars on both hemp oil and batteries.'

'A hybrid car 90 years before its time!' Carty teased. 'So what went wrong?'

'It seems that the industry barons of the age manoeuvred to ensure that crude oil and its distillate, petro-diesel, would become indispensable to the industrialising world, out-pricing and marginalising biodiesels, until recent times.'

'Another conspiracy theory?'

'It gets worse. In 1913, after successfully converting the French navy's submarine fleet from steam power, Diesel planned on meeting with the British Admiralty. He never made it. His body was found adrift some days later in the English Channel.'

'He obviously pissed someone off,' Carty hissed. 'Anyway, what's that got to do with this fabulous car of yours? Are you running it on peanut oil too?'

'No. Old, used cooking oil!'

'You're serious about this, aren't you?'

'Couldn't be more so.'

'So where are you filling up? Chip shops?'

'Not exactly! The oil needs to be processed first.'

Carty scratched his head, sighing inaudibly.

'Scott, the solution to energy efficiency and reduced emissions is not in reinventing the wheel, but in tinkering with it. Used cooking oil is both practical and cost-effective.' He nodded as if mentally confirming this to himself. 'Now, let me show you something that will really blow your mind.' He pointed under the bonnet to a metallic cylinder, the size of a thermos, sitting to one side of the engine. 'Take a closer look at that.'

Carty lent in, hesitantly hovering his face over the car's guts. 'It looks like some type of dynamo to me.'

'Looks can be deceptive.'

He turned his head in the cramped space, drilling his friend impatiently. 'Okay, what is it?'

'It's my black box...a *Tesla* device!'

'Tesla!' Carty groaned. 'Come on, Nick, you're not making sense today.'

'And why's that?'

'You know that Tesla's inventions were flawed.'

'Really? What about his AC motor? It completely revolutionised our world and is still in use today!'

'All right, I admit that it was a brilliant breakthrough, but that's all he ever did.'

'I'm afraid that's where you're wrong again. Nikola Tesla discovered and demonstrated certain electromagnetic phenomena that defied explanation by the scientific establishment of the early 20th century.'

'Yeah, and they still defy explanation today!'

'Not so.'

'Huh?' Carty uttered, pulling out from under the bonnet. 'What are you implying?'

'This device holds two powerful magnets which produce on their own, enough electrical power to run the car.'

'What do you mean, *run the car*?' Carty said, glaring back at his friend.

'I'm not sure if I can explain it, but I can certainly prove it.'

'You're not telling me that this contraption does something it's not supposed to, are you?'

'Sort of.' He looked sheepish, knowing that the comment would challenge his friend's intellect.

'Once the magnets are rotating at a critical speed, the diesel engine stops and the car runs by itself.'

'But the power is still supplied by the battery, right?'

'No, there's no external energy supply required.'

Irritated, Carty span back at him. 'Nick, what you're suggesting contradicts the first law of thermodynamics – one of physics most fundamental – energy can neither be created nor destroyed in a closed system. Of all people, you should know that!'

'I do, but you have to see it working.'

There was a short silence before Carty cracked an unenthusiastic grin. Nick pushed himself up off the superstructure and trotted to the door, swinging back to his friend.

'Come on. Get in!'

He reversed back up the lane. Carty groaned, clearly unimpressed by the silence of a vehicle running on batteries alone. Suddenly, though, the diesel engine jumped into life and a cloud of soot erupted behind them as they reached the main road. The pungent odour of cooking fat was nauseating.

'It should only be a minute before the magnets take over,' Hall announced, accelerating down the clear stretch of road.

'I can't believe I'm letting myself be taken in by this.'

'Just trust me and watch that gauge!' He indicated to a device haphazardly stuck to the dashboard with ducting tape.

'Very elegant, Nick!' Carty quipped, but as he did, the engine died and the gauge flipped into life.

'You see. We're now running on magnet power!'

'Hmm, isn't it just the car's battery kicking in again?'

'Absolutely not.' He pointed at the car's regular on-board monitor. 'See, the battery is fully charged but it's not running the car.'

'I'm still not convinced, Nick.'

'That's the problem with you left-brained types. You need proof that you're alive!' he snorted. 'Do you want to have a drive?'

'No thanks, but I wouldn't mind taking a look under the bonnet again when we stop, so I can explain to you very, very slowly, how this car is really working.'

Nick chuckled. 'We'd better head back.'

He slowed and spun the car around in a small lay-by.

'Scott, doesn't your searching mind find it a bit strange that over the last hundred or so years, the technology we humans use to ferry us about hasn't fundamentally changed at all?'

'You're referring to the internal combustion engine?'

'Of course. Over the same period we've seen the advent of wireless radio, telephone, television, mobile communications and the internet. We've developed incredible new materials and travelled to the moon, harnessed nuclear power – albeit primitively, and have gone from writing letters longhand and sending them by mail to communicating virtually in a fraction of a second. But in stark contrast, we're still tied to fossil-fuelled internal combustion engines.'

'That's because they work economically, Nick.'

'Even though they're less than 20 per cent efficient? Don't you think that there have been other inventions which could have replaced them entirely? Or perhaps they've simply been prevented from coming to market.'

Carty shrugged. The same thought had occurred to him only months before.

The drive back took minutes and they were again met by the dogs.

'There, take a look!' Hall insisted as he lifted the car's lid.

'Can I see inside that box of tricks?'

'Not when it's running.'

'Well, there you go, Nick. How can I explain it if I can't see it operating?'

'Sorry, mate, you'll have to take my word that it's genuine.'

'Ha, just like Tesla, claiming the impossible!'

'Fancy a cup of tea?' Nick offered, deflecting the comment.

'That's a bloody good idea, but none of that herbal rubbish just regular builder's tea with real milk and sugar!'

A warm aroma of freshly baked bread met them, a pleasant contrast to the smell of engine fumes.

'Wow, what's happening here?' Carty commented. The basic kitchen was surprisingly tidier than he remembered, despite the breakfast table being habitually littered with a selection of partially read textbooks.

'Magda's staying.'

'Who's Magda?'

'The Polish girl I met recently.'

'Oh, the poor thing! Fooled into doing your housework.'

'Not at all. She's smart, has a degree in microbiology, but can't find any work in Warsaw.'

Magda walked in at that precise moment, a willowy beauty in a long summer dress.

'Magda, this is my good friend Scott, Scott Carty.'

Carty was captivated, connotations of the maiden from his dream flickered again before his eyes. She smiled shyly as she poured tea, conscious of her effect.

'Here, take this tray,' Nick intervened. 'Let's go through to the sitting room. We can chat there.'

'You seem tired. Is business going well?' Nick asked, still registering the uncommon malaise in his friend as they sat down.

'Could be better, I'm a bit stressed.'

49

'By what?'

'A potential fight-in-the-making.'

'Who with?'

'Mark Boyd.' Carty picked at his fingers.

'Who's Mark Boyd?'

'The guy who brought down Brightwell Carter and ended up doing time, remember?'

'The criminal?'

Carty nodded. 'D'albo's giving him a second chance.'

'Maybe that's a sign of what's to come.'

'Of course it's a bloody sign. I could lose my team and my job!'

'Whoa! Calm down, Scott, what's the panic? You're financially stable and I'm sure the competition would be happy to snap you up, if you decide to leave Albion.'

'Yeah, I suppose you're right.'

'And you think all this is triggering the dreams?' Nick joked as he chomped on a dunked biscuit.

'I've no idea, but you may know better.'

'Sorry, Scott, I tinker with machines, not dreams.'

'But you can't resist a bit of amateur psychoanalysis, can you?' Carty grinned, recalling his friend's dalliance with dream interpretation in the past as a ruse to chat up girls and appear intellectually superior to his peer group.

Nick's expression had become deadly serious. 'Hmm, perhaps you haven't been listening to yourself for a while, and I would also hazard a guess that you'll have more dreams until you do.'

The comment railed against Carty's logic and the respect in which he usually held Nick's opinion. His friend wasn't the wealthiest guy he knew, but was probably the wisest.

'You know what?' Nick announced. 'You should meet Gordon Green. He can give you a much better insight into your dreams then I ever can.'

Carty's eyes widened. 'That's not the Gordon Green I think you mean? Is it?'

'You know him?'

'Well, if it is the same man, then I have no idea why I would want to discuss my dreams with him. He's a banker!'

'In a previous existence perhaps, but he's now a dream analyst.'

'I can't believe my ears, Nick,' Carty yowled, recalling an ill-fated meeting with Green years earlier. 'The man's a complete bastard.'

'Why is that?'

'He stymied an investment opportunity Albion was leading, despite its overwhelming business case. His inexplicable behaviour spooked everyone and we almost lost the deal. Luckily, D'albo managed to pull in private finance at the eleventh hour.'

'Well, that may have been,' Nick retorted defensively. 'Gordon is trusted with the dreams of some very important and influential clients.'

'Like who?'

'Members of the Royal family, MPs and business executives.'

'But that still doesn't vindicate his behaviour.'

'It does in my world.'

Carty looked skyward in an expression of bewilderment. 'I don't understand, Nick. How did you come to know Green? He has nothing to do with your world, does he?'

'He was at school with my father and is known to stick to his guns. That's probably why he left the banking world so suddenly.'

'He did? Why?'

'I'm not sure of the details.'

'Was it fraud?' Carty quizzed.

Nick shot him a look of distaste. 'Definitely not!'

Carty bit into a biscuit as he pondered this news. *What could Green have possibly done to damage his credibility so badly?*

Magda floated back in, expressionless, and topped up the teapot with hot water before leaving again.

'Cute, isn't she?' Nick quipped but Carty ignored him, intrigued. 'Sorry, Nick. I still find it hard to believe that Gordon Green is dabbling with dream analysis.'

'Well, he is for part of the time.'

'And for the rest?'

'He's busy arranging finance for renewable energy projects, mainly solar electricity.'

'Oh, I get it. He's another bloody green like you!' The pun was crude.

'Scott, I don't think he would care about these arbitrary name tags. He's more concerned in mitigating the damage we're doing to the climate. He's lobbying for a much larger investment in clean energy from government, to reduce the accelerated burning of fossil fuels. That's hardly a sustainable future for any of us.'

Nick's uncompromising conviction left a discreet sense of loathing in his friend.

'And I suppose you're also going to tell me that it's all downhill from now on.'

'Possibly,' Nick murmured. 'You know as well as I do that, as a society, as a civilisation, we've been weaned on fossil fuels as the primary energy source. Some people are now warning that we have already reached *peak oil*.'

Nick was referring to a tipping point in global crude oil production when no new large discoveries are made and consumption begins to rapidly outstrip demand. While there would be plenty of oil left in terms of volume, the lag in having alternatives in place to meet spiralling energy demands would cause prices to spike sharply. The knock on effect would trigger a global recession, making the depression of the 1930s trivial by comparison.

'So one problem might resolve the other: less oil burning, less global warming!' Carty hit back, pushing Nick onto the defensive.

'Gordon's company is just one of a number of new groups funding the alternatives, just in case.'

'But Nick, neither you nor he are being practical. Renewables such as solar and wind might be enjoying a spurt because global warming is making front-page headlines, but they will always be the poor relation. Their power output is unpredictable and can't be relied upon for the base load. No supplier in this deregulated market is going to risk losing its client base over such an inconsistent energy supply. And besides, there are stringent emissions controls in place to mitigate climate change.'

Nick waved the comment away, visibly disenchanted. 'Nice try, Scott, but the world doesn't spin on market forces. Don't you get it? It's not just about energy production. The planet's essential ecosystems are being driven to their limits by the unsustainable consumption of resources. We have probably less than 20 years to slow it down and reverse it, and if we don't, if we screw it up, then the invisible hand of the free market is not going to sweep in to save us!'

Exasperated, Carty downed his tea.

'Look, if science is sophisticated enough to send a man to the moon and develop nanotechnology, then pollution can be handled. Politicians and captains of industry are not suicidal because, like us, they are not excluded from spaceship Earth.'

'You think so?'

'Of course I do! In the real world only the dangling carrot of financial gain motivates investment and change, and that's the reason why the Kyoto Protocol was put in place. You see, Nick, everything boils down to plain old, economic gain. It makes sense.'

Nick sat back into his chair, grinning uncomfortably. 'Yes, Scott, I do see, but *does everything have to make sense?* Take my car running on magnets, for instance.'

Carty's face froze, horrified at hearing that phrase again. He couldn't believe it; the coincidence was implausible, illogical.

'What's wrong with you?'

'Nothing, nothing at all.' Carty stammered.

'Nothing? You look like you've seen a ghost.'

'It's what you just said '

'Really?'

'Yes. "Does everything have to make sense?" It was exactly the same phrase I heard in my dream.'

'Ha! Then all the more reason for you to meet Green!'

Carty attempted a smile, but his veneer of calm had been cracked by an irrational fear. 'All right, Nick, I give in. Arrange the time and the place but, just to let you know, I'm leaving for Kazakhstan at the weekend so it may have to wait until I'm back.'

'Well, if you want answers now, you can always consult the *I Ching.*'

Carty shook his head despairingly. The *I Ching* or the *Book of Changes* is one of the world's oldest treasures. Like *T'ai Chi Ch'uan*, it was a product of Taoism, the indigenous, shamanic tradition of ancient China. Essentially a book of wisdom, the *I Ching* had survived millennia of turbulent history to become a means of divining the future through its 64 images or hexagrams, which, according to Taoism, govern all eventualities of time and space.

Carty had flicked through the book before out of curiosity but had decided it was mumbo-jumbo, and relegated it to the realms of fantasy.

'The *I Ching* is not to be sneered at, Scott.'

Wringing his hands, Carty was dismayed. 'Come on, Nick, you have to agree, important decisions cannot be made by consulting an old book.'

Hall eyed his friend. 'That *old* book simply provides probabilities open to the questioner, based on the exact moment when it is consulted,' he said, attempting a grin and recalling a moment years before when, on a whim, he had consulted it to decide his fate with Diane Carty. Unwisely, he had ignored its advice.

Magda slipped in again and sat opposite him, resting her bare feet on Nick's lap.

Hall smiled. 'Magda has done some really interesting research work in drawing parallels between the structure of DNA and the binary code of the *I Ching*. There appears to be a link at a deeper level and that the Taoists somehow intuited the fractal code, centuries before Crick and Watson discovered the DNA double helix.'

She smiled coolly at the comment.

Sensing her jealousy for having taken up Nick's evening, he glanced down at his Seiko. 'Shit! Is that the time? I'd better get moving.'

'Wait for a moment, Scott, will you?' Nick jumped up and then left the room.

Magda remained mute looking at her fingernails for the little time it took Nick to return.

'Here, take this.' He passed Carty something wrapped in a plain brown paper bag. 'Don't open it until you get home.'

Carty followed his friend back out into the garage with the dogs in tow, their moist snouts nosing his hands.

'Magda's very nice, Nick, but take care. Those Eastern Europeans can be a handful.'

'She's just shy,' Nick winked. 'You, though, should concern yourself more with Diane!'

The roads were quiet on the journey back as *Losing My Religion*, one of his favourites, played. He usually sang along but today remained distant.

What was Nick trying to prove with his claims for that black box? Surely he didn't seriously think I would believe the car was powered on magnets alone?

He shook his head dismissively; they had known each other too long for that.

And what had he meant about Diane?

Carty had met his beautiful wife through Nick's introduction. But even with the security of marriage he could not dispel the notion that she still secretly carried a flame for Nick. He sensed his friend was tactfully avoiding it.

Pulling up in the driveway to his Hampstead townhouse, an SMS tone prompted. It was from Nick.

Green's free at 7:30 tomorrow evening. I'll text his address to you shortly.

Five

Almaty airport, Kazakhstan

All of the events had seemed like a weird dream, yet now, sitting in this suffocating room, something from within suddenly shook Carty. Those nights of running miles across Hampstead Heath and not cracking in the face of pain or exhaustion, had developed in him a strength of will he was unaware he possessed, until that moment. Feeling calmer, he decided that he would convince these officials of his innocence, trusting that Lena's contacts would soon extricate him.

A quarter of an hour dragged before a silhouette loomed behind the frosted-glass door panel.

Blondie sauntered in with two cronies in tow and pivoted a chair around on one leg before theatrically lifting a jack-boot to sit astride it. His cold uncompromising stare met the Englishman's as he leant against the backrest and fanned his lips with Carty's passport. A broad asymmetric nose dominated a hard, angular profile, suggesting a violent past. The impasse lasted a few seconds then he clicked his fingers, motioning with an outstretched arm for the briefcase to be dumped on the stained formica table. The guards acted promptly, opening it so that its contents faced their quarry.

'So, I'll ask you again. Who is this money for, *meester* Carty?' he said as he flashed a glance at the torn envelopes. Carty tried to avoid showing fear at the ploy to intimidate, but his heart raced. The self-belief he had experienced only minutes earlier was evaporating as he mentally fought to keep his cool and drilled a look straight back.

'I have been invited by my client, CentralniySib Energo, to a conference here in Almaty.' His posture straightened, projecting confidence. 'Its executives will be contacting the British Embassy as we speak, to ensure that I am released immediately.'

Blondie slammed his hand down on the table in anger. 'I know why you're here, but why are you smuggling this money into Kazakhstan?'

Sensing a lack of substance in his inquisitor, Carty blanked him.

'Do you recognise this signature?' Blondie growled, infuriated. He slid the declaration form that Lena had filled out, across the surface between them.

'It is yours? Am I correct?

'Yes,' Carty acknowledged, pursing his lips.

'It states that you're only carrying a thousand of your *Great* British pounds, so you have lied!' His voice rose to a crescendo. 'But if you tell me why you brought these dollars, I will release you without charge and you can leave on the next flight.'

'It is the initial cash advance stipulated in those contracts,' Carty bluffed, pointing to the plastic wallet still in the case. 'You can check that with my clients if you wish.'

The man pulled back. The rapid response had forced him to assess the possibility that he might be interfering in the affairs of powerful *biznismen.*

'Now, may I make a telephone call?' Carty pressed.

'No, you cannot!' He flushed, his psychological advantage lost.

'But it is usual practice to...'

'Stop *meester* Carty!' he snapped back violently. 'There will be no call.' He stood. 'I want you to count this money, now!'

'What? All of it! ' Carty stammered.

'Yes, all of it!'

Come on, Lena. Hurry up and get me out of here.

Carty picked up the first bundle of hundred dollar bills, rifling its end to gauge the amount before placing it flat on the table. Cramps tightened in his stomach as pulling up each corner, he began counting. The notes were new and crisp and disquiet stirred that they might be counterfeit.

'$10,000,' he murmured after some minutes, his fingers sweating in the stale environment as he stole a glimpse at the slouching guards' avaricious focus. For each, the pile of notes amounted to many life times' salary, but for a man of Kosechenko's wealth, it was pocket-money with which to bribe minor officials or to lavish on hookers.

It took some time for Carty to conclude the stressful task. He was left choked by the amount and D'albo's deception.

That fucking bastard!

The denigration of his trust had been so complete that it was as if the ability to rationalise the motive had been sucked from him, leaving him instead with an untold desire for vengeance.

Blondie flashed an unpleasant sneer. 'So, *meester* Carty. How much?'

'$500,000.'

'And why did you bring it into Kazakhstan? Are you a trafficker?' His rough accent probed harshly, as if sensing that the Englishman was beginning to falter.

Carty shook his head. 'I demand to see a representative of the British Embassy!'

'What makes you think that your government can intervene now in the affairs of the Republic of Kazakhstan? They will see you in prison tomorrow.'

'Prison?' he gawped.

'Yes, but before that, you will write down every serial number on these bills.'

'That's going to take forever.'

'And you have plenty of time!'

On instruction, one of the guards reached into his breast pocket and retrieved a small notepad, tossing it on the table. Carty smeared his brow on his sleeve before grabbing at a stack of dollars again. With perspiration now trickling down the small of his back, he took a silent breath and then began.

All sense of time was lost to him when the door suddenly flew open. The two guards sprang to attention, saluting to a uniformed army officer in a huge brimmed hat.

Startled, Blondie rose to his feet and attempted a polite exchange with the suited official who followed behind; a large Kazakh with almond shaped eyes set in a broad, copper face. The *suit* casually brushed him aside with a hand gesture and, turning to Carty, spoke in clear, precise English.

'Mister Carty, I must apologise for this inconvenience but you will understand that we have regulations to follow.' He smiled economically. 'Your clients have contacted my superiors to ask that these documents be handed to them personally.'

Documents? Carty observed the coded use of language.

The man swung to the interrogator and barked sternly. Blondie lowered his head and then spoke to his guards in a vain attempt at imposing his rank. The army officer, though, cut him dead with a shout. Now visibly demoralised, Blondie scowled at the Englishman before trudging out.

'May I ask who you are?' Carty questioned the *suit*, relieved as the two guards began to pack the money back into the case.

'Your clients know who I am,' he answered, handing him back his passport. 'We should not detain you further. Do you need to collect your luggage?'

'No. I have my bags with me.'

'In that case, my deputy here will escort you straight through customs and into the arrivals lobby.'

The officer passed the closed case to the *suit* and courteously ushered Carty out ahead of him.

As he stepped through customs, a fresh breeze raced across the concourse and the sight of Lena boosted his morale. Smiling, he walked over to her. Her slight frame was dwarfed by three minders, Italian dressed in grey tonic suits and matching open-necked shirts.

'Are you all right, Scott?' she asked, her manner brittle as she touched his arm.

'Just about, I thought I was going to spend the night in a cell!'

'What happened exactly?'

He broke into a brief recount of the last hour, but noticed that her attention had become distracted.

'Where's the case?'

'I was told that one of the officials will return it,' he responded.

Her eyes widened. 'Which official? What was his name?'

'He wouldn't tell me but, believe me, Lena, asking questions was the last thing on my mind. I was being accused of trafficking by that blonde arsehole before his seniors released me. I assumed you had pulled some strings to get me out.'

'You didn't get his name?' She stamped her foot in frustration at the effectiveness of the trick: he'd been fooled by the *suit.*

Breaking off into Russian, she explained the scam to her colleagues, their expressions slowly turning to scorn as the story unfolded.

'Let's go to the car,' she instructed. 'My friends here are going to find out exactly who took it.'

As they drove off, he attempted to explain himself.

'I'm sorry Lena, I didn't know that money was in the case, it was Arthur D'albo...'

She put a finger to her lips while discreetly pointing at the driver, indicating that it was not safe to speak.

He sank back into the leather seat as the approaching lights of Almaty paled against the early dawn.

I should never have agreed to bring the briefcase. A rising sense of anger was tempered only by the sudden and chilling realisation. *I could have been thrown in jail.* Yet through some strange sequence of events he was still free. In Carty's rational world, things like this never happened.

The hotel, part of a Russian boutique chain, was a grand Soviet building with a huge marble-floored lobby and ancient rugs hanging across the dark woodwork of its walls. They were met by a young woman with welcoming eyes, but a curt manner. Lena briskly filled in forms, and impatiently handed Carty a room key.

'Your passport will be held at reception and this registration document must be carried at all times while you're here in Almaty.'

He sighed a resigned affirmative.

'I will meet you at 11 o'clock in the lobby.' She waved to the porter to trolley her luggage after her.

Carty didn't move for a few seconds, staring at her beautiful form as she disappeared down the corridor.

I don't believe she could have known anything about the money, he concluded, recalling the look of horror on her face as the case exploded across the customs desk, hours earlier.

But will she be blamed for its loss?

Six

A persistent rap slowly roused him.

He sat up and reached for his watch. The sunlight squeezing through the narrow join in the curtains, screamed confusion at him until he remembered that he was still on British summer time.

The rap came again and he grabbed a towelling robe.

A pallid-faced Lena, in jeans and a white blouse stood in the doorway.

'Good morning, Scott.' Her breath was tinged with the hum of cigarettes and puffy lids encased her sapphire eyes as she strained a smile.

'Good morning, have you slept at all?'

She dipped her head.

'Let me guess. They haven't found the money?' He quipped, gently pulling her into the room and incongruously placing a finger gently under her chin to raise it. 'I'm sure your people will get it soon enough!'

She drew herself to him and rested her head against his chest, breaking an unspoken barrier. Taken aback, he wrapped his arms around her slight shoulders then slid a palm up along the nape of her neck. Cradling it back, his lips inched to hers. But she smoothly placed her fingers over them, halting his advance. A grin had now replaced her earlier sullenness.

'We must go soon otherwise we will miss the conference opening,' she whispered, pulling away.

'What's the rush? I'm not presenting until this afternoon.'

'I know, but I need to escort Kosechenko at the opening ceremony this morning. Anyway, you can come along and trial run your presentation on the big screen.'

'But I thought...' He was confused and attempted to pull her closer again, excited by their encounter. She pushed him back.

'I'll meet you in the lobby in one hour. Please be ready!'

He felt surprisingly alive, taking in the view of Almaty's bustling streets from behind the tinted windows. The ordeal at the airport was now forgotten as sun beams played through the leaves of the tree-lined *prospecti*.

So, this is the Paris of Central Asia, he reminded himself, recalling pictures from the internet site and comparing them with the eclectic mix of modern glass and metal constructions that overshadowed crumbling edifices, some still stained with faded Soviet propaganda. Then, as he cracked the window open, an exotic profusion of smells rushed in with the warm air, triggering his latent excitement. Here, the veneer of the modern world barely disguised a culture whose past was still accessible without censure. He felt robbed by comparison; his own now whitewashed by the trappings of ubiquitous consumerism.

'Tell me about your wife, Scott?' Lena asked coyly. Until that moment she had been strangely absent, perhaps because of their earlier physical closeness. But he had sensed her smouldering emotion and leant back against the door to take in her profile: high, chiselled cheekbones and a deportment that gave the impression of a noble heritage from which she had somehow been severed.

'Well?' she gently insisted. But his focus had drifted to the smiling images of Diane and James, brooding over how little he had seen of them recently.

'Would you mind if I smoked?' she asked, thinly disguising disbelief at his prevarication.

She lit a cigarette ignoring his silent distaste, and drew on it deeply.

Soon they were immersed in the entourage swarming around them in the conference centre lobby. Igor Kosechenko, her ultimate boss, had arrived, a short man expensively dressed in a beige Brioni suit, its oversized jacket barely covering his waistline. Carty had already studied the Russian's form: a former Soviet party man who had risen through the Politburo's ranks but had no discernible experience in power or energy. It was apparent that he was enjoying the privileges of capitalism.

Still feeling awkward with the loss of the case, Carty dived into the empty conference room to run through his presentation with the technicians at the podium.

As the delegates filtered in, his attention was drawn to the body language between Kosechenko and Lena: he was treating her like a servant. Angered, Carty paced over towards the balding Russian. A burly henchman blocked his path before Lena hastily ordered the hulk to let him through.

'Scott, this is Mr Kosechenko, the General Director of CentralinySib Energo.' She had become the cool-headed businesswoman again.

Carty thrust his hand out. 'I'm very pleased to meet you Mr Kosechenko. Mr D'albo asked me to give you his warmest regards.'

The Russian's palm was thick and sweaty and he eyed Carty up and down continuously talking to him as Lena struggled to keep up.

'Mr Kosechenko is eagerly awaiting your presentation,' she related.

Carty nodded politely, returning the stare.

'He is also sorry to hear that you were badly treated at the airport and is inviting you to visit our corporate *datchas* around Lake Baikal after the conference.'

'Lake Baikal? Is that near here?'

'No, Scott, it's in Russia,' she grinned.

'Da, da, *Rossiya!*' Kosechenko gruffly echoed.

Russia? The Englishman echoed back to himself, camouflaging his discomfort.

The place was now full of movers from the international energy circuit, all eager to meet the head of CentralinySib. Sensing that his few minutes were up, Carty made his excuses and the Russian was chaperoned away.

His presentation was the first of the afternoon. Its subject, emission-linked derivatives, seemed lost on an audience that appeared to be keen to re-establish the old Soviet network. Lucrative opportunities were emerging in exploiting the huge hydro-power potential of the mountainous *Stans* and supplying the strategic markets of Northwest China, Pakistan and, eventually, Afghanistan.

Perhaps it was due to nervousness, but it wasn't until the end of his presentation, after he had faced a number of difficult questions, that he realised how impressive the translator's colloquial use of technical vocabulary had been. Clearly the man had studied English for years.

Lena grabbed him on a short coffee break between further rounds of translation.

'You presented very well.' She smiled.

'Thanks, but it would have been a dismal failure without the translator...'

Her eyes flickered nervously as she cut him short. 'I'm sorry, Scott, I must go. Kosechenko is waiting for me. You can take the car back to the hotel.'

'Will we meet later?'

'Yes, get some sleep. I'll call your room before dinner,' she shouted, before turning briskly back into the crowd.

Her minder pointed Carty up a flight of stairs and, on reaching the balcony he stopped to snatch a glance back over the delegation. Lena's sensuous lips cracked open subtly, as she returned his look.

'Ha! Did they strip-search you, Scott?' Arthur D'albo roared as Carty recounted the news.

'Yes, virtually!'

'And did Kosechenko's people recover the package?'

'Not yet.'

There was a pause.

'Is it a problem?' D'albo added.

'Yes. It's likely it has been stolen.'

'That's not acceptable!'

'What could I do Arthur? I was threatened with imprisonment.'

'Come off it, Scott. That was a ploy to scare you. You're safe now, aren't you?'

'Yes, but you could have had the decency to let me know what was in that case before I left,' Carty fired back.

'And perhaps you better remember who you're talking to, Carty!'

Stunned, he lost track of the conversation: D'albo had never called him *Carty.*

'Are you still there?' D'albo bellowed.

'Yes, I'm here!'

'Right, listen. Just make sure that you stay close to Kosechenko. Ask that girl Lena to help you.'

'She has already,' he responded, 'and Kosechenko has asked me to join them at Lake Baikal after the conference.'

'Where the hell is that?'

'In Siberia. It's a corporate jolly for his select guests.'

'Well, you'd better go. I don't want the relationship soured further!'

'Thanks for your trust, Arthur.'

'Cut the sarcasm,' he barked. 'Call me before you leave, and not a word to anyone about the lost property. Do I make myself clear?'

Angry, Carty feigned platitudes then slammed down the phone and, in frustration tossed the computer bag off the bed. He stretched out, still smarting. Gordon Green's comments had been spot on the mark. D'albo's duplicitous nature was something that Carty had spent years denying.

Seven

Four days earlier – Highgate, London.

Cycling uphill took a greater toil on Carty's knee than he imagined and he stopped to grab a breather by The Flask pub.

Is it really worth meeting Green? I've better things to do with my time.

But cancelling wasn't his style. He always followed through on his commitments, regardless of the circumstances.

Unlike Mark Boyd! I can't believe he's coming back.

The notion was still raw and like everything else in the last couple of days, totally out of the ordinary. Something, though, a hunch perhaps, told him it wasn't.

He free-wheeled 50 metres down the private road, gripping the brakes so that he slowed to catch sight of the house numbers on the large gates. Stopping, he rechecked the address with Nick's text then pushed the bike up a shingle drive towards an Edwardian haunt.

Finding no bell, he gave a solitary knock which reverberated loudly, as if waking the place to his presence and obvious lack of enthusiasm. There was no response and stepping back to see if there were any lights on, he spied a hanging plaque, partially obscured beneath an overhang of elderly wisteria. Engraved beneath its peeling varnished layers, was one word.

τέμενος

Temenos? he mouthed. *Studying those Greek classics had some use after all.* But he had no idea what it meant.

A movement of the net curtains, covering a side window, startled him. Then, seconds later, a youth's face squeezed from behind the partially opened door to nervously scrutinise Carty.

'Is Gordon there?'

'I'm through here. Come on in!' a rich voice peeled from somewhere inside.

He followed the boy across a chequered marble hallway into a morning room and there, standing in expectation, was a relaxed Gordon Green, large and broad-shouldered, exactly as Carty remembered him.

'Nice to see you again, Scott!' His hazel-green eyes shone with the zest of a much younger man. 'This is Joanna.' He introduced his wife, 'and this is Joey.' His son hung close by, timid yet curious.

'We've just eaten, but would you like something?' Joanna offered, her smile radiating warmth.

'No, thank you, I've already had supper.' He was still struggling by misgivings over Green.

'Perhaps a coffee then?'

'Yes, please.'

'Can Scott play PlayStation with me?' Joey blurted.

'Not today,' Green gently reproached. 'Scott and I are going into the study to chat, and you need to finish your homework.'

Green led Carty back out across the hallway and into a spacious oak-panelled room. A shaft of evening sunlight had burst through the French windows, illuminating the ceiling-to-floor shelves. They were crammed with an eclectic mix of leather-bound first editions and dated paperbacks.

'Impressive!' Carty uttered.

'Yes, books are my friends. These are mainly a collection of esoteric works.'

'Really? I've only ever heard that word being used in the financial markets.'

'Believe me, Scott. There is a world beyond the City. Take a seat.'

Carty sank onto a Chesterfield, scanning the room's uncommon artefacts and framed pictures. The atmosphere felt awkward, leaving him uncertain what to expect as Joanna slipped in carrying a tray with two coffees. He thanked her.

'Fancy a cigar?' Green, still standing, opened a small humidor from an aged mahogany desk.

'I've given them up!'

'A brandy then, with your coffee?'

'No thanks,' he fought the urge to accept. 'I still have a lot of work to run through later.'

'Ah, yes, the schedules of the City: I used to think they were all-important too.'

Carty gazed at him quizzically. 'And you don't anymore?'

'No. All that rational thinking, it's far too limited.'

'Limited?'

'Yes. I use both heart and head to guide me through life. I suppose I've become like an old-world Native American.'

'It didn't get them very far, did it?' Carty's tone, while unintentionally provocative, drew Green's sigh.

'Well, that depends on your definition of *far*,' he conveyed, firmly, wiping a tanned hand across his large forehead. 'If it means living in harmony with the land for thousands of years, I have to disagree with you. The traditional ways of ancient cultures were to consult with the forces of the unconscious and look at the potential repercussions of their actions for several generations ahead. This required using both one's heart and head.' The older man's emphasis was deliberate. 'But nowadays, we seem to be trapped in a *rational irrationality*, collectively deceived by the illusion that we are independent from each other and the natural world when, in fact, we are more reliant on both than ever.'

Carty stared vacantly back in schoolboy silence.

'Anyway, Scott,' he perched on the corner of the desk. 'What's going on in your world? I see the energy derivatives business has grown considerably since we last met. How much are you and Arthur D'albo responsible for that?'

'Quite a bit, I suppose.'

'I can imagine!' Green shrugged, nurturing a Honduran cigar in his large fingers. 'And I wonder where that will lead us all?'

Carty frowned. 'I'm not sure I follow you.'

Green waved his palm as if having second thoughts. 'Sorry, I'm rambling. Forget it. Nick tells me you been having some eventful dreams lately.'

Carty cocked his head, puzzled by the bizarre switch of dialogue. 'I suppose they were more real than eventful.'

'You know, *real* is just a subjective concept. I remember Jung once asked himself if he was sitting on a rock on the shores of Lake Constance or if the rock was actually sitting beneath him. He wasn't sure which scenario was real.'

'Jung?' Carty exclaimed.

'Never heard of Carl Gustav Jung?' Green retorted. 'His picture's is over there on the wall.'

Carty turned to look at a grey-haired, moustached man, wearing glasses and an impish grin which deceptively, made his age hard to guess.

'Was he a friend of yours?'

'Hah! No, he wasn't, but I feel as though I had met him through his psychological work.'

'Oh, he's the psychoanalyst.'

'The *analytical psychologist* actually, as well as an empirical scientist and doctor of medicine, much maligned for having broken ranks with Freud in the early part of the 20th century.'

Carty forced back a yawn.

'More than anything, Jung was an explorer of the soul and coined many new terms for his findings: *collective unconscious, archetype, synchronicity, extrovert, introvert...*' Green ran the cigar under his prominent nose, savouring its aroma. '...he also

72

analysed tens of thousands of dreams during his life and was probably responsible for the resurgent interest in alchemy.'

Carty grinned sheepishly as he sipped his coffee, recognising a common reference point in what was otherwise a sea of verbiage.

'I suppose modern-day alchemists are particle physicists, bombarding matter and transmuting one element into another.'

'Yes, but the alchemy I'm talking about is more to do with the transformative process latent in us all. Jung rediscovered what the great alchemists of history had known for centuries; that the psyche of an individual can affect matter itself.'

Carty's posture sank. He had come to discuss the meaning of his dreams, not to listen to some metaphysical claptrap.

'I understand you're a physicist?' Green asked, snipping off the end of the Honduran.

'That's right. I have a doctorate from Cambridge.'

'Then you probably know that Neils Bohr, one of the founders of quantum physics, incorporated the *Yin-Yang* symbol into his family's coat of arms?' As he spoke, he leant back and pulled a framed picture from his desk to reinforce his point. 'Here we are.'

'Sorry, I didn't know that and I don't see the connection?'

'Most people familiar with this Taoist symbol believe that it signifies balance but, actually, it represents the tension of opposites in nature, creating growth as one ceaselessly transforms into the other. As simple as it appears, Bohr understood that this image yielded a critical key to the unlocking of matter.'

Carty replaced his cup. A compelling urge to cut short the meeting rumbled, quelled only by his recollection of what Nick had told him and an understanding that the older man did not have to humour him at all. Green sensed his unease and continued.

'Anyway, I find that many of my dreams, and those of the people I treat, reveal a latent world of energetic patterns or archetypes, which structure our physical and mental worlds. They open a door onto our own unconscious stories, stories which need to be understood in order to give life greater meaning.'

'Do these archetypes appear in dreams?' Carty's curiosity had been jolted.

'Most definitely! In every culture, particularly in myths and religions,' Green added. His expression seemed ancient as he struck a red-tipped match; its pungent odour pricked Carty's nostrils, reminding him of his father's love of cigars.

'Now, let's get down to the business, shall we?' He moved to sit on the twin sofa, nonchalantly puffing smoke into the air.

'You will need to write down all the associations that come to mind as you recollect your dreams,' he instructed, handing Carty a small pad and an HB pencil, crudely sharpened with a pen knife. Carty stared at it, befuddled.

'It's an old habit,' Green grinned. 'A pencil gives a greater sense of realism than a ball-point ever can.'

'Okay,' Carty shrugged.

He then began recounting the first dream.

'Mark Boyd forced his way into my office and dragged me by the hand, out in front of the team, before walking through a glass window and transforming into a woman!' He rolled his eyes and laughed nervously. 'She told me I had to go with her because "*my life depended on it*!"'

'Where to?'

'Into a forest that had magically materialised behind her.'

Green swilled his glass for some seconds as the shafts of the dying sunset panned through the smoke, revealing an invisible, energetic world of microscopic dust particles, dancing between them.

'Any thoughts?' he boomed, startling the younger man.

'Well, I was napping on the tube when I had the dream and it shook me up.'

'Yes, the unconscious will not let us ignore things forever,' Green uttered. 'Is Boyd someone you get along with?'

'No, there's a history between us. D'albo appears to be playing on it.'

'Why?'

'I am not entirely sure.'

'And the history?'

'He's the fraudster who caused the collapse of Brightwell Carter and almost cost me my career.'

'Ah, I remember that...and you feel uncomfortable in his presence?'

'I detest him.'

'So nothing in common?'

'Not at all!'

'Good. Make a note of that. It's important.'

'Is it?'

'Yes. Boyd obviously represents an unconscious aspect of yourself.'

Wide-eyed, Carty was stunned by the comment.

'Don't seem so surprised. We all have a dark side to our characters, don't we?' Green simpered. 'That's why Jung termed it the *shadow.*'

Is this a joke? Carty wondered, glancing over at the picture again.

'And when this shadow aspect is reflected upon and given attention, it becomes a friend, lifting a veil so that we can become more complete as individuals.'

Green gently rose, disturbing an inert strata of smoke. It eddied in his wake as he sauntered across the room to open a small window.

'Did you have any other dreams after that?'

Carty nodded. 'Yes, I had one as I fell asleep in front of the fire. There was a young girl – a child – standing at my front door. She seemed to be waiting to lead me outside into a heavy mist, then down some steps into to a cellar where she disappeared into its depths, leaving me alone...' he hesitated, 'a hooded figure then emerged from out of nowhere, scaring the life out of me.' He looked up for Green's acknowledgement, but found him gazing away into the haze, slowly nodding.

'It jolted me awake, and my brandy glass dropped and shattered in the hearth. The noise woke up my wife and I was terrified.

'Of course, you had an experience with the *Self.*'

'What do you mean, the *Self?*'

Green ignored him and continued. 'Have you discussed these dreams with your wife?'

'No, she'll think I've gone mad.'

'Will she really think that?' His eyes narrowed.

'She's not happy with me at the moment.' He reached for the coffee cup to avoid delving into the failing relationship.

'What associations do these images invoke in you?'

'Well, the mist was cold and damp which is unusual for the height of summer, and the steps and the cellar...neither exist in real life.'

'Ah! There's that word "real" again,' Green muttered. 'Is that all?'

'No, it's not. The hooded figure spoke to me!'

'It did!' Green became animated. 'What did it say?'

'"*Does everything have to make sense,*" and the odd thing was that Nick spoke those very same words to me the day after.'

'Had you already told him the dream?'

'Not in detail.'

'You're sure?'

'Absolutely!'

'Then that is meaningful: you know the spoken word in a dream has great significance. What do you think it was trying to tell you?'

Carty searched Green's face, puzzled. 'Perhaps it was because I thought none of it made any tangible sense.'

'Precisely! Very often, logical thinking alone, without the balance of the other three functions of consciousness – feeling, sensation and intuition, can hinder our growth as individuals.' Green leant forward to pick up his coffee. 'Anything else?'

'I'm not sure.'

'Then perhaps I can give you a clue. The dream-world is a place where the opposites of good and bad, night and day, man and woman, exist together, undifferentiated and autonomous, until we reflect upon them.'

Carty looked lost.

'Your shadow will always appear in a dream as a masculine figure. On a deeper level, though, sits an image of the opposite sex, a feminine image Jung called the *anima*. He borrowed it from the Latin word for soul although, etymologically, it comes from a much older Indo-European word – *ane*, meaning to *breathe*.

'Is that why Boyd turned into the young woman?'

'Very good, Scott! It was showing you that by making both figures separate, and then conscious, they can be united again as part of the whole personality. It's the *mysterium coniunctionis,*' he muttered the Latin as if reinforcing the point to himself, 'the alchemical marriage of opposites'

'You think alchemy has relevance to my dreams?'

'Absolutely. In the many thousands of dreams Jung analysed, he recognised the same symbolic stories arising time and again, as depicted in ancient myths, legends and medieval texts,' he said, smiling uncannily as he held the younger man's sombre stare. 'Since classical times, the alchemists were seeking the elixir, the true gold of the spirit, not the yellow stuff that comes out of the ground. They believed their art was a holy one, redeeming the base aspects of humanity, and that it required introspection, reflection, and prayer. For brief a period of history there was an uncommon overlap with traditional Christianity but then, it posed a threat to the Church and the alchemists were forced to form secret societies, hiding their profound work in arcane, almost indecipherable language.'

Green drew on the cigar butt. It glowed back into life in the darkening room as Carty moved uneasily in his chair. Memories beckoned of attending mass with his maternal grandmother as a young boy. He was often sent to stay with her to escape his mother's bouts of alcoholism.

'What was the young girl doing?' Green asked, his tone now avuncular as he switched on a brass desk lamp.

'She led me outside into the garden.'

'And to an instinctive side of your psyche, one which you've ignored for too long and which, like her, hasn't been allowed to grow up.'

'Really?'

'The psyche is alive and grows as we do, unless it is prevented from doing so by a trauma or other events.'

'Hmm, and the mist and the cellar?' Carty asked sheepishly.

'The mist probably represents being lost and unable to see your way forward in life. It's also cold, like your feelings. The cellar might represent your past, partially buried and dark.'

'But what about the hooded figure?'

'You tell me!'

Carty shrugged. 'It looked like a monk so I suppose it suggests religion.'

'But not dogmatic religion: a monk is somewhat of a hermit figure – introspective and living away of the world in order to perceive the divine. Jung called this archetype, the *Self – the two million year old man* – the part of each person that's linked to the eternal. Perhaps it's the part of God in all of us!' He had indirectly answered Carty's earlier question. 'You can count yourself both fortunate and cursed but you really have no choice other than to accept its message!'

Carty felt his hackles rise. He didn't like being told his fate but a sense of something greater quelled the urge to argue back.

'Would you like some more coffee?'

'Yes, I would.'

Carty sat alone, bathed in the green hue cast by the lamp's ornate glass shade.

What a bloody mess! He thought, glancing around at the eclectic clutter, disappointed that a man of Green's pedigree had such a disorganised study. A compulsion, though, drove him to wander over to the shelves and casually browse. Running a finger over the spines, a book leapt out as if animated, crashing loudly on the parquet floor.

'Looking for something to read?' Green quizzed, entering at that precise moment and laying down the tray.

'No, I wasn't.' Carty shamefacedly stooped to retrieve the book.

Green scanned its cover. '*Psyche and Matter*, that's a good choice!'

'Really?'

'Yes, it was written by Marie-Louise Von Franz, one of Jung's closest collaborators.'

He automatically poured two glasses from a bottle of Armenian Cognac and passed one to the younger man.

'Shall we continue?' Green asked, ritually relighting his cigar.

The study was eerily quiet in that moment, as if it was waiting for Carty's reply. He peeked at his watch, torn between the thought of making his excuses to leave and an inexplicable draw to resume the analysis.

'So, you think Mark Boyd is my shadow?' he asked as he sat back down.

'You could say that. Everything you dislike about him is just a projection of qualities latent within yourself. The dream tells you that it will be humiliating to connect with your shadow, but connect you must, "*your life depends upon it!*"'

Carty visibly reeled. 'But it's just a dream.'

'Scott, your dreams and their world are real, just as real as the one in which we are speaking to each other now.'

'Then what should I do about them?'

'Well, you could start by making a list of all those things you dislike about Boyd. Mull them over, work on them and see how many you recognise in yourself.'

'Does it have anything to do with my job?'

Green tilted his head, quizzically. 'Are you worried about losing it?'

'Possibly.'

'Be honest, Scott. You're driven by your career but does it really fulfil anything more than a superficial pursuit?'

'So you're suggesting I resign?'

'*Tertium non datum,*' Green resounded.

'Is that Latin as well?'

'Yes, it means "*the third not given,*" the resolution of two seemingly insoluble scenarios yielding a third, a solution not previously seen or understood but which can only be gained by effort, sweat and conscious reflection. Dreams usually guide you to this natural solution but it's not a path most people usually choose to follow, although in your case, you appear to have been chosen.'

'Chosen?' Carty's eyes widened with anxiety as his grip tightened on the leather arm of the sofa. 'I don't think Arthur D'albo would agree with your line of thinking Gordon.'

'Arthur D'albo!' Green's expression darkened. 'He's not exactly a moral compass, is he?'

'Why would you say that?'

'Brightwell Carter: ask yourself why it went down under such suspicious circumstances, without D'albo knowing anything about it.'

'But Boyd was found guilty.'

'Yes and your dream chose Boyd's image to shock you into understanding the events unfolding around you.'

'Which are?'

'D'albo is playing a game with you both.'

'A game?'

'Of course! You've been blinded by your own shadow. D'albo has a very questionable background.'

Carty tried to stifle a laugh. 'Do you know something that I don't, Gordon?'

'Let's just say that allegations have been made behind closed doors.'

'By whom?'

'Close, influential friends who do not utter without clear conviction.'

'But what is it that they know?'

Green shook his head dismissively. 'Tell me, what role is Boyd going to fill at Albion?'

'Supposedly, he's there to assist me but he's definitely not a derivatives man.'

'Then perhaps D'albo no longer has a need for your derivatives.'

'So you are suggesting that I resign?'

The older man raised a finger. 'Do nothing. Just listen to what your instincts are telling you and wait for D'albo to make his move.'

Carty slumped back into the leather upholstery and pored over the recent happenings. Green's allegations seemed to make a distorted sense in explaining D'albo's odd behaviour.

'Anyway, if you find yourself out of a job you can always work with us at *ReSourced*,' Green quipped, referring to the partnership Nick Hall had mentioned.

'Thanks, but I already told Nick what I think of renewables!' Carty countered, tactlessly. 'They cannot be relied upon to produce mainstream power.'

Green snorted. 'I'm sure I don't need to tell you that the earth's surface receives enough heat and light from the sun, in the space of a few minutes, to supply all of our energy needs for a whole year. I agree that harnessing it in bulk will present a challenge – the funding and technology already exist – but the will, though, is lacking.'

'I can't agree with you. There's plenty of research work being carried out and huge investment, but no major breakthroughs, yet. So it seems that we're stuck with fossil fuels, nuclear power and energy efficiency for the foreseeable future.'

'Well, that all depends on the zeitgeist, Scott. You're churning out the same old argument that has prevailed for more than 100 years since Rockefeller, Morgan and others established the framework for the modern industrial world. That structure was relevant in its day and has achieved many great things. But now it's out of date and is causing a paralysis which is stretching the sustainability of our planet to its limits.'

'So why hasn't anything else replaced it then?'

'Short-term profit and expediency!' he retorted, 'political parties looking to stay in administration while appeasing the vested interests of multinational globalisation. This is a shadow problem on a much grander scale.'

Carty sighed, exasperated. 'You and Nick really have a problem with conspiracy, don't you?'

'Yes, when it comes to the blind destruction of the very ecosystems that supports life.'

'Gordon, nature is dynamic and can adjust to the march of progress.'

'Everything on this planet is interconnected but progress, as you call it, is disturbing its balance. The story of the *Rainmaker of Kiao Chou* explains it very clearly.'

'Sorry, what is that?' Carty looked bewildered.

'Ah yes, sorry, it's in *Psyche and Matter.*' He pointed to the book. 'It's a true story. Perhaps that's the reason why it fell off the shelf so that when you've read it you'll understand things differently.'

'Well, I believe my emissions derivatives will, in part, help to mitigate climate change,' he said, feeling vindicated.

'You really believe that the world can trade its way out of the environmental issues that it's facing?'

'It's better than not doing anything at all.'

'On the contrary, it seems to me that carbon offsetting is just a modern form of absolution: purchasing someone else's right to commit the sin of polluting, just more cheaply.'

'That's very short-sighted and simply not true.'

'Ah, well, I guess I'm just not intelligent enough to understand how the emissions from raging forest fires or the methane leaking from thawing Siberian permafrost – such huge natural processes – can be alleviated by carbon trading?'

He's got a point, Carty silently affirmed.

'Scott,' he uttered quietly, 'the world's feminine soul – the *anima mundi* as the alchemists revered her – the maiden of your dream, depends on our responsible behaviour in order for us all to survive.' His eyes widened with emphasis. Carty noted a troubled sadness behind them and the sublime statements had left him bereft of his usual intellectual retorts. He fell into a numbed silence as the door clicked quietly open and Joanna peered in briefly, before closing it again.

'I think we should call it a night,' Green said brusquely. 'Don't forget your notes and the book.'

'Yes, yes, of course,' Carty staggered slightly as he rose.

'Problems with your leg?'

'Not really, it's an old knee strain that's recently started to play up again.'

'Hmm, I would look at the synchronicity of that as well.'

They walked out across the hallway to the front door.

'Thank you for your insights into the dreams, Gordon.'

'It's my pleasure. I suggest that you take them, and any more you have, very seriously.'

'I will.'

They shook hands firmly and then Carty strolled out into the cool night air.

'And try humbly to accept the words of the maiden and the *two million year old man.*' Carty turned to acknowledge the comment and caught sight of the plaque once again.

'By the way, what does "Temenos" mean?'

'It's Greek for a sacred place where ritual is held.'

'Really, and what ritual is held here?'

The older man dropped his eyes. 'Engaging with the unconscious,' he answered, almost inaudibly.

Carty nodded at his own faux pas and wheeled his bike out to the gate before turning to attempt a friendly wave. But Green had already gone.

The breeze was unusually chilly for the time of year and felt strangely foreign. He trembled and picked up the pace, mentally churning Green's numerous statements. He had been impressed, yet at the same time annoyed by the man's uncompromising nature.

Why is he so taken by Jung anyway? Surely his work hadn't been so all-encompassing? And how can alchemy and these dreams have any relevance to my life?

They were too far removed from his ordered everyday existence: two completely different worlds that could never be reconciled. *Or could they? "Tertium non datum, the third not given."* Green words echoed quietly against the tide of his normal world, flowing back in again.

Eight

Hotel: Almaty, Kazakhstan.

Carty propped himself up against the pillows. Jet-lagged, he had distracted himself by flicking through the various satellite channels before ordering a meal in the room.

He picked at the local *plov*, a dish of lamb and rice, his appetite sapped as he relived the drama that had unfolded that morning at the airport and then the meeting with Kosechenko. As he tried to relax his attention was momentarily drawn to the curtains billowing with the breeze from the balcony's tall windows. He didn't remember opening them earlier. Then he noticed the dog-eared cover of *Psyche and Matter* on the floor. It must have spilled out of his bag and lay open at a page that had obviously been referenced many times. One word stood out as he picked it up: *Rainmaker,* the story that Green had referred to. Curious, he began to skim-read the passage.

A serious drought had befallen a region of China during the latter part of the 19ʰ century. The town of Kiao Chou had been particularly badly hit, and desperate, its elders sent a messenger to the mountains to ask the Rainmaker, an elderly Taoist monk, for help.
He agreed but on arriving refused their best lodgings, asking only for a modest dwelling and to be left alone until he called for them.
The townsfolk waited nervously for three days and then, miraculously, it began to rain and then snow. The events were witnessed by Richard Wilhelm, the Jesuit

missionary who had translated the I Ching, and brought it to Jung's attention. Amazed by the events, Wilhelm interviewed the old Taoist, asking just how the impossible had been achieved. The sage simply replied that the inhabitants were not in harmony with nature – the Tao – and that, once there, having attained his own balance, it naturally rained!

Ordinarily, Carty's reaction would have been to cast it aside as bunkum but after the dreams and the meeting with Green, he was intrigued and flicked through its pages. There were a number of references to familiar themes drawing parallels between quantum physics with old-world traditions.

Was there really an all-pervading Tao? The thought swirled, *a link between matter and all life?* He cast his mind back to scientific papers published during his PhD years, dealing with the quest for a unified field, the Holy Grail of elementary particle physicists – the new alchemists. Some had veered away from the inorganic physics of *dead* matter, venturing instead into the vibratory world of energy, DNA and the essence of life itself.

The phone's shrill timbre jolted him, sending the plate and its unfinished contents onto the floor. He grabbed at the receiver.

'Hello, Scott, I am about to have a sauna, would you like to come too?' Lena asked. It seemed a strange question and he vacillated, momentarily unsure of her motives.

'Erh, no, I think I will politely decline. Thanks anyway.'

'All right then, I will be with you in an hour and a half. Please be ready.' Her tone seemed edgy.

Slowly, he pulled himself off the bed and stepped out onto the balcony to be greeted by the city's skyline and the backdrop of the snowy peaks of the *Tien Shan* – the celestial mountains, glinting in the sun's dying rays as darkness crept unceasingly up their slopes, to consume their magnificence for another day.

'So, Scott, how was your afternoon?' Lena asked as the lift descended. Her perfumed scent was delicious.

'Oh, not bad, I slept mainly and didn't see anything of Almaty.'

'That's a shame! There won't be a chance to do that tomorrow.'

'Why?'

'We leave for Baikal.'

'We're not staying for the conference?' A lump settled in his stomach.

'There's no need. You have already presented and Koshechenko never remains for more than a day at these functions.'

'But I thought he was joking! What about my flight back to London?'

'I will have my office re-book it.'

'For when?'

'A few days' time.'

'A few days!'

'Yes, we want to give our clients plenty of time to enjoy Siberia and to understand its huge potential for the energy business!'

'I'm really not keen to leave the warmth of Kazakhstan for the freezing snow.'

'Snow!' she spluttered. 'Central Siberia has a hot, continental summer and anyway you will enjoy being at Baikal. It's the Earth's Blue Eye.'

He frowned.

The lift doors parted. 'Ready to go to dinner?' She winked at him and then daintily stepped out.

A mixed bag of prominent local businessmen and dignitaries were hosted at an impressive local restaurant, boasting modern European cuisine. Carty was seated on the main table, placed away from the few international clients who might want to strike up a conversation about business. Instantly, though, he recognised the two Russians who he had met with D'albo, sitting opposite him and he raised a hand, smiling. They apathetically reciprocated.

Lena, having finished her greetings, sat down next to them, her eyes focused on Kosechenko who had remained standing with a champagne flute in hand and his bullet head perspiring profusely. His speech went on longer than it should have done and without Lena's translation. The two men had carried on their irritating mutterings between themselves, impervious to the host or the other guests.

After more than an hour of listening to a stream of toasts and with the vodka loosening Carty's stiffness, he felt Lena's hand on his shoulder. She had been making her way around the tables ensuring that all the clients were enjoying themselves and now she whispered something to him. Unable to hear, he strained his head backwards.

'Scott, you must make a toast.'

'I must?' he seemed surprised.

'Yes, it's customary!'

Sighing, he slowly rose with a raised his glass and waited for everyone's attention. Then he briefly gave his thanks to Kosechenko and the Russian energy business.

It was after midnight when the coach party returned back to the hotel. In the lobby Lena, forever the professional, schmoozed with a bunch of Americans who had arrived late. Carty sidled backwards a few paces and then slipped away to his room.

His mobile showed a number of missed calls and inebriated, he stripped and flopped down on to the bed to listen to the voice messages from the women in his life. Diane had wanted to know if he had arrived safely while Davina sounded uneasy. He mulled their words, half-listening, still preoccupied with the events of the evening.

Why had the two Russians ignored Kosechenko so blatantly?

The same single ring shook him again. It was Lena.

'I thought you would be asleep after all that translating!' he joked.

'I can't sleep. I want to talk with you.'

'Go ahead.'

'No, I meant that I would like to talk with you in person.' She paused deliberately. 'Come to my room.' Her soft tone was irresistible.

She was tipsy and pouting as she invited him in, nudging the door shut with her arse.

'You wanted to talk with me?'

His naïve comment drew her close and grinning, she ran a silky palm across his cheek. He grabbed her waist and she toppled forward in a moment that seemed timeless before resting her forehead against this shoulder. Carty gently puckered his lips along her slender neck. She tilted her head back, baring it to him, her blouse open just enough to expose the edge of her bra. He ran his hand brusquely over her breasts as he softly explored her ear. She panted, her hands squeezing his as he swept her up in his arms and laid her on the bed.

They kissed deeply and then suddenly she pushed him away, fixing him with a searching look. Behind her cool mask lay a vulnerable woman, one who wanted to be cherished, not consumed.

Their short passionate lovemaking left him struggling with confused feelings as he lay quietly with her blonde mane spilled across his chest. His relationship with Diane had grown stale and despite his guilt he now found himself strangely desperate for Lena's affection. She was unlike any other woman he had met. Her bold manner and deep emotional torrents were hard to fathom.

'Why me, Lena?' he murmured, kissing her head and wondering if a relationship with her would be any different, once the passion had waned.

She pulled herself up onto her elbows.

'There's a light that shines from you. It's warm and sincere and not stained by the world that I live in.'

He was stunned by her answer, not feeling particularly sincere having just cheated on his wife. She carried on as if reading his thoughts.

'You think you should be doing the right thing but you cannot know what that is without having explored your feelings. I knew that you were not fulfilled.' She pecked at his hairless chest.

'And just what is your world like?' he asked, reflecting on her words while combing his fingers through her unkempt strands.

'Kosechenko does whatever he wants to,' she murmured.

'But you don't have to work for him, do you?'

Her porcelain face remained unmoved but an almost imperceptible inhalation drew a second's hesitation.

'I cannot leave...' she buried her face in his chest, 'I know too much.'

Shocked, Carty cradled her cheeks with both hands.

'Lena, what are you saying?'

'You *do* know what we're doing in Russia, don't you?' she nodded slowly, as the words tumbled from her mouth.

'Actually we're in Kazakhstan,' he mocked.

'Ha!' she laughed hollowly, her face still reddened from the effects of the vodka.

He pulled his head off the pillow. 'Be clear, what do you mean?'

She pushed him back down and slipped her legs astride his waist, leaning to whisper in his ear.

'I mean that *your* Mr D'albo is not really interested in CentralniySib's risk management strategy.'

'He's not?' Carty stammered.

She shook her head, her tousled locks brushing his face, physically confirmed the negative.

'The money in the case...it was a trap to implicate you in trafficking...to have you deported and to destroy your reputation.'

Why? His eyes widened, searching hers as she dug her chin into his sternum. That moment at the airport shot through his mind again. At the time he had missed an obvious clue, but his unconscious hadn't and now he recalled just how quickly the guard had opened the locked case. He must have already known the combination.

'D'albo wanted to do this to me? How can you be sure of that?'

'I overheard Kosechenko discussing it yesterday.'

'With D'albo?' he countered.

'No, it was in Russian, but something went wrong with the plan.' She giggled, in a drunken hysterical way. 'Someone at the top level, here in Kazakhstan, intervened and had you released.'

'What? That's bullshit! I don't know anyone of that importance in England, let alone in Kazakhstan.'

'Well, someone's protecting you. Kosechenko is incensed and he's blaming D'albo.'

'But is Kosechenko in control?' His question hinted at desperation.

'No, the nephews are.'

'The nephews? You mean those two Russians?'

She put a finger over his lips. 'Don't you understand?' Her voice was hushed. 'It's not about the money in the case anymore, Scott. They think you're a spy.'

'A spy! That's absurd!'

He felt a tear fall onto his chest. 'They think you're interested in the *other* business,' she stuttered, 'the one that D'albo and Kosechenko are managing for the nephews.'

Carty's face had frozen. 'Other business?'

'You honestly don't know about it, do you?' Her fear was obvious.

'No, I don't. What is it?'

'The dumping of spent nuclear waste in Siberia!'

She began to sob.

For a moment he thought she had spoken in Russian. He stroked her milky cheek in disbelief but maintained a nonchalant smile.

Why is she telling me all this? he wondered, unsure that her comments weren't influenced by drink as her bloodshot eyes stared back at him. It all seemed too quixotic and railed against his *quant* instincts. The thought of D'albo being involved in the dumping of nuclear waste, entrepreneurial as it might seem, didn't fit, it just wasn't his style.

But then he suddenly remembered the Russian paper that Davina had left on his desk, referencing disposal strategies for European nuclear waste.

That's just too much of a coincidence.

A number of western nuclear power stations were fast approaching the end of their useful lives. Decommissioning them and removing the radioactive waste would place a strain on domestic storage facilities but dumping it elsewhere in the world, cheaply and out of sight, might be an attractive option as long as fingers couldn't be pointed.

He was heady with the surreal thoughts as Lena lay curled up beside him and his heart sank with the cold suspicion that she might have played him. Whatever her reasons, though, her confessions were irrevocable and that now put both of their liberties at risk.

Nine

Heavy footsteps along the corridor outside shook him from a febrile sleep. Irritated by the clinging sheets, damp with their sweat, he slid off the bed. His knee buckled under his weight and wincing, he struggled out on to the balcony.

A strong wind had lifted the night's muggy air and a hint of dawn was creeping from behind the *Tien Shan*. He drew a breath, still anxious about Lena's story. Whether D'albo was involved in this insane predicament or not, made little difference, he had lied to Carty about the case and trampled his trust into the ground. A mixture of anger and apprehension forced his breathing uncomfortably high into his chest, as his mind played ceaselessly over the options. Whichever way he juggled with them, though, he arrived at the same conclusion: to travel back to England as soon as possible that day, and face down D'albo.

He took another breath and hobbled back in to find his clothes.

'Where are you going?' Lena purred, holding out a sculpted arm to him.

'To my room,' he took her hand and bent to kiss her lips. A warm sensation filtered up from the pit of his stomach.

'What time is it?'

'Almost five. Sleep now and I will see you for breakfast.'

'Hmmm, that would be nice,' she beamed, her eyes still tightly closed.

But Lena missed breakfast.

He hurried back to his room suspicious that her superiors were now aware she had spent the night with him.

'Diane, hi, it's me.' He felt relieved at reaching his wife. Her warm face presented itself before him like a hologram as she spoke, reminding him of his responsibilities and his guilt.

'Scott, I thought you would never call!' Her voice was distorted by the satellite link. 'I had to speak with Davina to find out if you had arrived safely.'

'What did she say?' He strategically timed his question with the delay in the line.

'Nothing much, except that Arthur seemed to be upset. Is everything all right there?'

'Everything is fine, but the hospitality has been rather excessive!'

'How was the presentation?' Her question jumped ahead of his last response.

'It went fine. I'm heading back to London today. I'm finished here.'

'Oh, that's odd. Davina told me you were going on to Russia.'

'No, she's wrong!' he snapped, understanding that D'albo must have mentioned the invitation to Baikal.

'Is James well?'

'Yes, and he's missing you badly.'

'What's wrong, Diane?'

'We'll talk when you get back,' she said.

'C'mon, what is it?'

She was silent for some seconds. 'I know about Sally, Scott.'

'It's nothing!' he said, feeling no compunction to argue. 'Give James a hug and a kiss for me.'

As he hung up he caught the reflection of his swollen pallour in the mirror.

'I've left several voice messages on your Blackberry, Scott!' Davina's manner was defensive.

'Sorry, Davina, it's dead. I left the charger back in London and it's been hectic here.'

'So what exactly, has been going on?'

'I would love to discuss it but I urgently need you to do something for me.'

'What?'

'Find me a flight out of here today!'

She quickly reviewed the options with him, settling on an afternoon flight to Tashkent, a regional hub with a number of onward flights to Europe. Lena knocked and entered without waiting, taking him by surprise. He had left the door ajar by mistake.

'I'll call you back, Davina,' he uttered, stunned by the picture of Lena's red Chanel business suit and her stockinged legs, turned into patent stilettos of a matching shade.

'Where were you? I was waiting at breakfast for almost an hour.' Confused, he had no idea of the risks she had taken in being intimate with him.

'Sorry, I was just too tired,' Lena responded coolly, glancing at his suit-carrier lying open across the bed. Gone was the doe-eyed woman with whom he had shared the night.

'Scott, you are coming to Baikal, aren't you?' She bit her bottom lip, nervously.

'No, Lena. This whole thing is a farce: the interrogation at the airport, the cash in the case and now this insane story about dumping nuclear waste!' He gripped her upper arms gently but she had closed her eyes, halting his attempts to reach her.

'Lena, please, I need to get back to see my family and save my job. My responsibilities are there, not with CentralniySib or Kosechenko.' He turned and continued to pack.

'Scott, I'm scared!'

He stopped and looked up, worriedly. 'Of what?'

'I suspect that someone knows about our conversations last night.'

'So what, no one can hold it against you, it's hearsay.'

'You don't understand. This is not London. The freedoms you enjoy there will not protect me here or in Russia.'

'Do you want me to speak to Kosechenko?'

'Hah!' she blurted, hysterically. 'That would make matters much worse.'

He caught the deep-seated anguish in her expression. London would have to wait.

'So, tell me again.' He paused before slowly enquiring. 'How long will we stay at Baikal?'

She frowned, processing his response before breaking into a broad grin.

'Only a few days!' she blurted. 'The aircraft is chartered and we leave the hotel at midday. The Americans are coming too.'

'The Americans,' he taunted, recalling their brief introduction at dinner.

'Why?'

'Orders from Kosechenko!'

Ten

The drive to the airport provided him with another snapshot of Almaty's daily life and its myriad culture. Young street traders, garbed in silky track-suit bottoms and sleeveless jumpers badged with fake marques, exuded a frenetic energy as they shouted out to a fusion of Kazakh, Tartar and European faces. Others with lank black hair and dark weathered features dwelt on their haunches atop disintegrating kerbstones, chewing pine nuts, smoking and staring at the immaculately dressed young women squeezing past them.

'Here, women think nothing of spending a large amount of their monthly salaries on clothes,' she remarked. 'It's a cultural thing and besides, Almaty is the Paris of Central Asia.'

Carty smiled, his gaze switching to the groups of elderly men sipping tea in their oversized jackets and shrinking frames, sheltering from the sun on benches below the birch and European ash that lined the roads. They momentarily interrupted their domino games to glance up at the passing motorcade.

How simple their lives are, he thought.

The loaded invitation to visit Baikal meant Carty had been robbed of the opportunity to loiter as a tourist and visit the markets or sample traditional local dishes. The obvious charm of this place would be forever tainted by his experience at its airport.

Shortly, they pulled into a parking lot alongside a local landing strip. Lena briefly re-introduced the Americans but explanations as to their possible business interests were skirted in apparent urgency as she promptly ushered them aboard a newly refurbished Tupelov jet.

Kosechenko arrived soon after, accepting a whisky as his unmistakable bulk slumped down alone on a leather sofa in the forward cabin. The sight of the man made him nauseous and caused Lena's diabolical revelation to echo in his head again. He leant over and whispered to her.

'Where are the nephews?'

She turned to him, snatching a worried look as the laconic translator hovered in the aisle behind them, his wan, sunken cheeks and grey pallor projecting a morbid aura.

As soon as they had left the ground Tom, one of the Americans, piped up.

'How long is this flight going to take?'

Seated next to the Englishman, he had taken the liberty of leaning across him, in order to maintain a dialogue with the beautiful Russian.

'About four hours,' Lena shouted back against the roar of the engines.

The stewardess then began pointing out something below the starboard of the plane. Carty used this as an excuse to visit the toilet and taking a cursory glance out of a rear cabin window, he noticed that the lush vegetation of Almaty had been supplanted by an arid shrub-land and in the midst of the low sandstone mountains, arched an enormous lake. Its shimmering surface was obscured in part by a dense yellow haze billowing up from the chimney stacks of the Kazakh copper industry, a legacy of Stalin's *gulags*. Thousands of disenfranchised Koreans, Germans and other unfortunates had been shipped in, following the Second World War. That a place of such beauty could be so obviously violated disturbed Carty in a way he had never felt before. It triggered a realisation that he had been living in an academic bubble, impervious to the raw and chaotic interaction of industrial progress within the closed ecosystem of the planet. The vision of the maiden surfaced for a fleeting moment, beckoning him again into the woods of his dreams.

'There's a big lake down there,' he commented as he slipped back into his seat.

'It's called Balkhash,' Lena replied abruptly, 'and it's not that big!'

'It looks like it is.' Tom frowned.

'Not compared to Baikal – the deepest lake on the planet.'

'That's news to me. I thought the Caspian Sea was.'

She smiled pitifully at the American. 'The Caspian is salty, unlike Baikal's pristine water. Our cosmonauts see it from space as a thin blue eye the same deep shade as the oceans, not the light blue of other lakes,' she faltered for a moment, 'Baikal is awe-inspiring and you will soon see why.'

Her comments caused an inexplicable shiver to run through Carty.

'You seem to know a lot about it,' Tom added.

'Yes, I spent many summers there. My grandfather was a research scientist working at an institute near its shores.'

'And what was his line of research, hydro-electricity?' Carty interjected.

'Is the energy business all you think about?' Her raised voice caught the translator's unwanted attention again.

'This lake, Baikal, it can't be as big as Lake Superior!' Tom goaded, obviously turned on by her bold manner.

'Baikal contains more water than all of your so-called Great Lakes,' she glared. 'And it's more than 20 million years old!'

The American tried to smile off his embarrassment. Carty meanwhile had blanked the conversation and had sunk back into his chair, chewing uneasily again over Lena's confession of the night before and D'albo's possible involvement.

A sensation of pressure in his ears woke him as the aircraft banked to land. Minutes later they were on the ground, at a small private airport outside Irkutsk.

As they emerged into the late afternoon sunlight, the air smelt sweeter and fresher than in Almaty, and Carty's gaze was drawn beyond a huddle of ageing aircraft. Irkutsk, the 'Paris of Siberia', was just discernible in the distance through the haze, rippling off the tarmac.

'Mr Carty?' a trim man, bedecked in mirror-shades, called out as the Englishman stepped off the stairway. Carty nodded to him, forgetting for a split second where he was.

'This way please!' the Russian ordered, directing him to a waiting convoy of black Land Cruisers.

A feeling of unease sat with him some minutes into the journey, before it became evident exactly what was causing it.

'Lena, did you arrange a Russian visa for me?' he blurted, turning to catch his expression of doubt reflected back in her wrap-around sunglasses.

'Huh!' she uttered, casually lifting them, 'an official will visit the camp to issue all the foreigners with temporary tourist visas.'

'But isn't it mandatory to have one, to enter Russia?'

'Strictly speaking, yes, but a copy of your passport was forwarded to the customs authorities in advance to begin the process. Don't worry; it will be issued before you leave.'

He shrugged, feeling his concerns justified. If she screwed up he and the others would be deported.

'And is the camp far from here?'

'It's just up the lake.'

'Are we getting on a boat then?'

'No, a hydrofoil!'

'Really?' His tone ill disguised his impatience.

She slipped her fingers surreptitiously across the smooth leather to reassuringly touch his.

He grinned as his attention shifted to take in the scenery: rolling hills of grassland and large patchwork fields punctuated by dense copses of birch and pine. Small, sturdy timber cottages sat amongst the trees, their corrugated roofing and galvanised steel chimneys reminiscent of the pioneer houses still standing in the southern states of the USA. These *datchas*, though, held a greater sense of the eternal and their small gardens provided the city-dweller with vegetables, fruits of the forest, and eggs from poultry.

Irregular wooden picket-fences, some collapsed in places, separated each property from its neighbours while cows roamed freely along the muddy tracks, between stacks of chopped wood and roughly hewn telegraph poles carrying power lines to each dwelling. The great Soviet uprising had prided itself in supplying electricity to all but despite that, life here seemed not to have changed much in the last 70 years.

'This is Siberia.' She gently squeezed his hand.

'Yes, and it's pretty rustic!'

'Rustic?'

'I meant charming.'

'And now we're approaching Irkutsk.' Her comment was prompted by the increase in traffic.

Soon enough the convoy sped into the wide streets of the city, passing a mix of tired architecture and modern offices, some still partly finished. The bulbous steeple of a gleaming white church caught his eye, standing alone, gold topped and proud, proclaiming the rush to orthodoxy. It contrasted starkly with the brick-built tenements and their rotten concrete canopies exposing rusting steel-framed cores.

Nestled in all this were the traditional wooden lodges; grand affairs, newly painted in greens and dark blues with intricately carved, diamond-beaded eves that hung like jewellery above their windows. These homes were testament to the wealth of a town that had boomed more than a century before, trading fur pelts, prospecting gold and mining Mica. By the late 1880s, its entrepreneurs were rubbing shoulders with Czarist socialites, academics and exiled Decemberists, creating a cultural breathing space in the backwaters of Eurasia.

Carty was taken by the place's energy: newly erected kiosks selling everything from Tajik watermelons to imitation MP3 players. Blonde and redheaded girls hung aimlessly around in cheap copy-designer clothes, their faces evidence of a richly mixed ancestry. Older women with headscarves and unashamed gold teeth offered punnets of wild fox-berries. Less than a generation ago they had been youngsters in a very different system.

Shortly, the harbour emerged and with it, the first glimpse of the bizarre hulk they were to board.

'What the devil is that?' The words tumbled from Carty's gawping mouth. The vessel at the dock resembled a huge, technological platypus with a hull-bottomed fuselage, proportionally longer than it should have been. Two wing-like ears protruded from either side of the cockpit and its main wings were stunted and carried four massive engines that wouldn't have been out of place on a 747 Jumbo Jet.

'That isn't a hydrofoil,' he insisted with a hint of misgiving as he stepped out and offered her a hand. She refused him.

'No, it is called an *Ekranoplan,*' she said.

The vessel creaked worryingly against its moorings, and from its patchy, rust-bubbled paintwork he guessed it was more than 20 years old and probably built to military specifications. It was likely to continue running until it fell to pieces or sank. Aircraft kerosene was, after all, cheap for a Russian energy group.

'This Ekranoplan was a project of the Soviet industrial-military complex,' she explained. 'It flies undetectably, at aircraft speeds just above the water.'

Carty cocked an eyebrow.

'The airflow is forced between its wings and the water's surface which increases the lift and reduces the drag.'

'Spoken just like an engineer!' he said and was then just about to ask why she hadn't explained this earlier when he noticed a black Mercedes crawling up alongside them. The barely visible face of Kosechenko leered behind its tinted windows. She tensed and stepped forward to greet him.

'You seem like a lucky guy!' Hank, a handsome Alpha male and the self-proclaimed leader of the Americans, announced as he sidled up alongside Carty.

'Why's that?' The Englishman kept his gaze steadily on Lena.

'Oh come on, Scott! You get the girl all to yourself in the car. What is Albion doing that is so important to CentralniySib?'

'They're after insider information!'

'On what?'

'Synthetic weather derivatives!' Carty turned and grinned. The American's steely eyes lacked the warmth that his approach feigned.

The beast's engines coughed fiercely, drowning out their chance of conversation but both sensed in the other, a fear as to the purpose of this trip.

The craft swayed in the rapid currents making their gang-plank boarding, precarious. Then, passing through the access door into the cavernous interior, Carty caught sight of Lena through its portholes. She was still standing on the pier, her soft face hardened in defiance at her director but her head, though, dutifully bowed in deference. Carty wanted to go to her defence but was thrown as the craft lurched forward suddenly and craning his head back, he watched the entourage of vehicles pulling away from the quayside. He realised that he was now alone with a group of strangers, each one sporting the same expression of trepidation that perhaps this piece of Cold War junk might be a coffin. It took milliseconds for the thought to register on his face before the translator's smirking mask acknowledged the discomfort.

The sheer thrust and then elevation from the water was stupefying.

'Moves pretty fast, don't it?' Hank resumed his inquisitive streak with Carty. 'Do you think it will get us there?'

'Depends where *there* is!'

'Didn't your girlfriend tell you?' the American quipped, the other members of his group tuning in to his conversation.

'Not exactly.'

'So, why are you here then?' he delved again.

'Well,' the Englishman faltered for an instant. 'I come here every year and...'

The American snorted. 'Yes of course you do, but why have you been invited?'

'The same reason as you, I assume.' It was a calculated response, laid to draw his challenger out.

'Which is?'

Carty sighed, deciding to relinquish something he had no reason to defend. 'My CEO has a close relationship with CentralniySib. I'm here to hand-hold it on his behalf and perhaps get some derivatives sold.'

'You want to sell these Russians options!' Hank grinned in disbelief, seeking the unquestionable support of his subordinates. 'That's bunkum. They're only interested in hard cash, not in price protection and right now they want full market value for the commodities they're drilling for or digging up.' His colleagues looked on nodding, accepting his guru-like exposition. Carty pondered the dialogue as the drone of the engines became hypnotic and he found himself lapsing, strangely distanced from their stares, analysing the situation in a way that he would never have done just a few weeks earlier. Perhaps Hank was right, that his derivatives and mathematical modelling were too one-sided and divorced from the *real* world. His dreams and Gordon

Green explanations seemed to have given him a new perspective. He eyed the American and then aimed a question.

'Why are you really here, Hank?'

'Well...' the man stammered, taken off guard. 'We're working with the regional government on strategic energy projects.'

'No doubt you are. What kind?'

'We're looking at all opportunities.' His voice lowered.

'In this region?' Carty sought clarification. 'Well, I suppose there's plenty of coal and gas, or maybe you're looking at hydropower.'

'Possibly, but I am not at liberty to say.' His eyes were unblinking, as if he had been programmed to react to such searching questions.

Is he part of this dumping scam as well?

Carty's intuition was pricked, sensing that the American was playing dumb. Then he made a move worthy of any Russian chess master.

'Siberia is really at its limit for hydro-power,' he chimed. 'Any new power capacity would not be commercially viable and would lead to over-supply.' Pausing to gauge their reaction, he noted that they were hanging on his words. 'What would really make sense, though, is for US companies to deploy their world-class expertise in decommissioning old nuclear reactors.' Carty knew there were no nuclear plants in Eastern Siberia. 'It might also be possible to dispose of spent nuclear waste here, not only from Russian reactors but from foreign ones also.'

Hank eyed the Englishman, his visage a stony grey. 'It would be far easier to dump nuclear waste in Kazakhstan,' he replied with a practised cool. 'Lord knows there were so many nuclear tests carried out there in the past, it wouldn't make any difference!'

Carty stifled a smile: his ploy had worked. Hank's slip was a strong enough hint that he knew about the dumping scam.

'But in many ways we are in the same position as you,' the American continued, 'just keeping the relationship cosy for the bosses.'

'Good, so we're all in the same boat!' The pun was unintentional but it defused the loaded atmosphere. 'Let's drink to it, shall we?'

Shortly, servings of grain bread, salmon caviar and pickled cabbage, along with hot coffee and vodka, were forced on them by the translator.

An announcement then rang out over the intercom, instantly animated the Russians and causing them to clamber together around the small portholes like school kids.

'What are they so excited about?' Tom commented, raucously.

'We're finally on Baikal,' the translator answered.

'But I thought we were already on the lake?' He smugly fired back.

'You're wrong. We've been travelling on the Angara estuary but our Ekranoplan makes light work of a boat journey which normally takes twice as long.'

'Why's that?' Carty shrugged.

The translator wheeled around. 'The Angara is the only river that flows out of Baikal. It starts life, though, as a monster, more than one kilometre wide and its current is so rapid, that it never completely freezes over but steams instead, in our severe Siberian winter, then floods its banks unseasonably.' The light mustard hue of his eyeballs enforced Carty's disquiet for the man. He turned away and took in the sight of a horse lazily grazing at the water's edge alongside rusting farm equipment and a few outboard launches, bobbing in the tide-less wake.

Everything seems as if it's been stuck in a time warp, he thought, glancing back to find the Americans disappearing to the cockpit to absorb the immense view.

The journey seemed to have raced by, as the diminishing revs of the engines and the captain's blurted Russian indicated that they were nearing their destination.

The sharp landing back to the water's surface took them smartly up to within ten metres of a wooden jetty from where a launch had already set out to meet them, riding the waves of the craft's wake.

Carty was instantly taken by the extraordinary light and the fresh air and gazed around, soaking in the phenomenal natural beauty. Larch boughs hung low over the red-clay cliffs and the pebbled beach was swathed in a wispy mist.

That's unusual for this time of day, he mulled, stretching his eyes up along the coast to note several peaks jutting above the myriad green of the *taiga* – the Siberian forest.

An uncanny stillness stole the ambience, subtly unnerving the visitors as the colossal antiquity of this place smothered their casual arrogance. Carty now understood Lena's attachment to Baikal and the reasons for her emotional outburst on the aircraft.

'Quiet, isn't it?' Hank broke the calm. 'When I was a kid in Oregon my grandfather took us hunting in forests, alongside lakes like this. The silence is something you never forget and soon enough you know if you can handle it or not. Some people can't and cling to city life.'

Carty simpered in speechless agreement, chilled as his imagination fooled him for a moment into believing he had seen the hooded revenant again, hovering above the water's surface, in the distance.

Eleven

As they disembarked a Russian youth, dressed in gumboots and sporting a pubescent beard, met them on the shoreline. Embarrassed and unable to communicate, he picked up some of the bags and indicated ahead to a small clearing.

The acrid yet comforting smell of burning logs tainted the pristine air, greeting them before they caught sight of the recently constructed cabins, gently billowing smoke from their galvanised chimneys.

'Guess we'll see each other later,' Hank uttered as Carty was ushered inside one.

A single naked bulb lit the starkness of its interior.

'Hardly corporate entertainment!' he muttered, brushing off the bed before sinking down on its edge. The lad dropped Carty's suit carrier and stared blankly back at him, seeking a tip. It didn't come and he left the Englishman struggling to pull off his jacket, in the stifling warmth and overpowering scent of Siberian cedar. Physically and emotionally drained, the temptation to lie down had overcome Carty.

A sharp knock roused him. 'Come in!' he said, expecting the youth to have returned. But there was no reply. He rose cautiously and opened the door.

No one was there. Confused, he stepped out, squinting against the compound's floodlight. The evening's chill stung the back of his throat as he gawped at the unmistakable outline of the apparition, standing at the edge of the forest. It dipped its hood to turn away and, before he could think, he was in pursuit, running down the network of raised gangplanks criss-crossing the camp's rough terrain.

At the tree line, he was forced to leap blindly into the darkness. He landed awkwardly amongst the damp roots, scraping his shins. Struggling up, he pushed on for a further ten metres, into the dense foliage until a peel of thunder fixed him dead in his tracks and then he realised he was lost. Frantically, he turned to mark his route back to the compound but fell backwards sharply onto his hands, terrified. The ghostly figure was there once more, hovering between the trees.

'Finally you come to where it all begins!' the entity said. 'Lightning and thunder now clear the air and so you must empty your mind and see only those things which are real.'

Carty was speechless, hypnotised by the extraordinary blue eyes, staring through him from inside the cowl. And then, with a sharp rush of wind, the figure span rapidly within its cloak and it slumped to the ground, empty and lifeless.

Arthur D'albo paced the cobbled side street through the modernised warehouse complex of the old Victorian docks, just south of the Thames. Irritated by the lack of news, he fumbled with his mobile, hesitating with his indecision. But then impulsively, he dialled the number, breaking the rules that had been agreed.

'*Da,*' the heavily accented voice answered after some seconds.

'*Zavftra...*tomorrow!' The words were chilling and final.

It should all have happened so differently, he thought with a pang of remorse. But it hadn't. Somehow Scott Carty had foiled his simple plan, and in doing so had fallen foul of the Russians on their own territory.

He kicked a small stone and watched it bounce along the uneven road as a glint flashed from across the river, momentarily framing a figure. It could have been anyone in the crowd leaning on the embankment wall, watching the Thames roll by but the reflection had come from a pair of binoculars watching his every move.

Twelve

'Wake up Carty!' Hank jolted him. 'Dinner's being served!'

Dazed, he sat up. 'How long have I been sleeping for?'

'About two hours.'

He was muddled, but pulled himself off the caved-in mattress.

'Just what have you been doing?' the American blurted, shocked at the claret blood running freely from the grazes on Carty's shins. The Englishman stared at them in disbelief as they began to smart, and then a cool fear forced him to accept the only viable deduction.

Don't be a fool, it was just a dream!

'Carty, the Russians are getting agitated. They're expecting you!' Hank snapped as he prodded the air between them with an unlit cigar.

Carty was strangely glad that the American was there, inadvertently giving him a handle on reality.

'But I haven't even showered.' he said, shaking out his concertinaed jacket, trying to improve its appearance as he caught the American's bleary eyes.

'None of us have. We've just been drinking the god-damn awful beer!'

In the camp's main hall the maternal *babushki* were milling between the tables in their brightly coloured aprons and scarved heads, serving home-cooked food: jewel-coloured Russian salads, pickled mushrooms, *pilmeni* – Siberian dumplings filled with meat and *Borsch* beetroot broth. The smells were completely foreign to Carty but the combination of tastes was delicious. He ate well as an insurance against the effects of the *Kedrovka*, a lethal moonshine made from pine nuts, offered to him at every occasion by his hosts.

The initial frostiness between the foreigners had evaporated and the atmosphere was slowly tipping into that of a Western saloon bar. Loud cheers and screams came each time a winner emerged from rounds of low-stakes *hold'em* poker.

Carty sat calmly on the smoke-filled side lines, sipping beer. He had no nose for the game although he was fully familiar with its rules. Gambling was a risk he only took in the international derivatives market, where someone else's money and much higher risks were at play.

Sometime later, a low growl outside announced the arrival of a truck into the compound. Its occupants, all young women, jumped down one by one, in a melee of stockinged legs and short skirts, their fashion at odds with the raw environment. The babble from the games instantly died away as the foreigners gaped at this fascinating sight. There was a *sure thing* for each of them that evening.

Energetically, the women enticed with a well-practised routine; drinking and then pulling the foreigners up to dance to nondescript Europop.

'Hello, I am Natasha,' one introduced herself to Carty. He didn't respond.

'You're very handsome,' she persisted, draping her arms around his shoulders. 'You want to dance with me?'

'No, I can't dance,' he lied, nonchalantly glancing at her.

She sat next to him and took a small sip of the offered beer.

'Don't you like me?' she probed in a broken, deep accent, caressing the back of his head with her fingernails while attempting to captivate him with a self-promoting smile.

'Maybe, but I'm not dancing.'

'We go to your room instead?'

He smiled self-consciously into his glass, considering her question and weighing the consequences.

'We go?' she persisted, her voice echoing desperation. Carty looked up to catch some of the Americans filtering away with their new friends, leaving the Russian entourage brooding over their drinks. He stood up and held out a hand to her, reading in her face a contorted mix of pleasure and fear.

'Thank you!' she beamed, looping her arm in his, in front of the cold stares.

The cool air outside sobered him slightly as Natasha pigeon-stepped along the planks in her crème, thigh boots, hugging him as much for warmth as for balance.

At the cabin's porch, he hesitated, half expecting the apparition to appear out of the shadows but Natasha pushed the door open and then forced him forward, into the darkness.

She appeared to know the room well, and switched on a small lamp, throwing her scarf over the shade to soften its harsh light. The fire had been stoked by the staff but instinctively, she opened its oven door and tossed in a log. He watched her, a young woman in her prime, stuck with little options for work or the future. Looking up she read his eyes and moved towards him, gently leaning up and puckering her lips to his. He resisted her full kiss and she pulled back, theatrically peeling off the exquisite waist-length fur coat and laying it over the room's only chair. Her knowing grin spoke unquestionably of the reasons for her actions as her contour-hugging silk frock immediately dropped to the ground, leaving her slender dignity covered only by polka-dotted panties. Then, wrapping her willowy arms around his neck, she manoeuvred and pushed him gently down on the bed, its springs arguing as he slipped back under her control.

'You like me?' she sought his confirmation as she straddled him.

'Yes, you're very lovely,' he murmured, discovering up close, her beautiful face, damaged by the rough seasons and a tough existence. She giggled and nuzzled her soft lips against his. Carty

113

went with it for a few minutes but then, in a soft yet decisive move, held the nape of her neck and gently pulled back her head.

'I'm sorry but I don't want you tonight.'

Her stare locked onto his. She was suddenly helpless; rejection was not something she knew well.

'Please do not tell them.' Her trembling voice overtook her.

'I won't,' he looked caringly at her, 'but I need to sleep.' He soothed her, understanding that his hosts were brutes.

She undressed him, her cheap perfume diffusing the aroma of his unshowered sweat as she pulled the worn cotton duvet around them in a vain attempt at modesty.

Darkness suddenly befell the cabin, with the extinguishing of the compound's light and the stinging of his cut shins, only temporarily numbed by the effects of the alcohol, now resurfaced. *The spectre was trying to tell me something...but what?*

He squeezed Natasha's form close as he struggled with the consternation the image had invoked.

Thirteen

A mosquito's high-pitched whine roused him from the deepest sleep he had had for some time, and for an instant he was lost, unfamiliar with his surroundings. But then he registered the sunlight filtering through the heavy net curtains and suddenly remembered Natasha. He sat up abruptly. She was gone. He breathed in the sweet air and slipped back onto the pillow running through the events of the previous night. The creak of a floorboard, though, fractured his serene state. There was a presence in the room.

'Natasha, is that you?' he blurted.

'No,' a familiar voice answered.

Carty craned his head fully forward, straining to recognise the silhouetted figure against the light.

'Lena!' His fear melted. 'But I thought...'

'That I was Natasha?'

He pulled himself up as she offered a steaming cup.

'It's *chai*,' she said, 'an infusion of local herbs and flowers – excellent for hangovers!'

'Right! So you've come here this morning to make me a cup of tea?'

'Yes, I do it with all the Englishmen that I like!' She pouted theatrically and sat alongside him, her porcelain palm gently stroking his face. 'Did you sleep with her?'

'Who?'

'Natasha.' Her stare was unequivocal.

He grinned boyishly. 'I did fall asleep with her.'

'You know what I am asking, Scott,' she blazed.

'Look, she was scared and needed to be comforted. It seems to be something that I'm getting pretty good at doing, lately!'

She coolly scanned his body language. 'Good, that's what she said too.'

'You spoke with her!'

'It's part of my job to organise the women who work here.'

'Your job!'

'Yes. It's simple, either I act under instruction or I become one of them. What would you do in my position?'

'Is that why you didn't come on the hydrofoil?'

'No, I had to do something for Kosechenko and, by the way, it's called an Ekranoplan.'

He shrugged as she held her fingers under his chin.

'Natasha was swayed completely by your charm and kindness. Usually, men will do anything she wants.' She smiled. 'You *did* want her didn't you?'

'She's a sweet girl and yes, on another day I would have been tempted, but I was thinking of the end result.'

'The end result?' She looked puzzled.

'She was paid to sleep with me and I would have ended up exhausted and still in love with another woman.'

'Your wife?'

'No, you,' he whispered. It was a new experience to stare straight into her sapphire eyes and not feel guilty.

The mosquito's drone intensified in their moment of silence then she leaped at him, wrapping both arms tightly around his neck. He was lost in her volatility as he fell back.

'I fell in love with you the first time I saw you!' She said, kissing him passionately.

He pulled her close, gently gripping her hips, his intentions clear. She held back, screwing up her nose in a cute grin.

'Scott, the Americans are leaving at lunchtime and I must be courteous and entertain them until then.'

'Are you going to dance for them?' he taunted.

'*Mozshadbet,* maybe,' she smiled coyly.

'But why are they leaving so soon? I thought we were all flying back together?'

'There's been a change in the itinerary.'

'Anything to do with the dumping of waste?' he jibed.

She shook her head. 'Please don't mention that again.'

'So when will we leave?'

'Tomorrow, on the first Ekranoplan out of here,' she attempted a smile, pulling her flowing hair back and tucking it up into a bun. Their lips met again and his eyes closed as a myriad of wild thoughts swirled.

So what now? He questioned, struggling to reconcile his growing love for Lena with the impending pain of separation from his wife and son. Green had warned him that a seemingly insoluble unconscious situation was inevitable – *tertium non datum* – the third not given, its meaning now painfully obvious.

He opened his eyes to find hers gazing at back him.

'What's wrong?' she asked.

He sighed. 'I'm thinking about my family.'

'Will that stop us being together?'

'What do you mean?'

'In Russia many men have second wives. It's just the way things are.'

'I'm not that kind of man.'

'I think you are, you just don't know it yet!'

Most of the men he knew would have already thrown any pangs of guilt to the wind, given a chance to be with this woman.

An image of D'albo and Boyd conspiring together sprang up again as his thoughts turned to London and his job.

Shit!

He had completely forgotten to tell Davina where he was and when he would be returning.

'I really must call back to the office today but my Blackberry is dead.'

'The camp has a satellite phone, you can use that.'

'Thanks!' He was distracted by the large swellings appearing on his legs and arms. The mosquitoes had feasted well that night and scratching furiously at the bites, he caught Lena staring at the grazes on his shins.

'How did you get those?'

'I am afraid you wouldn't believe me if I told you!'

'Really!' she attempted a frown but her expression hid her sense of foreboding.

Fourteen

'Where are you?' Davina's voice was unusually welcoming as it crackled back down the line.

'Lake Baikal.'

'Where?'

'It's in Russia,' he answered coolly. 'How's everything there?'

'Bad! Boyd's already started pulling the team apart. We need you back here as soon as possible!' Her tone had quickly become despondent and Carty felt comforted to be wanted again.

'I'll talk to D'albo about it. Patch me through to him, would you?' He was still simmering over the set-up with the briefcase and his weakness in not fully confronting the man during the last call.

The line clicked silent for few seconds.

'Scott, he can't speak to you now but wants you in the office the minute you touch down in London.'

'Even if it's after hours?' he jibed.

A giggle exposed her inner warmth. 'I'll let Diane know that you're safe and there's been a change of plans.'

Am I safe, though, here with Lena? He wondered.

'By the way, Scott, when did you get an entry visa for Russia?' Davina continued, her intuition keen.

'In Kazakhstan,' he responded, disguising his own concern that the customs officer hadn't yet materialised, as Lena had promised.

119

It was early afternoon when a thunderous drone shook the bench he was sleeping on. He struggled to stand on his numbed calves, wincing as the tingling circulation throbbed back into them.

The Americans had gathered near the edge of the camp with their bags littered around, staring up at the sky. Lena stood nearby clawing her hair away from her face in the downdraught from the helicopter. Carty trotted up alongside her.

'Still can't tell me where they're going?' he shouted against the deafening noise. She shot him an annoyed look and he stood back to let the Americans play.

Each picked her up in a fireman's carry and threatened to take her with them. Then, Hank hugged her tightly for just a fraction longer than was polite.

'We're going home. Don't stay here too long,' he said, turning to Carty and patting his shoulder.

Within minutes the clatter of rotors took the copter above the canopy of trees.

It appeared again some minutes later, further down the lake, diminished in the enormity of the place.

Carty turned to find Lena but instead caught Tikhomirov's fixed stare from 15 metres away, his arm hanging with a cigarette characteristically poised between finger and thumb, observing everything as he slumped up against an aged birch. It lasted long enough to instil apprehension and then, distracted by the noise of a small outboard boat, he pushed himself away and walked down to meet its arrival at the shore.

Carty traced his movements against the magnificent backdrop. The sun was warm and he felt unusually attuned to the vibrations of this place as he rubbed his itching shins, reminded again of the spectre's words.

What did it mean? Why have I come to where it all begins? he mulled, uneasily.

'Would you like to take a boat ride?' Lena asked optimistically, severing his thoughts.

'Perhaps,' he commented as they both sauntered down towards the shore. A portrait of the carpet of green sentinels, covering the low mountains, reflected in the water's placid surface. He pulled a hand up over his brow, to shut out the sun.

'How far is it to the other shore?'

'25 kilometres, more or less.'

'And why exactly is Baikal so special to you?'

'There are so many reasons. Probably its immense age and that it holds one-fifth of the planet's fresh surface water. If emptied, it would take all of the world's rivers, one year to fill it again.' She paused to catch his expression. 'Its deepest point is more than one and half kilometres down and around 330 rivers fill it with pristine water which remains in the lake for about 400 years before it leaves through the Angara River.'

'They're stupefying statistics.'

'Yes, and 70 percent of the flora and fauna in and around its shores are endemic and found nowhere else on Earth. So, you see, it has always been held sacred by us Siberians.' Her tone rose with pride, remembering her early school days when she learned of its eximious features as generations had done so before her.

According to legend, Ghenghiz Khan was buried on *Olkhon*, the largest island in the lake but the ancient Chinese called Baikal the 'Northern Sea' and thought it a woeful place, far from civilisation. No wonder, then, that its watershed had been little explored until the late 1600s when the Czar's Cossacks mapped its immense contours and assimilated local stories of its mythical powers into an emerging empire's folklore.

'Is it always calm like this?'

'No. Its moods are temperamental and can be unexpectedly violent.'

'Hmm, then I think I'll decline your offer.'

She playfully pushed him against the trunk of a wind-sculpted pine and pulled back her hair to snatch a kiss.

'Ah, Mr and Mrs Carty!' The translator's sudden throaty exclamation pierced the ambience. Lena pulled away and nervously made polite exchanges in Russian but Carty was not taken in by the deliberate ploy to embarrass them. Tikhomirov read him and dumped his burning cigarette butt some seconds later, grinding it into the quartz granules before trudging back up the beach with the fish he had haggled over.

'What did he want?' Carty asked.

She looked up to ensure the man was out of earshot. 'Nothing in particular, just small-talk.'

'Are you sure?' His response vexed her.

'Scott, forget it. You have no idea what that man can do.' She lowered her voice to a whisper. 'Tikhomirov is the nephews' eyes and ears.'

'Does he suspect that you've told me about the dumping?'

'Possibly.' Her eyes glazed over as she stared out across the water again.

The lake had changed colour to a rich turquoise and clouds were building on the horizon. Intuitively, he sensed that the Americans' sudden departure was part of another ploy, one which Lena and he were unaware of. He also understood the urgent need to leave with her as soon as possible.

Fifteen

A mist hung listlessly in a sheet that had edged in from the lake and up into the dense *taiga*, shrouding a huge stone boulder atop which the Buryat sat, motionless.

Soon, he shivered, disturbing the filtered vastness and then, with a gentle out-breath, his eyes flickered open, breaking his meditation.

Slowly, he stretched his arms up over his head and rising gracefully, shook his legs for a few moments, to ease the blood circulation, before padding down the granite incline and onto the mossy ground. The sounds of foraging animals pricked his sensitive ears as he made his way along a rarely trodden path to Baikal's shore.

He stripped and strode out a few steps into the lake's freezing waters, before swimming smoothly and turning to float on his back under the fading light. The water's sheer cold almost consumed his limbs with numbness as the subtly powerful swell brought his pithy frame back into shore, minutes later.

Quickly dressing, he lit a small fire from pine bark and dead shrubs and perched on a petrified tree stump, munching on a handful of pine nuts, watching the fire take life. Its glow brought warmth back to his being and he slung a battered kettle over its flames to brew tea.

The hour was early and the embers dying when the Buryat woke to register moonlight permeating the tree canopy. It was time to leave.

He started off over the pebbles, to the small cabin. As he entered, he assumed the old man was asleep, but then caught his eyes blinking in the subdued light and understood that neither of them would get much rest that evening. Slinging on his belt, he set to work filling his pack with necessary essentials: a military knife, a flask of tea and some fresh buns wrapped in a towel, then he quietly slipped away.

Pushing the small outboard off into the tide-less shallows, he leapt in, setting out across the surface to test his forefathers' prophecy, one that might lead civilisation down a different path.

More than 300 kilometres to the southwest, a cargo train trundled unannounced into the far platform of a local railway station. The distinct outline of its cylinder wagons had gone unnoticed as had the rusted plaques, riveted to each of their chassis, obscuring the trefoil: three black blades on a yellow background – the international symbol for hazardous nuclear waste. But safety hardly mattered here as a rail-worker routinely tapped an oversized steel hammer against the carriage wheels, listening for the change in timbre that his tuned ear would recognise as a crack. He straightened, holding a palm over his lumbar and then started off along the weed-split asphalt to where his colleague was busy decoupling the engine and signalling for the driver to pull away.

It did, trundling back up the track to re-join the Trans-Siberian line to the north. Then the two men sat on a bench, to smoke and share a few words, all the while waiting.

Soon, a distant rumble brought them to their feet again.

A shunting locomotive, pulling a single carriage, had rounded the bend and slowed to an imperceptible speed as a small number of its armed crew jumped off.

A thud then signalled the engine's contact with the stationary wagons.

Some of the men oversaw the re-coupling while others expertly fanned out across the tracks to the edge of the *taiga*, scoping for any non-obvious signs that others may be watching.

The two railwaymen had witnessed this same practice, twice a month, for several years. Knowing that the stationmaster received a small bonus and some privileges for his silence, they preferred to keep their jobs and a pittance for turning a blind eye. There would be no reward for whistle blowing, only an unpleasant, premature death. No one would believe them anyway. A cargo of spent nuclear waste had no reason to be here, this far East, on a local rail line. The nearest nuclear storage facility was at Zheleznagorsk, 1,000 kilometres to the West.

The locomotive suddenly fired up, spewing out a cloud of black *mazut* as it lurched into motion, pushing ahead its deadly load. The paramilitaries retreated, leaping up onto the ladder system of the wagon, to ride shotgun as the train rattled out. They believed their operation had been covert and, on the ground, it had. But 400 miles above them, a satellite adjusted its co-ordinates into a stationary low earth orbit. The cargo's movements were being closely monitored from a remote observation station in Chinese Inner-Mongolia.

Sixteen

The gentle strum of guitars woke Scott Carty from a restless sleep. Foreign aromas hung insuperably in the cabin's still air and shivering, he lay watching the light from a campfire dance across the ceiling's peeling varnish.

Curious, he picked himself up and lumbered to the door, rubbing his eyes with half-formed fists. The sight of Lena took him by surprise. Her hair was hanging loosely down to her waist and her eyes were closed as she swayed in gentle rhythm to a Russian ballad, sung by her countrymen.

She's beautiful.

Stepping out onto the gangplanks, he wandered over and unobtrusively sat on a rough-hewn bench, hungrily accepting the barbequed fish offered.

Chewing heartily he turned his back to the warmth of the fire and casually scanned each member of the group, noting that the translator was absent. Lena's soft vocals quickly entranced him, sucking him into the cultural spirit of the moment. Then the whole group joined her, singing a folk song in melodic unison, full of metaphors about nature and life. The sad ubiquity of their tones carried a memory of a collective past, one that Carty could never possibly understand. Instead, it unnerved him, pulling at his mind in a strange way, as if opening a portal into his own short life and dredging up uncomfortable, repressed memories.

A log spitting violently, shook him from his meditation. A red hot ember had landed in the lap of one of the local men. His hilarious antics, frantically dancing around to shake it off, had the group roaring with laughter.

Carty grinned but felt excluded all the same as he glanced across into Lena's glazed eyes. *Whatever happened to that visa?* He swigged at the Kedrovka to numb a rising sense of urgency. She couldn't be questioned at this moment.

The guitars started up again and tired of feeling as only an outsider could, he ambled away across the planks, back to the cabin. The breeze had died down and the camp bathed in moonlight, held an eerie calm, like that before a storm.

'Scott,' Lena whispered as she touched his arm.

'What time is it?' he murmured, part awake.

'Late!'

She stripped and slithered underneath the covers.

Scott Carty smiled as he felt her soft nakedness and then the swath of hair brushing his face. It carried an acrid whiff of smoke, but otherwise she was perfect.

'Is the door locked?' he asked.

'We never lock doors here.'

'What about the bears?'

'Bears can't open doors!'

'And are the curtains shut?'

'Yes.' She giggled uncontrollably. 'Scott, you're so English, so conservative. I want you to take me now.'

A glint of lust in her eyes drew him into her arms and then, like a panther, she manoeuvred on top and began to rock herself into bliss.

They slept, entwined. He dreamed that he was back in England, walking hand in hand with a woman whom he felt he had known all his life.

'Who's at the door?' she asked, *turning to him, her shining face heavy with urgency.*

The question echoed, waking him and through his partially opened eyes, he registered an outline silhouetted against the curtains.

Is it one of the camp's instructors?

127

At that same moment a knife blade slipped in to lift the latch's securing bar.

No! An adrenalin rush had spiked him into a state of fearful alertness.

'Lena.' he whispered, shaking her. 'Lena, wake up.' But an alcoholic, passion-induced sleep had consumed her.

He slid urgently off the bed and into the shadows, his breath suspended as he watched a pistol's silencer appear though the gap. He reached for a log and panicking, struck out, knocking the weapon away as its muffled shot ricocheted across the room. But the assassin had already rolled inside, striking a forearm into the Englishman's windpipe. He reeled back choking, to see a second man smothering Lena's face and slamming her head back against the wall.

My God, they're going to kill us!

Instinctively, Carty brought his foot up into the attacker's groin. The grimacing face let out a putrid gasp and then smashed a fist into his floating ribs, doubling him onto a knee that rammed into his nose. He gasped, frantically struggling against the thick blood flooding his throat. The killer had locked his neck, in an attempt to snap it but Carty kicked against the wall and toppled them both backwards, out through the door and onto the gangplanks. The man's grip was lost and a torch beam flashed wildly across the campsite, picking them out as an instructor shouted to them from 70 metres away. But the assassin had already stamped a boot into Carty's kidneys and was brutishly dragging him up by his hair, away into the bushes. Barely conscious, and choking on plasma and mucus, Carty heard Lena's screams silenced with a dampened shot. Her assassin darted out from the cabin tossing a hunting knife to his comrade, swiping his fingers across his neck in a symbolic gesture, to finish the job. The blade flashed momentarily in the moonlight and as the man caught it, ready to tear into Carty's jugular, a rifle's shot rang out. The figure shuddered and dropped his weapon, clutching at the growing crimson patch on his shirt. Seconds passed, and then staggering in shock, he grabbed the Englishman's wrists and yanked him the few desperate steps to the cliff's edge. He stepped off, pulling Scott Carty with him to a certain death.

Plummeting uncontrollably, as the water's surface raced towards them, Carty rolled just milliseconds before impact to let the Russian's body take his fall.

Stunned, he lay suspended in the freezing darkness before his survival instincts kicked-in and he forced his head back up above the surface to suck in air in a huge guttural gasp. His lungs burned as his blurred mind laboured to keep himself afloat. The lifeless body of the killer had now slowly risen to the surface alongside, its leaking blood cocooning him with warmth.

Somewhere in the background, the distinctive whirr of the camp's generator, firing up, was followed almost immediately by a diffuse halo cast up behind the wall of trees, many metres above him.

A ball of light hovered out from the shoreline, across the water's surface and as it drew towards him, he saw that it contained the serene face of the dream maiden. Her soft brown eyes bestowed a pure wisdom and instinctively, he reached out to her.

She dived, though, into the depths, dragging him down with her, towards the whirling centre of a maelstrom whose intense spinning vortex seemed to be bending the light emanating from its source.

'The essence of all starts here,' he heard her say as his state of mind began to ease with the expectation of death.

'Stop!' the translator shouted, halting the systematic beating of the captured assassin by the woodsmen. 'Carty has fallen into the lake!'

Their faces registered the horror of what the statement meant: death from hypothermia before they could find him in its icy waters. The cliff walls prevented access to the shoreline, forcing them along an indirect route, down a tight track to reach the water's edge and the boats.

Seventeen

The gunshot had drawn the Buryat's attention and cutting the launch's engine he rowed stealthily, hugging the cliffs' face, towards the two floating figures. The small boat's keel cut through the bloodstained waters as he rounded on the first body.

Dead, he confirmed and left it to the *epishura,* the microscopic crustaceans inhabiting the lake. He then pulled the Englishman alongside with a pike hook and checked his pulse.

But this one isn't.

His strong frame, a genetic imprint from his Mongolian ancestors' millennia in the horse saddle, equipped him for bending low and lifting weight. He acted quickly and hauled Carty aboard.

Torch beams now panned down from the shore, scattering across the water's surface. The Buryat quickly rolled the motionless Englishman on his back, pinching his nose and blasting short sharp breaths into his mouth. But Carty was not responding. Grim-faced, he frantically stripped off the man's wet shirt and chest-pumped him for some minutes. Carty soon choked up water but his milky pallor indicated his failing condition and the Buryat acted, manhandling him into the coma position before covering him with a coarse hair blanket.

Then he turned and yanked on the ripcord, swinging the boat around with one arm on the rudder while supporting Carty's head gently in his lap as he hummed an ancient tune. It resonated through the night air, summoning all that was sacred to assist him in preserving the life of the Englishman.

Eighteen

Albion's Offices, London.

'Have you seen the news?' one of the young quants yelled as he raced in from the trading floor.

'What's happening?' Davina looked up from drafting a memo, surprised by the evident panic but Carty's team didn't need any prompting as instantly, they pulled up live news streams from Bloomberg and CNN.

'A Russian helicopter has gone down near Lake Baikal, in Siberia.' He drew breath. 'No survivors. The dead include American businessmen, a British man and some Russians.' His expression seemed perversely pleased at being the messenger.

Milliseconds passed before it registered with Don.

'Wasn't Scott at Lake Baikal?' he relayed loudly, turning to find Davina ashen-faced and busily hitting the speed-dial button programmed with Carty's mobile number.

'Scott, please call the office as soon as you get this message,' she blurted.

'Has anyone on the trading desk spoken to Centralniy Sib yet?' Don grilled the young man.

'I don't know!'

'Well, I suggest that you get Watts to do it now. Tell him that D'albo urgently needs to know where Scott is and has given a direct instruction.' He winked at the young man but restrained a smile. The situation, he sensed, was grave.

Davina was already on the phone again.

'Cynthia, it's Davina. We've just seen a news flash. There's been a helicopter crash in Russia, in the area that Scott Carty was visiting. We can't reach him and I'm worried he's been injured.'

'I am sorry Davina but I don't understand what you want me to do? I thought he was in Kazakhstan. Don't you two stay in contact?' Her condescending manner incensed Davina.

'Just let Arthur know!' She hung up and turned to Don. 'Where's Boyd?'

'Early lunch, I guess.' Don said, still maintaining an ice-cool reserve.

'Why do these executives always turn off their bloody mobile phones?' She had been redirected to Boyd's voice mail and desperation had begun to eat at her.

Watts then stepped in. 'I've just heard from CentralniySib's people. Scott didn't get on that helicopter.'

A collective sigh rang out from the team.

'Where the hell is he then?' Davina snapped, unimpressed. 'You better get your arse back to your desk and demand that those Russkies find out. You're sure as hell not leaving today until they have!'

Don shook his head as he ushered Watts out. 'Calm down, Davina! Why don't you call Cynthia back and tell her the good news.'

'Boyd can handle her!' she responded defiantly.

'Handle what?' Boyd articulated, sauntering back in.

'Oh, it's good to see that some senior management have their finger on the pulse.'

'What the hell do you mean, Davina?' he fired back, baited by her unbridled sarcasm.

Don leapt up to explain but was interrupted by D'albo's call, asking for Boyd.

'What is Arthur going to do?' Davina quizzed as Mark Boyd put down the receiver.

'He's asked Cynthia to get hold of Kosechenko's PA to clarify exactly where Scott is.' The comment, though, didn't warrant the look of fear that had registered in Boyd's eyes.

'I'll be back shortly,' Boyd uttered, clutching his mobile telephone.

Cynthia called Davina back a while later, in a more conciliatory tone, advising that D'albo had pulled some strings: the Foreign and Commonwealth Office had already requested direct assistance from the Russian Embassy in locating Scott Carty.

A tense hour culminated in a meeting with the police and Albion's human resources director, to commence a formal review of the facts. Exasperated, Davina weighed the options for a few minutes before making the call she had dreaded, to break the news to Diane Carty.

'Nick!'

'Diane?' Nick Hall immediately recognised her fraught voice.

'It's Scott. He's gone missing in Russia. There was a helicopter crash. Some Americans have died but Scott wasn't amongst them, thank God.'

'In Russia?' Nick queried. *But he was attending a conference in Kazakhstan.*

'Who told you this information?' he quizzed.

'Davina, Scott's P.A.'

'Look, Scott's sure to be fine,' he attempted to make light of her fears. 'He probably wandered off to inspect a power station and forgot to tell anyone. Don't worry. I'll call a friend who has some high level contacts in the government.' He calmed her with a promise to visit later that evening and then caught Magda's jealous glare as he closed the call.

'All we can do is to leave it with the UK authorities,' Gordon Green advised Nick, returning his call later that afternoon.

'Is that *all* we can do?'

'For the moment, yes. The Russians authorities aren't saying if Scott was on that helicopter or not and have pulled down a wall of silence over the incident until their crash investigators have finished at the scene.'

'What can I tell Diane?'

'Tell her that everything that can be done is being done and if Scott is in Russia, he'll be found.'

Green agreed to meet Nick in town the next day and having hung up, sat quietly in his study, running back over Carty's dreams and their portent. He had some reservations about making the next call but knew that he must speak with a higher authority.

A woman's impeccable English accent answered the phone.

'Jack please,' Green asked quietly. 'I need to speak to him urgently. Tell him it's Gordon Green.'

Nineteen

Wednesday 6th July 2005 – just over two weeks later.

Carty's eyes flickered open. Unfocused they squinted against the light.

Around him muted machinery whirred, and he could faintly smell disinfectant. Mechanical booms, reminiscent of his childhood dentist's surgery, hung overhead and from their nozzled armatures, beams of coloured light shone onto his skin, radiating tingling sensations.

Lowering his glance, he took in the swath of acupuncture needles protruding from his torso and limbs. Images of human experimentation rippled an immediate fear before recollections began slowly trickling back: Lena's smiling face, the camp, the Americans, and then his attacker's wild, emotionless stare. He relived each blow, sympathetically twitching and triggering off the monitor alarms.

A sharp clack of footsteps soon filled his ears and then he felt his arm being soothed by the hands of a young nurse as she urgently scanned the various screens positioned alongside. She then looked closely into each eye, repeating several phases in a language he did not recognise.

Shortly, an older man in a white doctor's coat appeared and smiled kindly at the Englishman.

'What do you want with me?' Carty's simple question summoned all of his strength. The man calmly repositioned the lasers.

'Relax, you are amongst friends,' he said, grasping Carty's hand. 'All your questions will be answered in time but first you need rest,' he relayed in a strongly accented, but clearly practised English.

Exhausted, Carty closed his eyes.

When he woke several hours later he was conscious of a greater sense of mobility.

'Ah, Scott, you are making good progress,' the older man greeted him, as the nurse busily replaced the fluid to an intravenous drip.

'Who are you?' he asked fragilely.

'My name is Lubimov – Oleg Matissevich Lubimov. I'm the Director of this Institute.'

'You speak English very well.'

'Coming from an Englishman I will take that as a compliment!' A grin lit up his craggy face. 'I learnt English when I was a student in order to present my scientific research to the international community.'

A sigh escaped Carty's lips. The comment fired up a reluctant memory of the conference and the briefcase.

'Where am I?'

Lubimov skirted the question. 'Do you have any idea how you came to be at Baikal and why you were attacked?'

'I was attending at a conference in Almaty.'

'Almaty?' The director's brows tangled, 'do you realise that you're now in Russia?'

He stared listlessly back at the Russian, slowly nodding his head, and attempting to move. The nurse rushed to prop up his pillows.

He smiled weakly at the young woman.

'I was invited to here by a client.'

'Alone?'

'No, there were also some Americans with us.'

'Americans?' Lubimov nodded inquisitively.

'Can you get word to my family that I am alive?'

Lubimov faltered. 'Not until you have made a full recovery. We cannot risk reporting your presence; it might lead to another attempt on your life.'

'But they will be worried sick about me!'

'Scott, please understand that things work very differently here in Russia. You will be able to speak with them as soon as you have made sufficient progress.'

'When will that be?'

'Weeks rather than days.'

'I can't wait that long...' his voice trailed off as a stranger entered.

The man made some exchanges in Russian with Lubimov before approaching the Englishman.

'Hello, Scott, I'm glad to see that you are recovering so fast,' he uttered unashamedly.

Carty stared back, vaguely recognising the face.

'Boris, here, saved you from Baikal.' Lubimov announced.

'Thank you,' Carty murmured, looking deeply into the stranger's russet eyes, unsure of why he sensed an uncommon bond with the man. 'And you also speak English.'

Boris simply smiled.

'But you're Russian, aren't you?' he quizzed, confused by the man's weathered Eurasian features which were more rounded than those of the Kazakhs he had met.

'I am a Buryat,' he announced.

'Buryatia is an autonomous region to the East of Baikal,' Lubimov gently interjected, 'one of the largest in the Russian Federation.'

Boris nodded. 'My ancestors were the nomads that made their home around Baikal, centuries before the Mongolian hordes of Genghis Khan arrived.'

'And now its time for Scott to rest!' Lubimov added firmly, placing his hand on Boris' shoulder. Carty's expression had become visibly spirited and Lubimov was worried that he would relapse. 'There is plenty of time to discuss these things,' he said as he began to reposition the booms.

The Buryat's smile broadened and then he hovered his palm inches above Carty's eyes. An uncanny sensation of warmth and electricity flickered from it.

As Carty succumbed to sleep, Boris watched the older man switch the lasers back on and warily stand back to view his patient. Lubimov should have been exuberant, knowing that his skills had saved the man but instead, his expression spoke of apprehension. Carty's story, while plausible, seemed unbelievable and it was merely a matter of time before he would be discovered by the authorities, leaving two possibilities, his escape or his death. Either way, Lubimov's position would be untenable and he would suffer the consequences for harbouring a fugitive. But a greater fear concerned the Russian: a search of his Institute.

Twenty

Arthur D'albo's office, London.

'Cynthia, ask Mark Boyd to come to my office will you?'

She smiled, unfolded her shapely legs and straightened her skirt before walking just a little too provocatively back out to her desk. D'albo was aware of the power he held over her and she played to it with expectation.

He sat, anxiously picking at the permanently tanned skin around his nails. Boyd's change in behaviour – grilling the quants with unusual questions and staying overly late to examine files – had made D'albo wary, forcing him to change tactics.

Boyd showed up after ten, unshaven.

'Hello, Mark,' D'albo announced, his countenance swollen with a brewing rage. 'Where have you been?' He pointed the man to the sofa.

'Apologies, Arthur. I was working rather late last night and had a number of personal issues that needed to be dealt with this morning.'

'I don't give a toss about your personal issues!' D'albo's green eyes glared, 'I haven't seen squat from you since you started.'

Boyd tensed. 'But I've spoken to you regularly about the obstacles I'm facing and...'

'I don't want any cosy chats,' D'albo fired back, cutting him off mid-sentence, 'I want some action. You get it?'

'Yes, of course!' Boyd flushed.

'I saved your arse. There's no way that anyone would employ you in this industry, not with your criminal record.' He rocked in his swivel chair from side to side and then cracked a bizarre grin.

'Cigar, Mark?' he offered the box to Boyd.

'No thanks, Arthur.'

'I will then.' The older man took one and then sidled over to sit opposite.

'Have you noticed anything strange since Scott went missing?'

'What do you mean?' Perspiration had begun to smear Boyd's acne-scarred forehead.

'You know, anything odd, strange phone calls, large positions being placed or closed?'

'No, nothing,' he bluffed, 'although I'm struggling to reconcile CentralniySib's book positions. Its BVI office is not returning any of my calls.'

'Tell me more.' D'albo feigned an interest, flicking his hair back with a shake of his head.

'Well, it seems that they only ever give execution orders to Duncan Watts. He's not been any help and the dealers are pissed off that he's handling such a key account. Scott was apparently unaware of all this.'

D'albo waved the comment aside. 'That's not unusual; Carty had nothing to do with the trading desk in recent years. Is there anything else?'

'Should there be?'

'I don't know, Mark, you tell me.' His response seemed loaded.

'Well, the only other thing I found strange was a paper in Carty's pending tray. It was in Russian but someone had highlighted an English footnote referencing the storage of spent nuclear waste.'

'Have you told the police about this?' he asked, blowing smoke between them.

'No, it didn't seem relevant.'

'You're right. It's not.'

'Mark,' he stalled for a moment staring unashamedly at Boyd as if weighing his next comment. 'I have a job for you.'

Boyd frowned.

'There's a high level meeting tomorrow, in Prague, between Albion's merger and acquisitions team and a regional energy producer.'

'What's the brief?'

'I want you to be my eyes and ears. Albion has already negotiated the management contract but the endgame is to take control. Make sure you know exactly what's being agreed.'

Strange! Boyd nodded, knowing that D'albo should have been attending such an important meeting himself, as Albion's Head of Europe.

'Cynthia will give you all the details,' D'albo added, smiling falsely and glancing down at his watch. 'Call me when you arrive and...good luck!'

Good luck? Boyd hid his confusion as he stood. There were no pleasantries, no handshakes.

To think he could try to fool me! D'albo fumed as the man sauntered out. He now understood that Boyd was operating for someone else, but that was inconsequential, he had become a liability.

'Take any calls for me, Cynthia. I'm going out for an hour.' His manner was charm itself as he carried his tall frame out of the office, moments later.

Crossing over London Bridge towards Borough High Street, he slipped down a side road, shooting a brief look around to ensure he hadn't been followed before stepping into an insignificant pub, one of a few that still had a coin-operated public telephone.

He dialled a number.

'He will be there tomorrow. Show him the town,' he whispered.

Twenty One

Carty woke early. The lasers and needles were now absent, leaving him unsure if it had all not been part of an absurd dream, but for the small red pin pricks dotting his skin and the intravenous drips still in his arm.

Lubimov silently entered some time later offering a small bowl.

'Thank you,' Carty murmured.

He took several mouthfuls, astounded at just how quickly his appetite had returned. The Russian sat quietly observing him for some minutes.

'Why did you use the lasers?' Carty asked unable to restrain his searching curiosity any longer.

'Ah yes, the lasers,' Lubimov sighed. 'They are the pinnacle of our healing methods here at *Sphinx*, the result of years of research into obscure acupuncture methods.' He removed his glasses, enthusiastically nodding at the achievement. 'The early tests were based on trial and error but the breakthrough came in experimenting with different coloured lasers on plant-life. We realised that correct doses, used at specific times of the day, stimulated their health and growth. It took meticulous research after that to perfect the techniques we use on our patients.'

'You had a good success rate?'

'Very good indeed!'

'And when you say energy, do you mean *Qi*?' Carty blurted, recalling his many conversations with Nick Hall about the mysterious life force.

Lubimov rubbed his chin, surprised. 'Yes, that's the Chinese word, but all cultures have a name for it.'

Carty frowned. 'And what is *Sphinx*?'

'That's the name our masters in Moscow gave us. It's ironic really, the institute was never meant to be anything more than an experimental laboratory.'

He pulled out a notebook and scribbled something down.

С.Ф.И.Н.К.С.

'S.F.I.N.K.S,' he spelled out the Cyrillic letters, 'it's an acronym for *Sibirsky Federalniy Institute Nauchno-Kognitivnich Strategiy*. The Russian alphabet doesn't use the letters *P* and *H* together as you do in English.'

'So it's an acronym, but what does it mean?'

'Let me see.' He scratched his head for a few seconds before breaking into a broad smile. 'It translates literally as *Siberian Federal Institute for Scientific Cognitive Strategies* but the title only hints at its purpose. The *Sphinx*, as you probably know from mythology, also had its riddle.'

'So it's only medical research then?'

Lubimov blew across his lenses and held them up to the light before slowly cleaning them with a faded handkerchief in a flourish of misdirection.

'During the early years of the Cold War, this institute was established to research the effects of electromagnetism on matter. Baikal was chosen because the Lake's immediate environment is probably one of the most pristine in the former Soviet Union.'

'What kind of matter?' Although still tired, Carty's instincts had kicked in. He sensed another agenda lurking, in the same way he had with the Americans at the camp.

'Mainly biological.' Lubimov replaced his glasses and stared out of the window. 'We were studying the effect of electromagnetism on DNA.'

'That's interesting,' Carty uttered, recalling his conversation with Nick.

'Is it?'

'Yes, I was once told by a friend that the structure of DNA mirrors the binary code of the *I Ching*, one of the world's oldest books. It seemed like nonsense at the time but, strangely, it makes sense now.'

'It does!' The older man's eyes were wide with excitement. 'DNA's binary code is a fractal archetype that continually gives birth to itself. This knowledge, along with the laser acupuncture, saved your life,' Lubimov said recognising the exhaustion in Carty's face. 'And this conversation can wait for another day. You must rest.'

But Carty was not having any of it and instead pushed in another direction.

'Mr Lubimov...Oleg, I am very grateful for all that you have done but I must let my family know that I'm safe.'

The Russian's eyes narrowed. 'Scott, that's not possible for the reasons I have already explained.'

'But what's stopping me from getting out of this bed and finding the nearest telephone?' Carty's rise in tone belied his frustration.

'You will only succeed in making two steps before you collapse. You're still not strong enough, even with my treatment.'

But a sensation of doubt had crept into Carty's head, that his host was not being completely honest. At that moment a knock announced the nurse's polite entrance.

She spoke quietly to Lubimov.

'Inna's asking if you're still hungry. Do you want more *kasha* – porridge?'

'No, no, this is enough, thank you.'

'Well then, I must leave you. I have some work to finish.'

He rose and left with the nurse.

Carty leaned back, slowly chewing as he mulled over the conversation and his predicament. Soon, he was absorbed by birdsong dancing in through the open window. James' faint laughter seemed to be carried in with it, triggering an image of them playing together in his Hampstead garden. Then a picture of Diane's gentle smile magically surfaced and with it a wave of emotion flooded in, focusing him acutely on his own rash stupidity.

Why did I put it all at risk?

He had taken everything for granted – his most precious possessions, his wife and his son – in the vain pursuits of pride and lust.

Twenty Two

His strength improved with each day, finding him falling into a pattern of waking at dawn, taking steps to walk with Boris' support for an hour and then sleeping after lunch until supper.

He woke late one afternoon, to find himself strangely refreshed; his mind placid and clear.

'How are you feeling?' a hushed voice came from the background. Startled, he craned his head, to find the Buryat's motionless frame standing nearby.

'Boris! Have you been here for a long time?'

'Just an hour,' he grinned.

'Why?' Carty uttered in astonishment.

'You needed me to be here,' he serenely replied. 'You're still physically weak but your spirit is strong and I'm worried that you'll try to leave your bed.'

'Are you holding me hostage?'

'No,' the Buryat's voice gently resonated. 'But nobody else can know that you're here. If they do, then it will mean certain death for both you and Oleg.' His words lacked any ambiguity. 'Your attackers were trained killers and it was either luck or fate that you survived.'

A sullen mood overtook Carty as he recalled the dream maiden's words of that night, alerting him to the impending attack. *Poor Lena,* he thought. The mere few days they were together had stirred an undiscovered passion in him. It was absent in the relationship with Diane and challenged his puerile ways, as if Lena had somehow revealed to him a hidden side to women. Her subtle balance of firm independence, tempered with a gentle sexual femininity had been unnerving yet irresistible.

Would she still be alive now had I forced her to return home from Almaty with me? He sighed, churning with a strange mixture of remorse and guilt. His marriage would have been in certain turmoil if she had.

Boris' eyes bore into his. 'I took a huge risk bringing you here but there was no option. Only Lubimov could have saved you.'

'And I am grateful for that, but when can I leave?'

'Not soon. My instincts tell me that this is not over yet. Someone wanted you silenced yet you are still breathing. If you want to continue to do so then you must be patient and trust us.'

'Well, I have nothing to hide,' the Englishman muttered, defiantly.

'Maybe, but that doesn't explain why they left you impersonating a *nerpa* in the lake!' He grinned at his own joke but stopped short on registering Carty's bemused look. 'A *nerpa* is the only species of freshwater seal on the planet. It lives in Baikal,' he explained.

A few more weeks and I will be strong enough to leave here.

'Please do not do anything rash,' Boris commented. Carty gaped. It was if the Buryat had directly read his thoughts. 'The *taiga* – the forest here, is deep and extremely dangerous. Brown bears can smell human scent from more than a mile away and once they decide to attack there is no escape. They can run faster than us and can climb trees, but they will not harm you, though, once you gain their trust.'

'And how do I do that?'

'Why don't you get dressed and we can talk about it when we are walking.' The Buryat smiled mischievously.

Carty was astounded. He hadn't answered his question and it seemed a ridiculous instruction, knowing that he struggled with the effort of making just a few dozen steps each day.

'Get dressed!' Boris repeated forcefully, throwing a full plastic carrier bag on the bed.

'Where are you going?' Carty shouted after the Buryat but the door was already closing.

Frustrated, he up-ended the bag. Its contents spilled across the bed; ex-combat fatigue trousers, a lumberjack shirt and worn trainers.

He is serious!

His limbs were still weak and he struggled to dress, recounting Boris' words. He did owe Lubimov his life, yet he was also naturally suspicious of how much these men might really know. Both could be unintentional pawns in the illegal dumping of nuclear waste in Siberia.

Boris returned almost a quarter of an hour later to escort the Englishman along a corridor of faded linoleum. It was cool to the touch despite the sticky summer day.

Lubimov, already standing ahead of them at the exit, scrutinised Carty's approach.

'Let me help you, Scott,' he offered, reaching under the Englishman's armpit and around his chest for support. Carty was hesitant but sensed a familiar closeness from the contact with the older man.

Outside was humid and bright and he stood for a moment to suck in the extraordinary freshness, thick with pleasant yet unfamiliar aromas.

'Let's walk, shall we?' Lubimov said.

They plodded along a roughly laid concrete path, shaded by mature silver birch, which led to a secluded vantage point overlooking an incult valley. Its sides dropped steeply away into a canopy of dense pine and cedar. Rising pillars of smoke pinpointed the small cabins of a hamlet a mile or so below them, and stretching his gaze down the valley towards its mouth, Carty noted a massive rock outcrop, several hundred feet high, obscuring the view of the lake beyond.

'It's a strange feature, isn't it?' Lubimov commented.

'The rock?'

'Yes, it's granite, and quite different from the local geology. It was either pushed here during the ice age or thrown up when Baikal was formed. Whatever its origin, it keeps our location well hidden.'

'Yes. It is an amazing sight.'

'The seismic shift between the eastern and western Siberian tectonic plates, 25 million years ago, was so massive that a ten kilometre deep chasm opened up. Baikal fills only the top 15 per cent of it but even so, it is still the deepest lake on the planet.' Lubimov smiled curiously at Boris as if they were sharing some clandestine secret. 'All of the rivers emptying into it have their watershed in the surrounding mountains and Russia's mightiest river, the *Lena,* begins from them, along the coast.' He raised a finger in the direction. 'And then runs for thousands of kilometres to the Arctic Ocean.'

Carty's heart had jumped at the mention of Lena's name, her smiling face appearing to him again, fleetingly as he stretched his gaze out over the panorama.

'And those cabins down there, are they part of *Sphinx?*'

'No, all research goes on in the Institute.'

'Have any other foreigners ever visited the Institute?'

The Russian turned to him, smiling economically. 'Scott, you're a guest and have no right to be asking such questions but I will give you an answer. You are the only foreigner to have ever set foot here, although, I am sure your British intelligence services are aware of the location of all former Soviet institutes.' He paused, as if pondering his next words and then lowered his voice. 'Are you part of that same system, Scott?'

'What! I've already explained who I am.'

'Yes, you did, but *is* that the truth?' The Russian squinted.

'You told me yourself how close I was to death. Do you think I faked that?'

'No, I don't, although it's quite possible that you've crossed either the British or the Russian agencies or both, and they ordered your assassination.'

'That's preposterous!' Carty flushed. 'I am an energy specialist, structuring emission-linked options that create wealth and alleviate poverty around the world – that's what I am about. Now, I should ask who you *really* are, and what else you are doing here at this Institute.'

Visibly offended, the Russian's calm demeanour had evaporated. 'I am a doctor. I heal people, including you. And now you show me such little respect.'

Carty was reluctant to back down despite the creeping exhaustion. 'Well, what do you expect? You're practically accusing me of spying.'

'But you must admit that the circumstances around how you came to be here are very unusual, aren't they?'

'Admittedly they are, but if you let me call back to London you'll find that I'm telling the truth.'

Lubimov cut him dead with a sullen glance. 'You really don't understand the danger that is facing us, do you?'

All this time Boris had been quietly standing in the sun, but prompted by the heated conversation, he stepped between them and softly held the Westerner's gaze.

'Scott, you are not who you think you are.'

What does he mean? Puzzled by the statement, Carty stared back, his blue eyes unblinking.

'How can you possibly know who I am?' he said, in disbelief.

'Very simply by the things you do not say and the messages your body tells me. Please release your anger otherwise it will consume you. You have had several special experiences in a short space of time and your mind is still confused. Your spirit, though, knows exactly why they have occurred, even if they make little sense to you now.'

'How can you know all this?'

'I know that you have come here to learn something.' His blended accent lent an uncanny air to the statement.

Lubimov meanwhile, had wandered away toward the railing and then stood entranced as if re-living a memory.

'Is he all right?' the Englishman asked, regretting his outburst.

'He's carrying the weight of things that the modern world has yet to fully grasp,' Boris replied.

'Really? What?'

'His work.'

'But how can his work be so revolutionary?'

'All it takes is one person, openly sharing conscious knowledge, to make a change.'

'Conscious knowledge?' Carty's face contorted, partly through tiredness.

'That's right. The unlimited latent knowledge of nature can only really be absorbed consciously when the time is ripe. A person may have a hunch about something for many years but only through persistence, can it be grasped clearly at the right moment.'

'In a flash of inspiration?'

'Yes. We all use knowledge that has been realised in this way and recorded by pioneers for the rest of humanity. The paradox, though, is that like a double-edged sword, it can either benefit or cause suffering depending on how it is consciously used. Lubimov has developed his discoveries with great responsibility.' He paused gathering his thoughts. 'The former Soviet Union, despite its failings, was a breeding ground for academic excellence, a meritocracy in which people excelled in pushing forward the frontiers of knowledge.'

'And so was the free world,' Carty fired back.

'Neither system is, or was, superior. I am simply giving you the background from where Lubimov inherited his technology. In his hands it can change the world.'

Carty cracked a cynical smile, one that echoed his doubts. *He can't surely mean the laser acupuncture?*

The scientist had strolled back on hearing his name, his mood now more settled.

'Unfortunately, while you're here the other parts of the Institute must remain off-limits to you, Scott. You will be conspicuous and people will talk, especially if there's a price on your head.

'Is there a price on my head?'

'Possibly,' he retorted. 'Shall we walk back to your room, now? The fresh air is good for you but you still require much rest.' He put his arm under Carty's again.

'Oleg, I am sorry if I appeared ungrateful. I owe you my life.'

Lubimov looked kindly at him. 'Nonsense, young man, everything has its reasons.'

Something was still subliminally troubling Carty, it had been for the last few days yet he wasn't able to put his finger on it. Now, outside, it suddenly dawned on him what it was. At the CentralniySib camp he had been irritated by the fumes and intermittent drone of a diesel-powered generator, but both of those were oddly missing here. It prompted his curiosity.

'How is electricity provided to the Institute?' he enquired.

Lubimov looked straight ahead. 'There are a series of micro-hydro turbines in the mountains.'

'That's interesting. Could I see them?'

'Not until you're in a fit enough condition to go trekking,' Lubimov answered dismissively.

'That's strange,' Carty halted. 'I can't see any overhead power transmission lines.'

'That's because they aren't any: they're buried underground.'

'Buried! Isn't that impractical?'

Lubimov grinned, quietly impressed by Carty's intelligence. 'Scott, there is something you should know.'

'Something?' Carty's eyes flashed wildly back – *nuclear?* The word instantly sprang into his head.

'Yes, take a look over there at the roof of the hospital wing,' he pointed.

Carty switched his focus to the extruded aluminium strips running down from the asbestos roof ridge to the dilapidated gutters. A bank of skylights filled its middle section.

'What should I be looking for?' he asked.

'That roof powers the building.'

Carty let out a spurt of laughter in disbelief. 'Oleg. I do not wish any disrespect, but that roof cannot generate enough energy for this Institute.'

'It does...well, most of it!'

'How?'

'They are actually part of a hybrid heat-pump system,' Lubimov explained, 'converting both light and heat energy from the sun, into useful electricity, but I do not expect you to be conversant with these concepts.'

Hah! Another amateur expounding the virtues of renewables. Surprising, really, for a medical doctor.

'Is it too advanced even for a doctor of physics?' Carty announced, validating his academic credentials.

The Russian grinned. 'So you'll understand that there's nothing new in the technology, but simply in the materials and the engineering.'

'And I suppose they also provide the parasitic electricity for the necessary compressors?'

'There are no compressors!'

'Hmm, I find that hard to believe, I am afraid!'

Nick would love this guy! He recalled his friend's eccentricities as they began walking again.

'What's the overall efficiency of your system?' Carty probed, clearly humouring the man.

'Approximately 70 percent.'

'That's unbelievable! Current photo-cells are only 18 per cent efficient in converting sunlight into useful energy.'

'Yes, but that's because they are made from silicon and you will probably know that it's inefficient above a critical temperature.'

'So are you using *CIGS* then?' Carty knew that a new generation of semi-conductor alloys; copper-indium-gallium-diselinide – were being rapidly commercialised, but were still nowhere near as cost competitive as silicon.

'No, the collector's surface is manufactured from a more advanced photo-responsive alloy, five microns thick. It was developed here in the early 90s as part of a research study, until the funding stopped.'

'Is it patented?'

The Russian grinned in the strong sunlight, shaking his head.

'Well, if it's as effectual as you say it is, then with today's low manufacturing costs the commercial pay-back should be only a few years. Have you sought any foreign investment?'

'No, that is not my field of expertise,' Lubimov sighed. 'Besides, what point is there in trying to fight the world's love affair with fossil fuels? The time is not yet ready for an energy revolution.'

Carty smiled nonchalantly back. *How can he possibly understand? The emissions market and energy efficiency are the solutions to climate change, not an energy revolution.*

'Are there any results published? You must have recorded data proving all this?'

'Yes, of course, but all in good time.'

The comment seemed to lack any doubt but Carty sensed it did as they stepped back in.

Twenty Three

Lubimov met him after breakfast, tapping him lightly on the shoulder with a rolled up document. 'I think you are strong enough to accompany me on my walk today.'

'Where to?' Carty was bemused. A couple of weeks had passed since recovering and he was now itching to leave.

'To see how my technology works. This paper quantifies the output data from the heat pumps.' He beamed, failing to conceal his relish.

'Well, I am interested to see where you've made a mistake in calibrating your instruments!' Carty chimed back. 'Is Boris coming too?'

'No, he's gone trekking. Now, if you'll get dressed, I will be waiting outside.'

They set off, ambling over the raised walkways and then up a gentle incline into the forest, following a trodden-down route, overgrown with a spongy carpet of sphagnum moss. To each side sprawled bilberry and foxberry shrubs, heavy with morning dew which washed over Carty's cumbersome gum boots. Further along, peony sprang between the chaotic 'shin-tangle' of rotting timber. The air was extraordinary, tinged with the subtle aroma of unknown flora, and sunlight infused the dense canopy above, bathing all in a strange green hue, softening the raw reality of this place.

'This is the wild *taiga*,' the Russian announced.

Carty now understood. *There's no way of escaping without an intimate knowledge of this forest.*

'Be careful of the *slepni*, the horse flies. They can give an unpleasant bite!'

Carty kept his head down constantly waving away the profusion of insects that had descended to feast on the two men.

The half hour trudge took its toll and he came close to fading as Lubimov finally stopped and turned.

'Here we are!' He proudly pointed back to a small cabin nestling next to a huge boulder partly shielded by rhododendron. Unhurriedly, he released the several padlocks and ushered Carty into a small, musty den filled mainly by banks of dated dials and flickering lights. An oversize printer on a far cabinet held a roll of green-and-white banded computer paper, the type that he hadn't seen since his university days.

'So which is which?' Carty asked, peering over the meters in the dim light.

'These to the left are monitoring the output,' the Russian indicated with his oversized index finger. Carty stepped closer and pondered the oscillating needles for some minutes.

'Hmm, they're showing rather a large power output. How big is the total area of the solar collectors covering that roof?'

Lubimov, now seated, was silently turning the pages of his paper. 'It's all in this. The data needs no translation.' He pointed out a table of figures. Carty took the pages and pored over them, making some basic mental calculations.

'If these meters are calibrated correctly, then there is an unbelievable amount of energy being harnessed from the sun, although I would like to see the readings during the winter months here.'

Lubimov squinted back through his glasses. 'The temperature drops to 40 degrees below zero, but there is sunlight and those collectors convert as much of its spectrum as possible.'

'But how do you prevent the heat pumps from freezing up?' Carty probed, still dubious.

'We use a low boiling-point antifreeze.'

'And the lack of any compressors? How can you explain that away?'

'I am afraid I cannot divulge that to you.'

'Proprietary technology, I suppose?'

The older man smiled. 'It's a reworking of the thermodynamic cycle with a novel twist.'

'And was it also developed here?'

'Yes, by my father. He discovered the forgotten concept, by chance, in a pre-war engineering document.'

'So he wasn't a doctor like you?'

'No. He was an engineer given the specific task of setting up this Institute in the late 1950s.'

'But didn't you tell me that *Sphinx* researched the effects of electromagnetism on DNA?'

'I did and my role here has always been in medical research but my first degree was in power engineering. It was my father's great love.'

Carty felt himself flush, ashamed at having erroneously assumed Lubimov to be simply a medical man.

'The Institute's main focus was alternative energy technologies including some of Tesla's research work.'

'Tesla!' Carty uttered, shocked by the mention of the name again and the instant image it conjured up of Nick Hall's rotating magnetic motors.

That's another bizarre coincidence.

'I don't believe Tesla did anything out of the ordinary,' Carty scoffed.

'I have heard many people say the same thing,' Lubimov replied, 'probably because many of his discoveries did not fit the zeitgeist of the day and were rejected by the scientific community. There will come a time soon, though, when they will become commonplace, out of necessity.'

Carty forwent the argument and changed topics. 'Your laser acupuncture technology is quite remarkable – my old knee injury seems to have disappeared completely.'

'It does have a profound effect,' the Russian quietly grinned. 'My father's position allowed certain privileges and during the 70s I was offered a chance to set up the research unit here, to pioneer its techniques through a formal exchange of information between China and the Soviet Union.'

'And is that what you wanted?'

'At first, yes, I was very keen to pursue it but I soon understood that I was being persuaded to develop other areas of research that would be used for negative purposes. Opposing the state was a crime in the Soviet Union and I had no option but to comply...' His voice faltered. The Englishman had noted the Russian's stare become morose and he quickly veered back to one of the meters at the end of the bank, noticing its pointer arm flicking over the maximum reading. He pointed at it.

'Can I take a closer look at this?'

'If you wish.' The reply seemed guarded.

'Huh, that's just impossible! This meter alone is registering the equivalent output of a small power station. Are you sure that you're not plugged into a dam high in these mountains?'

'I can guarantee that we're not.'

'But as I said before this amount of power would usually be transmitted by overhead power cables.'

'There are many caverns and underground passageways around here. The power lines were put in place before my time.'

'But as the Institute's Director, surely you have a blue print of its overall infrastructure, for its long-term maintenance?'

The absence of words was telling as Lubimov shifted his gaze to the window and into the mass of the *taiga* outside. Carty understood that the man was being evasive. It would have been impractical, and far too costly, to isolate high-voltage power cables underground for such a small and remote institute.

But why is he showing me these instruments? Is he testing me?

For the briefest of moments he wanted to spill his thoughts but Lubimov's kind expression prevented him. It spoke volumes of a man not unlike himself: intelligent, inventive and possibly, in his younger days, competitive.

'Have you seen enough?'

Carty slapped his neck, killing a gorging insect. The Russian accepted this for his answer and moved back to the door.

As they strolled back, Carty pored over the possible reasons why he had been taken to the lodge and shown the engineering paper. A chilling thought then filtered up:

Was the meter measuring the output from a research size nuclear reactor, hidden somewhere in the forest?

'Scott!' Lubimov's hushed command was accompanied by a raised hand thrust abruptly in front of him. Carty halted.

'What is it?'

'A small group is approaching on the trail ahead.'

Carty glimpsed through the rhododendron, spying several bobbing heads.

'Hunters?'

'Possibly. Don't make any eye contact and say nothing, absolutely nothing!'

He skilfully negotiated the path, partially shielding the Englishman as they stood off to allow the four unshaven men to pass.

'*Zdravstvuitie,*' Lubimov's quiet salutation was met by a chorus.

'*Zdravstvuitie.*'

Though he kept his sight lowered, Carty felt the suspicious scan from the last man and glanced up instinctively, catching the emaciated weathered-reddened face glaring back at him.

'*Priviyet!*' the man slurred.

Carty ignored the comment but sensed trouble.

'I've never seen those men before,' Lubimov announced on reaching the edge of the *taiga*. 'They're strangers. It was clear from their accents.'

160

'Perhaps they're just visiting.'

'Unlikely!' The Russian's creased face failed to conceal his concern.

Twenty Four

Following a lunch of salted *Omul*, Carty sat outside overlooking the valley, mesmerised by the activities of two chipmunks playing just metres from him. He had discovered to his surprise, just days before an English version of *The Adventures of Sherlock Holmes* in the ward. Reading through the stories that he had so loved in his youth, he rediscovered the elegance of the plots. Conan Doyle's thought process and experience of human nature had enabled him to capture both the romance and the squalor of the late Victorian era while weaving an elaborate story that, on the face of it, could only be solved by a genius.

Inna's urgent appearance, though, surprised him.

'Quick, you come!' she said breathlessly while simultaneously lobbing a lightweight jacket to him.

'Where are we going?' he attempted to quiz her but she was already in the corridor expecting him to follow.

He scrambled on the jacket and trotted down to the door to find her outside with Lubimov. The Russian looked tense and was speaking hurriedly with her. Then he turned to Carty.

'They are on their way here. Inna will take you out into the forest to a safe place and Boris will meet you in a day or so.'

'But *who* is coming?'

The Russian waved a finger. 'There's no time to explain. You must leave now. Boris will explain everything to you.'

Inna was already grasping his arm pulling him outside.

They dashed into the tree line and waded through the squat bushes until they met a path. Inna, being a local woman, knew the terrain well and negotiated the damp tree roots and small sharp rocks with ease. Carty, though, struggled to keep up with her, panting audibly, his heart drumming in his ears as he focused on where she was stepping.

She finally stopped almost an hour later in a small glade and removed her rucksack. Carty collapsed on his knees beside an outcrop of wild thyme, its pungent smell reviving him. She smiled and checked his pulse and pupils before producing a thermos to pour some tea. He had survived his first real physical test and taking the cup gratefully from her, now slipped onto a mossy bank to regain his strength. An even breath slowly returned as he drank.

Below, the vastness of the lake beyond the rock filled his vision. It seemed unreal that here inland, such a body of water could exist and its presence imbued a deep sense of solemnity.

He woke alone and shivering in the waning sun. Lumps from insect bites festooned his exposed skin, causing him to itch frantically at his neck and shins. The scars, incurred from chasing after the apparition on the first night at Baikal were still visible and he grew insecure again, looking around for signs of Inna. Only her rucksack sat where she had left it nearby, but as his mind juggled with the various options open to him, her silhouetted frame emerged from out of the trees, her hands crammed with herbs. A contented grin lit her face as she stuffed them in her sack and pointed up the mountain to a group of boulders, speaking to him very positively in Russian. Obviously that was where they were heading. Despite a clear lack of enthusiasm in climbing another hundred or so metres in the diminishing light, he made a thumbs-up sign and then grabbed her outstretched hand to haul himself up.

The trail quickly broke out across huge granite slabs, separated by deep crevices. Negotiating them required his full exertion and some manhandling by Inna but eventually they reached the outcrop. He couldn't immediately see any place where they could shelter for the night but Inna, though, had disappeared under an overhang of stunted pine. He followed her and was amazed to find a path snaking between the upright slabs that led to the door of a lodge, virtually undetectable from outside.

Inside, it was dim, the only light coming through an ageing glass window facing down the valley into the darkening eastern sky. Inna lit an oil lamp and stripping down to her T shirt, moved straight into a practised routine of stocking the small furnace oven and then preparing the food. Shattered, Carty slumped down on a bunk and rested against the wall. His senses slowly began to shut down with exhaustion.

He was back at the CentralniySib camp with Lena, in the same cabin, lightning filling the sky as rain battered the windows. She was peering outside at someone or something and he rose from the bed. Then, in an instant, she had vanished and desperate, he ran outside into the storm in search of her, only to be met by the familiar hooded figure once again.

'You must prove yourself worthy and then I will bring her to you!' it uttered.

'No!' Carty screamed as he jolted awake.

Inna dived over to grasp him. *'Harasho?'* she asked searchingly, her acrid body odour rousing him from the dream state.

'Yes...yes,' He appreciated her presence.

Rising, she smoothly picked up his legs, swinging them around so that he was forced to lie back down on the bunk.

'Eat!' Inna insisted, offering a bowl of broth and a heel of black bread, spread thick with a white, fatty cheese.

'Thank you,' he mumbled, still numb. *Why should I have to prove myself worthy?* It seemed that the spectre only spoke to him in the form of stark messages.

Within the hour, fatigue had overcome him and having wrapped him in blankets, Inna extinguished the lantern. He lay in the darkness, timorous with the thought of losing control to his dreams once again.

During the night, he became acutely aware of a heightening of his senses and as his eyes opened, a face appeared behind the wavering light of a small candle. Startled, he jumped, his heart racing before the message from his brain told him it was Boris.

'Sshh...she's trying to sleep,' the Buryat whispered, pointing to Inna.

'What are you doing here?'

'Why shouldn't I be here?' he responded. 'I only heard from Lubimov a few hours ago that you were coming to this *isbushka*, so I came straight away.'

'What's happening back at the Institute?'

'Lubimov is being cautious. The local mayor believes that he's sitting on money from Moscow and has organised a spot check to pressure him into paying fines. The truth is that the medical funding stopped years ago.'

'And I suppose my presence would have been dangerous for everyone?'

'Yes, information about you may have been sold to the authorities and others know about this lodge, so we will need to move on tomorrow.'

Apprehension swept over Carty's face. 'Where to?'

'How do you feel?' Boris changed the subject.

'Dead tired.'

'Rest now and I will wake you early,' he winked and turned to make up a bed on the floor.

Twenty Five

Dawn hadn't yet broken as the Buryat softly shook him. Minutes later he nudged Carty forcefully with a foot, leaving him no option but to sit up.

'We need to be packed and gone in 30 minutes,' Boris ordered.

Barely able to keep his eyes open, Carty didn't appreciate the tone but understood that there was no arguing. His breath stank and the simplicity of the Institute's aging showers now seemed like a lost luxury.

Eating warmed buckwheat with butter he watched Inna pack. She grasped her rucksack and held Carty's shoulder in a show of affection before turning to Boris, passionately cupping his face between her hands and kissing his lips. Boris held her tightly in a hug and whispered to her.

'Where's Inna going?' Carty asked, embarrassed by their closeness.

'Back to the Institute.'

Carty watched her as she set off, back down the same trail over the boulders. A feeling of fear settled in his stomach.

'What about you Boris? Won't your absence be suspicious?'

'I don't work at *Sphinx*,' the Buryat grinned, picking up his things to lead Carty out.

They moved off in the opposite direction up through the damp undergrowth.

'So what *do* you do?' Carty persisted. Until this moment he had not spent any real time with this man.

'Many things, but I suppose you could call me a healer using the traditional medical practices suppressed by the Soviet authorities.'

'And what kind are they?'

'My ancestors were shamans, indigenous people, and their healing arts were passed down through a culture that has existed here since ancient times.' He paused momentarily, raising a hand as if he was listening for something.

'What is it?'

'Nothing.' He beckoned a struggling Carty to follow.

'So why do you spend time at *Sphinx*?'

'Lubimov has a need of my ancestral skills. In these changing times there will be a great need for this ancient knowledge.'

With the Buryat's openness, Carty sensed that this was now the time to field his own suspicions.

'You know, Boris, I think there's something rather strange going on at *Sphinx*.'

'You think so?' Boris stopped dead and crouched down again, this time to examine some animal tracks before swivelling around on his haunches and tilting his head up to face the foreigner.

'Are you talking about the *PSI* experiments, Scott?'

Carty's breath lapsed momentarily. The response wasn't what he had expected. 'Does it involve power generation?' he asked urgently, suspecting that Boris was alluding to the source he believed must exist in the *taiga*.

'Not exactly, *PSI* was the name of a secretive Soviet research programme, manipulating psychological and extrasensory abilities of the human mind.'

Carty remained silent. The Buryat continued.

'From the earliest days, there were many reports about the unusual abilities of some of the indigenous peoples of Russia. Lubimov was given the responsibility of investigating these phenomena and it led him to develop a form of synthetic telepathy.'

'How?' Carty was aghast that he was even entertaining this conversation.

'Simple. You take a naturally gifted telepath and wire that person up to see what part of the brain is stimulated during telepathy. Then you take another sensitive, intuitive patient and stimulate the same part of the brain to encourage the same ability.'

'It sounds pretty dangerous.'

'It is. You see, nature doesn't bestow these gifts to just anyone. If they're forced upon a person with a weak ego then it is catastrophic.'

'You said it *is* catastrophic. Did people suffer because of these experiments?'

'Yes, they did.'

'And Lubimov was responsible.'

'Although he was the leader of the team, he was personally crushed by the very negative effects on his research subjects and had a nervous breakdown. My uncle brought him back to a sense of himself through the practices of the shaman. By the time he had recovered, the research had been transferred to another institute.'

Carty was visibly angered. 'But Lubimov can't deny involvement.'

'If he hadn't complied he would have been imprisoned and become part of the experiment himself. It's something which you will not easily understand being an outsider.'

'That's a convenient excuse!'

'I don't spend time thinking about it.'

'No, but you choose to turn your back on it instead,' he blurted, indignantly, 'hoping that it will erase the horror of what Lubimov might have done?'

'No, I chose to hold those horrors within my psyche and neutralise their effects by being conscious of them.'

'How can anyone do that?'

'Ah, maybe the reason you are here is to understand that. Anyway, the benefit of his work was the experimentation with lasers and acupuncture. This, allowed Lubimov to positively deal with his guilt. It also saved your life.'

A squirrel, jumping through the trees, startled Carty momentarily.

'Can we stop for a few minutes?' He sighed, as he knelt on the thick moss, taking in the shards of light playing through the latticework of branches. The emerald iridescence was more than just calming: it pervaded his being, allowing him to forget this disturbing news of Lubimov's past and also the madness that had landed him here. He understood that he was now completely dependent upon the Buryat in this vast wilderness.

All around, pine and larch stood silently like living *stupas*. Nothing stirred for seconds. The ambience was thick and tangible as if the forest had taken its own breather before it was disturbed by the flutter of a solitary green woodpecker. Carty then recalled something that an acquaintance at a London-based timber fund had told him – more trees in the Siberian *taiga* die and fall, than are cut down. It had, at the time, left him with the notion to cash-in and develop a forestry-linked emissions product. Now, though, sitting in the majestic presence of the world's largest continuous forest, the idea seemed foreign and ludicrous. *A rational irrationality*, he recalled Green's rebuke.

Sap lines of amber resin dribbled down the myriad trunks, part of the abundance of the short summer here, its odour a blend of rich pine and sweet honey. Boris broke off a hardened part of the sticky flow from a larch and chewed it like gum.

'It's *sera*, an antiseptic which helps clean the gums,' he uttered in response to Carty's disparaging look.

The Englishman stretched back again into the soft foliage, allowing it to comfort him as a mother might.

'Boris, for how long was I in a comatose state?' The question seemed out of place but needed an answer. He had to know just how much time he had lost and if anyone was still looking for him, or had given up.

'About fourteen days: at one stage we thought we had lost you, but Lubimov never lacked faith.' His expression left Carty in no doubt as to the older man's integrity.

'Here take some of these.' The Buryat passed some small berries in his thick, stained palm. 'They're *Chernika*, packed with vitamin C!'

'They're bilberries!' he exclaimed, pleasantly surprised by the tart flavour. As he knelt, his focus adjusted and it seemed that a sea of the same berries materialised as if by magic hanging hidden beneath the bushes' petite leaves.

He joined Boris in harvesting them. It was backbreaking and after some time he straightened awkwardly, seeking to register his joy at such as satisfying task with his friend. But as he turned, horror took away his breath. He was facing down the barrel of a rifle, raised to the cocked head of the same hunter he had seen the previous morning. The figure's bloodshot eyes seemed hesitant as if confused at the apparent ease with which he was about to take the Englishman's life. Then, he squeezed the trigger. The barrel suddenly flew skyward, rattling off a blast that sent unseen birds fluttering. Boris had swept the stranger's legs away, dropping him, winded amongst the roots.

'Scott, stay back!' the Buryat coolly commanded as the stranger leapt up and a glint of a metal blade flashed menacingly between their bodies. Carty froze, unable to help his friend but it wasn't needed. Boris had already spun, trapping the weapon against the hunter's ribs while the momentum caused him to topple backwards and fall. A pained gasp chilled the Englishman. The killer had fallen on his own knife, piercing his spleen.

Boris knelt to support the dying man and gently asked him questions. The hunter pointed at Carty as he desperately spluttered an answer and then expired.

Head hung, the Buryat wiped his wide brow. 'This man was not a killer and his death could have been avoided.'

'Who is he?

'He was hunting bear when he learned that there was a ransom for you.'

Carty turned ashen. 'Lubimov and I saw him yesterday, on the trail near *Sphinx*. There were three others with him.'

'Well, they're not around now.'

'But how can you know that?'

The Buryat stared at him, calmly. 'I just do. Now help me lift the body, we need to remove all signs that he was ever here.'

Staring at the dead man's placid countenance, Carty shuddered, disturbed that the hunter had been about to commit cold-blooded murder for a reward.

'Come on, help me!' the Buryat insisted, tersely.

Twenty Six

Finishing the job, they set off on a different path.

'We need to move faster and get into hiding. We're a target out here in the open.' The Buryat picked up his pace against a strong wind. What began as a still summer's day was now building into a storm. Carty strained to keep up all the while frantically reliving the episode again and again in his head.

Why had there been a ransom issued for my death?

Finally the Buryat dropped his pack in a clearing and began scouring the ground for signs of any other visitors while intermittently smelling and picking some leaves.

'Anything I can do to help?' Carty called out as he squatted down, weakened but absorbed by the sight of Boris' hunter-gather instincts. The Buryat then held up a soiled root.

'What's that?'

'Siberian ginseng – good for men!' he chuckled quietly. 'Some people were here a few days ago, two men; one fat, a cigarette smoker, the other tall.'

Carty was immediately reminded of Sherlock Holmes' methods again and how his reading had been interrupted in the rush to leave. He shivered.

'Follow me.' Boris led him under the draping bough of an aged European ash, to a cabin, partially hidden by an outcrop of granite.

'Is anybody in there?'

'I am not sure yet. Wait here.'

Boris' countenance was noticeably relaxed as he reappeared some moments later.

'Is it safe?'

'Yes, for some time. Why don't you build a fire and I'll see if there is any salted fish,' he instructed. Carty followed him in to see him pulling up some of the floorboards and disappearing beneath them.

'Do you have any matches?' Carty asked as he prepared the small branches and logs.

'No!' the muffled response came back. A brown paper parcel tied with old gardening yarn then flew up out of the hole, followed by the man's head and arms. He hauled himself back out and secured the boards, all the while muttering to himself in a language unlike the Russian he had spoken with Lubimov or Inna.

Having inspected Carty's fire preparation, and rearranging part of it, Boris stripped the papery thin bark from a birch log to use as tinder and stuffed it into the assembled pile. Then, taking a small amount and cupping it in his hands, he calmly closed his eyes and audibly exhaled. The bark caught alight. He quickly tossed it into the fire watching it take life, ignoring Carty's shocked glare.

'How did you do that?' The Englishman scowled, guessing that the local man had played a trick. 'Was it a match in your hands or just friction when you rubbed it?'

'Neither.'

'Boris, please don't play mind games with me.'

'I'm not!' Boris cut him dead with a glare. 'Take some more bark and place it on the floor.'

Carty did as directed and the Buryat slowly placed his outstretched palm, face down, some ten centimetres above the bark and closed his eyes again. He remained motionless for some seconds and then exhaled forcefully. His hand quivered and then the bark instantly ignited. Carty's mouth gaped open, astounded by what he knew to be impossible.

'Boris, did you really light the bark with...'

'With my energy?' he murmured.

'But *really*, how did you do it?'

'I concentrated the yin and yang energies of my body together as one.'

'Is that *Qi*?' Carty quizzed, still in shock and trying to rationalise what he had just seen.

'Yes, if you want to call it that. Why don't we eat lunch? I'm sure you're hungry,' he teased, leaving the effect to play on the psyche of his doubting friend.

They proceeded to prepare a simple meal of fish soup, pickled sour cabbage and some dry biscuits. Boris had added a number of the herbs to the salted fish and hung the pot over the fire to heat the liquid. Carty was silent, just tossing the soiled ginseng root from hand to hand, exhausted as he ruminated on the mad events.

The open fire flared sporadically with the storm's draught as it whistled through gaps in the cabin's woodwork.

'Are you all right?'

'Yes, just tired.' Carty lifted his head, acknowledging him with a smile. 'And still logically trying to understand what just happened.'

'Don't bother. It's just a side-effect of the energy exercises I've been practising, daily, for most of my life.'

'Energy exercises?'

'Yes, they're also part of my heritage.'

'The Buryat culture?'

'In part: my mother's family are from Buryatia.' He swigged some coffee from a stained enamel mug.

'My father, though, is descended from Manchurian Chinese. His grandfather was a Taoist abbot, a master of the *neijia,* the internal healing arts. He passed his knowledge on to his son, my grandfather, who became a bodyguard at the court of the Empress Dowager. With her death, in the early 1900s, came the fall of the hated Ching dynasty and many Manchurians associated with the royal court had to flee in fear of their lives.' Boris dipped a biscuit into the drink. 'So he left for Harbin city in northern China, becoming a doctor to many of the wealthy Europeans and Russians living there.'

'And did he then come to Siberia?'

'Yes, following the growing unrest in China he moved the family to the new Soviet Union and ended up in Irkutsk. His first wife died early but he married again to a local woman and treated many of the new *apparatchiki*. My father was born shortly after.'

'And the teachings were passed on to him as well?'

'He kept the traditions of both cultures alive, despite Stalin's brutal attempts to stamp out anything which hinted at a non-Russian past and because of that, his family were forced to live in a small collective settlement around Baikal.'

'Did he practise acupuncture as well?'

'Of course, it was literally in his veins. When I was a boy I spent time in the mountains with him and my grandfather, meditating and practising the martial skills of their Taoist heritage.'

'And is your father still alive?'

'No, he's not.'

'I'm sorry.'

'Don't be.' The local man paused, reliving a memory as he stared into the fire: the light, mirrored against his copper face, captured the latent emotion. 'He was asked to help a sick friend, a member of the local Communist Party who had been abandoned by doctors as incurable. He did and the man fully recovered.' His voice lowered. 'But the authorities soon found out and set a trap. I was in my late teens when I saw my father being attacked by five men with axes. He moved through them like a whirlwind. It remains as clear to me as the day it happened. I can't remember seeing him touch any one of them but they dropped like stones, two of them dying several days later from their injuries.'

'And what happened to him?'

'What was expected for an ethnic-Chinese, killing two local Russians who had been ordered to assassinate him – he faced charges of murder and so fled to the mountains. Months later they found a skeleton, stripped by animals. It clearly wasn't his and we remained hopeful that he was still alive.'

'Have you seen him since?'

'Only his spirit: he has passed from this world.' Boris' expression said everything.

'I understand how you feel. My father left early one morning to play golf. He had a massive heart attack and died doing the thing he loved most.'

The atmosphere was strangely light despite the weight of the conversation.

Boris rose to test the soup before pouring it into two bowls.

'That day when you put your palm on my face, it felt like a low electric current, pleasant and warm. It sent me to sleep.'

'Good. That was the intention.'

'So do you use this energy to heal people?'

'Yes, but again it's a side effect. Intuitively I know when someone is *dis-eased* and what is causing it. I can only help, though, if they consciously want to recover.'

'But if it's only a side effect, then why are you practising these disciplines at all?'

'To maintain a sacred space where I have a conscious dialogue with my inner self: I find it relieves the collective psyche.'

'But what benefit is that?'

'That is too difficult a question for me to answer in words. One has to experience it.'

'Experience it?'

'Probably the easiest way is through the unbiased messages of dreams. I know that you face great difficulties with yours.' The Buryat's bright gaze met Carty's astonishment.

'How do you know that?'

'I have seen the shadow that follows you. The wake-up call for you was the first attempt on your life but you still haven't decided to take responsibility. You are destined for other things, but first you must allow your dreams and intuitions to show you who you really are and your way forward in life.'

'You sound like Green,' Carty muttered, scratching at his thickening stubble.

'Green?'

'A friend: I should have listened to him and then I might not have ended up here.' He shrugged.

'Scott,' Boris' manner was stern. 'You were coming here anyway!'

Carty remained silent, spooning the soup and pensively watching Boris go onto his haunches to play with the fire, adding and rearranging logs so that they would burn more evenly.

After the humble meal, he passed Carty a small bowl of potatoes and a crude old knife.

'Peel these. You'll be hungry later,' he insisted.

Carty accepted the chore. It felt perversely satisfying to sink the knife into the crisp flesh and then render the skin, leaving as much of the potato intact as possible.

The Siberian summer day was darkening into early evening and with it Carty remembered their unfinished conversation from the trail.

'Boris, I believe I can trust you fully. You saved my life and I suspect that your wisdom would put you beyond corruption.'

'Well, the *taiga* does provide me with all that I need and I earn a little money through my healing work with the locals. If you wish to share something with me then that is your choice.'

Carty nodded. 'Lena Isotova, the young woman murdered at the Baikal camp, disclosed to me that nuclear waste is being dumped in Siberia. It was sanctioned by her director who's working covertly with my boss back in London.'

Boris' expression turned grave. 'Just suspecting that you know this information was a good enough reason to order your deaths.'

'Anyway,' he uttered, collecting himself. 'I suspect Lubimov is covering up a something.'

'Ha ha!' Boris laughed.

'Boris, I'm serious! I saw the meters in his cabin. The power output was enormous and couldn't possibly have been produced by the heat-pumps on that roof.'

'Scott, why do you think Lubimov showed you those?'

'I've no idea but I don't believe his story about mini-hydro turbines up in the mountains. There has to be another feasible explanation as to how all that energy is being produced and I suspect that it's nuclear.'

'Nuclear,' Boris muttered, grinning mischievously. 'That is very far from Lubimov's ethics.'

'Is it? So can you explain what's going on, then?'

'Yes.' He pulled himself up into a cross-legged position on the wooden chair. 'His energy source is all around us.'

The crackling of the fire resonated with the Englishman's inaudible gasp of amazement.

What other energy source could he mean?

His commonsense told him it was ridiculous and as crazy perhaps, as Boris lighting the birch bark with his bare hands – not once but twice.

'What are you trying to tell me?' he blurted.

Boris winked at him. 'Have you finished with the potatoes?' He wasn't about to open up any further.

Twenty Seven

Arthur D'albo pulled uneasily on a cigar as he stared out of the window at the view across the Thames. The situation had now taken a new turn. Mark Boyd had failed to show up for work for the best part of a week. D'albo had had no choice but to report his suspicions to the Board that Carty, and possibly Boyd, had instigated fraudulent trades against CentralniySib Energo. The extent of the embezzlement had not yet been determined but he knew exactly that it ran into tens of millions of US dollars, misappropriated during the few months leading up to Carty's disappearance.

Having made the mistake of employing Boyd, D'albo would be expected to graciously fall on his sword and resign. It was a small price to pay for the wealth awaiting him. The expectation raised a cruel smile.

And no one will even suspect me!

A sharp knock disturbed him and he shuddered as the light threw back his dark reflection in the glass pane.

'Inspectors Church and Cooke are here to see you.' Cynthia effortlessly introduced the two men. He swung around, switching on his slick persona once more.

'Thank you for agreeing to meet with us, Mr D'albo,' Church, the senior of the two remarked.

'Well, I would say it's a pleasure, gentlemen, but I fear that's never really the case with Scotland Yard's finest,' he uttered smugly as he shook their hands.

'Why's that, Mr D'albo?' Church quizzed.

'Because it means something's gone badly wrong. I spend my whole day, every day, trying to ensure that we're managing this business effectively, looking after the shareholders' interests. Yet two of my team have absconded, apparently having embezzled funds from our most important client.'

'Mr D'albo.' Cooke seemed puzzled. 'I apologise if there's been any confusion. We are simply here on a routine investigation pertaining to a missing person's report filed by Mark Boyd's family and your own office.'

D'albo stumbled over the response for a second. 'But surely the disappearance of both Boyd and Carty and the recent discovery of unauthorised trades are too much of a coincidence?'

'That may seem coincidental, but making assumptions is not our business.'

'I suppose you're correct. But I did advise the investigating officers that we had been suspicious of Carty's activities for some time.'

'We have been made aware of those facts, sir, but has Albion uncovered any hard evidence which could directly implicate these two men in fraudulent activity?' the detective probed further.

'Not yet,' D'albo countered. 'You see, these exotic derivatives, they're complicated. It may take months to unravel them and fully evaluate the losses and the money trail. Until then, we won't have a clear picture of what they were up to.'

Cynthia re-entered carrying a sterling silver tray. Her form momentarily took their attention as she served.

'I must admit, Mr D'albo, we do find the circumstances rather unusual.'

'Unusual, why?'

'Both men previously worked at Brightwell Carter and one of them, Boyd, was convicted of a fraud which brought the company down.' Church said, stirring sugar into his coffee and watching as the intent of his remark bit.

'Yes, I suppose you would find it odd, not knowing what these two young men are capable of in business. Carty is a brilliant derivatives originator with tremendous foresight and Boyd, unsurpassed as a client-man despite the previous conviction.'

'But some would ask if it was a good management decision to have employed Boyd at all, given his history.'

'People make mistakes in life and need a second chance. Carty persuaded me that we needed Boyd and I agreed to it on a trial basis. I'm regretting that decision now, though!' He feigned a sigh. 'I've made a recommendation to the Board for a full forensic examination of Carty's department and the trading positions he took.'

'You didn't make a routine investigation after Carty's disappearance?' Cooke posed.

'No. As I explained to the detectives then, I was waiting for Boyd's report. I expected him to get to the bottom of any trading discrepancies quickly and without causing undue panic.'

'And did he find anything?'

'Nothing. He seemed to go off the boil.'

'You seem to be referring to Boyd in the past tense, Mr D'albo.'

'That's because he's bloody well history at Albion, even if he does turn up somewhere.'

'But there may be other reasons why he went missing,' Cooke chided.

'All I meant was that if he's been involved in this scam with Carty then its curtains for them both!'

'You seem confident of that, sir!'

'I have traded all of my business life and can tell when there's something fishy going on.'

'So, you believed Scott Carty was acting fraudulently and you asked another member of staff to investigate it secretly?' Cooke's expression underlined his disbelief.

'Yes, and I've already discussed all this with your detectives.'

'Just for the record, sir, what exactly did you tell them?'

D'albo's ruddy face grew agitated. 'That I had asked Boyd to take over the responsibilities of the team when Carty was promoted, just before he left for Kazakhstan. Because of my suspicion I thought it best to review the department by stealth so that no one would get wise and destroy any incriminating evidence. We also wanted to ensure minimum disruption and eliminate the chance of our clientele hearing rumours of a problem.'

'That implies that you had a special relationship with Boyd, being able to trust him like that?'

'That's a bloody strange remark, isn't it?' D'albo riled. 'I've known him since he was a young man.'

'Longer than you have known Carty?'

'Yes.'

'And you didn't think it unwise; asking him to look into Carty's trading activities?'

'Just what are you driving at?' D'albo glared.

'The facts, sir: I'm trying to understand what might have driven either of these two men to have committed a crime.'

'Look, we didn't exactly understand how these derivative positions were set up. I had to be sure before I formally reported my suspicions. Could you imagine the repercussions, if I had got it wrong?'

Cooke wouldn't let it go. 'I understand that, Mr D'albo, but surely you know that an executive officer of a company has a fiduciary duty to report any suspicion of fraud, no matter how insignificant it appears, at the earliest opportunity.'

'In this team we handle our problems ourselves, holding back on shaking out the dirty linen until we have to. Anyway, now it's official, okay!' He was rattled. 'The Board will have a full report in a matter of days and will take the appropriate action then.'

'Can I recommend that you ask the Serious Fraud Office to assist in any investigation?' Cooke's words implied that whatever the Albion Board decided, Scotland Yard, for its own reasons, would want to be involved.

D'albo had read the implied intent and visibly backed down. 'Of course! The FSA's input would be most welcome,' he countered. 'Now, gentlemen, if there's nothing else I would like to get on with the activity of keeping this company afloat.'

The two detectives glanced at each other, puzzled.

'As I mentioned earlier, we are here to discuss Mark Boyd's disappearance,' Church reminded him. 'There are some questions we wanted to ask you if you have a few minutes, Mr D'albo?'

He eyed them, his interest suddenly aroused. 'Yes, what are they?'

'Do you have any reason to suspect that Mark Boyd may have led a secret life?'

'I don't know what you mean?' A frown rippled his forehead.

'Often with missing persons, we discover that they have something to hide; an affair, a love-child, being blackmailed, etcetera.'

'You're not serious, are you?'

'It's not as bizarre as you may think, and could explain his disappearance. Was Boyd acting strange in any way?'

D'albo leant forward to pour more coffee into the cups, slickly continuing his dialogue. 'No, although he did seem distracted after Carty went missing.'

Cooke locked onto the comment. 'Exactly why did he go to Prague?'

'We have an important client there. I sent him in with the US team organising the package of finance and options.'

'Would that involve complex derivatives?' Church asked, attempting to sound intelligent.

'Generally, yes, if a client is hungry for a cash investment or working capital, then we include options at an increased cost. The client tends not to care too much and it may work in their favour in the long term. It also gives our quant team a reason to exist and a chance to run their models in a real scenario.'

'I see,' Cooke grinned quietly at what seemed to him to be a legitimate fraud in all but name.

'I asked Boyd to represent me. I should never have trusted him.'

'We shall see, Mr D'albo.' Church coughed, clearing his throat. 'Now, can I also ask you about the young lady, Elena Isotova, who travelled with Scott Carty to Russia?'

'I met her once, briefly, at a lunch meeting with her senior management. Why?'

'It's just that her apartment in London was broken into before she left. Nothing was stolen.'

'And?' D'albo replied, disinterestedly.

'It implies that the burglar was looking for something and didn't find it. We would like to interview some of her colleagues at CentralniySib in Moscow, including a Mr Kosechenko, who we believe to be one of the last persons to have seen both her and Scott Carty before they went missing.'

'Didn't she get on that helicopter with the Americans?'

'Not according to the Russian authorities.'

'So what do you want from me?'

'Well, we were hoping that you could assist us in setting up an interview with Mr Kosechenko?' Church's tone wavered.

'I would have thought that Scotland Yard had the resources to do that!'

'It's proving to be difficult, sir.'

'Despite the fact that Mr Kosechenko is a director of one of Albion's largest clients and that his company is likely to be serving a court order against Albion very shortly, I am afraid that I cannot assist you. I don't think I have to, do I, Inspector Church?'

'No, sir, you do not.'

'Why hasn't anyone requested this earlier?'

'We wanted to explore all the leads we had in London first.'

'And have you?'

'After today, yes we have.'

'Good! Then, gentlemen, I bid you good day,' he gesticulated to the door.

Cynthia had already entered.

'Thank you, Mr D'albo.' Cooke shook his hand. 'We'll leave our cards with your assistant. Please feel free to contact us should anything come up that you think may be useful.'

Twenty Eight

The high pitched note of a mosquito, settling on Carty's face, woke him. He struggled to sit up with his cramped arms and as he did, he noticed Boris' empty bunk across the small cabin.

Next to the fire he found a coffee pot still warm.

Boris must have left recently, he reasoned as a hazy recollection of the fire-lighting episode persisted against his fresh doubts.

'Harrh!' An unusual short, muffled shout, splintered the calm.

Startled, he ran outside and cautiously scanned the immediate area.

'Harrh!' The noise came again from beyond a cluster of pink granite boulders sitting upright like petrified feathers. His heart started to pound with an immediate concern for his friend and he raced over to tackle the irregular stones. His stiff muscles struggled to respond as he scrambled up between their fractured surfaces and as his feet pushed against a discrete layer of scree, they slid away from under him. He fell hard, gouging his shins.

'Yah...shit!' He stifled a squeal for fear of giving away his position and then, ignoring the stinging pain, grittily hauled himself back up.

From the vantage point on the top boulder, he crouched to catch his breath and gaze over a vast panorama. A mist listlessly transpired in the dawn's rays, shrouding a mass of evergreen foliage and smoothing out the contours of the landscape to the horizon. Granite tips roosted by huddled crows, poked through here and there and momentarily, he felt himself hypnotically drawn in by the belief that he could step out on to this apparent substantiality.

'Harrh!' The sound pierced the damp air, pulling his focus back down to a small sandy arena beyond the interlaced rocks. The Buryat was rapidly walking, almost gliding, around in a wide imaginary circle, his arms held out, facing towards its virtual centre.

Every four or five steps the movements switched direction as he whirled off into smaller circles, his body actions meshing tightly in a pattern of superb order.

A low heel kick darted out followed by whipping palm strikes and then a sudden leap, spinning rapidly backwards in a blur of movement. Carty's gaze was drawn to the point where he expected the Buryat to return to terra firma but instead he appeared to hover longer than feasibly possible before landing some metres away. Carty stood up, gawping in amazement.

It has to be a trick of the morning light, his rational mind screamed back at him.

The Buryat then stood quietly and slowly raised his hands in two simultaneous arcs up over his head and down his torso centre line as if gathering the energy he had expended.

'It's called *Baguazhang,*' he placidly stated without looking up.

Carty gingerly slid down the crag as Boris turned.

'You've hurt yourself,' he said, pointing at the claret-red stains on the Englishman's leg.

'Oh, it's not serious,' Carty replied, dismissing the distraction. 'But did I really see you defy gravity just then?' His expression begged an answer.

'Ah...just a side effect.' The man sunk gently onto his haunches, scouting around the undergrowth next to them.

'Come off it, Boris, was there something in that soup we had yesterday? Hallucinogenic herbs perhaps?'

The Buryat glared at him. 'Why would I need to deceive you?' He passed him a large leaf. 'Now wipe your cut with that!' he ordered, swiftly rising to walk away.

'Wait, Boris, I didn't mean to insult you. You have to understand that for a man of science, the things that you have been doing just don't make any sense.'

'Science!' Boris scoffed. 'You speak as if science can explain everything.'

Capitulation registered in Carty's expression. 'All right, I agree, but please understand. One day you're lighting a piece of bark with your bare hands, and the next you're floating a metre above the ground without any feasible explanation!'

A beam broke across the Buryat's broad face as his mood transformed. 'Do you want try it?'

'I'll give it a go!' The words had left Carty's mouth before he had a chance to give it any real thought.

'So what exactly is *Baguazhang*?' the Englishman asked.

'Essentially, it's a meditation developed centuries ago by the monks of the *Dragon Door* Taoist sect. During their daily chanting practice they 'walked the circle', consciously focusing the breath to open the energy pathways of the body.

He contorted Carty into low stance: weight sunk upon the bent rear leg with the forward foot placed a half step in front, toes slightly turned-in.

'It enhances both physical and spiritual well-being but is very challenging and can take the performer into a trance-like state, a condition in which many things are possible.'

'Like levitation?'

'Hah!' the Buryat snorted, 'like the control and summoning of one's *Qi* at will.'

'But isn't it a martial art, the one you were taught by your grandfather?'

'Yes. Over the generations the monks also incorporated fighting techniques into the system, probably shown to them by retired military officers who had chosen to atone for their bloody lives, evolving it into a unique martial art. By the late 18th century, it began to be taught to outsiders including my family.'

He twisted the Englishman's torso and pulled his leading hand forward. 'Once the basic postures have become natural and much stronger, then the martial aspects can be developed. *Zhang* is the Mandarin word, meaning palm. There are no fist techniques in this system.'

'But isn't a fist stronger and more powerful?'

'Not really; an open palm allows the *Qi* to flow more easily.' Boris demonstrated with a beautifully fluid movement of his hands as he spoke. 'And the *Ba Gua*, are the eight trigrams from the *I Ching*, an ancient book of wisdom.

'Yes, I know it,' Carty gasped, 'but I thought it just was an oracle?'

'It's much more than that. Each of the eight *Gua* represents an archetypal state of energy transcending time and space and which manifest in nature through the changing cycle of the seasons. That's why they are used to predict the various probabilities of future events.'

Carty frowned at the comment. 'But how does all that have any relevance to fighting?'

'There are eight martial principles which, when incorporated with the rapid stepping and spiralling movements of the torso and arms, create a supremely efficient system of health and self-defence.'

He ran a finger firmly up the ridge of the Englishman's backbone. 'The spine is of major focus. It must be held straight at all times.'

Carty flinched. His weighted leg had become too much to bear.

'Your knee will be fine,' Boris whispered.

'How did you know I was worried about my knee?'

'Your body has been compensating for it throughout the journey but don't worry, this exercise will help.'

Carty had only just learnt not to cynically question Boris and instead, he sought his advice.

'So why, exactly, am I compensating for my knee?'

'You probably work too hard intellectually and you're frightened of losing power over your life. In traditional Chinese medicine, the kidney's energy pathway runs up the inside of the leg, through the knee. Yours has been depleted because you persist in maintaining a demanding regime and an overactive sex life, which drains, rather than replenishes, your *Qi.* That's why the energy has temporarily collapsed at the point of most stress.'

Collapsed! He was shocked at the diagnosis. 'My knee?'

'Yes. Lubimov fully examined you during the coma.' He grinned.

'But how did you know about my job and the sexual relationships?'

'A wild guess really but the kidney controls the emotion of fear, and houses the sexual pre-birth *Qi* in the body.'

'Pre-birth *Qi?*'

'It's the body's hereditary storehouse of power, generally wasted away by life's excesses. Taoist *neijia* exercises focus on mixing this with the *Qi* contained in air, water, and food, to nourish the body's organs and sustain life. It's a kind of alchemy.'

Carty looked bemused as his bent leg began to tremor wildly under its weight. Boris lightly pulled him forward.

'Shake it to relieve the pain and let's wait for a few minutes before we focus on the training, shall we?'

The sun invigorated rather than sapped his strength, and over the course of a few hours, he had walked a circle, two metres in diameter, more than 50 times. At first he was clumsy, awkwardly transferring his weight from one leg to the other. Eventually, though, he moved smoothly with his spine upright.

Boris' expression voiced a pleasure at the determination shown, and his quick skyward glance, to gauge the time from the sun's position, caused him to halt the training.

'That's enough; you have the basic walking technique. We may as well have lunch now and then rest before the storm comes.'

Carty was relieved. His calves and thighs throbbed from the low postures.

'That has to be one of the most challenging exercises I have ever attempted!' he exclaimed as he struggled to pull off the sweat-soaked shirt sucking at his skin. 'I need to take a dip.' He indicated to the stream running alongside the clearing.

'Not yet, it's dangerous!'

'Dangerous!'

'Yes. Your *Qi* is full and close to the skin. To have a cold shower or bath now will reverse all the good progress you have made. Rest here in the cool shade, instead.'

The two sat down next to each other on a grassy bed below the birch, their backs to the area where they had been training.

'Cross your legs and gently hold your head up, as if its crown is suspended from the sky.' Boris' demonstrated as he spoke.

'Now breathe, very slowly, like a child. Suck the air in gently through your nose, in a continuous stream without breaking the flow. Expand the stomach and let it fill your whole body. Do not strain. Let the action be natural and as you reach fullness, pause for a moment and then...gently let it out through your mouth.' His voice had descended to a whisper as the chatter of the brook subtly played across his words.

'Imagine that the hot energy you have generated is sinking back to a point just below your navel.'

Carty's eyes began to close.

'Keep your eyes open.'

A hint of a smile crept across the Englishman's face. He lowered his eyelids just enough to filter the light through them and instantly became aware of the beat of his heart and the flow of air through his nostrils. He was feeling cautious but willing to experience his own barriers as his mind gently teased, tempting him to stop breathing altogether. Then a surge of energy, like a hot liquid, shot past his tail bone and up his back, bursting out along his limbs to the centre of his palms.

A light seemed to form around him, touching everything with a luminescence. Entranced, he gazed out into the forest and caught the silhouette of a figure moving towards him. It was Lena, bare foot and smiling.

'Scott,' she uttered but it was not her voice. 'Basilides has left your fate with me.'

'Basilides?'

'The hooded one,' her voice resonated. 'He brought you here.'

'But why?'

'So that you can bring the experience you will have back to those who have lost their way.'

'And then?' he asked, calmly.

'And then, watch the world change. I will lend you my strength.'

As her words ended her image began to fade imperceptibly into the backdrop and in seconds, she was gone.

Twenty Nine

A breeze had whipped up dust into small funnels as Carty slowly lifted his eyelids, allowing the light to pour back into his temporal cocoon. With an effort of purpose, he forced out his legs and a burning rush brought an almost unbearable tingling back into them.

It took him several minutes to clamber to his feet and trace his route back to the rocky outcrop. The circling exercise had proved to be more demanding than he had imagined and the boulders, greater obstacles than some hours before. He laboured the last few steps and collapsed in a weathered chair near the lodge's entrance as dark clouds bloomed above the tree cover.

'The storm will be here shortly,' Boris quietly acknowledged while skinning a squirrel as it hung from a branch. An eye had already been removed to drain the blood. Carty sat and watched for some minutes, brimming with questions but strangely more interested pondering them himself than in asking his friend.

'Here!' The Buryat flung the bloodied carcass to Carty. 'Take it inside.'

Like a student with his new master, Carty followed the instruction.

He was then given the chore of cutting the meat into small chunks and placing them into a boiling pot of herbs as Boris stoked up the small stove and furiously fanned the fire.

'You need to drink plenty of fluids. You have been sweating excessively.' He passed Carty a mug of hot tea, his manner avuncular in ironic contrast of character to the martial warrior of that morning.

A sudden sheet of rain shook him.

'Strange things certainly happen here,' Carty muttered, nursing the mug in his bloodied hands.

'Strange?' Boris asked, quizzically.

Carty looked up, 'Yes, I had a vision during the meditation. Did you see the light in the forest?' he quizzed.

'If you are asking me if I saw what you perceived, no, I didn't.' his voice was suddenly drowned out by a peel of thunder, raging above the cabin.

'I saw a woman emerge from the *taiga* bearing an uncanny resemblance to Lena Isotova. She told me that my fate had been left with her.' He faltered with the recollection of her passionate sigh as their lips first met in that hotel room.

A sizzling of water meeting fire – the boiling-over of the stew – roused him and he dived to the stove.

'Don't touch it!' Boris barked, simultaneously throwing a small towel across his path. Deftly the Englishman caught it and spun around to grab the pot away and place it on a stone slab.

'Well done!' The Buryat was impressed. 'The exercises today have sharpened your reflexes. You moved like a cat.'

Carty beamed briefly but then a stinging sensation drew his focus to the gash on his leg. The deep wound was oozing from under its dried red crust, visible through the tear in his trousers.

Boris knelt to examine it. 'This needs treating. We cannot be careful enough out here in the wild, infection can kill.' His facial expression was that of a sage as he started to squeeze out the old blood. 'The shaman's traditional treatment is to chew some specific forest herbs into a mush and then apply them with the saliva to the wound.'

Carty screwed up his face.

'But we'll use some hot water and an antiseptic spray instead.'

Wincing, as the local man set to work, Carty tried to switch his mind from the pain. 'So what do you think it meant – the vision, I mean?'

The Buryat gazed up at him. 'Perhaps its suggesting your fate is not in being a....what is it that you said you are?'

'An energy trader, I suppose.'

'And do you believe you can return to doing that?'

'Not really, but I guess everything is relative.'

'Relative!' Boris roared with laughter, shaking his head.

'Do you really think I still need to remain hidden?'

'All my senses tell me that there are forces still searching for you.' He looked up. 'They know that you didn't die in Baikal so we now have to create the illusion that you've perished in the *taiga*, until we can get you safely home.'

The hint of fear washed over the Englishman. 'I guess I was too big-mouthed with those Americans.'

'Well, if you were they're no longer any threat.'

'Why?'

'They're dead.'

'What?' The blunt statement left him stunned.

'That's right. The helicopter they left in, crash-landed. But I can see that this is news to you.'

Carty sensed a deception and became irritated. 'It is, but I suppose Lubimov told you to keep it from me?'

'No, actually I thought I would keep it quiet until the right moment.'

'Ah, thanks,' he muttered sarcastically. 'So how did you find out about it?'

'My friends fly regular helicopter journeys for the military. They were called in to deal with the accident.'

'Was it an accident?'

'Unlikely!'

Thirty

The Buryat yanked the door open with a sharp tug and the sweet fragrances of the wet foliage inundated their senses.

They served the stew outside, under the overhanging trees. Carty tentatively tried it fearing that squirrel would taste awful, but it didn't.

'Some more training?' the Buryat ventured after they had rested for a short while. The Englishman looked down at the yellow-brown streaks of iodine on his leg and nodded, following him out into a clearing a few metres away.

He stood quietly, allowing his posture to be adjusted once again.

'This exercise is called *zhan zhuang* – standing like a post,' Boris said softly, encouraging Carty to bend his legs as he pulled lightly on the Englishman's thinning crown hair.

'The stance should be held upright, naturally, not with force but with the mind,' Boris advised. 'It's a paradox which can only be understood by continual practice.'

'For how long?'

'I've been doing it for about 25 years,' Boris winked. 'But I doubt if you will last ten minutes on your first try.'

'It's not easy at all!' Carty sighed. 'What are its benefits?' He expected to be told about special powers, the type he had witnessed in the last days. Boris sensed the meaning.

'Like the *Baguazhang*, it develops the body's quiet force through the use of breath and imagination and takes the individual into a zone of inner stillness, a place where the alchemical process of looking at ourselves can begin.' He had placed a palm on Carty's chest, rubbing it and forcing it to be more relaxed.

'But how is that alchemy?'

'The true man breaths from his *tan tien,* his centre of gravity. That's where the pre-birth *Qi* mixes with the *Qi* of the air to create a deep internal heat that tempers the bone marrow, stimulating blood cell and antibody production. The Taoist classics claim that this process reverses aging and brings immortality.'

'And you believe that?' Carty baulked.

'Well, at least it helps me light fires!' Boris simpered, raising a finger to his lips to halt any further questioning.

Silence then engulfed them, as time itself seemed to warp and slow down.

After a short time Carty's arms felt intolerably heavy and his legs began to shudder uncontrollably again. Sensing this, Boris gently eased himself from his own posture.

'Are you feeling tired?'

'Yes, and quite dizzy.'

'Then that's enough for today!' He slapped him gently on the shoulder. 'Now come with me,' he instructed as he wandered off towards the trees. Carty shook his aching limbs to relieve them as he tried to keep up.

They stopped some way in, alongside the naked frame of an old lodge, its timbers worn and cracked with age. Piled up at one end, to a height of a man, were large river stones, heaped over a cast-iron stove. The arrangement resembled a modern sculpture.

'What's that?' Carty questioned but was ignored as the Buryat lifted a tarpaulin to reveal chopped fire logs. He threw a small one at Carty who, unprepared, missed the catch and stumbled forward.

'Just what exactly are we trying to achieve here?' Carty asked, petulantly. Boris began stacking the logs crosswise in his arms.

'We're going to build a fire to heat those stones and then much later, we'll cover this frame with canvasses to create a *banya*.'

'A *banya*?'

'A sweat lodge!'

'Why?'

'Too many questions!' Boris dumped them down and arranged the kindling. He then disappeared, emerging minutes later with paper and some burning embers balanced on a flat piece of slate.

'No hand-lighting tricks then?' Carty jibed.

'Not this time.'

Shortly, he had the fire roaring into life.

'Now we can go down there to collect water.' He indicated to a torrent gushing through a gully a hundred or so metres below them and then grabbed two disused cooking-oil buckets leaving no time for Carty to rest.

'Are you coming?' he yelled back as he effortlessly glided down a slope.

Carty followed unenthusiastically. The ground underfoot, sodden by the storm, caused him to slide several times leaving him gasping and peeved that he was being tested to the limits of his endurance.

When he caught up, he found Boris standing precipitously near the point where the young stream cascaded over a cliff edge.

'Amazing, isn't it? All this energy, it's just *free*,' Boris chimed, in awe of its magnificent raw power. 'We'll leave the buckets here.'

The Buryat then sped off again, sliding more than stepping down a bank of overgrown grass and shrubs, which camouflaged a perilous terrain of loose rocks underfoot. Carty dragged behind, unable to keep up but eventually slid down a bank on to a narrow ledge where the falls met a huge plunge pool. Its waters lapped against Boris' boots as he squatted, cat-like, focusing into its depths.

'Are you okay?' Carty asked, panting as he drew alongside

Immediately, the Buryat's palm flew up behind him, imposing a silence.

'Move very slowly,' he whispered and then put an arm around Carty, forcing him to sink to his knees. 'Stay low, the refraction of light through the water means that the trout can easily see us back here.'

Carty was well versed in the laws of light propagation and picked out the shimmering image of a large mature fish in the rapidly moving water.

'Interesting isn't it? How it can hold its position against the strong current without any effort?' the Buryat murmured. 'How do you think it does it?'

But before Carty could respond, the man had sprung out into the shallows, one arm darting out as the other simultaneously scooped up in a forward motion. Up to his waist in the pool and struggling like a juggler, the Buryat pulled the fish firmly to his chest. It writhed incessantly in his thick fingers and holding the gasping mouth close to his face, he waded back, gently humming to his catch. The creature had begun to grow calmer, yielding to its captor and fate.

'Wow, that was incredible!' Carty boomed.

'Not so incredible: when I was a boy my grandfather taught me to practise *calming* fish every summer.'

'But I have never seen anything like that.'

'Actually this trout has claimed the remarkable act,' Boris quipped as he reached the shore.

'What do you mean?'

He grinned quietly to himself, his face round like a full moon as he laid the fish on the pebbled bank and pulled a piece of fabric from his pocket to wrap around it.

Mystified, Carty stared on, silently.

'This fish is giving up its life for us so that we can survive,' Boris explained. 'It has also revealed its secret, its ability to suspend itself motionless when it could have sped off upstream. Now, how do you explain that?'

Carty shook his head, his mouth down-turned. 'I can't.'

'Scott, I'm not trying to make a fool of you, I just want you to challenge your intellect.'

'Well, can you explain it?'

'Yes, I think I probably can, but not in terms you may understand or accept.'

'That's a very convenient answer!'

'But it's the truth!'

Thirty One

They started back up the trodden-down track, to where the buckets sat. Carty was close to totally spent. Boris filled them and then carefully laid the fish into one, watching it slowly come to life again, its tail thrashing in the sunlight.

'Now let's check on that *banya*, shall we?'

The flames had already died out but the white-hot stone pile threw out an unbearable shimmering heat, halting them in their tracks, just a short distance away.

'Here, take this.' Boris passed him the corner of an old tent canvas and moved to haul it over the wooden frame. Carty copied on his side. Repeating the process with several more, they created a breathable, yet sealed membrane.

'Right, let's strip off and then we'll take the buckets in,' Boris said, flinging back a flap to form a makeshift door, revealing a dark cave-like interior.

Carty did so, embarrassed as he compared his sluggish figure with the local's bronzed physique, toned, but not overly muscled.

'Don't worry, your eyes will soon become accustomed to the dark,' he laughed, pushing the Englishman in.

'Thanks!' Carty uttered with obvious insincerity as a wall of hot air hit him.

'We call this a *banya po-chernomu* – a black *banya*!' he uttered, dropping the canvas closed behind them, leaving it only just possible to see an outline of his friend silhouetted against the dull glow of the stones.

He was able to isolate specific aromas in the menagerie of the flora from the *taiga* and, gradually, adjusting to the dark, he noticed that the floor was scattered with pine fronds on which Boris had assumed a crossed leg posture.

'It's bloody warm in here!' he gasped. The dry heat had already begun to tease small beads of sweat across the smooth skin of his back and shoulders.

'You can leave at any time but I suggest that you stay in here as long as you can bear it, to gain the maximum benefit.'

'I'll try.' The dryness had already stilted his breathing

'Good, just let everything go, and then see what happens.'

In the wake of the absence of words, the Buryat's odd comment repeatedly sounded in his head. Carty narrowed his eyes as formless images appeared, swimming in the haze, suddenly shape-shifting into figures and faces from the past. They triggered a melee of buried feelings, which added to the pain of the suffocating environment. He tried to move his limbs to wave them away but they didn't respond.

The young girl of his dream surfaced again, beaming as her eyes held his. He blinked and found himself transported back to his garden in a summer many years before, playing with a ball, throwing it back and forth to her.

'She's your friend,' a voice said from somewhere behind him and he turned to catch the loving image of his mother's face, smiling back from the kitchen window.

Was it a dream? He wondered. His eyes had now fully opened, searching for Boris. Instead, they found another figure in his place, its dropped head lifting unhurriedly, to show its face.

'Dad?' he called out, his skin rippling with goose bumps in recognition of the familiar contours. No words came but just a calm, peaceful stare.

And then Carty understood. Nothing he could do could change anything that had passed. The burden that he had been carrying since childhood was of his own making and his own choice.

He shook himself.

'Are you well?' the Buryat asked, now sitting before him again, motionless.

Carty sought the man's face and found the muted reflection of the glowing stones glinting back in his unblinking eyes.

'Yes, I think so.'

'You spoke.'

'I know.'

'What did your father tell you?'

'Nothing.'

'And is that what has been holding you back from understanding yourself?'

'I suppose it has.'

'Well, that's what the sweat lodge is for.'

Carty was at a loss for words and wondered if he had come all this way just to learn about himself.

'Often, when we are challenged by a strange and unusual set of circumstances outside of our comfort zone, we find the point of greatest weakness in ourselves.'

'And like yin-yang, can that can become our greatest strength?'

'You see, you already know this. It's not a mystery but the real art is in not forgetting it in those moments when we're confused by the illusion of things happening around us.' His words seemed to hang in the hot mist, enforcing the point that he was uninterested in outer appearances or prestige, but only with a path of truth and the inner man.

'You know, I miss my son James so much. I talk to him in my mind almost every day as if he was here sharing my experience.'

'That's good. Maybe if he has inherited your talent he will be close by in spirit. I will get you back to him as soon as I can. I give you my word.'

After some minutes the place felt markedly cooler and Boris' question of the previous day resurfaced. *Why had Lubimov even bothered to show me those meters?* The issue hovered, refusing to go away and then, as if he had walked out of a fog, an answer was suddenly upon him.

Tesla! He recalled again the conversation with Lubimov in the *taiga*.

Had Tesla's incredible claims been realised, here in Siberia?

'Boris. I think I now understand.'

'You do?'

'Yes, the tricks, lighting that paper, the levitation and the fish remaining motionless.'

Boris' tantalising silence spurred him on.

'They all use the same energy source.'

The Buryat flexed his legs muscles and rose deliberately to dip a battered saucepan into one of the buckets.

'And Lubimov has found a way to harness it, right?'

'Cover your head with the towel,' Boris warned.

Carty obeyed, frustrated at the man's evasiveness.

The ambience was suddenly shattered by a loud hiss accompanied by a blanket of burning steam. Boris had cast the water over the stones.

'Oh my god, have you gone mad!' Carty screamed, 'I can't bear it.'

It took him several minutes to acclimatise. Gasping but undeterred, he continued. 'Can you explain to me in simple terms what Lubimov is doing?' he asked.

Boris' head hung low, contemplating a response, unsure if the Englishman could rationally handle the truth.

But that is why he is here, he reminded himself.

'Boris.' The pitch of his voice commanded the Buryat's attention. 'How, exactly, does Lubimov power *Sphinx* and the village?'

'With spiralling water.' The words slipped from the man's lips.

The parched environment had become a mere annoyance as Carty's shadowy face told a story of confusion.

'Do you mean turbines, hydro turbines?' he asked, believing that Boris had meant *spinning* water.

'No. If I meant hydro power I would have said it!'

'Okay then, how does he spiral water? Have you seen it?'

'I haven't, but it's likely that the Americans were looking for his technology.'

'And that's why they died – they were spying?'

'Probably.'

'But I thought they were only interested in dumping nuclear waste in Siberia?' He scratched at his unshaven growth that was rapidly becoming a beard.

'There is a link between the two, and I believe that is what interested them more.'

'I don't understand.'

'Perhaps they realised that the waste is no longer radioactive when it's disposed of.'

Carty's glistening forehead furrowed, as he laboured with the comment. 'How do you know that?'

'Lubimov's machine... it transmutes the waste so that it isn't radioactive anymore,' Boris murmured back.

'What!' the swollen Englishman yelled.

He sprang up, forcing his way back out into the sunlight. There, squinting and gulping in the refreshing air, he remained in a state of incredulity as an aura of steam hung listlessly around his body.

'Throw cold water on your face.' the Buryat shouted to him. 'And close the flap, the heat is escaping!'

Carty dutifully complied and then bent to take a handful of water from a bucket, rubbing its shocking cold into his face.

Has the heat sent Boris completely mad?

He wanted to believe him but was still struggling with the levitation stunt that morning. Ordinarily, that would have been unbelievable, had it not been for similar experiences documented throughout history. Mystics of the East and their flying carpets had been known to defy gravity, and in European monasteries Carty had seen for himself the rusting remains of iron hoops embedded into stone floors. These, the guide had advised, had anchored the cords of the monks' cassocks to prevent them floating away during the ecstatic bliss of their prayers.

Perhaps Lubimov is lying, even to Boris and covering up for a small-scale nuclear plant, processing old soviet warheads. What better to keep it secret than to extol the virtues of an incredible technology, one that transmutes spent nuclear waste.

An eagle crying out to its mate as it scouted overhead propelled him back to the reality of where he now was and a familiar loathing for his boss resurfaced.

But D'albo can't possibly be involved in all this.

Shuddering with the sheer madness of his thoughts, Carty ventured back into the sanctum.

'Did you cool your face?' Boris asked, unruffled.

'Why is that so important?'

'Because the *yang* energy meridians end in the face and that's why it can withstand extremes of hot and cold, unlike the rest of the body: cooling it reduces the build-up of heat, enhancing the health effects of the *banya.*'

The Englishman sat motionless, taken by this fact – it intuitively seemed to make sense. Nick Hall, he guessed, would have given anything to be here, exposed to this strange man's talents.

'Are you finding it difficult to accept what I told you?'

'Totally. Is Lubimov processing nuclear waste at *Sphinx*?'

'No, but we know that the same technology is being used elsewhere in the Irkutsk region. The Americans were probably trying to locate it and you were used as a decoy to throw them off the scent.'

'But this business must be worth billions!'

'It's a charade, pretending to store the waste paid for by international budgets when actually, the costs are minimal. Too much was at stake in risking that you might have found this out, so you had to be eliminated.'

Carty silently acknowledged his friend, closing his eyes against the heat to reflect on the incredible import of their conversation. But then they shot open again, just as quickly.

'Boris, can you persuade Lubimov to let me see his technology?' he asked excitedly.

'Hmm, possibly; I believe that you are here at Baikal for a reason but I'll have to convince him of that.'

'I have to see it to understand how it works. A spinning water technology would be gyroscopic, creating its own gravity and generating a large amount of energy.'

'More energy than is required to keep it operational.' The local man grinned.

'What? You know that's impossible, Boris,' Carty riled. 'The first law of thermodynamics doesn't allow it.'

'Do you think nature cares about a law that applies to only a limited part of this existence?'

'Well, it's been scientifically proven and is reproducible at any place, at any time.'

'I could argue that but I would rather just enjoy the *banya*,' the Buryat retorted, running his hands down his arms and flicking the sweat off. It sizzled on the hot stones. 'It's interesting, isn't it, that we know so little about this sea of consciousness that we exist within, and yet we still attempt to explain events and phenomena through a limited set of rules instead of challenging the paradigm?'

'Boris, you've studied science.' He struggled to speak as the parched air hit the back of his throat. 'You must know that energy can neither be created nor destroyed in a closed system!'

'Yes, Scott, but you're forgetting one important point.' A drop of sweat ran along his flat nose. 'Where and what is the *closed* system? We live in a universe which, as far as we know, is infinite.'

Carty hung onto the words, trying to hide his disquiet. The temperature had disturbed his thought processes, preventing him from responding in a measured way.

Boris continued. 'The manner in which energy is currently generated to drive the wheels of industry, transportation and in heating our cities is unnatural. It's manufactured inefficiently through explosive *hot* forces driving combustion engines or turbines. Nature, on the contrary, uses a cool implosive, centripetal energy to nurture life. In this way, energy appears seemingly from nowhere and then disappears as if it were a spectre. It defies being harnessed in bulk by mankind.'

'But that's not an argument for the existence of *free* energy, is it!'

'No, but the Earth's ecosystem is so huge it would be impossible to disprove.' He took a sip from a small wooden ladle before handing it to Carty. The spring water was still cool and sweet and it revived his senses as he mulled the statement, recalling an incident from the past.

It was in the late 1980s when Stanley Ponds and Martin Fleischman, two chemists working at the University of Utah, allegedly stumbled across an impossible phenomenon: *cold fusion*: the room temperature fusing of hydrogen atoms, a process which generated the release of tremendous amounts of energy and which could, ordinarily, only ever occur in the ultra-high temperatures of a star's interior. Their discovery triggered a media furore as well as a plethora of copy-cat experiments, carried out by global research teams. But, unable to reproduce the same results, the international scientific community refuted the claim as 'bad science' leaving the reputations of both men in tatters.

'Is it similar to cold fusion?' Carty asked eagerly.

'I'm not sure. Lubimov uses the term *zero point energy*; others call it *overunity*.'

A mad grin lit Carty's face. He was well aware that at minus 273 degrees Celsius – the absolute zero-point temperature – matter should theoretically cease vibrating. Modern physics, however, had been stumped to find that this was not the case and that a flicker of free energy still remained, as if accessed from another dimension.

'What are you thinking about?' Boris asked, but Carty didn't reply. His mind was whirling again with a melee of distorted thoughts.

The emissions market and my business will be redundant if energy can be produced so abundantly, without pollution. His fleetingly selfish wants, though, were replaced by a more sobering deduction. *But if he's telling the truth and Lubimov has a free energy machine, then the world is about to change forever.*

Thirty Two

Some time later the two men emerged, their steaming bodies bathed in the gold-suffused light of the early evening.

'Arrghh!' Carty squealed as suddenly, freezing cold water rained down. Boris had doused him with a bucket of river water.

'It's your turn now!' he beamed, pointing at the other bucket, as he stood motionless.

The Englishman drenched him and they stood there laughing like schoolboys, shivering. Boris then threw a playful but powerful punch at Carty's ribs. He instinctively side-stepped, deflecting the blow and forcing the Buryat to adjust his step to maintain his balance.

'That was incredible!' he blurted, taken by surprise. 'I shouldn't have underestimated your ability to understand the techniques of *Baguazhang* at the unconscious level.' He put a hand on Carty's shoulder. 'You see. It's never too late for me to learn a lesson – from a complete beginner!'

'Yes, but it's not quite the same thing as lighting paper with my hands though, is it?'

Boris rolled his eyes. 'You're missing the point – the synchronicity of our discussions, the spiralling water creating its own energy and gravity. You just demonstrated how it works in practice without consciously meaning to!'

'But weren't you just playing?'

'That's irrelevant. Did you see how you easily disturbed my balance with your relaxed instinctive movement?' Boris' eyes shone with excitement. 'That is the essence of the *neijia,* to meet hard with soft, using the minimum amount of energy to remain centred.'

The comment took Carty aback. Perhaps the Buryat had been trying before to teach these techniques to others without success. Now, in this unscheduled moment, he had met a kindred spirit who had demonstrated the potential of understanding his art.

'So synchronising my body and arm movements deflected your force?'

'Spoken like a true physicist! In a real confrontation, even when your life might be threatened, the key is to be like water: yielding and able to support great weight. Then, when you strike, you act like a tidal wave, carrying all before it.'

'Water being the feminine principle, I suppose?'

'Exactly!'

Carty sniffed the air and smiled.

Is this why Basilides has left my destiny in the hands of the earth maiden – the feminine? It confirmed a hunch he had had as to why *Sphinx* was situated where it was, next to the greatest and oldest body of fresh water on the planet.

Thirty Three

Green leaned back in his studded Captain's chair and sucked on a cigar, engrossed by the pieces sitting on the chessboard table separating him from Arthur D'albo.

Scott Carty watched on silently from the shadows, an invisible, unheard spectator. But then a shaft of light from a dying sunset burst through the huge Gothic windows to reveal a full-length mirror on the far wall. The image of the hooded revenant, reflected back at him, shook Carty to the core.

'Basilides! But I thought you were...'

'Gone?' the darkly figure retorted.

'Yes, the maiden told me that you had finished your work.'

'And so I have.' He pulled back his hood, 'and it is you who stands before the mirror!'

Carty shuddered. 'Have I become you?'

'You have become yourself,' a voice echoed back from somewhere in the shadows.

'You know, this game could continue for his lifetime,' D'albo suddenly commented, still indifferent to Carty's presence.

'Perhaps longer,' Green responded.

'Whose lifetime?' Carty feared, recognising that some of the pieces carved in the white and brown soapstone were caricatures of his own family members.

'Are they playing chess with my life?' he blurted.

'The game cannot be won on the chessboard,' Basilides' voice resonated once more. 'Only when the King and Queen are united is there a chance of consciousness.'

Carty spun around frantically, seeking the apparition.

'Am I telling myself this? Am I Basilides?'

'*Checkmate!*' D'albo announced, forcing Carty's attention back to the board. It was indeed the end of the game and he panicked.

'*Is this the end of my life?*'

'*The game appears illusory yet you must not discard it, for it is where the work is done, the work that cuts into your skin, which wearies you, but which you then make your own. Take great care.*'

As Basilides' voice faded away, Green and D'albo stood and then, as if he has suddenly became visible to them, they both turned to Carty and silently bowed.

Thirty Four

The short Siberian summer was inexorably shifting to autumn and a colder wind now whipped up from the lake and along the valleys.

Training each morning until midday, he had developed some stamina for the *zhan zhuang*, able to stand for 20 minutes at a time, overcoming the intense burning sensation in his legs and glimpsing, temporarily, the ecstasy of a truly quiet mind.

With the circle walking he had managed to increase to three metres in diameter and for twice as long as he had on his first attempt. It seemed that Boris' floating stunt had triggered a reaction, spurring in him a desire to explore the possibilities of these arts, even though their extraordinary conversations in the *banya* still remained anathema to his reasoning. It was easier to believe that Lubimov was covering up something far less extraordinary.

He lay, waiting for dawn to creep into the cabin as a certain anti-climax in learning these incredible things had left him yearning for home.

They may have already forgotten me by now, he feared, sitting up and glancing across at Boris – still safely asleep – before swinging his legs sideways to remove himself quietly from the warmth of his makeshift bunk.

Pulling on his simple clothes he then strained the cold remains of the previous evening's tea into a cup.

Outside, the chilly morning mist reeled down between the pine fronds and wafted low on the ground, causing him to shiver uncontrollably. But he wasn't to be put off and positioning himself to face east, to a place where he would glimpse the sun's first rays, he sank into the standing posture once again.

Quietening his mind was a challenge, and his notion of time seemed to become distorted – almost lost – as he quelled his persistent questioning of Green's odd dialogue with D'albo during the dream and let a more natural process give him the answers he sought.

Many minutes had passed before the pain in his legs had become a dull, monotonous throb and his heightened state perceived a movement, some distance ahead, in the rhododendron. He assumed it was a large animal, a bear, or an elk, and remained stock still. A red insect had landed on his shirt and began slowly crawling up his chest, drawing his attention. It lacked any shape and his instincts screamed that there was something wrong with the way it moved. Then, in a blur, an object hurtled across his line of sight, into the same bushes.

'Down! Get down, Scott!' Boris yelled out as the insect flew up towards Carty's face, revealing itself as the dot of a laser-sight rifle. His weight shifted, in the same infinitesimal quanta of time, and he sensed the passage of a bullet skim his aura and thud into the wall behind him. Another cry, one of death, followed almost simultaneously. Without having time to react, he saw a figure in blue combats stumble out of the foliage, his head split open with the wood axe Boris had hurled seconds earlier.

The Buryat dashed across the open space towards the fallen assassin.

'Down, Scott!' he screamed again. But Carty had already dived into the soft moss, his pounding heart restricting his breathing. A sharp crack from another gun echoed across the small distance, scattering birds. From his position he had seen the Buryat spin high, evading a bullet and landing a kick into the floating ribs of a gunman before locking the man around the throat. With an abrupt crack, the assailant folded, his neck snapped.

There was a split-second's calm and the Englishman was up racing to his friend who had turned to deflect a third man's machete blow with his upper arm. As Carty reached the stranger he launched his foot into the back of his knees, taking him down heavily and sending the weapon flying. The man expertly rolled away, disappearing into the bushes, leaving him an instant to register the Buryat's pained grimace and the cherry-coloured blood pumping through his jacket's sleeve.

'Duck!' Boris growled, launching the fallen machete like a propeller. Carty instinctively understood, slamming himself forward below its arc, onto the ground and then rolling over. The stranger was staggering over him, vainly grasping at the blade embedded in his chest, his eyes vacant as he crumpled to his knees and slumped face down, gurgling, just feet away.

Unsure if there were more assassins, he urgently scrambled on his hands and knees through the stunted bushes to reach Boris who was slumped onto one knee, gripping a soaked tricep.

'There are no others,' the Buryat grunted.

'How can you be sure?'

'I was stalking them since before dawn.'

'What? You were fast asleep when I left!'

'No, I was just resting,' he growled, tearing at his sleeve to allow Carty a clearer look. The wound was pumping, forcing the Englishman to prop a knee into his friend's back for support. He needed to act quickly.

'I'm going to use your sleeve to make a tourniquet and stem the bleeding. Then you're going to tell me where you keep the antiseptic and bandages!'

'Scott.' The Buryat fixed him with a severe stare. 'You saved my life today!'

'I'm just paying you back as you always knew I would,' he grinned, trying to raise the spirits of his friend who was close to passing out.

Forced to improvise, he used a small branch as a fulcrum to twist and tighten the bandage just above the gash. The Buryat gritted his teeth as it clamped his limb and the branch was tucked under one of the turns to maintain the pressure.

'There, that should do it!' the Englishman announced, helping his partner to his feet.

'Are you hurt, Scott?'

He shrugged. 'No. Just shocked and bruised; those shrubs were tough to land on!'

'Well, how you handled that killer was impressive. You would have been no match for him, face to face.'

Carty looked deflated.

'They wouldn't have stopped until they had killed us both!' he added, bending over the corpse to remove a wallet from a shirt pocket with his good hand.

'As I thought: ex-military. I recognised the techniques these men were using this morning.'

'That's interesting!' Carty cocked his head. 'Did you let them shoot at me deliberately before you decided to attack?'

'We're lucky,' Boris scowled. 'They were around during the night but waited to strike when you left the cabin.'

'But how did you know they were coming?'

'I noticed their tracks yesterday and waited for them to show themselves.'

Carty couldn't disguise his bewilderment. 'You've got some nerve, Boris!'

'I created the distraction drawing two others away from the camp just after you left the cabin. They tried to use their hunting knives to finish me off but that was their mistake.'

He slouched and Carty grabbed him. 'We should get back inside.'

The Englishman had water boiling and was sifting through the ancient medical kit, deciding on what to use, when a female voice broke his concentration.

'*Zdrastvuitie.*'

Boris already had his knife in hand as both men instantly reacted, twisting around to face its source. It was Inna.

'News certainly does travel fast in the *taiga*,' Carty quipped, relieved to see her familiar face.

She took a brief yet detailed look at Boris' arm and then hastily left the two men. Returning after minutes her hands were full of flora some of which she used to make a compress to suppress the blood flow while noisily masticating the rest. Turning native, she then applied the chewed mash and saliva mix into the wound before wrapping another bandage around it, securing all in place. The arm looked ugly, swollen and smeared with congealed blood. All the while Boris munched on local ginseng as she affectionately spoke to him in a distinctly different tongue.

'Inna has brought the horses,' he advised.

'But how did she know about the attack?'

'She didn't.'

Carty laid down in one of the bunks and suddenly began to shiver, exhausted from the trauma of another attempt on his life.

Inna offered him some fresh tea and then wrapped a blanket around him.

'Scott!' Boris' effort to console his friend made no ground and it was Inna who instinctively grasped the Englishmen to her breast, humming a tune almost inaudibly under her breath to soothe him.

Thirty Five

The sun was sinking behind the trees when Carty came around.

'How are you feeling?' Boris inquired. He stood perched in the doorway with two rustically dressed men.

'I'm not sure,' he responded, timorously scanning the strangers' faces and stunned that his friend seemed so energetic for a man who had nearly lost an arm.

'These are my friends Igor and Sergei.'

They smiled reassuringly on hearing their names.

'Svetlana, Inna and Oleg are outside, so that's seven of us,' he continued.

'Lubimov?' Carty eyed him.

'No. It's another friend called Oleg!' His face creased into a broad grin. 'We're going back to *Sphinx* shortly, on horseback.'

'How long will that take?'

'We'll get as far as we can and then camp in the *taiga* overnight. We will be there for breakfast tomorrow.'

Carty nodded. 'How's your arm?'

'Painful!' He wheeled around to show a simple sling. Any signs of blood had been washed away, leaving only a tell-tale red trace in the centre of the bandage, directly over the wound. The swelling was impossibly reduced.

'I'm finding it hard to believe that you're acting as if nothing happened this morning. Don't tell me Inna's magic saliva and herbs have healed your arm!' Carty snorted.

The Buryat moved forward, reaching out with his good arm to pull Carty up in one quick movement, indefatigable despite the trauma.

Outside, he was introduced to the others who clearly spoke little English. Inna pushed Svetlana forward, announcing her name. She was younger than the rest, in her mid-20s with a slight stature yet seemingly strong and exuberant.

'Can you ride?' Boris questioned.

'I used to ride a little when I was a boy.'

Svetlana walked a steed close alongside him, steadying the horse as Carty pulled himself up into the saddle. The pungent smell of the beast and the worn leather stirrups and saddle, felt strangely familiar.

'There, I can still do it!' Relieved, he smiled at the foreign faces that had also mounted up.

'Good. I'm now going to scout ahead. Svetlana will take care of you,' Boris shouted as he cantered away. Already mounted she yanked on Carty's reins to bring his horse closer in to hers.

A while later they had caught up with a stationary Buryat, who let the group pass him on the forest path. He, unlike the rest, did not carry a rifle. Carty noticed this, fearing that a lone killer might be waiting to finish the job that the assassins had failed to accomplish that morning. News that he had not died at the Baikal camp had by now become common currency. He flinched at the recollection of the red dot – a sign of death – moving up his chest and how the silent gunshot had narrowly missed him. Boris' instincts had been sharp and Carty was thankful despite his anger at being used as bait.

But was it just another coincidence that I survived?

The journey along the trail was laboured and the dimming light forced the group more tightly together as gusts harried the tree tops, a constant flux driven by Baikal's temperamental moods.

A muffled light beam from Sergei's torch dispersed through the rising mist, revealing a thinning of the trees into a dell some metres ahead. It seemed that, with night fall, the team would camp here. Sergei rounded and dismounted, surveying the forest's carpet for tracks as he strode over to a ramshackle recluse hut.

His disappearance inside threw the space around them into darkness, save for the intermittent flash of torchlight through the structure's window pane.

'This is where you will stay tonight,' Boris uttered.

'And everyone else?' Carty grunted.

'Igor, Sergei and Svetlana will stay with you. Oleg, Inna and I will ride on to *Sphinx*.'

'No thanks,' Carty announced firmly. 'I'd rather go back with you.'

'That's not a good idea, Scott; we're going to pick up the pace.' While his voice was still strong, Boris' energy levels had visibly deteriorated.

'And you think I can't manage the pace?'

'It's another three hours down this trail.'

'Sorry, Boris, I'm not hanging around here.' The Englishman's resolve was unshakable.

Sergei reappeared, his torch-beam picking out the group huddled against the ancient *singing* cedars. He shouted something, prompting Boris to turn to Carty.

'We're going to spend 15 minutes inside to have coffee and then we'll move on.'

'Good!' he announced decisively, fuelled by the desire to see his friend receiving care but equally to quiz Lubimov. The need to determine if the technology Boris had alluded to actually existed, was overwhelming.

He took a swig of the hot, bitter coffee offered, silently viewing the others.

They live here, in this wilderness, without the trappings of the modern world, yet seem so happy within themselves, he mused, taken by their perennially warm expressions. Each possessed a quality that was lacking in Carty's life, a unique humility which paradoxically gave them their strength.

The air now had a decisive chill and filtered by the canopy, the moon-light created a haunting theatre. For an instant the Englishman thought he had heard James' infectious chuckle sound across the emptiness, causing him to beam before a pain in his heart tempered his joy.

What has he been told? That I drowned in the deepest lake on the planet?

His head dropped, drawing the attention of the Buryat.

'You okay?' he grunted still chewing.

Carty nodded. But he wasn't. All he wanted was to be quiet in his own garden with his son. He had learned of too many things that had challenged his world. Green and D'albo had been playing chess with his life and *Basilides'* warning, to *"take great care"'* echoed again. More disturbing, though, was his discovery that the revenants' image was in fact his own.

The mirror must symbolise a need to reflect upon my life's actions.

Perhaps a higher aspect of his nature had been there at all times, guiding him in this journey which might take a lifetime to make sense of, or *"perhaps longer"* as Green had said. The words sounded in his head as a revelation then hit. *Of course – the marriage of opposites! –* the 64 black and white squares of the chessboard had been staring at him all the time, *the same number of hexagrams in the I Ching, and permutations of the building blocks of DNA.* His steed reared up, whinnying as if to confirm his thoughts.

This dream was pointing him towards his own genetic complexes, his *karma* as Nick preferred to call them, and bringing them into consciousness. Emboldened by these revelations, he was keen to reach *Sphinx* and note them down before their memory had evaporated with the morning's first mist.

The group remounted.

'Now hold on!' Boris commanded, grabbing Carty's reins and heeling his own mare, into a cantor.

The trail gradually broadened out into a valley littered with cubic-limestone boulders, some as big as a house and strewn about as if discarded by some giant's hand. This move out into the open left Carty apprehensive and he looked over at the Buryat registering the weakening of his friend's posture.

'How are you feeling?' he asked.

'I will be when we get to *Sphinx*.'

It was, by Carty's guess, 1:30 in the morning when lights flickering through the trees, signalled that they were close to the hamlet skirting the Institute.

'Wait here.' Boris commanded as he pulled up his steed in a small copse. They all swiftly dismounted.

'We need to check first if it's safe. The girls will wait with you,' he instructed to Carty, squeezing his shoulder gently.

The band of men walked their horses through the Institute's main gate and disappeared.

Time dragged before Igor finally reappeared from the rear, startling them. He placed a finger on his lips, signalling for quiet and then led them back the way he had come.

Thirty Six

The hassock afforded little comfort as he knelt in the freezing Norman church. Footsteps had stopped in the aisle alongside him and he glanced up, startled. A shrouded monk stood silently for some seconds then effortlessly moved away towards the font where it momentarily peered back at him before disappearing inside a gothic panelled doorway.

Green quickly rose, understanding that he was being invited to follow and found that it opened into a low-ceiling tunnel, which snaked off in both directions.

'Which way?' he hesitated momentarily. 'Left – into the unconscious.'

Its air was dank and a light breeze played against his forehead, carrying with it the sound of footsteps ahead of him. His decision had been correct.

Soon, he arrived in a small hall lit by numerous flaming torches and straightening up, he gazed about at the medieval tapestries hanging on ancient stone walls. There was no obvious exit except for a set of stairs dropping away into a subterranean chamber, leaving him uneasy and without a choice. It was either down these or to turn back.

Descending into the scant light, his eyes quickly adjusted, making out the monk standing just a few steps ahead of him. Expectant, it unfurled its long sleeves. Green moved forward, in search of a face inside the hood but was unable to find one. He shuddered and steeled himself, looking at where its finger was pointing; to a stretch of cell doors. Each had their hatches shuttered except for the last and evidently, there was something on the other side that he was supposed to see. He stole a look

224

back at the motionless figure and then walked resignedly towards the door.

The picture of sunlight pouring through the canopy of an ancient forest, accompanied by the distinct smell of pine, filling his nose left him stunned. His ears then picked out the music of river water running over a group of flat boulders, way below.

'He is still with us,' said the monk.

'Who is?' Green questioned now conscious that he was dreaming.

'Look again,' it instructed.

He felt his heart beat pick up as he scanned the scene more closely. A man was sitting in full lotus on one of the rocks with eyes lightly closed in meditation. Then the meaning of the monk's words registered.

'Scott Carty! But it can't be!' Green uttered.

It had merely been a mid-afternoon nap, yet one of the most memorable dreams of Gordon Green's life had left him struggling to pull himself from its draw. He lit up a Honduran and gazed over at the picture of Jung, wondering just how this Swiss doctor of medicine and pathfinder of the unconscious had managed so much in his lifetime. *Remarkable!* He mused, considering the professor's 20 or so tomes of research work, covering not only the mundane practise of psychology, but also the more sublime studies of mythology, alchemy, and quantum physics.

An inkling of what the message might mean then came to him.

Scott had also had a dream about the monk. Is he about to emerge from his meditations and return?

A surge of adrenalin propelled him from his wicker chair to make a telephone call.

'Hi, Gordon, what's up?' Nick had recognised Green's number flashing up on his mobile.

'It's about Scott.' Green's agitation was obvious.

'You're joking, aren't you?'

Nick Hall had descended into a depression after his best friend's disappearance but then, hearing the rumours of the fraud at Albion, had become confused, unable to reconcile the emotions of grief with those of anger at being betrayed. Only Diane understood him and they had found solace together in sharing their loss.

'Still hurt?' Green quipped.

'Don't be off-hand Gordon or I'll hang up.'

'I understand Nick but I had a very explicit dream this afternoon, which suggested he's alive.'

'Ha! I wonder when the fraudster will show up?'

'He's no fraudster!' Green resounded.

'Well, if you believe that then you should get your Whitehall buddies to have Interpol look for him. He can't hide forever.'

'Interpol have already drawn a blank. Anyway, how is Diane taking it all?'

'She's devastated. It's easier for her to believe he's dead.'

'Why? Is that for your own selfish reasons?'

'Fuck off, Gordon.'

'Be careful, Nick. You've been through too much to let your shadow blind you now.'

'What bullshit are you talking about?'

'Diane Carty – she's not yours!'

The phone clicked dead.

Bewildered, Green closed his eyes. It occurred to him that oddly, Nick and Carty seemed to have changed places in life, both psychologically and physically. Nick had always been the enthusiast with whom Green cherished conversing but it had been Carty, a man Green had initially considered as cynical and greedy who, in the days prior to his leaving, had accepted that dreams and visions had a place in his life.

Thirty Seven

29 July 2005: Sphinx.

'Good morning, Scott.'

The composed, craggy face of Oleg Lubimov came into the slumbering Englishman's blurred vision as he rubbed his eyes.

'How are you feeling?'

'I'm fine,' he replied, pleased to see the familiar smile. 'But how's Boris.'

'He's strong and we're treating him well.' Lubimov nodded as if to confirm his diagnosis. 'And you, my young friend, we have much to talk about.' His expression widened into a grin as he placed a steaming cup of tea on the sun-bleached cabinet.

Carty pulled himself up, confused.

Does he mean the machine?

'Drink up. I will meet you outside shortly.'

A weird mix of trepidation and excitement bristled as he scrambled to dress, sensing that something of tremendous import was about to unfold. Even with the aftershock of the attack, his desire to verify Boris' incredulous story had not diminished.

Soon, they were strolling back through the *taiga* once more.

Lubimov eyed him. 'Boris told me about the unusual events in the mountains.'

'You mean the two attempts on my life?'

'Obviously those, but I also understand you witnessed something extraordinary.'

'Ah, the stunts; lighting fires with his bare hands!'

Lubimov seemed flummoxed by the response. 'No, I meant the trout!' he retorted, stopping by the lodge they had visited previously.

Surely he's not going to show me the meters again!

'Are you still trying to convince me about the solar heat pumps?'

The Russian flouted the comment and pulled the padlocks off. 'Shall we go in?'

Inside, the stale environment smelt odd, not dissimilar to the odour of damp air after a lightning storm.

'Stand back please,' Lubimov quietly instructed as he knelt down and threw back a rug to expose the rough larch flooring. Then with a sharp slap, one of the boards flipped down on a sprung hinge into a void below. Carty surmised that it might be where the Russian kept the secret records of his experiments but then Lubimov reached under the adjacent board and a creak sounded. Six of the boards, moving as one, swung down and slid smartly underneath the flooring with precision engineering. The result was a neat metre-square hole in the floor.

Glancing back up, Lubimov's subtle smile told a story.

'Boris has persuaded me to reveal the facts,' he said.

'I'm honoured!'

'I have already told you that during the Cold War my father established *Sphinx*.'

'Yeah, and you also mentioned that he was dabbling with Tesla's experimental work.'

'And that's the reason the Institute is situated here at Baikal.'

'Why exactly?'

'Because of its water.'

I thought so.

'I am sure you're aware of the race to isolate *heavy water* in order to develop the atomic bomb during the Second World War, aren't you?'

Carty grinned half-heartedly, unsure where the director's story was leading. Then he recalled seeing *The Heroes of Telemark*, and the Norwegian resistance attempts to sabotage the factory in which the Nazis were producing heavy water.

'Baikal's water exhibits a range of exceptionally strange properties.'

'Like what?'

'You're about to find out!' His forefinger indicated down, under the floor. Carty knelt and peered cautiously into the hole. Roughly constructed concrete steps dropped away some two metres into darkness. A chill pricked his spine as he recalled that first dream in which he had been led down into the cellar.

Is this what it meant? A ploy to eliminate me for being guilty of a secret I haven't yet learnt.

Green's associations then echoed back at him and he understood that its message had been symbolic, not a premonition.

'I'd rather you went first. I am a foreigner and might get lost!'

The Russian snorted at the lax remark and crouching, he gripped the edge of the boards to lower himself into the hole. Once down he flicked on a single fluorescent bulb.

'There, it's safe. Are you coming down?'

Curious, he descended and found himself in a stark, rendered room in which he was barely able to stand upright. Its walls were filled with shelves holding jars of pickled vegetables and jams. Lubimov darted back up the steps with the energy of a much younger man, to pull the rug back over the entrance. Then, with a quick upward thrust he swung the hinged boards back. A sharp click signalled that the two of them were now sealed inside the room.

Carty took a deep breath. The smell of ozone had grown stronger.

'So you've brought me into a cellar,' he chided.

'Take a closer look,' instructed Lubimov, reaching into his jacket pocket to fumble with something. As he did, the stone wall at the end of the cellar began to move, rattling the jars as it trundled back.

What is he doing?

'Go on, take a look!'

Carty moved gingerly forward to glance along the length of the shelves, sighting a small passage to his right where the walls had separated, just wide enough for a man to squeeze through. A faint blue glow suffused the space from somewhere beyond its end. It forced a memory of once being trapped in an office during a power cut and a similar blue emergency light had led him down a stairwell to safety.

'Why is there such a strong smell of ozone?' he quizzed, his eyes beginning to smart in the overpowering atmosphere.

Lubimov handed the Englishman an ex-army gas mask. 'Put this on and don't worry, it's not what you think!' he reassured, registering Carty's alarm. 'You'll need it if you're to witness the machine.'

The word triggered a sweeping tide of goose bumps over his skin. Boris had not been lying. He pulled on the mask, adjusting the straps so that its seal pressed closely to his flesh. A sickly smell of aged rubber filled his nose. *But if there is ozone, then this is better than risking my lungs,* he reasoned, familiar with how dangerous the gas could be. Normally found only in the Earth's high atmosphere, it had in recent decades, become commonplace in the ground-level smog of polluted cities.

An alien mechanical drone began to trouble him as he stayed close behind the Russian, inching themselves through the tight access passage and then finally out into a cave system.

The sight bordered on the ghostly, lit more intensely now by the same eerie blue glow, which seemed to emanate from beyond a natural stone archway. He stepped gingerly through it and the scene filled him with awe: a cavernous hall hung with the brilliance of countless quartz crystals.

'Scott.' Lubimov had leant towards him, sliding his mask away slightly. 'What you are about to witness here is real and must remain totally secret. Do you understand?'

Carty stared back into the Russian's blue eyes, barely able to affirm the comment as he searched for a father figure in facing the unknown. His breath had become unbearably audible and minute beads of sweat oozed around his temples.

Will it condemn me forever?

'Follow me,' Lubimov uttered, his form silhouetted against the luminosity.

They trod on, negotiating a narrow concrete plinth, proud of the shallow pools that lay on the near-impervious granite floor. Ahead the acute luminescence pulsed more heavily, in synchrony with the low-frequency drone, which resonated disturbingly, through Carty's chest cavity. He struggled to keep his breath centred but nothing he had experienced in his short life, not even Boris's amazing talents, could prepare him for what lay behind an opening in the rock face just a hundred feet away.

At the cavern's wall, the Russian turned and caught the nervousness in his young friend's expression. He smiled and formed his thumb and forefinger into an *O* sign before signalling for Carty to climb up alone.

The Englishman legs were leaden and salty sweat stung his eyes as he ran his hands over the ledge above him until he found purchase. Then he leaned back to snatch a desperate look at Lubimov, seeking confirmation that he had understood correctly. The Russian's solitary nod verified that he had. He made one huge exertion, hauling himself up through the gap and into the blue light.

What in God's name is that?!

Still on his knees in the secluded grotto, he gawped at the Orwellian sight as he sought to make sense of what his eyes were telling him. There, bathed in its own brilliant aura, was a metallic egg-shaped orb, roughly two metres across, pulsating with an intense vibration that now shook his whole body. It appeared to be alive and shielding his eyes, he frantically scanned it again. Two stainless pipes ran up along the wall to the contraption, *too large to be electricity cabling,* his strained mind reasoned, noting that they coiled around the orb and converged at a common point beneath it.

A massive steel clamp, descending from the grotto's ceiling, 15 feet above him, appeared to be holding the machine in place. But a looming doubt refused him to accept what his brain was telling him; the orb looked to be hovering imperceptibly.

There's no visible means of support!

The deduction uncomfortably shook his reasoning. He trembled.

It's levitating!

Lubimov's hand suddenly touched Carty's shoulder, causing him to flinch. He snapped his head sideways at the man and desperately struggled to remove his mask. The choking environment attacked his throat, forcing him to pull it back on.

Then, once again he was sucked back into the impossible spectacle. It invoked in him both elation and fear, challenging everything he held sacred. All his instincts told him this could not be happening.

Yet why couldn't it?

Nick's magnetic motors and then Boris's demonstration of inexplicable feats in the *taiga,* had also confronted his rational senses in a similar way.

An urge then overtook him to move closer and raise a hand, as if in touching it he could verify its existence but the Russian's grip tightened, dragging him back to face him.

Thirty Eight

'Now you know,' Lubimov uttered removing his mask as they slid back into the cellar. Carty did the same.

'Oleg, what is going on in there? That machine...was it levitating?' He was visibly shaken.

'*Zero point energy* utilisation, Scott.' His countenance held a conspicuous relief in having finally revealed the technology. 'The ozone, glowing light and levitation are purely incidental.'

'But how?'

'By the implosion of water spun against itself at super-high velocities. The contraption is fabricated from a titanium-vanadium alloy, the same as is used in the compressor section of a jet engine. Anything with a lower tensile modulus would be torn apart by the internal stresses. Water is pumped in unfiltered from Baikal and fed directly into a series of implosion baffles.'

'In the tubes running around the outside?'

'No, the implosion occurs inside the machine and the tubes simply allow the water to be recovered before it goes through the cycle again.'

'How many cycles?'

'Four and then it is replenished with a new intake.'

'So there must be some auxiliary power to pump the water.'

'None, all the power is supplied by the machine. It exhibits *overunity*, generating more energy than is required to run it.'

'But that's *perpetuum mobile* – it's impossible!' Carty was referring to perpetual motion, a theoretical ideal, which had intrigued natural philosophers for centuries. Some of them had claimed inventions that had displayed it.

'Not quite! It will run down and eventually stop, one day.'

'When?'

'We're not quite sure but probably in another 20 years' time.'

'20 years! When was it switched on?'

'At approximately 7:15 on the morning of the 2nd April 1993.'

'But that was over 12 years ago! Are you sure? With all due respect, someone could be deceiving you!'

'Really!' His brows knitted. 'What about the levitation and the luminescence? Why would anyone go to all that trouble to fake it when I am the only person who knows of its whereabouts?'

'Not Boris?' Carty asked, astounded by the remark.

The Russian shook his head deliberately. 'Boris is from another culture where trust is everything and questions can be avoided by the use of delicate perception.'

'But I just don't understand how this machine could have been manufactured and constructed. It would require the resources of an international corporation with advanced engineering know-how, access to capital finance and...'

'The resources of the former Soviet Union!' Lubimov's words cut him dead.

Whether as a result of being in the choking atmosphere or the shock at having his cherished laws of physics severely pummelled, Carty felt his head spinning and knew that he needed fresh air. Lubimov registered his pale complexion and decided that it would be easier for both of them to talk elsewhere.

Shortly, the wall had creaked back into place on its mechanism and the two men were hauling themselves up, above the floorboards, and into the sanctity of the cabin. Carty helped pull the rug back into place all the time shaking his head and grinning wildly in disbelief.

'The Soviet department that authorised the building of this place, they must know about its location. It must be recorded somewhere?'

'Not anymore.'

'Why not?'

'The original machine, developed in that cavern by the team that included my father, was decommissioned in 1991 and removed. The main entrance was then dynamited, sealing it with tons of rock. But the bunker entrance below this floor was known only to my father.'

'So you're saying that thing I just saw, is not the original?'

'Correct, it's not.' Lubimov grinned. 'In the early 1990s, with the disintegration of the command economy, salaries were going unpaid but the State was still following the entrenched five-year plans, one of which was the commissioning of a new prototype machine. The components for its construction were delivered to the Institute, but at the time anything of value, particularly industrial machinery, was being sold for scrap. It's likely that the responsible department simply assumed that the parts had ended up in a re-melt shop in the West.'

'Seems hard to believe!' Sarcasm crept into Carty's voice.

'Yes, it does. The crumbling Soviet system had bigger worries at the time with the loss of its territories and their nuclear arsenals.'

'But surely your superiors would have visited this place and discovered the new prototype working.'

'Why? The programme had been stopped and the cavern sealed, remember?'

'But didn't they suspect you knew about it?'

'As far as the authorities knew, and still know, I am simply a research doctor working on the advancement of acupuncture. My father, though, had been threatened never to speak of his research.'

'And he told you?'

'Through this entrance, he had secretly shown me the original operating over a number of years and had explained the underlying physics.'

Carty faltered, his blue eyes searching the Russian's as he contemplated his next question.

'Is your father still alive?'

'No, he died in a hunting accident shortly after the cave was closed.'

'I am sorry.'

The older man's facial creases deepened. 'He and his colleague died prematurely. Boris, though, told me that his spirit still wished for me to continue his work, to build the second machine.'

'So that's how Boris knows about it?'

'Yes.'

'And the original was re-assembled in another part of Russia?'

A shrug gave Carty his answer.

'But you must have an idea if it's still operational or not?'

'How would I know that? I am a doctor; remember? The Institute took me in for my degree in medical research.'

The conversation stalled, the Russian's expression now registering the muted anguish of memories he wished he could forget. He poured tea from a thermos into two mugs and passed one to the Englishman to wash the remains of the ozone's acrid taste from his mouth.

'The genius of the team,' Lubimov then continued, 'was Ivan Yegorovich Isotov, an extraordinary man who had worked on the early Soviet nuclear programmes. Initially, he pushed for the development of *fusion* reactors as the ultimate source of energy to satisfy the world's energy needs.'

'No one has achieved that, yet.'

'No, but instead he stumbled upon a greater secret, *overunity*. His peer group, though, wouldn't accept his findings and ostracised him. The State couldn't be seen to support his claims either but was unable to dismiss his talent and unremitting intellect so he was banished here to Baikal to secretly continue the work. He and my father built the first *trout* engine.'

'And what happened to Isotov?'

'He was retired.'

'Did he help you build the second device?'

'He advised me on its construction.'

'So I presume from your comments that he's still alive?'

Lubimov gulped his tea and swilled it around before swallowing it. Carty was now familiar with the man's tactics and sought to pick up the question at another time.

'Well, it's an amazing story, and one that I would never have believed if I hadn't seen that machine down there with my own eyes!' Carty indicated ominously, as if he meant Hell.

'How on Earth did they discover this phenomenon?'

Lubimov lent back against the desk, running a hand through the strands of silky grey hair, looking decidedly younger than his near 70 years.

'It had already been discovered by Viktor Schauberger, an Austrian forester, before the Second World War. It was his initial work that inspired my father's team to develop the technology successfully.'

'An Austrian forester!'

'It does sound absurd, doesn't it? But as history has shown us, it is often nature that reveals the biggest secrets, not experiments performed in a laboratory. Living in the Alps, in one of the last remaining ancient forests of Europe, Schauberger experienced the raw power of mountain rivers, naturally creating eddies and vortices, transporting minerals and sustaining life. In doing so he was challenged by a trout remaining motionless in the rapids.'

'As I was!' Carty chimed.

'Schauberger was a gifted man and very probably receiving information in the form of visions and dreams. He realised that flowing water was spiralling around itself in a complex yet ordered pattern, creating a *still* central vortex, which the trout instinctively sought. He made a working model of a trout engine and, so it is said, when he set it in motion it broke free of its fixings and levitated. It is also likely that the Nazi war machine funded his experiments.'

'What!'

'Yes. Schauberger was probably a little naïve and thankfully the war ended before the Nazis could really experiment with it.'

'But how did his technology end up here in Siberia?'

'Ivan Yegorovich met with him several times when he was seeking financial support to develop the technology. He admitted to me that Schauberger had revealed its secrets before he died.'

'When was that?'

'In the 1950s, shortly after he returned from America where he was virtually held under house arrest and forced to give up some of his information.'

'Ah, that explains why the Americans were at the CentralniySib camp.'

'Not really; they were probably interested in the other phenomenon.'

'The other phenomenon?' Puzzlement swept over Carty's face.

'Its ability to transmute radioactive nuclear materials.'

'Ah yes!' In the excitement Carty had forgotten this vital piece of information.

'It was discovered by mistake, but it was this that led to the machine's decommissioning.'

'It was too dangerous a technology to leave in Isotov's hands?'

'Most definitely!'

'Then why was the second, smaller machine commissioned in the first place?'

'That was planned well before they dismantled the first.'

'Why? It doesn't make any sense.'

'It does. A controlled research programme on *overunity* was conceived with the new machine while the transmutation phenomenon was to be researched using the original, elsewhere, by a new team who had no knowledge of its previous history.' The older man shook his head in disgust.

'And this original, it also produced free energy?'

'Yes, it did.'

The Englishman hesitated, contemplating the response. 'But, Oleg; there must be a concrete theory to explain how a spinning vortex can generate limitless energy?'

'At the quantum level it can be easily explained.'

'Can it?'

'Yes. Matter is mainly comprised of space. The sub-atomic particles – the nucleons and electrons – occupy just a tiny volume of the atom by comparison.'

'I am aware of that.'

'So, if the solidity of your hand is mainly made up of space, and so is that desk, then it should be a simple task to push one straight through the other, right?'

Carty looked back blankly.

'But we know that's impossible because of the different frequencies at which atoms vibrate. The reality of matter is essentially a function of these different vibrations.'

'And the vortex strips away those frequencies?'

'It modifies them allowing them to resonate as one so that the potential energy of the space, around and inside the atom, can be unleashed. At the subatomic level, matter behaves very differently to the laws of mechanics laid down by Newton.'

'Quantum physics.'

'That term is frequently thrown around but science is, as yet, still struggling to explain, outside the language of complex mathematics, the nature of reality as we humans perceive it. What is plainly obvious, though, is that *overunity* is a measurable phenomenon and is probably a key to unlocking the unified field theory.'

The Englishman scratched at his stubble. The conversation and its implications raised more questions than answers.

'Can I ask how the electrical energy is being generated by the machine?'

'Direct induction, it by-passes the need for turbines.'

'So where was all that free power being utilised before they dismantled the original?'

Lubimov sighed. 'It was kept a secret, but we believe it was sent to the many underground military cities in Siberia. Transmission losses were not really an issue.'

'But there are many hydro-plants in Siberia, surely they were generating enough power for the military-industrial complex?'

'Abundant free energy was the ultimate secret weapon in a Cold War scenario, particularly when the State was gearing up for further space and military programmes.'

'That makes sense,' Carty chimed, pausing momentarily to consider his next question. 'Oleg, what is really bothering me is why did they go to all that trouble to develop such a ground-breaking technology only to keep it quiet?'

'It's a good question and one that deserves a better answer than the one I am going to give you.' He paused, removing his glasses to hold them up to the light and peer through them. 'The seniors in Moscow were starting to realise that the Soviet Union could not exist as an empire based on the disintegrating ideology of communism. Isotov persuaded them that mankind was not yet sufficiently conscious to use *overunity*, productively. Science had not then even begun to understand its underlying principles and the potential negative side-effects of its long term use. It seems that someone saw the huge financial value in continuing to use it only for transmuting the waste.'

Carty smiled unconvincing but was willing to leave the statement unchallenged.

'Now, we should be getting back to *Sphinx.*'

A choir of birdsong greeted them as they cautiously exited the cabin and scanned the immediate area. Lubimov fastened the door with two huge, battered padlocks.

Hardly secure! Carty grinned mutedly.

It was now late morning and overcast with cloud. The impact of the spectacle, back in the cavern, overshadowed his thoughts so much so that he couldn't speak as they strolled. Instead, he silently processed it, coldly acknowledging the danger of being associated with this technology. Lena had lost her life because of it and he suspected that others might still be seeking his.

Now they had a reason to!

Most, who had known of the machine's secret had already been silenced.

Thirty Nine

Lubimov left the Englishman on their return to *Sphinx*, professing that unfinished work required his immediate attention.

Carty paced the disinfected corridors and hospital wards in search of Boris, ignoring pangs of hunger and only stopping intermittently to question the nurses. Before long, dizziness had replaced frustration and he was forced to step out into the overgrown gardens for fresh air.

'You want *Boreece*?' a middle-aged woman called after him.

'Yes. Where is he?'

She spun smartly about and he shadowed her back into the Institute. The cut of her dress restricted the length of her strides as she smoothly navigated the maze of hallways before abruptly stopping outside an unmarked door. Raising a hand for him to remain where he was, she opened it and entered. Seconds later she motioned him inside.

'Boris; am I glad to see you!' His excitement was obvious.

'Lubimov wanted me to be checked over by his *ladies*.' The Buryat chuckled from a bed, nodding cheekily in the direction of a young nurse. Crimson-soaked medical swabs were strategically placed as she worked on the wound. Two oversized acupuncture needles had been inserted deeply into one side of his chest and lasers were focused on specific parts of his torso.

'She's just sewing back the tendons so they heal faster. I can't feel a thing and it's interesting to see the various muscle groups up so close,' he quipped.

Carty was stunned. 'No anaesthetic?'

'None. Have you seen Oleg today?'

'Yes...I did,' Carty stuttered, his expression indicating that he wouldn't discuss anything in front of the nurse. Boris quietly spoke in Russian to the woman, graciously handling her so that she was gone in minutes.

'So?' probed Boris as the door clicked shut. 'Did you see his secret?'

'I did but I still cannot accept it. It's as if an alien spacecraft had landed in front of me.'

'Ha!' he laughed. 'The trout engine is Lubimov's baby.'

'I can see that, but why choose to show me and not you.'

'His *daemons.*'

'*Daemons?*' Carty stuttered.

'When I first brought you here, in a coma and close to dying, he suspected that you might be a spy and then, when we fled into the *taiga*, he faced the dilemma whether or not to turn you over to the authorities, in order to preserve his secret.'

Carty flushed. 'And is that why we were attacked?'

'No, Scott, that was a result of your own karma. Lubimov chose to trust his intuition and trust you. He carries a great burden in guarding the machine's secret for the benefit of all humanity.'

'But, Boris, surely it can't still be a secret?' his voice trembled. 'You told me yourself that the same technology is operating commercially, elsewhere in this region!'

Boris nodded. 'Nevertheless, you must understand the enormous responsibility he's taken in revealing it to you.'

Both men fell silent as the door creaked open and Lubimov's head nudged into the room, his eyes wide beneath the distinctive spectacles. He had clearly heard his name being mentioned.

'Sorry to disturb you, gentlemen, I'll come back later.'

'Oleg!' Boris broke into Russian, obviously pleading for him to stay. He did, straightening his posture as he entered to face them both.

'So, Boris; how was the treatment?'

'Good, thanks,' he deflected, 'but Scott has just told me of this morning's activities.'

Lubimov lowered himself slowly onto a chair next to the bed, draping one leg over the other knee and brushing off his shiny, worn charcoal trousers. The movements were measured and unhurried as he maintained his gaze at the two men.

'Scott, it's now simply a matter of time before the authorities arrive here, looking for you, and when they cannot find you, they will fully debrief me.' His expression belied an acceptance of his fate. 'The existence of the second machine will then be exposed and that's why I have shown it to you.'

'Will they shut it down as well?'

'You will be going back to your world soon and must keep this secret until a time comes when it may need to be revealed,' he uttered in a hushed tone.

'Why?' Carty was ecstatic to hear that he was going home but shocked by the poisoned chalice he had been given. 'Surely, others already know that *overunity* is the main function of the machine.'

'Possibly, at the highest levels, but no one is going to divulge that and live to tell the tale. Not here in Russia!'

Carty shuddered at the frankness of the remark and it prompted another question. 'If this technology already exists with the Americans, the Russians and possibly even the British, then why hasn't it already been commercialised?' he probed. 'I understand your fears that there may be very serious negative side effects but the only way to find out is to test the machine, full-scale, in a real working environment.'

'Your thinking is rational but lacks wisdom. You believe, as I once did, that science holds the keys to solving humanity's problems and securing its future wellbeing. This is partly true, but only when the psychology is a match for the technology.'

'What are you saying?'

'What Oleg means,' Boris offered, 'is that we seem to be stuck in a technological dead end, a *cul de sac.* I think that's the French expression, isn't it?'

'I totally disagree! Look at the inventions and the skills that have emerged in the past century alone.'

'We're not talking here about scientific developments per se but the inability of the collective psyche to handle the possibilities of those developments,' Lubimov added. 'Unleashing a technology such as this would not halt climate change overnight, as you believe is possible, because science, nowadays, is not wholly serving mankind.'

'It's not?' Carty frowned.

'No. Instead it seems intoxicated with giving technology a new face-lift every year or so, to supply an unsustainable consumer circus. This, with its thirst for natural resources will very likely cause the failure of essential ecosystems – the complex systems that support humanity's existence in this paradise.'

'Okay, I see your point but what if the machine was used secretly, inside the shell of a conventional power station?'

Lubimov shook his head, gently frustrated at the suggestion. 'Even if *overunity* could be integrated into established power networks, covertly, it would generate an impetus that could not be stopped.'

'But didn't you just state that it might be needed.'

'I meant that it may have to be used as the last resort, if the world stands on the brink. I pray that we never reach that point.'

The brink of what? Goose bumps reared on Carty's skin.

Fiddling with the lenses of his glasses, Lubimov hung his balding head as he quietly contemplated a thought. Then, his eyes flashed up at Carty.

'Scott, how much have you heard about global dimming?'

'*Global dimming?*' He was flummoxed. 'Nothing. What is it?'

'It's a factor that has been completely overlooked in the models predicting the extent of climate change.' He drew a breath, wiping a handkerchief across his forehead and then down over his eyes. 'Immediately after the attacks of 9/11, all flights over the USA were grounded for approximately three days. It was during this time that scientists noticed something very strange had occurred.'

'I'm not sure what you're driving at.'

'It's very simple. For more than a century, US agricultural scientists have been carrying out pan-evaporation rate experiments on a daily basis. They're a tried-and-tested method to measure how much water evaporates from a known volume, a pan of water for example, in one day. From this, the evaporation rate is easily calculated and the data is irrefutable.' He replaced his spectacles, and eyed the Englishman solemnly. 'In those three days, with hardly any aircraft vapour trails in the skies, evaporation rates increased dramatically. In fact, the net average temperature over the USA increased by one degree centigrade. A significant increase, wouldn't you agree?'

'Yes, I would.'

'And that revealed a more alarming problem which may be masking the true effect of climate change.'

'Global dimming?' the Englishman muttered.

'Correct! The pollution created by industry, transport and aircraft carries small particles of soot and fuel high into the atmosphere. There, they nucleate microscopic raindrops into an aerosol, which acts like a giant mirror, reflecting sunlight back into space and keeping the planet cool.'

Boris grunted in accord and then picked up the conversation. 'Over the past 20 years the volume of sunlight falling to Earth has fallen by approximately 16 per cent over Europe and about 30 per cent over Siberia.'

'So what you're saying, in effect, is that the huge efforts to curb greenhouse gas emissions are actually exacerbating climate change. Is that why we're seeing so much disruption in weather across the world – the droughts and floods?' His voice trailed away.

'It's very likely,' Lubimov's lips tightened, 'and combined with the increase in solar flare activity and a reduction in the Earth's magnetic shield, it might be the beginning of a runaway scenario. Then, the machine may be civilisation's only salvation, in a dramatically changing world.'

'But we can't wait for that. There are good people out there who would be delighted to lobby governments and bring this technology into the public domain. It would end the reign of fossil fuel overnight.'

'Yes, and then the world's economies would falter disastrously. The fragile balance of power that we all now enjoy would change abruptly before a utopia could emerge where energy is truly free. Millions would lose jobs, stock markets would collapse, and civil rioting, wars and famine would result. It's not in any country's interests to allow that.'

'So you're talking about nothing short of an economic and political revolution before *overunity* can even be considered?'

'You could put it that way. I would prefer to call it a paradigm shift – a change in consciousness. It's less melodramatic.' The older man smiled, he had lived with the possibilities of the machine for too many years.

'And you're prepared to stay quiet about the solution to an energy-hungry world's needs and its urgency to reduce emissions?'

'Yes. There are simpler solutions.'

'And just what are those?'

'Renewables.'

'Renewables!'

'Why not? We do not have to give up entirely on conventional power sources just yet, but with the budget many times less than that of global armaments programmes, a new generation of highly efficient renewables could easily provide the solutions. Take for example, my simple hybrid heat-pumps and the energy that they generate.'

Carty sighed. Green and Nick Hall had said the same, in so many words, just weeks before.

'But I just can't believe that the machine's real potential is going to be squandered transmuting nuclear waste, for the wealth of a few!'

'It would appear that it will and those that control it will do anything to prevent its secret from being exposed.'

Anything. The word rang in Carty's mind, conjuring up again, the cold callousness in the eyes of the men who had tried to assassinate him. He reluctantly accepted Lubimov's statement. The machine would perhaps always remain a haunting enigma unless he could manage to slip out of Russia successfully. He had no idea how that was going to happen but guessed that the Russian already had a strategy.

Forty

Carty hardly slept that night, his mind re-running, time and time again, the sight of the machine as he constantly questioned its actual existence and what the ramifications of that might be. He was troubled by the news that it could never see the light of day, unless a global disaster struck. *In which case it might be too late,* he mused.

A mosquito's whine steadily increased as it closed in on his face, not unlike the rising pitch of a fast-moving train, approaching a station. The metaphor triggered a repressed emotion causing his hand to sympathetically clench into a fist as he was transported back to his young boyhood again. Waiting on a platform he would frantically squeeze his grandmother's hand, fearful of being be sucked into the carriages' wake as they passed. It was an ordeal he faced twice a month, visiting his mother at the sanatorium.

I wonder what she would make of all this if she was still alive?

The insect had landed ghostlike on his ear and slapping at it in the dim light, it floated off to land on the rough whitewashed wall. Following it with a muted death wish, Carty's unfocused gaze fell on a familiar object, squeezed into a narrow space next to the cabinet. He stared hopelessly at it for a second.

That can't be my suit carrier? he reasoned, struggling to understand quite how the bag he had left at the CentralniySib camp had materialised here. Confused, and believing he was still dreaming, he leapt up and hauled it across the bed. He hastily pulled open the two-way zip and a short sweep of its contents confirmed that his senses were not playing tricks on him.

It is mine.

His shirts, shoes, and spare suit were all there, as he had left them, before making love to Lena on that last night. It was obvious that Lubimov had something to do with its return but exactly what, he couldn't fathom. He ran a hand into the inside pocket.

Shit! His passport was missing.

Dropping back onto the bed, he sat bewildered, stretching his gaze out of the window into the trees, ruminating again over the events at the Baikal camp. As he did, something stirred in his peripheral vision, at the Institute's hinterland with the *taiga*. He ducked, fearful that it was another assassin. But it was Boris.

Incredibly, the man was practising his vigorous exercises so soon after the operation and itching to be with him, Carty threw on his combats, leaving the carrier lying open on the bed.

Outside, he homed in on the Buryat's outline ahead of him through the shrubbery. Then, as he neared the spot he inexplicably lost sight of the man and swung around panicking and wondering if it was a trap to lure him out alone.

'Scott.' The Buryat's distinctive voice echoed seconds later somewhere behind him.

How did he get there?

Startled, Carty turned in annoyance. The local man seemed to enjoy vacillating between game playing and being deadly serious.

'How did you manage to creep up behind me?'

'Just keeping you alert, Scott. You weren't scared we're you?' His big moon-face smiled soberly.

'No!'

'Good. Here, place your hand on my stomach.'

'Why?' The air was chilly and he wanted to return indoors.

'Do it!' the Buryat demanded.

Carty obeyed and as he did Boris slowly rolled down his eyelids and let out a sigh.

'Ahhh!' Carty flinched, pulling his hand rapidly away from what felt like a sharp bolt of electricity, racing up his arm.

'What just happened?' Carty was stunned.

'Why are you so surprised? An electric eel can do the same thing.'

Unable to counter, a wide grin split his face. 'Is that the same force you used to light the birch bark?'

'Yes, but what you just felt was a jolt from my centre. It's a far more powerful *yang* force.' Boris paused, leaving Carty to ask the obvious.

'So what does a *yin* force feel like?'

'I'll show you. Hold my wrist.'

Carty did so, tensing noticeably.

'Relax and move your hand away.'

He tried but couldn't and instead felt a cooling sensation ripple eerily along his arm to his shoulder. The sensation became chilling, and scared, he instinctively pushed back. But the Buryat, reading his move, had instantly yielded and without any obvious movement, shot Carty off his feet, landing him more than a car's length away.

He was upon the winded Englishman in seconds, pulling him back on to his feet.

'Sorry, I read your intention before you acted.'

'I see. Did you use these powers when we were attacked in the *taiga*?'

'Of course, but it's much more difficult during combat, when confronted with skilled opponents.'

'You're still bloody invincible!' Carty laughed out loud.

'Obviously not!' he nodded down at his bandaged arm. 'But what I do know is that you have the potential to develop the same sensitive abilities, given time and practice.'

'What! You are joking, aren't you?'

'No, I'm not. But you're limited by your emotions swaying your mental states. This leads to confusion about who we are and our place in the world.'

'So how do I control my emotions?'

'By quietly acknowledging them each time they attempt to possess your actions and thoughts. Very often, when developing *Qi*, emotions erupt spontaneously, causing us to act in strange ways. In the martial arts, that can be deadly.'

'Why? I thought they are supposed to develop aggression.'

'Not aggression: control of power, so that one acts according to the situation. Remember how you acted in the *taiga*, when we were attacked?'

He nodded, flicking back to the moment when that red dot flashed in his face.

'A part of you was very calm under real pressure and that's what I recognised. Once the emotions are acknowledged and have no control, then you will have absorbed the shadow aspects of your own nature. That is when you will be able to use these powers to their full extent, to help others.'

How can I possibly return to Albion now that I've experienced such things?

'Are you pleased to be returning home?' Boris caught him mid-thought.

'I will be pleased when I get there but I'm doubtful.'

'There's a way, believe me.'

'Is that why my suit carrier was left in the room?' Carty eyed him. The comment was dual-edged.

'Ah, you've seen it then?'

'Yes. How did you find it?'

'The woodsmen at the camp kept it safe.'

'These woodsmen, are they friends of yours?'

'They belong to the same ancestral tribe as my mother. We have a bond of blood.'

'And they just handed it over!'

'Not really. I went there some days after.'

'You went into the camp!' he gawped.

'Yes. I needed to get a sense of what went on that night.'

'And you just took the case?'

'Yes.'

'And my laptop?'

Boris' wry expression confirmed the negative. 'One of the assassins was captured and badly beaten. Before dying of his injuries he admitted that he had instructions to eliminate both you and the woman, Lena Isotova.'

A repugnant look broke across Carty's face; shocked both by the unemotional manner in which it had been delivered.

'She *was* a beautiful woman.' The words tumbled out as he recalled the image of Lena's subtle smile and understood how he had impossibly fallen in love with her.

'Did Lubimov tell you about her grandfather?'

'No?'

'Ivan Yegorovich Isotov.'

'The man who developed the machine...is Lena's grandfather!'

'That's right.'

'Lubimov hinted that he is in hiding but wouldn't say much more than that.'

Boris acknowledged him only with a smile.

'Now, we still have some training to do before you leave, so let's get started!'

Forty One

Lubimov was conspicuously absent in those next few days, only appearing late for the collective supper in the darkening evenings. Carty assumed that he was researching acupuncture techniques, and perhaps experimenting with the machine in the cavernous vault behind the Institute.

The Russian finally surfaced one lunch time, inviting both Carty and Boris to join him in his office.

'Take a seat,' he offered the two odd wooden chairs in front of his desk.

'Scott, I have been reviewing all the practical means to ensure your safe passage home,' he casually announced. 'I am afraid there is only one.'

'Which is?' Carty quizzed, apprehensively shooting looks between the two men.

'Taking a direct flight from Almaty back to London.'

A lump hit his throat as the image of *Blondie* reared again.

'Are you out of your mind? I don't have a passport.'

Lubimov, clearly irritated at the retort, took something from a drawer and tossed it across the desk.

'It appears that you do and it still has a valid three month entry visa for Kazakhstan.'

Carty's face registered disbelief as he picked it up. It was his passport. He flicked through it, examining the impressive embossed visa. *Why had it been issued for so long?* It was still a mystery. *Lena couldn't possibly have known about it in advance.*

'So you've had my passport here all this time. If I had known that, I could have...'

'Left us?' Lubimov cut him off. 'You were only ever on a one-way trip here. You don't have a Russian visa!'

'Scott.' The Buryat lent across and squeezed his friend's arm. 'Do you want to learn how you are going to get home to your family?'

'Of course I do.'

There was a hesitant pause as Lubimov collected his thoughts. Then he began.

'Tomorrow evening you will leave by helicopter to travel west, across the Sayan Mountains. Boris will travel with you. The flight is connected with a military operation and the pilot is a friend. He has agreed to take you on the condition that you remain hidden and don't ask questions.' Lubimov pushed his spectacles back up on to the brow of his nose.

'You'll land in Gorno-Altai near Kazakhstan and will be smuggled across the border.'

'Isn't that dangerous? I don't want to be caught and interrogated again.'

'Don't worry. We have good connections there, friends who will ensure you get on to the TurkSib.'

'Turksib?'

'Turkish Siberian railway,' Boris added.

'Are you coming as well?' Carty asked, turning to the Buryat.

'Boris will give you the names of the contacts on the way. They will ensure that you reach Almaty and from there, take a flight to London. Does that all make sense?' The older man seemed somewhat smug with his plan. Carty, however, was still looking for flaws.

'There are so many things that could go wrong.'

'That's possible,' Boris cut in, 'but then think of all the things that have gone wrong for you in the last few months. They have, in fact, all worked out in your favour!' he beamed. 'If the right man has the wrong means, the wrong means work in the right way. It's an old Taoist proverb, which my father used to tell me. I believe it puts your experience here into perspective.'

Carty contemplated the words and slowly grinned. 'I suppose you're right, as usual, Boris, but who will pay for all this? The helicopter flights, train fares and airplane tickets.'

Lubimov sank back in his chair, judiciously surveying Carty. 'That's simple, Scott – you will!'

'I don't understand?'

'With the travellers cheques from your case: there's more than £1,000. You can cash them when you arrive in Almaty and then pay the contact yourself.'

The Englishman had forgotten that he had kept them in case of emergency – there had never been one, until now.

'So that's it?'

'No, not quite,' Lubimov uttered, passing him an envelope. 'Your business class ticket entitles you to an open return up to three months. Our contact will investigate if there are available seats before you commit to a flight.'

Visibly surprised, Carty pulled out the ticket and glanced over its details.

'Can I ask, just how long have I been away from home?'

'According to the date of the custom's entry stamp in your passport, it's been approximately 45 days.'

The news was sobering.

'Well, the ticket might still be valid, but the customs authority will definitely ask questions.'

'Possibly, so that's why we will make sure you have a backdated letter from a Kazakh company supporting your stay.'

'For that long? – no one will believe it.'

'Yes, they will. Mining engineers often spend months in the field, and you could have taken a holiday to meet some friends. It will all be explained to you by the contacts.'

Carty fiddled with the ticket, clearly still nervous. 'What if I am recognised? The Kazakhs will hand me over to the Russian authorities.'

'Why would they do that? You're a British citizen with a valid visa to be in Kazakhstan. If you're recognised and held, then our contact will have instructions to go straight to the British Consulate. Your government would be keen to get you back as soon as possible after all the fuss you have caused.'

'I have?'

'Of course! Your face was shown repeatedly on Russian television for many days, after you went missing. You were a celebrity!'

'I was?' Carty responded coyly.

'Yes, the connotation was that you might be a spy. Anyway, most people's memories are short and they have a greater propensity to recall football results or who is having an affair in a soap opera than to remember the name and face of an Englishman who they probably believe is dead anyway.' His comments tempered Carty's unsettled manner.

'So, shall I show you the route you will take?' Boris sprang to his feet, pointing at the wall map.

'Where do we start?' Carty cheekily probed, hoping that they would unwittingly give away the location of *Sphinx.* Neither did.

'You will land here,' Boris traced his finger across the map.

'How far away is that?'

'Six or seven hours in the helicopter with a short stop for refuelling,' Boris confirmed, 'and once in Kazakhstan the journey by train to Almaty should take one full day, if there aren't any problems!'

A knock drew their attention. Inna had arrived with a tray bearing three cups of green tea. She laid it down on the table and left.

Lubimov customarily dropped two large sugar cubes into his and slowly stirred it.

'Scott,' he eyed Carty,' I hope you don't mind, I took the liberty of reading through the book that was in your case.'

Carty was at a loss. 'Which book is that?'

'*Psyche and Matter.*' The Russian lifted its tattered form from the same drawer and passed it back. 'Thank you!'

'Ah yes!' He stared once more at its cover and recalled the dialogue with Green. 'This was lent to me by a good friend.'

'It's an interesting book. It touches on areas that I have demonstrated to be true.'

'It does, how?'

'The machine!'

Boris lent forward and tapped Carty on the shoulder.

'Scott, let's go down to the lake now. We can discuss the trip further with Oleg tonight.'

Forty Two

1st August 2005. England.

Nick Hall's dogs were snarling and scratching at the gate. Their unusual behaviour and the approaching footsteps brought with them a sense of anxiety, forcing him to stop the fluid movements of *T'ai Chi Ch'uan* and take a deep breath.

'Down!' he boomed as the dogs bounded at the strangers. They obeyed, instantly cowering back at his bare feet. He stared curiously at the two beige Burberry macintoshes on his doorstep. It was late summer and neither rainy nor cold.

'Mr Hall?' the taller of the two men enquired firmly.

'That's right. Sorry about the dogs.'

'Can we ask you some questions?'

Their odd manner concerned him. 'I would need to see some identification first.'

They smartly flicked open leather wallets in tandem, to reveal ID photographs vaguely resembling themselves. Neither mentioned their names but Hall sized up the first, noting his washed-out grey complexion. His younger colleague was posturing cockily to the side, sporting a sandy crop and a strong physique.

'It's not every day that I get a visit from Special Branch. What can I help you with?' He probed as he unenthusiastically ushered them into the kitchen and then settled the dogs.

'Thank you,' the older man uttered, nervously scanning the animals. 'We want to ask you about your friend Scott Carty.'

'I suppose that you know he's dead,' Hall quipped. 'We held a memorial service for him a week ago.'

'Yes, we know. Did you speak with him before he left the country?'

'I spoke to him a lot before he left the country, why?'

'Was he worried about anything?'

'I told the detectives everything just after his disappearance.' Hall avoided mentioning the fraud. 'Is Special Branch now investigating this?'

'Yes, we have our reasons.' The man's dark expression hinted a threat. 'Think clearly, Mr Hall. Try to remember if there was anything unusual that he might have told you?'

'No, nothing that comes to mind,' he answered after a short pause.

'We understand that you took him to the airport on the day that he left for Kazakhstan,' Sandy blurted.

'That's right, I did.'

'He wasn't asked to carry anything with him?'

'Not that I knew about.'

Realising that Nick Hall was not easily intimidated, the man smoothly changed tactics, adopting a tone of frankness.

'Did he ever mention anything about nuclear waste to you?'

'No. Not at all, why?'

'It appears he was discussing its reprocessing with a number of his clients.'

'I don't know anything about that, I'm afraid. I was just his best friend!'

'That's why we're here. It's usually the best friend or a family member who knows the most.'

'You're wrong on this occasion, gentlemen!' Hall enunciated clearly, feeling an uncomfortable cramp in his stomach. Despite their probing he could not defend his friend's character against the allegations of fraud and then sudden disappearance. Perhaps it was easier on Diane that he had gone along with the accepted story, giving her closure, and selfishly, allowing himself the chance to be with her. These two strangers, though, were implying that Scott Carty had been involved in something far more sinister.

He pondered their comments for some seconds. It went against his instincts. Carty was not a nuclear man, even though he had accepted it had served a limited purpose in supplying power until now.

He collected himself from his thoughts. 'I have to get back to my work, so unfortunately I must ask you to leave. But before you go, can I have your names again?'

'You've seen our IDs, but for the sake of repeating myself, I'm Lambie and my colleague here is Wade,' the older man answered brashly. No ranks were mentioned and Hall remained silent, preferring that they left quickly.

'So, Mr Hall, what is it that's keeping you so busy?' Lambie asked bluntly as they stopped just short of the front door.

'I'm working on my one of my car engines.'

'That's interesting. What kind?' Wade eyed him with a practised frostiness.

'A standard diesel from a Land Rover.'

'Hah, diesel!' he scoffed. 'Very topical at the moment.'

'Why's that?' The ignoramus' comment had surprised him.

'I know someone who was fuelling his vehicle on used cooking oil instead of regular diesel.'

'You mean *biofuel.*'

'Yeah, and he was convicted for the deliberate evasion of fuel tax after the Inland Revenue caught up with him,' he mocked. He obviously knew too much about Nick's activities and was scaremongering.

Agitated, the beasts began circling the strangers again.

'I understand you're the ex-boyfriend of Carty's wife?' Wade sneered as they stepped out.

'Could I have your cards in case I need to call you with any information?' Nick Hall calmly sidestepped the comment.

'No need, Mr Hall,' Lambie cut back. 'We'll be in contact again soon.'

He watched them leave, their faces hidden behind the heavily tinted windows of a BMW jeep, not a vehicle Hall associated with Special Branch's foot soldiers. But the visit had served its purpose: that of blatant intimidation and he juggled with it for some time as he laboured over the engine.

It was no good, he couldn't focus. The dogs we're still disturbed and his instincts were driving him to a conclusion that he was struggling to accept.

Scott might have been completely innocent.

He had an uncanny feeling that Gordon Green should know about the visit.

'I need a drink please, Gordon,' Nick clamoured as he sat on the Chesterfield later that afternoon.

'Brandy?'

'Yes, please.'

'You don't normally drink brandy?' Green uttered, direct and to the point.

'I do now! Those two creeps, today, have completely spooked me.'

'Did they have names?'

'Lambie and Wade. But they were probably false ones anyway.'

Green moved to his desk and scribbled them down as Hall nursed his glass.

'They're implying Scott was involved in some nuclear waste business.'

'And what did you tell them?'

'Nothing, of course! I didn't know Albion was active in that sector.'

'It isn't,' Green confirmed coolly, 'although, with Albion's allegations against Scott, and this visit to you today, my instincts tell me that something very irregular is going on. It's even more suspicious with the discovery of Mark Boyd's body.'

'He's dead too?'

'He was pulled out of the Vltava River, near Prague, recently. The news is being kept under wraps for the moment but I'll find out more soon. I'm having lunch with a friend tomorrow. I'll also mention the visit of the two *coats*. He'll know how to deal with them.'

Nick Hall squinted back. 'And you still believe Scott is alive somewhere?'

Green laughed loudly. 'Funny, whenever I hear that word *believe*, I always think of Jung's response to John Freeman, during his famous BBC interview, when asked if he believed in the existence of God.'

Nick sighed, used to Green's tales. 'And what did he say?'

'That belief was not enough. He had to *know*. His lifetime's work had proven that an intelligent and benevolent force was striving to be understood through the unconscious of humanity,' Green faltered, as if the statement's apparent heresy weighed upon him. 'But to return to your question – as a betting man, then I would have to say yes. The dream I had was too real to be ignored.'

Forty Three

Parting with Lubimov at the edge of the *taiga,* they paced uphill through a pathless forest of sculptured pine, perched precariously on the edge of low cliffs against which Baikal's temperamental waters had lapped for aeons.

Walking along the ridge, any sense of time seemed stalled as if its hold had been severed leaving a void that couldn't be articulated, only experienced.

Finally, Boris aimed a finger at a partly collapsed dwelling resting against some small cliffs at the edge of the beach, its tin chimney billowing smoke.

'Is that where we're going?' Carty asked expectantly but found the Buryat's usual bonhomie attitude absent, replaced instead by one of apprehension.

'You must not tell Lubimov that I have brought you here. This is not his story.'

Not his story?

As their footsteps sounded on the loose shingles, a welcoming odour of smoked fish wafted around them and then drawing around the shack, he caught sight of a white-haired man, sitting alone. Carty placed him somewhere in his eighth decade and felt irresistibly drawn towards him.

Boris walked up and shook his hand before turning to introduce the foreigner.

'Hello, I'm Scott...Scott Carty.'

'Yes,' the stranger replied with a heavy accent, his face creasing into a deep smile, as he stood upright to greet the Englishman. 'And I am Ivan Yegorovich.' His grip was firm and for a fraction of a second Carty just stared back in disbelief before a surge of excitement took him.

'You're Lena's grandfather?' he blurted.

'I am and I believe you're the man she was in love with.'

'Well,' he stammered, 'in the short time we knew each other we became very close. I am so sorry...'

'Please,' Isotov interjected, waving the apology away with a thin hand. 'Boris has already told me everything.'

'He has?' Carty searched his friend's face, confused by the statement.

'Come.' Isotov ushered them to sit on the rickety wooden stools.

'So, what do you think of Baikal?' he said, placing down a plate of smoked *Omul* and raising his open arms to the panorama.

'It's magnificent!' Carty cautiously answered, sitting.

'And it's much more than that.' He closed his eyes, breathing deeply.

The Englishman, tempted by hunger, broke off a piece of the fish with a tired aluminium fork. Its smell and the taste were delicious and as he chewed he gazed at Isotov with sense of awe.

After some seconds the Russian's eyes popped open, his expression now brimming with the animated impatience of someone much younger.

'Have you seen the machine yet?' he asked.

Carty ran both hands through his wavy locks, contemplating his answer. Lubimov had sworn him to secrecy.

But this man is its inventor for God sakes!

The thought forced him to seek confirmation but the Buryat was focused on his plate, busy eating in apparent ignorance.

'Yes, Lubimov showed it to me.'

'Aha. Oleg Matissevich, he's a good man, and that machine – it's special, isn't it?'

'I have trouble accepting its existence, accepting the science. It's beyond anything I could have imagined.'

Isotov let out a raucous snort. 'And so did I all those years ago, but now it seems totally natural and in harmony with this big machine that we live on.'

'How long did you work on it for?' The question left Carty's lips automatically as if he had been practising it for days.

'A lifetime, a lifetime's work that could change our world,' the old man uttered, as if conversing with himself. 'Tell me, what would you do now, if you were me?'

'I guess I would blow the technology wide open and tell the world.'

'You would?' A hint of the mischievous sparkled in his eyes.

Moments passed before Isotov spoke again, as if gripped by a thought he had to share.

'Tell me, Scott, are you aware of the Schumann Resonance?'

'No, I'm not.'

'You might want to look into it when you research the technology.'

Carty shrugged. It was unlikely he would ever be researching *overunity* during his lifetime and thought it presumptuous that Isotov had even suggested it.

'What exactly is the Schumann Resonance?'

'It's the standing vibration of the planet,' Boris interjected. 'Its electrical heartbeat, eight cycles per second.'

Hmm, that archetype of eight again, he thought, taken with the synchronicity as he tapped the fork against the small table.

'Once my team understood the fundamental importance of the Schumann Resonance in producing *overunity*, then it was simply a matter of finding the exact location in which to position the machine.'

'You're saying that *overunity* can only occur at specific co-ordinates on the Earth's surface?' Carty blurted, stunned by his own comment. The significance was more than startling; it was radical. The Russian's warm gaze confirmed his question.

'We found, by accident or serendipity, that Baikal was the perfect spot. The cavern is situated on a powerful energetic node that resonates in geomagnetic harmony with the Schumann Resonance.'

'Like the positive and negative poles of a battery?'

'More like two giant waves joining to form one gigantic tidal wave,' Boris added, registering his friend's obvious hunger for more information. 'The machine is simply the gateway through which the energy manifests itself.'

'Lubimov told me that your original machine had been decommissioned and removed in the early 1990s,' Carty said gently, as if quizzing the man.

'And it's still operating somewhere in Russia,' Isotov whispered back.

'Transmuting radioactive waste?'

'Probably, but that's not the high science.'

'You mean *overunity* – limitless energy?'

'Yes, there are only a handful of places on Earth where the vortex energies are powerful enough to be harnessed. Unless the technology is situated on one of these node-points, the *overunity* will be almost negligible and only enough to cause the transmutation phenomenon.'

Carty smiled. 'And only you, Lubimov and Boris know this.'

'And now you,' he murmured back.

'What about Lena?'

Isotov's expression hardened as he pulled a withered hand back through his white locks. In the momentary silence, Carty scanned him recognising the noble profile that was so attractive in his granddaughter. He was well presented in polished brogues and a dogtooth jacket over a soft cotton shirt, its collars frayed with the years. It was inspiring that he had maintained his appearance and clarity of mind under the circumstances in which he was obliged to live.

'No, she never knew about the machine's existence.'

Carty felt embarrassed that he had imposed and looked out over the great blue mass before them. A mist had started to gather just off the shore and then a glaring contradiction suddenly occurred to him.

'Lubimov also said that his new prototype could not transmute radioactive waste,' the Englishman blurted, implying that an untruth had been told. The Buryat recognised it and glared angrily at him.

'Ha!' Isotov laughed it off. 'In theory it can, but it never has. Lubimov is too much of a purist! I discovered the transmutation phenomenon in the late 1980s.'

'And did it cause excitement?'

'Absolutely! It was deemed of high military importance, to be kept an absolute secret. Senior personnel and specialists were sent in to experiment with small quantities of nuclear waste materials. My team were ordered to take a holiday but we refused to leave in case our cherished technology was stolen from under our noses.'

'How long did the experiments last?'

'About two years and then they suddenly stopped. No further nuclear materials arrived after that, although the total amount actually brought to the cavern during that time was minimal. We had maintained a rigorous daily discipline of sweeping the site with Geiger counters and within several days, any radiation signal had dropped below that of the background level, emanating from the granite bedrock.'

'The radioactivity had almost disappeared?'

'Yes, and the waste had been transmuted, not just into safer isotopes but into harmless elements.'

'Your original machine did this?'

The old man nodded.

'That's just incredible! he said in disbelief. 'But don't you think that civilisation might benefit from this technology, to completely eradicate the dumping of nuclear waste?'

'Of course, but it would directly threaten international businesses controlling the current funding programmes for nuclear waste management. They, along with governments, are spinning the fallacy that reprocessing it into mixed oxide and using storage will diminish the problem altogether.' He rubbed his small tired eyes as he spoke. 'This also covers up another possible factor.'

'Which is?'

'The financial opportunity in reprocessing the many thousands of decommissioned nuclear warheads in Russia and overseas.'

'That would seem to make sense! It's a cheap solution that reduces the reliance on mined uranium from unstable regimes!' Carty chimed.

'Then do you consider nuclear to be a practical solution to the world's energy needs?' His question drew the Englishman.

'I believed that nuclear *fusion* may hold the answer to that,' Carty grinned half-heartedly, 'that was until I witnessed the machine.'

Isotov gulped down the tea and then refilled the blue-rimmed enamel mug, as gulls shrieked over the cabin, seeking scraps.

'Scott, there is a much greater problem looming.'

'Are you referring to global dimming?' Carty added, expecting a regurgitation of Lubimov's story of earlier that day.

'No.' Isotov pointed a wizened finger towards Boris, signalling to him to explain.

'Scientific data shows that the Schumann Resonance's frequency has dramatically increased in the last few years,' the Buryat articulated, seemingly weighed down by the statement.

'So what does that mean?'

'It has many implications but it could be linked to a weakening in the Earth's magnetic field, an effect which has no observable cause.'

'Hasn't that been the case for centuries?'

'Yes, but recently, the magnetosphere has diminished more rapidly than at any time in the past 100 years.'

'Where are you going with all this, Boris?'

'I don't want to insult your intelligence,' the man grinned coldly back, 'but my culture speaks of a coming event when time, as we understand it, will stop.'

'Stop? What are you talking about?'

'Many ancient cultures perceived time in a very different way to how we do now. The Mayan civilisation's long-count calendar is probably the most well-known with its cyclical epochs of around 5,000 years.' His gaze hardened. 'This current epoch, we're living in, is believed to reach a turning point – a singularity, sometime after the Winter solstice in December 2012.'

Carty rolled his eyes, forgetting that he now might be insulting his friend's intelligence.

'Boris, these are all just stories.'

'Just like your dreams and the synchronicity of surviving three attempts on your life?' the Buryat said, cocking an eyebrow. 'Scientists are baffled at just how accurately constructed the Mayan calendar is – well beyond the technical capability of a civilisation in the fifth century BC. So that leaves two questions: how and why did they construct it?'

'To keep a track of time I suppose. Is there any evidence that this event was predicted by other ancient cultures too?'

'There's plenty: the pre-Inca *Olmec* civilisation, the *Qero* of Peru, the *Hopi* of North America all mention this same end point. Even the *I Ching* exhibits a diminishing time wave based on *novelty* – events in history that have completely changed the course of humanity. What's interesting is that their frequency seems to occur 64 times faster than in the preceding period.'

'The same number of hexagrams as in the *I Ching*! Does its time wave also stop in 2012?'

Boris nodded knowingly as Isotov picked up the thread.

'The most alarming news is the dramatic increase in sunspot activity. Every eleven or so years, CMEs, coronal mass ejections

– huge eruptions from the Sun's surface – reach a maximum intensity, spewing enormous quantities of electromagnetic particles into space.'

'Yes, I am a physicist and I know what solar flares are.' His response, unintentionally indignant, was wasted on the old man who continued as if he hadn't spoken.

'It's the increased frequency and intensity of these solar flares that's causing worry amongst scientists. In January this year an unexpected eruption on the far side of the sun blacked-out radio transmissions around the globe.'

'I'm not sure what your point is.'

'We're in 2005, which is a *minimum* point in the Sun's eleven year cycle.'

'I see, but that eruption might have just been an anomaly. What real scientific evidence is there to show that these flares are becoming more intense?'

'In 1989, which was also a minimum year, a huge solar eruption projected a proton cloud directly at the Earth, shutting down part of the Canadian power grid and fusing many of its transformers.'

'And the Earth's magnetic field couldn't deflect it?'

'Only partially: a super flare would disrupt much of the communications and power systems as well as having serious implications for human health.'

'You mean radiation effects: cancers and eye damage.'

'Very probably: the Halloween eruptions, during October and November 2003 – the most powerful in recent times – ejected electromagnetic particles at velocities approaching the speed of light, almost 50 times faster than a normal flare. More worrying, though, was that their relative masses had greatly increased, transforming them from peas into bullets. Thankfully they just skirted the Earth. A direct hit would have been disastrous.'

'Incapacitating electrical grid systems in minutes!' Carty shuddered at the unimaginable. 'Does the data predict that a super eruption is likely soon?'

Isotov remained stony faced. 'Solar Cycle 24 is predicted to reach its maximum sometime before the end of 2014. Cost modelling analyses have shown that a direct hit would cause damage running into trillions of US dollars. But more frightening is that it might take years, not months, to repair and reconnect power systems.'

'And after 48 hours, essential systems would begin to fail: safe drinking water, sewage treatment, refrigerated food supplies, air-conditioning!' Carty uttered what came immediately to mind, dropping his head pensively.

'Without these things that define our modern civilisation, humanity would be set back temporarily into the Middle Ages; time literally would have gone backwards and our so-called technological sophistry shown to be very fragile indeed.'

'And the machine, it wouldn't be affected by these coronal mass ejections?'

'No,' the Russian replied, instantly.

'But electrical power still needs to run through a grid infrastructure,' Carty announced. 'If that grid system is taken down by these CMEs then it doesn't matter how the electricity is generated – it couldn't be deployed anyway!'

'You're correct, but in the chaos of rebuilding our world there will be a chance for new technologies to be implemented, changing the direction of civilisation forever.'

'Do you really think that will happen?'

'Large grid systems are not the most efficient means of supplying power. It would be far more effective to have each town, village or community producing energy for its own needs and providing any surplus to a much smaller, local grid system.'

'Decentralising the grid into a cellular structure?'

'Potentially. And at those node-points on the planet, where *overunity* –virtually limitless energy – can be accessed, there would be manufacturing industries providing the essentials for the world's population, ushering in a revolution of Copernican magnitude.'

'A new energy era?'

'Every aspect of life as we know it would drastically change. Food supplies will no longer rely on expensive, energy-intensive growing techniques and transportation. Through inexpensive desalination and water pumping, deserts would be transformed, flourishing as vast forests or grain fields. More incredible, though, would be the transmutation of matter. Hydrocarbons such as gas and oil, used in making plastics, could be synthesised from their constituent elements at no cost, removing the need to drill for and process crude oil.'

'Sounds like alchemy in its purest form,' Carty added. 'But I suppose none of this will be achievable unless there is a disaster first. Does Lubimov know any of this?'

'He has great faith in human nature and the emerging consciousness.'

'And you don't?'

'I am old and responsible for this machine's emergence. It is my legacy to mankind, whatever happens,' Isotov replied quietly, standing up to stretch.

What would Nick and Green make of all this? Carty pondered. He was in familiar territory. It seemed that the few wise men he had met in his life all shared similar eschatological visions of the future.

'Perhaps Boris should take you down to the lake so that you may say goodbye.'

The Buryat smiled knowingly and Carty politely picked up the plates.

'Leave them there,' Isotov ordered gently.

'Thank you, Ivan Yegorovich, the fish was delicious.'

The old man remained silent.

'And it has been a pleasure to have met you and to have learnt about the technology's history. It is a great achievement.'

'And I'm pleased that it has been shared with someone who is worthy enough to understand its full implications.' He held onto Carty's hand momentarily longer than was usual before turning to the Buryat. Boris tenderly hugged the old man, whispering something in Russian.

Trudging away across the beach towards the forest, Carty looked back, waving at an unknown legend whose work he considered to be the equivalent of any of the giants of physics.

Isotov acknowledged him with an outstretched palm.

Forty Four

'What an exceptional man: does he live here all year round?'

'Only in the summer months, soaking up the sun, and swimming early in the morning. Baikal rarely warms up but even so, many older people bathe. It's a good tonic and helps their circulation.'

'He certainly looks healthy enough, Boris, but what happened to him? Why was he retired?'

'He had to disappear quickly when it was obvious that those in power wanted to take control of the original machine.'

'And they were not satisfied that Isotov would just walk away?'

'Not with that information in his head!'

'But where did he disappear to?'

'We Buryats hid him in the *taiga*.'

A *nerpa*'s bark broke their conversation, its head bobbing above the surface of the shallows, catching Carty's eye.

However did a seal population colonise this lake, so far inland?

Like everything else about Baikal, it was extraordinary.

Then a different thought surfaced.

Hah, so obvious!

It should have been one of the first things to enter his head on meeting the old man.

'Tell me, Boris.' He grinned, impishly. 'You've known Ivan Yegorovich since you were a young man, haven't you?'

'Yes, I have,' he murmured.

'Then you must have met Lena.'

Boris' dark complexion could not hide his embarrassment. 'Yes. I met her.'

'Why didn't you tell me then?'

'Because Lubimov expressly asked me not to.'

'Oleg is really quite a tyrant, isn't he?'

'No, he was worried that you were not who you said you were,' he coyly countered. 'Lena was worshipped by the people here. As a child she was a little blond angel who possessed a great power.'

'Really, what?'

'The ability to make people laugh, one of nature's highest healing arts. After her parents moved away to Novosibirsk she came back here every summer to visit her grandparents.'

Carty grinned, recalling Isotov's earlier comment. *But how did the old man know that Lena was in love with me? Boris must have told him.*

He shrugged, recalling the seriousness of the conversation with Isotov and how he now felt, left holding a poisoned chalice.

'What do you believe, Boris?' he switched tack.

'What, Lena being aware of the machine's existence or not?'

'No, I mean all this nonsense about 2012. Do you believe it all?'

'Scott, those ancient cultures were not predicting a terrible event that would wipe out humanity on a certain date.'

'Really? That's not what I heard you say.'

'I was simply giving you the myths. Ivan Yegorovich, though, was stating the facts: that one day, a solar super-flare will envelope the Earth again, as it did in the mid-19th century.'

'But didn't Lubimov say the Halloween eruptions were the largest ever?'

'In modern times, yes, but the Carrington Event of 1859 was several times more intense.'

'Then why didn't he mention that?'

'Probably because little scientific data exists, although there are many newspaper accounts of its widespread impact.'

'What happened?'

'The night sky was lit up for days, confusing wildlife. Telegraph systems across the globe were downed and compasses span uselessly, incapacitating shipping fleets. Fortunately, daily life was hardly reliant on electricity, and communities were far more self-sufficient.'

'Unlike today!'

'That's right. Such an event in current times would irrevocably change the way we live and that's what I meant earlier. The Mayans understood that this current epoch of human history will come to a natural turning point, the exact nature of which they could not predict.'

'So, why are you so convinced of it?'

'Because we seem to have lost our way and prefer to believe we can exist outside of the harmony and order of nature, by depending on a sophisticated framework which is susceptible to failure.'

Boris' statement had caught Carty off guard, igniting memories again of the *Rainmaker* story and its real relevance to their conversation.

'The surprising thing is that huge changes are not required,' Boris continued. 'Only small ones, made by each person in understanding that security cannot be had through the accumulation of material wealth, but in sharing knowledge and wisdom.'

Carty eyed him. 'You're referring to more than just climate change and solar eruptions, aren't you?'

'I'm more fearful of the relentless desecration of the environment in the name of progress. Pristine areas such as Baikal may soon be under threat, and this will signal the turning point when nature will have come to its limit in sustaining our current system.'

'The paradigm shift?'

'Yes. The shamans tell us that in their dreamtime they can now hear a new cultural tune emerging – one that has no root in earlier songs – and that it is humanity that must harmonise with this new vibration, in order to evolve.'

They had now reached the water and Boris produced a small glass phial sealed with a plastic cap, the sort Carty had not seen since his school days.

'What are we going to do now?'

'A small ritual.' A familiar expression had returned to the Buryat's face: he was at ease again.

The weather was fine and he squatted so that the waves broke over his shoes and then beckoned for Carty to join him. The Englishman grinned, ruminating that only a month or so earlier he would have considered the act both ludicrous and humiliating. The many strange ordeals he had experienced on this journey in Siberia, though, had totally changed his view of the world and he was glad for the closeness he felt with this man.

Raising his arms and hands out wide, symbolically embracing the lake, Boris then began to chant in a continuous earthy tone from deep in his throat. Carty looked on, his body inexorably resonating with the sound's rising pitch, until it engulfed his senses. The mist had mysteriously reappeared along the edge of the beach and he was transfixed, unable to move as it wafted down, blotting out the sun and robbing him of warmth. Its white mass swirled around them and as he looked more deeply, he could see the familiar figure of the maiden drawing towards him. A longing to be with her surged but as Boris' song waned so did the mist and her form.

'Take this' Boris calmly pronounced, presenting the phial, now full with the lake's water. 'You will need it when you arrive home.'

Forty Five

There was a mass of activity at *Sphinx*, in preparing for the farewell dinner and Carty, temporarily ignored, busied himself, ensuring that his suit and newly pressed shirts were packed in the best possible way to prevent creasing.

With anxiety hovering, he then uneasily wandered about the Institute, ending up on the same veranda where he first took a walk with Lubimov. The vista was stupefying, a monument to the last vestiges of ancient scenery on this planet, and he wondered why it was, that he, a mere spectator, had been allowed the humbling privilege of observing this beauty and its enigma. It was an image to be mentally framed in order to remember the lessons learnt here.

The late afternoon dragged as he cogitated again upon the bizarre sequence of events that had led him to Baikal and those that had unfolded since. Experiencing Lena's love had revealed to him Diane's mature understanding of his deep-seated flaws. She had sacrificed her way of life and her love in the vain hope of him changing. He had, but at what cost? His love for her was irrevocably altered, like brushstrokes on the unfinished canvas of his life, colourful but lacking real depth. He had been an insecure man who had hidden behind the persona of a city academic in the vain belief that his world of trading ran the big show. How painful the process had been, in uncovering this to be a fallacy and discovering D'albo's deceit.

Perhaps this has all been just a dream and I'll soon wake up to analyse it with Green.

But the thought then brought home the realities of Lena's death, the attempts on his life and the constant worry about his family's suffering.

He sat, captured by virtual images of his vision in the *banya*, recalling that the past was done and that he now had to walk his own destiny, to be whole and content.

He shook himself from his reverie, smiling at the whole madness of this adventure and then challenged himself to run through the *Baguazhang* one last time.

Forty minutes in, drenched in his own sweat, he stopped and strained at a distant whirring. Soon it had become a deafening noise, one that he recognised belonged to a helicopter – like the one at the Baikal camp, and the last flight that the Americans made. He hoped his fate would be different.

'Are you ready to eat?' Boris' sudden question took him by surprise.

'I suppose I am.'

'Good! We'll pick up your things later before we fly out.'

'When will that be?'

'In about three hours.'

It seemed so final.

They wandered down to the outside tables where a small group was gathered, including the team that had ridden back with him to the Institute. Copious bottles of vodka were lined up on the table and it was clear his departure was an excuse for a party that would be going on for long after.

Svetlana was the first to stand up and hug him, kissing him profusely on the cheeks. *That's out of character,* he thought but his grin was big and generous.

Soon, all the guests were seated and the first of the toasts began. Inna presented a solemn, tearful speech and they all gulped down the full shot glasses. Then, before they started the soup,

Tatiana Ivanovna one of the sturdy ladies who had fed him, stopped to raise a glass to the Englishman.

As the dishes were served, others continually stood in turn to give anecdotes or to praise the Englishman. Eventually Oleg Lubimov winked at Boris who slowly rose and waited, allowing the moment to choose itself. With a broad grin he spoke in Russian. It was short and sincere, stating that he would miss his *brother*. Lubimov translated in a hushed voice and then after refilling the shot-glass, stood straight up, to address the group, statuesque in his best jacket and combed hair.

'My friends, we're here to wish our *tavarish*, Scott Carty, a safe journey back to his family. It was a battle to save him but with his indomitable spirit and the skill of the team around this table, he pulled through. We have all been blessed with his presence at *Sphinx*. Let us hope that he will remember us and tell the world of our work here.' He turned to Carty and raised his glass as Boris finished translating.

Carty, now clearly emotional, rose slowly. 'Dear friends,' he began. 'You have all said so many kind things about me that I am at a loss for words and feel that I must address every one of you individually.' He then proceeded around the table, striving to remember the names of each person so that he might thank them personally, before coming to Lubimov.

'Dear Oleg Matissevich,' he uttered as he placed a hand on the man's shoulder. 'Your sense of grace and your gift of wisdom have shown me that a balance in all things is the only truth. Thank you for making this place what it is: a centre of excellence in the sciences of tomorrow. I hope to return one day!'

Lubimov wiped his tearful eyes as the crowd clapped loudly.

Carty let them finish.

'Then there is Boris.' He fought back a wavering of his voice. 'Boris. You are the brother I never had and what you have shown me here, I could not have learned in a lifetime of encounters with mystics or holy men. Thank you for sharing and teaching me these things. I will always remember them and thus I can never forget you.' He faltered but Boris had immediately sprung up to grasp him in a bear hug.

The gathering quietened again, waiting for Carty to raise his glass to them. He momentarily halted.

'And there is also one other person who is not with us tonight who brought me to Baikal and whom I grew to love.' He paused as Lubimov translated.

'Lena Isotova!'

'Lena Isotova!' Everyone solemnly repeated her name. Boris was right; she was loved.

Bowls of thick ice cream followed along with instant coffee sweetened with a dollop of sweet *scushornoyeh moloko* – a creamy yellow, condensed milk – resting in the bottom of each glass.

The party drank and loudly chatted over guitars mutely strumming to local songs, impervious to the dusk settling in. Then, Sergei gave a great impersonation of Cossack dancing around a lively bonfire, to cheers and clapping.

Boris, who had been heavily in conversation with a colleague, turned to Carty, his body language restless as he introduced the stranger.

'Scott, this is Slava, our taxi ride tonight. We need to leave in 15 minutes.'

The comment set the Englishman's stomach churning. This was the moment he was dreading.

He wandered around the crowd of faces, shaking hands and politely refusing the glasses of moonshine offered. Then, he made a short run back to the room to pick up his few things as the chopper fired up.

A blast of wind raced across the small open space outside the Institute, blowing about the team who had gathered to send him off.

One by one they kissed or hugged him and finally he came to Lubimov.

'A small gift for you,' said the director, passing him a large-faced military watch.

'It's the *Komandirski* from my military service. Don't forget us!' he shouted.

Carty winked at him and forced something into his hands. 'And for you: *Psyche and Matter*. Don't forget me!' he yelled back.

Boris grabbed his arm and led him in a crouching run beneath the spinning rotors.

He turned at its entry hatch to wave, and then climbed in.

Forty Six

The deafening whirr of the five rotors smothered his screamed farewells as the helicopter rapidly gained height, leaving the tiny cluster of buildings holding a vast secret.

Boris slid the hatch firmly into place, instantly giving respite from the raw sound. Thirty seconds later they were moving over the vastness of Baikal, into the darkening sky.

'This is a Mil 8 *vertolert* – the workhorse of the Soviet air force. It's not comfortable but it will get us there,' Boris yelled, leaning back over his co-pilot's seat.

'What's the plan?' Carty shouted as he inspected the empty fuselage behind him.

'We'll fly south initially, and then bear due west for about three hours before stopping to refuel.'

The Englishman, though, was drawn from the specifics by the sight of the sunset's deep orange aurora over the Selenga river delta, mirroring itself magnificently in Baikal's surface, creating the illusion that the lake was ablaze.

'In my language *Baikal* means a shaft of fire.' Boris pointed at the spectacle. 'Perhaps that is the reason why.'

Carty grinned, hoping that he would be back one day, but for now he was carrying memories and experiences he could never allow himself to forget. The *Blue Eye of the Earth* was reason enough for the native people of Siberia to be humbly proud.

The vista then slipped from view. The helicopter had dropped altitude to hug the contours of a sharp valley cutting through the mountains.

'Does anybody know that Slava's flying this helicopter?'

'You mean do his superiors know?' Boris answered.

'Yeah, can he just take it for a spin whenever he wishes, without orders?'

'His base is fully aware he's flying tonight. It's routine but what they don't know is that he's taking a detour.'

'Is that going to cause us a problem?'

'Only if they find out!' he stated curtly. 'His colleagues believe that he's moving some businessmen around on a private flight.'

'Is that common?'

'Officially, no, but it happens.'

The monotonous drone of the engine and the encroaching darkness left Carty mulling his thoughts as Boris and Slava sat chatting, ahead of him.

A gentle nudge brought Carty from his slumber and now, muzzy-headed, he had forgotten where he was.

'We're landing in a few minutes to refuel. You need to move to the back and lay down across the seats.'

He shuddered in the crisp environment. 'Exactly how long do I need to stay there for?'

'About 30 minutes: Slava doesn't know the ground team here so you mustn't be seen!'

Hearing his name, Slava turned, waving with his hand frantically, conveying the urgency for Carty to drop out of sight.

'No more questions, you need to disappear!'

Carty did as he was told, covering himself with a rough blanket, suffused with the sickening odour of fuel oil.

The craft oscillated in its descent, shuddering wildly as it settled down in the small clearing.

The Russians left him alone with only the mechanical tick of the *Komandirski* as he rested his head on his tucked arm. *11:30 already!* He noted from its luminescent face, stunned that he had slept for so long.

Secure in his lair, he had become accustomed to his own quiet heartbeat but was soon jolted by heavy voices around the craft and then the clunk of metal on metal. The refuelling had begun.

A little while later the side door was pulled back and thinking it was Boris returning, Carty pulled the blanket away from his head.

'Shto eta!' a foreign voice called out. Carty froze as torch light fixed the lifeless-looking bundle of cloth. His discovery had caused him to re-live again the cold fear of looking down that rifle barrel in the *taiga*. A prod from the torch's shaft sank into his spine. He flinched and then the blanket was yanked from him. Burying his head he expected shouting but instead an obscure clicking noise filled the fuselage's vacuous space followed by a weird low pitched, guttural tone. Carty slowly looked up to view the remarkable sight. Boris had appeared beside the vacant mechanic, whispering something while leading the tranced Russian back out through the open cargo door. Outside he slapped his hands, sharply in front of the young man's face and instantly the Russian came around again, as if nothing had happened.

Carty breathed a sigh of relief and quickly covered himself again.

Forty Seven

A sensation of pressure in his eardrums roused him and he pulled away the cover, his breath instantly condensing in the freezing air.

'Coffee?' the Buryat offered, waving a thermos.

'Thanks,' he muttered as he struggled up from the awkward position and rubbed the numb sensation in the small of his back caused by the steel frame of the seat.

'Where are we?' He was taken by the sight of icy peaks, jutting above the low cloud base.

'Gorno Altaisk region,' Boris barked. 'Beautiful isn't it? The Altay mountains are said to be the ancestral home of the Aryan race.'

'I thought the Aryans came from Central Asia.'

'It's probably just a story. The range splits just south from here: one part branches into Mongolia and the other meets the *Tien Shan* range near Almaty.'

Almaty! The mention of the city triggered a buried trepidation.

Soon a crackle from the radio was followed by a Russian voice. Boris bent to listen more carefully. Slava passed him a headset and he took charge of the conversation with the other party, winking at Carty to allay his obvious anxiety.

Is it a call from Slava's base?

Slava then joined in minutes later, seeming to ask a number of questions.

'That was Yulia, our rendezvous,' Boris stated finally.

'Yulia...a woman?'

'That's right, any problems with that?'

'Not at all!'

The next two hours passed quickly, the mountainous landscape softening into undulating hills. The chopper changed course again, descending against a buffeting wind, towards the lights from a small settlement.

'We're going in to land,' Slava called out.

Carty's adrenalin began pumping.

Minutes later they were hovering over a clearing in the forest, lit up by a waiting car's headlamps and then, they touched down.

A woman ran up to hug Boris, passionately kissing him on the lips. He held her full hips, unabashed by her actions.

What is it with this guy and women? Carty questioned as he was introduced to her.

'Hallo, Scott, I'm Yulia.' She offered in accented English, bowing theatrically and pulling back the shaggy peroxide-blonde fringe partially covering her high-set eyes.

'Hello, Yulia, it's very good to meet you,' Carty responded, tugging up the collar of his combat jacket against the wind.

Slava handed several boxes from the chopper to Maxim, her driver, who busily loaded them into the rear space of a Lada Niva.

'Get in please, Scott!' she pointed.

Carty turned to Boris. 'Are you coming with us?'

'No. I need to return to help Lubimov.' A sadness seized his expression. 'And anyway, Slava has a tight schedule. He can't wait.'

'Not even to the border?' Carty begged, now noticeably shaken by the finality of it all.

'Not even to the border,' he echoed.

'Then, I think this is good bye.'

'There are no goodbyes, just beginnings and ends.' He squeezed Carty's triceps. 'It's the natural course of events. We'll see each other sooner than you think.'

Maxim had already started up the vehicle, signalling that their departure was imminent.

'Here, take this.' As if by magic, Boris had produced a small stone and, grasping Carty's hand, laid the gem on his palm. 'It is said that these gold quartz crystals are charged with Baikal's energy. Carry it with you and you will always have access to its power wherever you are in the world.'

Carty grabbed him and held him close. 'Thanks,' he whispered. 'I will not forget you.'

As the car slowly moved out across the clearing the Englishman squinted back through the window, barely able to make out the figures of the two men re-boarding the chopper. Neither had glanced back.

Forty Eight

'We will soon be arriving at the main road to the border,' Yulia advised, craning her head back from the front seat. 'We'll stop there and you will hide in the back of the jeep,' she instructed boldly. He found her strange accent comforting.

True to her word they shortly arrived on a large carriageway and Maxim swerved up onto the overgrown verge to park.

'Now we have coffee,' she said enthusiastically, switching on the car's interior light against the pitch black outside.

They silently took turns sipping the overly sweet brew from the same enamelled cup until it was finished. Then Maxim climbed out and opened the rear door to haul aside the boxes and various bags in the boot space, hurriedly indicating to Carty to climb over the back seat. As he did a worry began to gnaw at him.

Yulia was now out of the car. 'Curl up,' she whispered, her warm, stale breath meeting his face, 'and whatever happens do not move or make any sound until I tell you that we are clear.' Her expression contrasted sharply with her earlier, frothy nature. 'Don't worry, I've done this before.' She winked reassuringly, sealing the conversation as Maxim laid a rug and then two lightly filled canvas bags over him.

The ride was short and uncomfortable. Several times he was thrown up off the boot's floor and landed awkwardly, knocking the wind out of him.

'Are you all right?' Yulia called out.

'Yes.'

'Good. Now be quiet!'

The car slowed.

The crossing was far quicker than he had imagined it would be, and then they were into no-man's-land between the two countries. A shout from outside, though, soon caused the car to halt abruptly and Carty's heart raced as he frantically rolled the smooth quartz stone around in his pocket.

Yulia wound the window down and responded harshly in Kazakh while Maxim kept the engine running. The car's interior was lit up by the guard's search light, flitting across the back seat and into the boot space. There was a deathly pause and then the jeep slowly cranked up its speed again. They were finally out of Russia.

Carty was shaken violently as the jeep swerved to avoid the gaping pot-holes, caught at the last minute in the headlights. Now flagging with exhaustion he lapsed into a memory slideshow, imagining he was recounting the adventures with Boris to his son. A sense of urgency gripped his shattered mind, focusing on the end game – to get back home.

Gravity then abruptly shifted him and the bags forwards as the vehicle pulled rapidly to a stop. Yulia opened the back up and offered her hand. He took it, finding it difficult to feel his legs as he laboured to climb out. Maxim grabbed him and slung an arm across his back, helping him onto the rear passenger seat.

'Are you hungry?' Yulia enquired gently, her sharp body odour filling his nostrils. Carty was dazed and seemed not be responding.

'Thirsty?' She placed a cup to his lips and then checked his pupils to ensure he was not concussed.

'Thank you.'

The car lurched into gear as Yulia covered him. He drifted into a slumber, vaguely recognising his name peppered throughout the Russians' dialogue.

Forty Nine

The City of London.

Jack better have a good reason for meeting here. Gordon Green harped as he cautiously trod down the aged spiral staircase in his rain-soaked soles, wary that he might slip on its varnished steps.

Forgotten in the developers' sprawl and defying the past, the old drinking house was not a place he would naturally choose but he understood the risks *Whitehall Jack* took in meeting him.

He turned the last wind of the stairs and noticed a pair of senior City men settling their bill and preparing to leave. His friend, sitting discreetly in a recessed booth, calmly raised a palm to acknowledge him, his eyes radiating a sense of trust that had drawn Green to like him from the first.

'How are you, Jack?' Green asked quietly, firmly grasping the man's hand as he slipped across the leather bench-seat.

'Fine, thanks, Gordon,' his beady brown eyes flashed back. Jack's appearance hadn't changed: slim and of average build with a distinct aquiline nose upon which thick-rimmed glasses were perched. With his classic pin-stripe suit and mirror-finished shoes, he carried the air of a TV commentator about him. The two men had remained close after leaving university despite their very different occupations. Jack had joined the civil service and there had been a five-year period when he had disappeared without contact. It was never raised, although Green suspected an intelligence programme overseas. They met infrequently and occasionally holidayed together with their wives and children.

'A bottle of Merlot, Gordon?' His question resonated with its crisp syllables.

'Sounds good; steak and kidney pies?'

It took only a few moments for them to order and the simple act of asking the waiter to rope off the bottom of the staircase meant that they wouldn't be disturbed.

Jack pulled a routine smile while running his hands over his greased black hair and then meshing his fingers to rest them on the table. Green sensed a story about to unfold.

'The coats who visited Nick Hall were not Special Branch. They were impostors, probably working for a foreign agency. We're not sure which yet.'

'Isn't that a little odd?'

'Not really: we know Arthur D'albo has been, and still is, a facilitator in the dumping of spent nuclear waste in Russia.'

'What!' Green shook his head, disbelievingly.

'Yes, that's right, Gordon, incredible isn't it? The coats were probably probing Nick Hall to find out if he knew anything that might incriminate D'albo and his Russian friends.'

'Then Nick might be in grave danger.' Green's composure dropped visibly.

'He's safe and we know all of the coats' moves,' he said locking stares over the rim of his glasses. 'Gordon, as always, not a word to anyone.'

'Of course not, you know that I would never...'

'I must confess,' Jack interrupted, 'I was in two minds about meeting you today.' He casually pushed the spectacles back up on to the bridge of his nose.

'It appears your friend, Scott Carty, was totally unaware of the trap set for him by D'albo,' he announced, unblinking. 'During the SFO investigation into the fraud at Brightwell Carter, Mark Boyd cracked...' Jack stopped abruptly in mid-stream, spotting the waiter hovering apprehensively nearby, ready to pour the wine. He motioned for him to continue.

Green took a brief nose and then a sip, 'Excellent!' he uttered.

Jack's clinical gesture to the man signalled that they should be left alone again.

'Mark Boyd was acting for the security services, acting for us.'

'He was?'

'Yes, he did a deal after he learnt that D'albo had set him up as the fall guy.'

'Didn't Boyd have a share in the takings?'

'No, but he did admit to operating the bogus trading positions that perpetrated the fraud. He was either stupid or naïve in circumventing statutory compliance procedures with the Russian client whom, he believed, was the owner of the company and so the Serious Fraud Office threw the book at him.'

'And D'albo?'

'His alibi was too well-polished and while it was inconceivable that he had known nothing about Boyd's activities, there was insufficient evidence to prove he had siphoned off any of the funds.'

'So when did you develop an interest in D'albo?'

'The services have been tracking his movements since the fraud. We were worried for a time, that with his American upbringing, he had another agenda.'

'Spying?' Green whispered.

'We can never be too careful. Neither the US intelligence services nor Albion have been alerted to our suspicions. They would knee-jerk and shut D'albo down, preventing us from ultimately discovering what he's up to.'

'Ahem,' the waiter softly cleared his throat. He planted two plates safely on the table. The delicious waft of the pies masked the cellar's musky odour.

'Jack,' Green waved his fork at his friend. 'Can we get to the point?'

'Which is?' Jack mouthed as he blew on a chunk of steaming pastry.

'Scott Carty: do you know what happened to him?'

'I am coming to that shortly!' he snapped back. 'Boyd was offered a chance to avoid a lengthy prison stay on the condition that he agreed to help us uncover D'albo's *nuclear* activities. He served a short custodial sentence in order to avoid suspicion, before being released.' Jack paused momentarily, as he chomped on a kidney.

'D'albo bided his time but then took the bait, re-employing Boyd as an unwitting helper in a much larger scam – and framing Carty in the process.'

'The bastard! And what exactly was Boyd meant to do for the agencies?' Green asked impatiently.

Jack looked around to check the status of the cellar. 'We feared that D'albo was trading weapons-grade Plutonium, but Boyd soon told us otherwise, having learned that the man was negotiating the removal of spent nuclear waste from various foreign states.'

'Which ones?'

'Sorry that's classified.'

'So D'albo is acting as a middle-man?'

'Of a sort, and his Russian friends organise the rest – dumping the waste.' Jack's eyes narrowed with a clear distaste for the whole set up. 'There's one point that defies explanation, though. The intelligence shows that its final destination is the Irkutsk region, in Eastern Siberia.'

Green looked puzzled. 'Does that mean something?'

'Implicitly, yes, there are no nuclear waste storage facilities anywhere near there.'

'Couldn't it be going to a military base instead?'

'Unlikely. We know all of them! It just doesn't make sense. And what's more, just before Boyd's death he alerted us to a trip D'albo made to Moscow, to meet with the senior executives of an obscure Japanese trade house. The relevance of that meeting only emerged when we remembered the recent closure of T.H.O.R.P, the UK's nuclear reprocessing plant, earlier this year.'

Green nodded. 'Yes, I read about that. It was due to a leak, serious enough to be classified by the International Atomic Energy Authority as a major incident!'

'Let's not get distracted by that. The Japanese have, for many years, been sending spent waste to T.H.O.R.P for reprocessing into MOX – a mixed oxide which can then be re-used in modern reactors, as a fuel.'

'And let me guess. D'albo's providing an alternative while T.H.O.R.P is shut, right?'

'The Japanese executives believe that D'albo was and still is, acting, in some unofficial capacity for the UK, as a back door solution.'

'How do you know all this?'

'We have our methods.'

'And D'albo has negotiated the dumping of this Japanese waste in Siberia?'

'Yes; leaving the logistics to his Russian partners. It's a hugely profitable business.'

Green let out a muted sigh. 'Why haven't the Japanese approached the Russians through the official channels?'

'Probably to avoid bringing attention to such a sensitive issue and the ensuing embarrassment.'

'And you're not going to break any of this to your Russian counterparts, right?'

Jack clasped his hands in front of his face, his eyes scanning his friend's as he mentally measured his next sentence. 'With their suspicions that Scott Carty was a spy, we cannot go to them. They will simply pay us lip service while tipping off D'albo's Russians and ultimately him.'

'But can't the Japanese help at all?'

'If we openly ask, then that might threaten the good bilateral relationship that exists.'

'Does it matter?'

'Of course it does and anyway, we would be no closer to understanding exactly what is happening to the waste and at what level, inside Russia, D'albo's partners are operating.'

Puzzlement washed over Green's face. He drummed his fingertips together, pondering the comment. 'Jack. I'm not very experienced in these matters but clearly you're going to need some inside help.'

'Actually, we already have it.'

'You do!'

'Yes, from the Chinese!' A wry smile crept across the Whitehall man's lips.

'You've asked the Chinese!'

'They actually alerted us, concerned by D'albo's approach; floating commercial terms for the lifting of spent waste from China. Since then, they have been monitoring the movements of the Japanese cargos to their final destination in Russia.' He paused to cross his legs and brush off the sharp creases of his trousers.

'I sense, though, that the Chinese are more interested in something else, and I've been in this game far too long not to listen to my hunches.'

'So what is it?'

'No idea, but D'albo is the key to whatever it might be and he probably discovered that Boyd was a mole seeking this information.'

Green pulled back from the table. 'But you don't suspect that Scott has anything to do with all this?'

'No. It appears Carty never planned to go to Russia and it's unlikely that he died in the helicopter crash. We do know, though, that at least two of the Americans who did, were spies.'

'Did the Russians or the Chinese tell you this?'

Jack neatly swerved the question. 'D'albo timed Carty's disappearance perfectly to frame him with the fraud at Albion.'

'But your information will exonerate him of that, right?'

'Possibly. I'm no expert in trading derivatives but from what Boyd told us and the deductions of our forensics thus far, this is my understanding of how D'albo's scam operated.' Jack sat back and began his hypothesis.

'CentralniySib's trading relationship with Albion was handled through a special purpose vehicle, a small commodity company, based in the BVI – The British Virgin Islands. We know that its nominee shareholders were acting for D'albo and others, mainly Russians. It was used to place two-way business, fraudulently, on behalf of CentralniySib without its management's knowledge.'

'*Two-way* business?' Green blurted, absentmindedly sliding an over-sized signet ring back and forth along his little finger.

'That's right. The BVI company credit line was underwritten with a Letter of Comfort, supposedly issued by CentralniySib. This essentially acted as a parent guarantee, allowing it to purchase options granted by Albion, on credit without having to pay any upfront premiums for them.' Jack grinned sublimely. 'But the problem is that the Letter of Comfort was a fake.'

'Hah!'

'And it gets worse. In the two months before Carty disappeared, Albion began purchasing a huge number of crude oil call options, supposedly granted by CentralniySib. Albion's management, though, had insisted on a performance guarantee as collateral, to give assurance that these options would be performed upon by the Russians.'

'Don't tell me. They issued a dummy guarantee?'

'Well done, Gordon. Albion paid millions for the oil option premiums, straight into the BVI entity's bank account.'

'That's unbelievable! And no one in Albion questioned this at the time?'

'Not deeply enough and there are two explanations why. D'albo had instigated a shadow trading operation, allowing one of Albion's directors to buy these options outside of its systems.'

'And the other?'

'There was a high turnover of back office staff, particularly those handling this account. D'albo regularly moved people around and Boyd suspected that a number were in the man's pocket. Boyd also revealed that the option positions had been closed out just before Carty's disappearance. More worrying, though, is what he found in a locked cabinet in Carty's office...the original copies of CentralniySib's contracts, all conveniently countersigned by Scott Carty, implicating him in the fraud.'

Green gently swirled the Merlot around his glass. 'Was it Carty's signature?' he asked sombrely.

'Unlikely.' Jack swept a hand over his glistening hair again.

'Do you think Albion will go down because of the fraud?'

'Probably not, but it's a huge dent to the bottom line and shareholders will be seeking heads. The Board has already appointed external forensic investigators and the SFO has been called in. Whatever the outcome it begs the question, *who* is Albion going to chase? CentralniySib insists it's a fraud committed by Carty and is in the process of filing legal proceedings in London and New York for full disclosure of Albion's records. It is stating that it never had any knowledge of these trades or the fraudulent guarantees. Albion's legal counsel and compliance team are crying the same.'

'That's ironic.'

'Yes, it is, especially as D'albo has recently produced the diligence paperwork on the BVI entity – all signed-off by Scott Carty, again!'

'Giving him a perfect alibi – the pig!'

'D'albo will no doubt lose his job but he and his partners have got away with defrauding CentralniySib and Albion out of millions and leaving Carty, Boyd and Elena Isotova as the prime suspects. Conveniently, all three are dead or missing. Without them it's going to be virtually impossible to finger D'albo.'

The waiter hovered again. Jack acknowledged him as Green pushed his glass out, holding its stem close to the base. The young man filled both glasses and then collected the gravy-soaked plates. As he did they sat silently, gazing at each other. Green knew Jack's methods were based on a *quid pro quo* sharing of information. So far he had volunteered nothing and had not been asked to, yet he sensed something else.

'Gordon, we've intercepted some other information.'

'More intelligence?' Green made light of the comment.

'A Russian special forces team, operating in the forests around Lake Baikal, were under instruction to eliminate an English foreigner – a spy.'

'But isn't that where Scott was last seen before he disappeared?' Green retorted.

'Exactly! The intelligence is hazy but we understand that the whole team were wiped out.'

An inexorable smile grew on Green's face.

'Do you have anything you should be telling me, Gordon?'

'It's just a hunch but just like yours, mine often point at truths.'

'And just what is your hunch telling you?'

'I had a dream that Scott is alive and needs help.'

'We can't act on dreams, Gordon, but if he has survived, he is the one person who might know what D'albo is doing with that nuclear waste and why the Chinese are so damn interested in it.'

'So you're not worried about him being missing or dead, or the pain that his family are going through!'

'Gordon, these are matters of strategic importance to the country.'

'A loss of business for T.H.O.R.P you mean!'

Jack shrugged. 'The agencies are exploring all avenues. We're aware that Carty was having an off and on affair with a wealthy young woman.'

'Yes, he hinted at that to me.'

'The police have brought her in for questioning. In any event, all the people closely associated with him will be under surveillance for some time, partly for their own protection. Gordon, if you know anything...'

'Yes, Jack, I understand. You've made that quite clear!'

Fifty

Semey railway station, North-Eastern Kazakhstan.

'Stop, James!' Carty called out. Waking and startled, he found Yulia's bright eyes gazing down on him. He had fallen asleep with his head on her lap.

'Good morning,' she said coolly, unravelling strands of her hair.

He quickly sat up and winced at the sharp stabbing pain under his ribs.

'What is wrong?'

'I hurt myself in the back of the jeep.'

'Let me see.' She pulled up his shirt and ran her warm fingers along his lower ribcage, pressing gently. He yelped.

'It is not serious, but I do not know how you say it in English?'

Carty glanced down at her hands and saw the tell-tale dark blue colour emerging below his skin.

'It's what we call a bruise.'

'Yes, a *bruise*,' she slowly repeated the word, locking it into her vocabulary.

He smiled back, taken by the sight of her shaggy bleached mane clashing with a washed-out, pea-green polo neck, zipped to top. She fluttered her long lashes and steadily poured a coffee, conscious of his attentions.

'Who's James?'

'My son.'

'Do you have any other children?'

'No, just the one.'

'But are you married?'

'Yes. It's been a long time since I saw my wife.'

Her honey-coloured eyebrows arched at the response. 'How long?'

'More than a month, I think,' he answered, distracted by people milling around near the car. 'Where are we?'

'The station at Semey: we will catch the train from here shortly.' She handed him a chipped enamel cup.

'Semey?'

'The local town: its name comes from the indigenous peoples' word for the seven-halled Buddhist temple that once stood nearby.

'*Dobre Utra!* Maxim's throaty voice erupted in as he woke from a nap in the front seat. The unshaven Russian seemed to be in continual state of semi-consciousness, his bleary eyes straining through heavy swollen lids. He lit up a cigarette and began a conversation with Yulia, juggling a large map across the space between the seats and pointing at what Carty recognised to be a rail network. A subdued fear stirred at the prospect of the journey awaiting them across this vast, landlocked country.

'Are you from around here?' Carty asked her.

'I was born just south of Semey – Semipalatinsk, as it was originally called.'

'Semipalatinsk – you mean the Soviet nuclear testing facility?' His eyes widened.

'Yes.' Her eyes dropped. 'Over 100 atomic tests were carried out near here, first above ground and then below, before they were stopped at the end of the 1980s. Even now children are still being born deformed from its legacy.' A tear erupted and trickled down her cheek. 'Chinese companies have traded clothes and plastic furniture in exchange for scrap copper cable from the test sites. Melted down, it is made into cheap alloy jewellery and exported, spreading radioactive harm across the world to other innocents,' her voice broke.

The Englishman put a hand on her shoulder, coughing as the acrid smoke of the cheap tobacco caught the back of his throat.

Yulia immediately barked at Maxim, forcing him to open a window and sheepishly flick the lit cigarette out.

'It's now time we were going.' She boldly rubbed her moist eyes and produced two beige tickets from her bag, waving them in his face to conceal her temporary weakness. Carty's eyes caught hers and his heart sank with the recognition that behind the steely resolve sat the same raw tenderness he had found and loved in Lena.

A dousing of rain earlier that morning had left huge puddles lapping at their feet as they hurriedly took their bags from Maxim and dashed into the station.

She halted momentarily to scan the flicking departures board.

'Quickly, Scott!' she yelled and then pelted down the platform.

'This carriage.' She stopped abruptly, checking its number before urging him to climb up its chipped, cast iron steps. Almost immediately the train lurched forward causing hapless passengers in front of him to stumble and grab out at anything fixed down. Carty locked his legs and held the door handle, catching Yulia on his chest as she stuttered back a step, before steadying herself. His free arm naturally caught her around her midriff. Instinctively she held onto it and tilted her head back, her hair sweeping his face.

'Thank you.'

'My pleasure.' He grinned.

'Here we are, on the Turk Sib railway!' she announced, ushering him into the compartment.

'This isn't too bad!' he exclaimed, looking around and noticing two small bundles of clean linen and blankets on the bench seat. 'Back in England we call this a *sleeper*,' he nonchalantly uttered.

'It's a *coupe*,' she stated, stepping up and straddling across the two seats, close to his face as she threw her rucksack onto the storage space above the door. 'We can fold down these to sleep on later.' She matter-of-factly tapped at one of the upper benches still latched back to the cabin wall.

'How long will it take to get to Almaty?'

'Officially 22 hours, but who knows!' She jumped down and pulled off her top, her nipples were now clearly visible through the smooth white vest.

'I will fetch some hot water so that we can make tea.' She winked at him and then disappeared into the corridor.

Carty perched down on the edge of the seat to remove his boots and relax. The temperature was warmer than Siberia and the hustle outside in the corridor unsettled him as did the stifling smoke from desperate passengers lighting up. Leaning over, he slid shut the compartment's door.

The calm hypnotic sway of the carriage urged him to lie back on the tan leatherette, propping his head on the rough blankets as the sun's brilliance now suffused through the net curtain. A pink, plastic rose in a vase on the flip-up table below the window drew his smile. It seemed so perfect and yet so false, rather like his life up until his experience at Baikal.

He found himself in a familiar place, his old sixth-form mess room. A throng of fellow students had gathered there, cheering as they congregated around a visitor.

'It's Tycho Brahe, the noted 16th century astronomer!' one of them told him, excitedly.

'Tycho Brahe!' Unable to believe what he had heard, he pushed into the crowd, eager to get a closer view.

The students were raising hands and taking turns to ask questions of Brahe and then listen, in awe, to his answers. Soon enough, a hushed silence replaced the clamour, as all eyes focused on Brahe's finger, aimed directly at Scott Carty.

Embarrassed, Carty looked around at the staring eyes for some seconds, and then indignantly blurted his doubts.

'How can you be Tycho Brahe? He died over 400 years ago?'

There was a collective gasp of shock but the stranger smiled, sagaciously.

'The answer to that lies not in who I am but in my name.'

Slowly, he emerged from the nap, rubbing his eyes, momentarily confused by his surroundings. Yulia had been sitting with her shoes removed and legs tucked supplely into a lotus position.

'Here you are.' She offered him a glass of tea, in a decorative silver holder. 'You were mumbling in your sleep.'

Sitting up he felt stiffness along his neck muscles.

'Were you dreaming?' she asked.

'Yes, yes, I was.'

'What was it about?'

Carty's expression was one of surprise as he took the glass.

'I believe that dreams are important.' Her gaze lingered on the Englishman. 'Will you tell me it?' she asked coyly already moving over to sit next to him, her intimacy unassuming.

As he recounted the dream to her, he simultaneously noted down the main points.

'This astronomer, Brahe,' she paused. 'Can you write his name for me?'

He stared at her questioningly for a second. 'Why?'

'Because he said that it would give an answer.'

Carty couldn't argue. Green had told him that the spoken word in a dream held tremendous importance. He scribbled out the letters that spelled the name.

TYCHO BRAHE

She moved closer to him. 'Hmm, that's interesting. Some of these letters can be pronounced differently depending if they're spoken in Russian or English.'

'Really, which?'

'Well,' she pointed, 'the *Y* is pronounced as *OO*, *H* as an *N*, and the *C* like your English *S*,' she said, sounding the letter through her teeth.

A wry grin accompanied his nod, recognising the first letter from *СФИНКС* – *Sphinx*'s Cyrillic spelling.

She persisted. '*B* can be pronounced like the English *V* and *E* is *YEH*.' She paused momentarily, pondering something. 'Hah! And all of the letters of *CARTY* are contained in the name *TYCHO BRAHE!*' she blurted.

Is she right?

He wrote out his surname and then proceeded to cross out each letter that matched, looking blankly over those remaining.

HOBHE

'Does this mean anything in Russian?' he probed.

She scanned it briefly, shaking her head. 'It's pronounced *Novney* but it means nothing...although,' her voice hovered as she mouthed the word silently again.

'What is it?' Carty sensed that she had hit on something.

'Well, it's one letter different to another word.' She took the pencil and wrote briskly.

HOBOE

'This word is pronounced *Noveyeh*, which means *new*.'

Carty quietly tapped the end of a pencil against his teeth, mulling a clue.

'You said that the Cyrillic *E* is actually *YEH* when it's spoken, right?'

'Yes.'

A shot of excitement raced across his face. 'Then *HOBHE* does mean new!' Instinctively he understood the message of the dream.

'It does? How?' She seemed puzzled.

'Yes. In *HOBHE* the last two letters, *H* and *E*, are the same as in the surname *BRAHE*, where they are pronounced in English as one sound – *YEH!*'

She frowned, still not fully understanding.

'The dream was speaking to me in code. *TYCHO BRAHE* is an anagram. It means *NEW CARTY* in a mixture of both English and Russian – a marriage of the two languages!'

The thrill in his eyes was suddenly quelled by the sound of a rigid tap-tap on the door. Yulia shot a worried look at him and putting her finger to her mouth to indicate silence, she rose and slowly slid the door back. A stout, middle-aged woman in a bright blue uniform flashed with daffodil-yellow epaulettes filled the space

'*Documenti!*' she uttered, curtly.

'She wants to see our passports. Let me do the talking,' Yulia announced as she stroked his cheek, lovingly.

Carty smiled, sensing a passion lurking in Yulia's play-acting. She held his hand, letting it tantalisingly slip away so that the tips of their fingers hovered together for a split second. Then he reached into his case and handed the passport over.

The official scrutinised Carty's photograph, looking at him several times before breaking off into an exchange with Yulia. The veneer of the conversation appeared polite but carried an obvious tension.

'She's asking why you've been in Kazakhstan for such a long time,' Yulia calmly advised before turning back to the woman, to continue her patter. The guard's granite expression suddenly cracked into a curious smile and she handed back the documents.

'*Spasibo.*' Yulia thanked her and immediately turned to straddle Carty's lap, placing her arms around his neck and nuzzling her lips to his. Tenderly, she slipped her tongue into his mouth. Carty closed his eyes and played along as the door slid firmly shut.

Yulia pulled away seconds later, chuckling. 'I'm sorry but I needed to make sure she understood.'

'Understood what?'

'I told her that we were getting married and that I had insisted that you come with me to Semey to meet my family. She was surprised that you had remained so long in the country.'

'Married!' Carty was astonished at the blithe comment. The kiss, though, had seemed genuine enough.

'Yes, it was necessary to give that cover story. She was suspicious and I was worried that she might have remembered the newspaper reports.'

That's what Lubimov said might happen.

'What did they say?'

'That there was a helicopter accident but an Englishman was not among the dead. It was assumed that you were a spy.'

'Pure James Bond!' he cracked in his defence. She giggled.

'Then the television news suggested that you had faked your own death after committing fraud, stealing millions from your company.'

'Fraud!' Desperation froze his face.

'That's a shame. I was hoping it was true!' She grinned.

'Is that why you kissed me?'

'No!' She shot him a deflated look. 'One of your accomplices went missing in Eastern Europe. They assumed that he would try to contact you in Russia.'

'That's a stupid thing to assume.'

'Yes, it is. He was found dead – drowned!'

Drowned! The word bounced around his head. *Who did she mean?*

'Do you remember the man's name?'

'It was short and sounded British.'

'D'albo?'

She shook her head.

'Boyd?' The word leaked timorously from his lips.

'Yes, yes, I think that was it!'

Carty's frame shuddered as he buried his head in his hands.

My God, am I indirectly responsible for the death of Mark Boyd?

'Boyd, was your friend?' she asked, running her long fingers gently across his scalp.

'Yes. I can't believe it,' he stuttered.

A few seconds passed before Yulia swung a toned leg balletically over his head and behind his back so that she could fully embrace him.

Green had tried to warn him about D'albo as had *Basilides*, yet he had allowed his own pursuit of power to ignore the danger and realise the depths to which D'albo had sunk. It was far worse than he believed it could have ever been and it reared a terrifying fear that the man might go to any lengths if he knew Carty was still alive.

Diane and James would then be in danger. His home had probably been turned over by the police, searching for clues to his disappearance and the location of the supposed embezzled funds. It felt as if the floor of his world had disappeared beneath his feet and he was suspended in that awful moment, before the drop into the abyss. The bitter taste of gall flooded his mouth as helplessness mixed with anger consumed him. He closed his eyes.

Patience. A woman's voice reassured him.

Fifty One

A light lunch of sardines, black bread, and coffee sweetened with condensed milk, left Carty feeling more optimistic. Yulia silently slipped out of the carriage, removing the empty cans and rubbish. He had enjoyed the simple meal and the fact that she respected his unspoken need for quiet.

Albion thinks that I'm a criminal.

He began churning over and over what he would tell his interrogators, if and when he arrived in London. The fact that he had been in Russia was irrefutable -- he had made calls to Davina using the satellite phone.

But why would they believe my story? It's just too incredible.

The image of the machine darted again into his mind, bringing a smile to his face. He had already forgotten about it, in his mad journey out of Russia.

The grinding of the wheels, and then a jolt, signalled that they were approaching a major stop. He moved over to the window, taking in the panorama of the vast, flat scrub-land. Numerous small holdings stood out, the homes of peasant farmers whose forebears had been forced into Kruschev's *virgin lands* programme in the mid 1950s, collectively growing food in exchange for basic housing, electricity and education.

'You were away for some time,' he commented as Yulia re-entered. Her bra-less form had attracted the attention of two grizzled Kyrghiz men hanging around in the corridor, cigarettes drooping from their gaping mouths. She slid the door closed.

'I've been talking to the guard again,' she answered. 'I was gently testing her to see if she knew anything about you.'

'And did she?'

'No, I don't think so.'

There were a countless number of stops during the afternoon. Carty wiled away time between dozing and wandering up and down the carriage, apprehensively gnawing over the information Yulia had dropped on him and suspicious that passengers might recognise him.

The sky was darkening when he re-entered the coupe.

'This is Tom and Tobias from Germany.' Yulia licked at a spoonful of honey. She had been sharing tea and Russian chocolates with a couple of European back-packers, young men in their early 20s exploring the old silk route through Kazakhstan.

'Hi, I'm Dave,' Carty said, shaking hands cautiously. They were infants when the Berlin wall had been torn down, but were keen to explore the remnants of the Soviet world in an attempt to understand the effect that regime had had on their home country.

As they made polite goodbyes, Yulia flirted, pecking them each on the check. Carty waited impatiently for them to leave.

'Yulia,' he looked pensively at her. 'Isn't it time you told me about the arrangements in Almaty?'

She shifted along the seat to casually peer both ways along the corridor before sliding the door shut and flipping the security latch. Then, she sat back, her hands underneath her thighs.

'We will arrive in Almaty early tomorrow morning.'

Carty stole nearer, openly hungry for the details.

'And will be driven straight to the airport.'

'How far is it from the station?'

'Probably 30 minutes.'

'And the flight?'

'You have a business class ticket, don't you?'

'I do. But what if there are no available seats?' His voice seemed panicky.

She leant forward and placed a finger delicately over his lips.

'We will wait. It will be safe.' Then reaching past his cheek she pushed back the flaking, chrome-plated catch, releasing the bunk and gently lowering it down to the horizontal.

'Sleep?' she offered.

He smiled, thankful that this woman was with him and able to calm his fears.

'If you need the bathroom, you should go now, the condition of the toilet will only get worse.'

His eyebrows arched at the remark and quickly, he grabbed one of the small towels before slipping back out into the corridor.

The coupe's light was extinguished when he returned and Yulia was already curled up on her bunk, eyes shut. The blind was down obscuring the last light of dusk but even so, he felt conspicuous as he took off his combats and clambered up onto the narrow bunk.

'Make sure that you lock all your belongings away in your bag. There are plenty of thieves on these trains,' she murmured.

'I will. Good night, Yulia.'

She was silent.

The stolid atmosphere had rapidly cooled with the breeze through the dropped window. Spreading a blanket over his torso, he propped the rough pillow against the wall and rested back with both hands under his head.

A perverse excitement filled him. Tomorrow would be the last day of this journey and he pored over the things he wanted to share with his son. He had been a poor father in James' developing years: the only activity in which he had shown any interest was coaching him to kick a football. In his self-absorbed way he had sacrificed his family by putting his career first. A pang of guilt found him gazing unfocused at the light squeezing in through the gap beneath the door and straining to hear Yulia's soft breaths, hardly audible above the rhythmical trundle of the wheels.

Periodically, his slumber would be disturbed by an approaching train's distinctive horn, accompanied by the dramatic suction of the carriages as it passed.

A pressure suddenly descended on Carty's bruised ribs. Startled, his eyes shot open to find a gloved hand smothering his mouth and a knife blade simultaneously pressed into his throat. Petrified, he expected the end but the weapon was immediately yanked away. Yulia had wrestled back the intruder only to be thrown back forcefully onto the hard lino floor. Carty instantly slid off the bunk, quickly scanning his friend's slumped form before the stranger lunged the knife at him. *Spin!* a voice in his head commanded. He twisted his torso, deflecting the thrust to his abdomen while simultaneously chopping at the attacker's throat. The figure reeled back momentarily and then slashed out again but Carty anticipated it and dodged, slamming his heel onto the intruder's knee. The figure stalled and in the muted light, Carty picked out its desperate eyes. Something about them looked odd, as if they didn't belong. But then the blade was being aimed towards his heart and he tensed, knocking away the attacking arm, forgetting Boris' crucial training. The knife span to the floor but the assassin had already grabbed Carty's hair and slammed his head back against the metal bunk. Dazed, the Englishman crumpled, waiting for the killer to collect the cold steel and sever his life. But instead, the attacker hovered, frozen for a second before crashing down by his feet.

How? He was momentarily confused. Yulia flicked on the light.

'Are you okay?' she asked.

Carty silently gazed down at the lifeless figure. A hunter's knife was protruding from its lower back and Yulia was squatting alongside, removing the impromptu stocking mask. She shook her head in confusion, glancing back up at the Englishman.

'It's a woman!'

'What!'

'We're lucky she wasn't a professional otherwise we would both have bullets in our brains.'

'Was she simply an opportunist then?'

'Probably. But now we need to dispose of the body.'

Fifty Two

As he wound up the blind to meet the crack of daybreak, the coupe's atmosphere hung heavy with the sense of death.

Will this ever end? Carty asked himself, gently rubbing the swollen base of his skull as he slowly churned over the night's madness.

Yulia had waited until a number of passengers had left the train in the early hours and then dumped the body off between stations. All traces of blood had been mopped up using bed sheets, which were also disposed of out the window.

He shuddered with the stark realisation that he was now an accessory to murder and that if he couldn't exit this country today it was likely he would be found. The Kazakhs would then have a good reason to hold him.

'We have almost an hour before we arrive,' Yulia, looking strained, broke his train of thought.

'I need to visit the bathroom,' he responded, tentatively dropping a foot down to meet the lower bunk.

Shaven and with a plaster covering the wound to his neck, he began the ritual of changing into his suit and polished shoes. As he did, forgotten memories of his former incarnation at Albion, stirred again and he distracted himself by looking out of the window.

A rich green wilderness, vastly different from the dusty arena over which the sun had set the previous day now presented itself, and in the distance the *Tien Shan* awaited his return. *Datchas* and farm buildings had become more numerous, and a plethora of overhead cables and shunted wagons, sitting in a tangle of sidings, indicated their approach into Almaty's hinterland.

'You won't need these anymore.' She took the fatigues and lumber shirt from him and pulled down the window to toss them out, along with his trainers.

'Forget what happened here last night. You're alive and going home today, *New* Carty!' She hugged him and then, picking up her rucksack, slid the door open to meet the throng already gathered in the corridor. Their expressions showed open resentment as Yulia pushed into the rough queue and without any qualms, turned to hurriedly pull him in behind her.

The station was a grand but tired building, hinting at a history of romance and excitement. On the main concourse, mop-headed men claiming to be taxi drivers gesticulated to the Englishman, clearly a magnet for their services. He scanned them nervously, fearful that any of them could be a potential killer.

Yulia forced him on ahead, towards a squat local man with kind black eyes and a full-moon face. Outside, he ushered the two of them into a customised jeep, its centre of gravity sitting precariously high on oversized wheels and its body covered in a patchwork of spot-welded panels. Inside, it reeked of diesel. Yulia gave Carty a reassuring wink before breaking off into local dialect with the driver who immediately crunched into gear and accelerated away.

Here he was, in Almaty once again. Its local Kazakh name, *Alma Ata* – the city of big apples, originated from the famous white-skinned variety that grew in the region: the original gene pool for all of the world's sweet apples.

'How do you feel?'

'Nervous,' he replied sharply, attempting a smile. His eyes, though, showed trepidation.

'We will be there soon!' Yulia's arm slipped over the back of the seat and reached for his hand.

An aircraft flying low in the distance signalled that they were near and shortly the vehicle swung off the road into the airport's car park. Yulia stepped out, thanking the humble driver as she struggled to fasten her hair in the gusty breeze.

'When we are at the check-in counter just let me do the talking,' she instructed, leading Carty past the guards and onto the concourse. 'Our officials are experts in making innocent citizens feel guilty here.'

'Don't I know it!'

'We'll avoid the European staff.' She directed him over to a small queue forming for the Economy class. Carty lowered his face and they both slunk into its ranks.

Soon they were invited forward. Yulia indicated to the young female representative in her local tongue that only the Englishman would be travelling.

'Can I have your documents, please?' the representative requested, tilting her head quaintly. Surprised at her polished English, Carty produced his passport and ticket as Yulia strained across the counter, chatting persuasively with the woman. It was clear that she was replaying the 'marriage' story again and as she did Carty caught the woman's name tag and silently mouthed her name, *Rosa*. The woman smiled economically at Yulia and looked over to him, as if seeking his confirmation of the yarn. His warm smile melted her doubt.

'I'm sorry, Mr Carty, but this is not the Business Class check-in.'

He raised his sandy brows and shrugged.

'It shouldn't be a problem,' she said, beaming and tapping on the keyboard for some seconds. 'There are seats available but there's an additional charge of $200. The tariff has recently increased.'

'Why?' Yulia argued.

Carty touched her arm, distracting her. 'Do you take travellers cheques, Rosa?' he countered.

'No, sir, you will need to exchange them on the concourse,' – she indicated behind them – 'and then pay with cash at the airline desk. Please present this.' She passed him a docket.

'Would you keep my seat while I do that?' His question was charm itself.

'Yes, of course, I have already entered you into the system. But please, Mr Carty, do not be too long.'

'Thank you so very much, Rosa,' he said, grabbing Yulia's hand to walk away.

It took 15 minutes. A boarding pass had already been prepared and was waiting for him but as Rosa flicked through his passport again, a discreet frown emerged over her sculpted eyebrows. She looked up to wave at an official across the way.

'What's wrong?' he asked, squeezing Yulia's hand.

'Your passport needs to be checked. It shouldn't take long.'

Carty looked over his shoulder to spy a swarthy official whose features hinted of Caucasian descent. The man nodded as he unhurriedly dispensed with his duties to purposefully amble towards them.

'This gentleman will ask you some questions.' Rosa's announcement caused the passengers waiting in line behind them to audibly moan. Yulia's body language was clearly agitated by the man's manner and she shot an uneasy glance at Carty.

'Mr Carty, why do you not have a *propiska* in your passport?' The official mocked a stern air as he flicked through the pages. He was referring to the official stamp that should have been made by the local authority in Semey, allowing Carty to remain in its jurisdiction.

'I told you, Yulia,' Carty volubly announced, cocking his head and grinning. He then turned back the official, spotting his name tag. 'But I am coming back to marry her!'

Yulia had meanwhile searched in her bag and handed over a prepared letter. The man took it reluctantly. It explained that

Carty had been invited to visit the small, regionally owned power station outside Semey, as a consultant.

'Are you married, Mr Kornobaev?' he humoured, clearly not concerned by the charade. Kornabaev understood and awkwardly straightening himself, handed back the passport and letter, bowing his head slightly forward. 'Thank you, Mr Carty, have a safe flight.'

'I recommend that you pass through immigration as quickly as possible,' Rosa pronounced, smiling and utterly taken by the Englishman's cool composure.

'What did you do back there?' A stunned Yulia probed as they headed back towards departures.

'New Carty.' He winked, swinging his arm around her midriff.

'Well, Mr New Carty, you're going to need this when you go through passport control.' She grinned and passed him a filled-out immigration form, already pre-stamped and dated.

'Now.' She paused, screwing up her nose into a grin that filled her delicate face. '*Dengi Davay!*'

'What?' Carty was lost.

Her voice lowered. 'It means, hand over the money.'

He beamed and reached inside his jacket to slide the grimy wad of Tenge notes down its lining and into her palm. She casually looked around and then slipped it into her jeans pocket.

'I hope it's enough,' he murmured

'It will be.'

He flicked his wrist over to note the time. 'I think I should be going.'

Her eyes lowered; she had become emotionally interested in the Englishman and as they joined the thinning departures line, she turned to him to hold his cheeks in her palms and gently peck his lips.

'Please remember me.'

He searched her eyes, understanding that they had shared a priceless time. 'I will.'

'Yes, of course you will.' She smiled cynically back.

He passed swiftly through the gate and lingered in its hinterland beyond long enough to wave to the raw beauty who had cared for him in these last days. She blew a kiss back.

The Business Class cabin rang with excited chatter and a glass of Bollinger lifted his spirits as the aircraft settled at its cruising altitude. He quietly slipped on a pair of headphones, relishing the first taste of a film after his long sojourn. A meal followed and the alcohol soon took its effect, allowing the impact of all that had transpired in these last months to fully sink in. He had become a new man, *but at what cost?* An innocent fugitive, he had survived assassination. *I should be dead.*

An image of Boris' rich grin lit up his dark thoughts. *He is the brother I never had.*

His eyes flickered closed and an ironic smile washed over his face as he sensed the ticking of the *Komandirski* on his wrist, triggering a thought of his friend Lubimov and the machine.

Was it just a hoax? He mused as its glowing, surreal picture irrupted once more – *a technology that might change the world forever?*

Yet, even if Ivan Yegorovich's prediction of solar eruptions engulfing the Earth were to be taken seriously, the machine would still be inaccessible, hidden in the depths of Siberia. It seemed an impossible dichotomy that he, Scott Carty, could do nothing to change.

And then an anxiety reared, denying him sleep.

What lies ahead in London?

Fifty Three

Heathrow Airport, London.

His breath quickened on moving forward to hand over his passport. This moment, arriving home, was one he had lived and relived in his head many times in the Siberian *taiga* and scanning the immigration official's blank face he felt a perverse need for recognition.

Then, as he was waved through on to British soil he felt strangely lost, the longing he had anticipated in being reunited with Diane and James, dowsed by the expectation of being branded a criminal in absentia.

Head lowered, he ambled down through the customs hall, his tunnel vision rendering him oblivious to the two ill-suited officials sauntering obliquely towards him.

'Excuse me, sir,' one asked, his dead eyes panning Carty. 'Could we look through your luggage?'

'Why? It's a suit-carrier.'

'We can see that sir. Please place it on the counter.'

He complied, his hands trembling.

'Can I ask where you came from today, sir?' he asked while indicating for Carty to open the bag.

'Almaty...Kazakhstan.' Carty unzipped it.

The man rummaged through his scant possessions.

'Thank you: now, could I see your passport?'

'Why? Are you a customs official?'

'That's what my identity card says.' He curtly flashed the talisman hanging around his neck.

Carty shrugged and reluctantly complied.

The official thumbed through it and then suddenly stopped. He glared up. 'Mr Carty...you're Scott Carty!'

Hearing his name spoken in English, seemed unfamiliar, and for a moment he was disorientated and not quite sure if it was he they were addressing.

'You're a missing person.'

'Not anymore!' he quipped, attempting to play down the situation but the non-descript bureaucrat wasn't buying it.

'Please will you come with us?' The other man had moved into his space and indicated towards the far end of the customs hall.

The instinct to challenge raced as Carty sized him up, but then decided against it, noticing a uniformed policeman slunk in the shadows with a Heckler & Koch MP5 submachine gun slung across his body armour. Carty signalled a muted despair to the officer but it was met with impartiality.

'Sit down, Mr Carty.' The instruction was firm. Carty submitted, now perspiring copiously as he recalled the bare interview room in Almaty. He took some comfort, though, that at least he was now in his home country.

Soon a sharp rap at the door jarred him.

'Mr Carty?' a dishevelled, plain-clothes officer asked as he stepped in. 'You are Scott Carty, correct?'

'Yes, that's right.'

'I am D.I. Johnson. Do you understand why you're being held?'

'Is it because I have been missing for some time?' he uttered, pulling a face.

Johnson grinned meagrely as he shook his head. 'Yes, and you're suspected of conspiracy to a fraud.'

'But that's simply rubbish!'

'And you're also under suspicion for the murder of Mark Boyd. I'm going to read you your rights.'

'It's all bullshit. I'm not guilty of these charges and I don't appreciate your insinuations,' his temper flared. 'You can put that on the record!'

'Very well, that's noted,' Johnson stated, indicating for the uniformed officer to move in and cuff Carty.

'What about a lawyer and a telephone call?' Bewilderment had now supplanted his anger.

'You will get those later, after you have answered some questions.'

He was brusquely escorted out and into fire-exit stair case, which went down several floors into a dimly lit car park. It was his first breath of English fresh air for many months and although it was tinged with aviation fuel and body odour, he still savoured its damp signature.

A Mercedes people-carrier was waiting, its engine humming.

That's odd! He reasoned, having spied its new number plate and tinted windows. As he approached, the vehicle's side door slid open. A seated stranger glared insidiously back.

'Get in!' the man rasped.

This isn't right. Carty resisted but he was shoved forward, sprawling onto his cuffed wrists. A thug stepped from the driver's side to haul him up onto the seat.

'Who are you?' Carty shouted angrily, scrutinising the stranger's vulpine features and lank hair.

'All of your questions will be answered shortly.'

Carty quickly scanned the interior, noticing a glass partition behind him, separating them from the driver. He baulked.

'Just so you know. I've just been read my rights and there are several witnesses to prove that I arrived at Heathrow, in case anything happens to me.'

There was no reply just a cold, merciless stare.

'What you're doing is immoral!'

'Perhaps,' the man smirked. 'But no more immoral than the crimes you've committed?'

'I'm innocent!'

'Yes, Scott, but technically you're dead!'

Having a complete stranger address him by his first name sounded sinister.

'No one expects you suddenly to show up after your own memorial service.' His top lip curled into a cruel smile. 'Only the Russians know you're alive and they want you back.'

'Hah, that's rich! There is no extradition treaty between Britain and Russia.'

'You've heard of rendition, haven't you?'

The comment chilled. He had heard the term before. Suspected terrorists had been *ghosted* through European capitals, held captive in transit, to be rendered to other regimes where torture was the norm.

'You're abusing my human rights and you have no evidence against me.'

'We will see,' he glowered, rubbing his strawberry-blonde stubble and relishing the effects his words had. 'Perhaps the Kazakhs will want to question you first, though.'

Does he know about the attack on the TurkSib?

A realisation had set in: the stranger and his cronies were acting in interests other than Her Majesty's Government.

But what do they want from me?

Carty steeled himself as he caught the sight of the west London skyline.

The car shortly pulled off the Cromwell Road and dived underground into another car park before stopping abruptly. As Carty stepped out the same lout grasped at his jacket lapel to yank him forward. Sensing the intention, Carty yielded, flowing with the force and twisting in concert with his own momentum to break the grip. The thug stumbled for an instant and then physically smothered Carty with his huge arms, flinging him through an emergency exit door. The impact shot a knifing pain across Carty's ribs, triggering the same anxiety he had experienced in crossing the Kazakhstan border, only a day or so before. But it was transient, lost as he was bundled into a service lift and taken up several floors.

Then, dragged out, one of his arms was cuffed to a chair before being wheeled into a darkened room.

The place hummed of stale air and for a moment hushed voices spoke outside.

It's Almaty airport all over again. He attempted humour but it did little to allay his fears. The situation was grave and he closed his eyes, seeking support from another place. Boris' voice sounded in his head, instantly transporting him back to that cool glade. Its familiar smells and fresh air re-energised him.

'So, Scott, have you decided yet?' the man uttered as he strolled in, smoking.

'Decided what?'

'If you want to go back to Russia?'

'You're making a massive mistake holding me like this.'

The laconic figure sat, rocking back in his chair to throw his feet up on the desk between them. 'So you don't deny it?'

'Deny what?'

'The fraud: we have the proof: you left a paper trail at Albion.'

'If that's the case, then I will be formally charged by the police.'

'You've already been charged.'

'Who by? You haven't revealed who you are. There's no formal interview process and no tape recorder. You and your cronies are not working for any recognised authority.'

'Believe me, we are,' he chuckled emptily. 'And we know the reasons why you were in Russia, Scott. We know all about the other business. Why don't you tell us who else was involved then you'll be released without charges.'

'Other business? Is this to do with the Americans?'

'Yes, the Americans!' the man reacted, suddenly pulling his feet back down and leaning forward on the desk.

'What do you know about them?'

'Not much: they wouldn't discuss their business.'

'So, you had them killed.'

Carty slowly shook his head as his eyes stung from the smoke.

That's Russian tobacco. He had recognised the distinct cloying aroma of Maxim's cigarettes.

'It's all right, Scott. You're going to have plenty of time to change your mind and tell us what we want to know!' the man sneered callously and then called out to his friends.

The thug re-entered and trolleyed Carty out, and down the corridor still cuffed to the chair. At its end, he was rammed into a small cell room and the cuffs were released. Then, in retaliation for Carty's earlier stunt, the brute struck him across the chin. The force of the blow sent him reeling back onto the steel-framed bed and he slumped down concussed, on the un-sheeted mattress.

Fifty Four

Shouting from just short of the cell door, roused Carty and still groggy, he lay there rubbing his face with his sweaty palms. His jaw was now badly swollen and his trousers stank of urine.

Then the noise died, rendering an anxiety.

Suddenly, a pistol-brandishing officer burst in followed by a suited man who stood in the open doorway, scoping the room.

'Okay Mr Carty, everything is under control now.' the suit uttered, seemingly satisfied before hurriedly turning to conduct affairs again in the corridor.

Carty was helped up and walked out to witness the strained expression of his former aggressor – the callous interrogator – now struggling under restraint by armed officers. Confused, Carty believed this was all a joke, a mind game to break his spirit through the staging of a pretend siege and escape.

'Who are you?' he brazenly yelled after the suit.

'Hedditch is the name,' the figure answered without turning his head.

Within minutes he was sitting on a small sofa facing his new *holder.* Plain-suited of average height with thinning brown hair, greying at the temples, Hedditch could have passed unnoticed on any London street.

'Water, Mr Carty?' He offered a bottle.

'Yes.' He held its rim to his lips but something stopped him. Did the water contain a drug that would cause him to spill all that he knew? He gingerly played with the cap. Hedditch, though, was staring beyond him to another part of the room.

'Drink it, Scott,' a familiar voice instructed, one he could vaguely place.

But it can't be! He froze and then slowly turned. There, behind him, sat the unmistakable figure of Gordon Green.

'Gordon!' Carty was lost for words, leaping up, his face drained with exhaustion.

'Scott, my boy!' Green stood and grabbed Carty's arms, pushing him back in order to examine him. 'We thought you were dead!' His emotions were reserved but clear.

'So did I!' he gasped, sensing that Green wanted to convey something more.

'Now, Mr Carty,' Hedditch announced in a tone that enforced his authority. 'Drink some water, please. Food and a doctor are on the way.'

'How are Diane and James?' Carty asked as he sat staring at his friend in disbelief.

'They're both very well but they don't know you're alive. It's best that we wait a few days and deal with the issues first.'

'Issues?'

'Yes, I am afraid there are a few things that need explaining.'

A young man entered with coffee.

'What time is it?' Carty pulled back his sleeve to reveal the face of the *Komandirksi*. Its luminous hands sat over the image of a MIG fighter aircraft, still showing the hour of the day at Baikal.

If only this could speak, he grinned inwardly.

'It's now 7:20 in the evening. You landed early this afternoon,' Hedditch answered.

'But what is this place?'

'It's a safe house and those men who held you were, let's say, a rogue cell, acting autonomously within the intelligence services. They have been closely linked to a Russian operation.'

Carty flexed his jaw, flinching at the pain.

'No one could believe that Scott Carty had arrived back at Heathrow,' Green added. 'That's why it took some time for MI5 to mobilise and get here.'

'And the police at the airport?'

'They were bogus,' Hedditch piped in. 'The cell wanted to understand exactly what you knew before eliminating you.' He laughed hollowly.

'But I haven't committed any crime.'

'We know, Scott,' Green chimed in. 'It's clear, though, that D'albo has implicated you in a huge web of deceit and his greed and lust for power has cost the lives of both Mark Boyd and Lena Isotova but thankfully, not yours.'

'Mark's dead?' Carty frowned, playing dumb but still staggered by the fact.

'Yes, he drowned...very likely murdered.'

'That's enough, Gordon, thanks,' Hedditch butted in. 'I'll take it from here. Right, we need to get you cleaned up, Scott,' he instructed, turning to his deputies to escort Carty out to the waiting doctor.

'No funny ideas now,' Green quipped, 'we can't have you disappearing on us again, can we!'

A brief examination revealed that his jaw was badly bruised but not broken. He showered and changed into a pair of worn, ill-fitting jeans and a T-shirt, before being escorted back to the room.

Gordon Green was there waiting for him.

'I can't believe you're back,' Green sighed.

'Nor can I. Have you seen Diane, or spoken to her?'

'Not recently.'

'Gordon, you must understand, I have to see them!' his voice cracked in desperation.

Green held his arm. 'I know, but be patient...' he was stopped short by Hedditch's sudden entrance.

'I do believe you need some more coffee, my boy,' Green loudly announced, turning his back to the MI5 officer while simultaneously raising a finger to his lips. The message was clear: *Don't say too much.* Carty guessed that they were being recorded and possibly filmed to compromise him at a later date.

Hedditch coughed. 'Now, Scott, for good order, can I have your side of events please.'

Carty flushed. 'What do you mean?'

'It's all right, Scott.' Green said. 'Just tell us in your own words what happened from the time you went missing.'

'Well, back in June, I was invited by CentralniySib Energo to speak at an energy conference in Almaty. It was at D'albo's insistence, although at the time I couldn't understand why. It all went smoothly until Kosechenko, CentralniySib's General Director, invited me to travel into Russia with a group of hand-picked guests, including some Americans and Lena Isotova.'

'When was that planned for?'

'The day after my presentation...it was all very rushed.'

'But was the trip for business?' Hedditch's character had morphed into that of a sleuth.

'It didn't seem to serve any purpose other than being a corporate jolly. I was reluctant to go but D'albo insisted on it.'

'And did Elena Isotova accompany you at that time?'

'Yes.'

Carty stopped to sip the coffee. Green caught his eye as the MI5 man glanced up from his notes, beckoning for him to continue.

'She was also frightened.'

'Of what?'

'Of Kosechenko. She thought his people had overheard her, in a drunken moment, telling me that he was directly involved in the dumping of nuclear waste in Siberia.'

'I see,' Hedditch scribbled animatedly. 'And had you been intimate with her?'

Carty hesitated. 'Why is that important?'

'Well?' he pressed.

'If you're asking if we screwed, then yes we did.'

He nodded. 'Please continue.'

'We landed in Siberia, at place called Irkutsk. There weren't any customs formalities.' He looked for acknowledgement of that fact but received none. 'And then we travelled up Lake Baikal to stay at a camp. It was there that I met with the Americans who –' He stopped abruptly in his tracks, unsure if he should admit to knowing of their deaths.

'What?'

'Who seemed cagey when I began to ask them about their business interests in Russia. Their answers weren't tangible and being in oil and gas, they were too familiar with certain facets of the nuclear industry. I sensed that they also knew about the dumping.' He yawned, wincing at the stabbing pain of his jaw.

'And then?'

'They left the next day, by helicopter.'

'Why didn't you leave with them?'

'I wasn't invited.'

'Did you have any idea where they were going?'

'None.'

'And Elena Isotova didn't tell you?' Hedditch's eyes narrowed, searching for snippets from Carty's narrative, which might paint a different story to the one he was recounting.

'She had no knowledge of their destination.'

'Really? She could have simply been a clever actress, testing you to see how much you knew about the dumping.'

'No, that's not possible!' Carty blurted, shaking his head forcefully as he screwed up his face in dissent. Memories flooded back of her enchanting girlish ways and the spell she had cast. Her innocence was palpable to him.

'But you did just admit to having slept with her.'

'I think it's probably more important at this stage to hear what Scott has to tell rather than to cross-examine him,' Green objected.

'All right, Gordon,' Heddich sighed, clearly rankled as he nodded at Carty to resume.

'That last evening, Lena and I were asleep together in a cabin but I woke up,' he paused, dropping his head into his palms as he recalled the images of the vision; the maiden diving with him into the vortex while he was fighting for his life.

'Here.' Green passed a bottle of water to his young friend, taking his attention and giving him focus. Carty swigged from it and caught Hedditch's emotionless stare. The MI5 man was chary, having seen many instances of assets faking fits or their own madness, to avoid questioning. It never got them far; he always flushed out the truth.

'I need to see my wife and child,' Carty blurted out, fighting back tears.

Hedditch shuffled uneasily. 'Can you continue or do you need more time?'

'Just get through this part, Scott, and then we can take a break,' Green supported.

Wiping his forehead he took a breath and resumed. 'Lena had drunk too much and I couldn't wake her when I realised killers had broken into the room. One overpowered me and then I heard Lena scream. There was a pistol shot and then she was silent.' Carty's expression was sullen.

'Did you see her being shot?'

'No, I was barely conscious and had been dragged outside. I vaguely remember an assassin holding a knife, about to kill me and then he was shot.'

'Someone shot him as well?'

'Yes, probably by one of the camp's hunters; he collapsed and pulled me over a cliff edge, into the lake.'

Hedditch smiled in a manner that mocked. 'So, you're suggesting that because Lena told you something she shouldn't have, both of your deaths were ordered?'

'Yes, there's no other explanation.' Carty's frustration was plain. 'I don't remember anything else.' He leant forward to grasp the lukewarm coffee, gazing blankly at the two men.

'Apparently I was in the freezing water for too long and fell into a coma. It was more than a fortnight before I came around and was too weak to move for some time after. That's when I learned that I had been pulled out from the lake by local fishermen and taken to a cottage hospital. The men caring for me were all skilled hunters.'

Green looked away, stifling a grin. Whitehall Jack's story, that a renegade Special Forces team had been slaughtered while searching for an English spy, seemed to match the account.

'Can you tell us some more about these men, their names and descriptions for example?' Hedditch's manner was impatient.

'You're joking, aren't you?'

'I agree. Scott's had enough for now,' Green interjected, noting Carty's weariness.

'All right!' Hedditch snapped, 'if you don't mind, though, telling me one more thing?'

'Yes,' Carty flinched.

'How did you get back into Kazakhstan?'

'I was smuggled across the border in a truck.'

Hedditch gazed blankly at his asset. 'Well, you're either one of the luckiest men alive, or you're a very good storyteller.'

'Hedditch, this can wait. He needs rest.' Green was insistent.

Nodding reluctantly the man called in his deputy.

'Take Mr Carty to his room and make sure he's checked over again by the doctor. I don't like the look of that jaw!'

Carty rose to his feet, shattered. Another glance at the *Komandirksi* told him he had been awake for too long.

'What do you think?' Green said, mocking concern moments after Carty had left.

'He's hiding something. I'm not sure if he's protecting D'albo or somebody else, but we'll find out soon enough!'

Fifty Five

He was woken by the clatter of a tray dumped in his room, carrying a poor excuse for an English breakfast.

'Thirty minutes, Mr Carty.' Hedditch's deputy announced.

Confused by the lack of daylight and sensing it was morning he sat up. The coarse fabric of the blanket left a tingling sensation across his inflamed cheek and Boris' gold quartz was still clasped in his palm.

He began to eat, quickly savouring the rich taste of grease and meat. Then he remembered the phial of Baikal's water and searched through his carrier to find it still intact. He downed the contents, and held it in his mouth allowing it to cool the back of his throat, recalling Boris' comment that he would need it.

Still in his crumpled clothes he was walked back to the same interview room. A strained Gordon Green stood waiting for him.

'Gordon!' Carty exclaimed in a no nonsense mood. 'I'm being held against my will and I demand having a solicitor present when being interviewed.'

'Of course, Scott, I've already arranged for that after Hedditch's debriefing today.' He held Carty's shoulder, calming him. 'I told you that D'albo was a villain but I could never have imagined that he would have done what he has.'

Hedditch appeared in the doorway, unshaven, and wearing a naff sweatshirt. His expression was more relaxed than the previous night but he got straight down to business.

'How well did you know Mark Boyd?' The question seemed ordinary enough but Carty remained cautious.

'Reasonably well. I worked with him some years ago at Brightwell Carter.'

'And did you know that he was actually set up by D'albo for the fraud?'

'No, I didn't. Is that why he was murdered?'

'Not directly.' Hedditch allowed no time for sentimentality. 'He was working for us, monitoring D'albo's activities from inside Albion.'

Carty, stunned, shook his head in astonishment.

'And you thought Boyd was trying to oust you,' Green uttered.

'Our intelligence had known for some time that D'albo was actively involved in an operation handling nuclear waste,' Hedditch rejoined. 'We now know that the shipments have been ending up in the region of Siberia where you were last seen before you disappeared. You see our predicament?' His smug expression was unnerving.

'And you believe I am involved in all this with D'albo?'

Hedditch wagged a finger. 'Scott, you have a choice to make and a duty to perform.'

'A duty?'

'That's right. Now that Mark Boyd is dead, you're going to help your country and expose Arthur D'albo at the same time.'

'Do I have any choice?'

'If you chose not to –,' his tone became hollow, '– it's likely you'll be tried for conspiracy to commit fraud.'

'Even though you've all but admitted that I am not a suspect!'

'Did I? What about the case of cash you took into Kazakhstan?'

How does he know about that? Carty dropped his head in capitulation.

'Shortly, you're going to be handed over to the police and formally arrested on suspicion of fraud. There will be a brief court appearance followed by a press announcement stating you have been found alive and well but are being held, pending trial.'

335

'Trial! But I need to see my wife and son, to explain what happened and where I have been.'

'Naturally. The Serious Fraud Office will recommend to the court that you be released on bail. It will better serve the case if you cooperate in the investigation with the appointed forensic auditors.'

'What about D'albo? He's the real fraudster in all this.'

'D'albo's going to be more slippery than you can imagine. You'll tell him that you believe Boyd and Elena Isotova were responsible together for instigating the fraud.'

'But that would be a lie and immoral.'

'It would only be immoral if it was true and D'albo knows that it's not.' The MI5 man's voice rose to a crescendo. 'You will not give any interviews without permission and there will be no direct contact with my organisation. Shuttle, my colleague, will brief you on how to avoid surveillance by other parties.'

'Surveillance?'

'Yes, mobile phones are notoriously easy to eavesdrop, and it's likely you will be followed and bugged!'

Carty smiled incredulously.

'I'm warning you now, Scott. This *will* happen. One careless word or action and you'll blow the whole operation and your ticket to freedom.'

'So there's really no choice.'

'Did I say there was? We need to know who D'albo is collaborating with and what's happening to that nuclear waste.'

'And the fraud?'

'D'albo must think your sole objective is to clear your name.'

'He's not a fool, he'll never trust me.'

'Well, he's certainly going to be suspicious of your bail release and will begin to cover his tracks. We're hoping that he'll make some mistakes when he does.'

'And if I discover any information?'

'Shuttle will brief you on how any intelligence can be passed on to us covertly.'

'So when does all this begin?'

'After lunch. You'll be going to Paddington Green police station. This is the last time we will meet, so I suggest you erase me from your memory. This meeting never happened. And I might remind you again, Scott, if you try to breathe one word of this...'

'All right Hedditch,' Green boomed. 'I think he's got the point!'

Carty quietly contemplated his options. There was only one and while the challenge seemed daunting it paled in comparison to those that he had faced in the *taiga*: escaping death twice and now carrying the burden of the machine's secret.

'Hedditch. Why don't you give me some time with Scott?' Green delivered his request as a thinly veiled instruction.

'Fine, but not too long; we need to be moving out soon.' The MI5 man's politeness was paper thin as he stood to leave, still unsure of Green's connection with his superiors.

'Well, Scott,' Green grinned. '*Tertium non datum* – your situation is rather like a dream, isn't it?'

'I guess you can say that,' Carty sighed. 'I don't suppose I will get that phone call, though?'

Green shook his head. 'Not just yet.'

Fifty Six

Leaden scuds shifted rapidly across the skyline as the unmarked police car drove into Paddington to a waiting audience of uniformed police, holstering pistols.

'Mr Carty?' The lead officer leaned in through the opened window.

'Yes!' Carty smiled, relieved in the knowledge that this was a genuine arrest.

'I am going to read you your rights,' he announced as he grasped Carty's wrists and cuffed them.

A muted excitement bristled among the crowd of officers as he was escorted past them. Expressions were mixed: some were cold, convinced of his guilt, others confused at how he had returned, seemingly from the dead.

Quickly marched into an interview room, he was charged in front of Green and his solicitor, David Foreman. It took ten minutes and then he found himself in the cells.

'There's a media swell outside. Everyone's looking for information,' Green announced trying to keep his friend in a positive frame of mind.

'Do James and Diane know I am back?'

'Yes. They're on their way here.'

'And Nick?'

'I don't know,' Green shrugged, avoiding direct eye contact. 'We need to get on with the brief before you go into court this afternoon.'

The court appearance was less daunting then he had expected: bailed with his passport surrendered, indefinitely. He felt a temporary release from the prospect of the circus that was waiting.

First, though, he was led away to a small meeting room and reunited with his wife and son. It was a private affair that lasted no more than a quarter of an hour. James remained mostly silent, sitting on his father's lap as Diane touched Carty's face and wept. He held them close. Words were furthermost from any of their minds. She thought that she had lost him forever but was now challenged by dormant feelings, conflicting with her new-found love for Nick Hall.

Carty then walked out to meet the press, holding her hand amidst a hail of flash photography. Green and Foreman had already briefed him on how he should answer their questions: "*Keep everything truthful but short, and be careful not to denounce Albion or its staff.*"

A brief introduction, made by the senior Inspector handling the case, explained that while Carty had been bailed, the Court had ruled that he was to assist both the SFO and Albion in various aspects of the investigation.

'Scott, are you guilty of defrauding Albion Light and Power?' A well-known journalist launched his question almost immediately.

'No,' he answered calmly.

'Why did you disappear?' came another.

'I didn't plan to.'

'So how do you explain it?'

'I attended a conference in Kazakhstan and shortly after was flown out to Siberia,' he sidestepped the question.

'Who arranged this trip?'

He hesitated. 'One of Albion's clients.'

'Was it the Russian company – the claimant in the fraud?'

'I've not been briefed about any *alleged* fraud, yet.'

'Are you aware that Mark Boyd's body was recently found?'

'I've only just been informed of his death and my sympathies go to his family.'

'Did you two get along well?'

'I respected him.'

'Even though he was convicted of an earlier fraud?'

'Mark Boyd served prison time for that.' His voice had risen indignantly at the lack of respect shown for the man, whom he now understood to have been a silent comrade.

'Do you believe he was involved in this fraud?'

'No, of course not!'

'And yourself?'

Foreman intervened. 'I would like to remind the press that my client is not on trial here. This line of questioning is inappropriate and may jeopardise his case.'

There was a collective moan from the press before a flurry of hands went up again. The inspector chose another.

'Scott, can you tell us something about the helicopter crash in Russia?

'I don't remember what happened. I was pulled out of the wreckage in a coma,' he uttered, repeating the story that Shuttle had briefed him to say.

'Why do you think that no one reported your presence to the local authorities?'

'I really don't know. As I said, I was in a coma.'

'But surely after you recovered you would have wanted to ring home!' The cocky comment raised a chorus of laughter. Carty grinned.

'Easier said than done. I found myself recuperating in a small settlement with no means of communication with the outside world.'

'No telephones?'

'No, none.'

'But who were the people taking care of you?'

'It was a small pseudo-Christian community.'

Green's wide-eyed expression echoed the collective shock. Carty had improvised. Boris had explained the existence of such isolated groups in the *taiga*. No one here could disprove it.

'Did you ask to be taken to the authorities?'

'Yes, but these people believed that my life would have been in greater danger if they had done so.'

'Why didn't you try to escape?'

'Because I quickly understood that I would perish in the Siberian forest.'

A momentary pause sucked in the excitement of the audience before another pundit fired at him. 'Scott, are you aware that Russian Embassy officials wish you to help them with certain enquiries over the disappearance of Elena Isotova?'

Carty flinched. Diane read it and squeezed his hand.

'No, I am not.'

'And would you be willing to meet with them?'

He shrugged as Foreman intervened again. 'This question is not relevant at present. My client is the subject of a UK fraud investigation, not a missing person's case!'

'But how or why could she have disappeared at the same time as you?'

'I wish I knew.'

'So, exactly how did you get back to England?' a young woman journalist then quizzed.

'I flew back.'

His answer was met with an incredulous stare from the questioner. She grinned cynically. 'Wouldn't you agree that your story seems a little far-fetched, considering the allegations made against you? You disappear in Russia, don't attempt to contact anyone and then, more than six weeks later, suddenly board a plane and arrive at Heathrow!'

'Maybe it does, but I have already explained myself to the authorities. I am innocent and will clear my name.'

'Mr Carty *is* still under investigation while he is assisting us,' the inspector clarified, leaning forward to the microphone.

'There are some suggestions that you are an operative for the British Secret Services.' More laughter followed the statement. 'What do you say to that?'

'Pure James Bond,' he muttered.

The crowd roared. They smelt something more to his story as Foreman's nod to the inspector signalled an end to the session.

'One last question, please,' the inspector offered, pointing to a journalist at the back.

'Did Elena Isotova get on that helicopter with you?'

'No, she didn't,' his voice trailed.

Gordon Green was observing his friend's expression closely. *What is he hiding?* He wondered.

'Thank you, ladies and gentlemen, that will be all.'

Two police officers took the cue to step up to the rostrum and escort Carty away. He was not entirely a free man, yet.

That evening the media camped outside Carty's house. His apparent resurrection had fired the public's imagination.

Diane had had the place spring-cleaned to welcome her husband home. After his disappearance and with her rekindled feelings for Nick, she had found it impossible to spend time there, preferring to stay with her parents.

'Daddy will read for you and then you must settle down and go to sleep.' She pulled the duvet up over James' shoulders and kissed his head.

Carty beamed as he opened his son's book glad to be sharing this moment again. James had grown accustomed to being with his grandparents and was susceptible to the swing in his mother's emotions following the trauma of losing his father.

'How do you feel?' Diane probed, sensing Carty's mood as he wandered back downstairs almost an hour later. Visibly drawn, she had curled up on the chaise longue in the conservatory and was nursing a large glass of Bordeaux. She had noticed a change in her husband's manner but couldn't pinpoint what it was.

'Weird, I guess. I was so long in strange and uncomfortable surroundings that it will take some getting used to, being home.' He gazed warmly back, harbouring a concern at how much thinner she had become and missing the shapely figure he used to love to hug. Her quirky smile sparked a loving memory of the first time he caught her eye at Nick Hall's party and knew that she was interested in him. That same look was still there, no matter how hard she tried to hide it.

'You will have to tell me everything that happened, one day!' she said, nervously tossing her flecked chestnut hair.

'I will try to, one day.'

An odd calm followed as she self-consciously sipped her wine.

'Do you still love me?' her voice cracked as she slipped the words out. He met her stare.

'Of course!'

The inevitable question then broke his lips. 'And me? Do you still love me?'

She faltered, gazing down into the glass, as if seeking fortification. 'I'm confused.'

'By what?'

'Scott. I thought you were dead. I was lost without you. Nick was there to comfort me.'

Her top lip trembled and she began to sob. Carty now understood why his oldest friend had been strangely absent since his arrival. The old Carty might have reacted differently, but wisdom had since tempered his character.

'I can never stop loving you, Scott, I just need some time to understand if we can work it out.'

He moved to sit and embrace her and a wave of emotion overcame him.

She turned her head, her moist eyes meeting his as she searched for the words that would release her from this torment. 'Did you have anyone?'

He couldn't lie to her. 'I met someone. It was very brief, but what I felt confused me also.'

'Do you want to be with her?'

'No.' His head sunk, 'she died.'

343

She stared at him, sensing that it had been Lena. 'Scott, we cannot pretend, not with that mob outside the door.'

'I know.'

'James and I will leave tomorrow. You have so much to do. I'll make sure you see him every weekend. Let's just see how things work out.'

He shrugged in acceptance, comprehending that there could be no returning to the past, to how they had been.

Fifty Seven

His arrival the next morning at Albion Gas Light & Power Plc was worthy of celebrity status: surviving death in an attempt to escape his crime and now coming home to face the music. It was all hyperbole but then the media would spin it again, if Carty proved innocent.

Escorted by a junior Scotland Yard minder up the escalator to the trading floor, Carty clapped eyes on Arthur D'albo standing firmly ahead of him, in front of a gawping crowd. Rumour of fraud and the threat of the enormous damage to Albion's credibility had sent critical money earners deserting, but those remaining wanted to catch a glimpse of the rogue responsible. A small group, consisting of Albion's legal counsel, a forensic auditor, and two trading directors, remained in the background, po-faced.

'Scott, my boy! How are you?' D'albo boomed in an unmistakable tone, nervously fastening the single button of his blazer. He appeared less imposing than Carty remembered, his posture seeming to stoop under an invisible burden. Carty's new understanding of the body's sensitive energies enabled him to read D'albo's: the lying and deceit had taken their toll.

'I am well, Arthur.' His blue eyes flickered, concealing a basket of unvented emotions.

'Good. We're all glad you're safe and that you're here where you belong.' He firmly shook Carty's hand for all to see. 'Together we'll put this company back at the forefront of what it does best!'

'We'll try, Arthur.'

D'albo turned to face the others. 'Are we ready then, gentlemen? Let's meet the press!'

In front of the media, D'albo shone. Public appearances and speaking were his forte.

He would have made an indomitable politician, Carty thought as he looked on.

Then, when it was Carty's turn to speak, D'albo poignantly interrupted where he felt necessary and had blatantly arranged staged questions for which he had rehearsed responses. The outcome was a positive spin for Albion in which both he and Scott Carty would vindicate it of any fraud and pinpoint the real culprits.

Carty left the meeting with a mild headache, sickened by the sheer mendacity of his former mentor but clear on one thing: D'albo, if trapped, would be highly resourceful and stop at nothing to elude guilt.

'Scott, let's have a chat, shall we?' D'albo's subtle insistence prompted a look of hesitation from Carty's minder.

'Mr D'albo, I must advise against remaining alone with Mr Carty given the seriousness of the allegations.'

'Don't worry!' D'albo ushered the man away and invited Carty through into the familiar surroundings of the executive suite.

'The press conference went well, don't you think?'

'I'm not sure what to think anymore, Arthur.'

'Hmmm. Fancy a drink?'

'At ten in the morning? No thanks!'

D'albo poured himself a scotch.

'Damned tragedy about Mark's suicide, isn't it? I keep asking myself why he would have done that.'

'Was it suicide?'

'That's what the newspapers reported. Maybe he couldn't handle the guilt.'

'What guilt?'

'For slipping back into his old ways and stealing from us like that.'

'Ah, I see what you mean but was he acting alone or was Lena Isotova also involved?' Carty played along, in accordance with Hedditch's ploy.

'There's no doubt that he had help on the Russian side.'

'And how is CentralniySib taking it?'

'Bad! They've filed a claim against Albion for damages. The trouble is, Scott, your signature is on every one of the fraudulent documents.'

'How could that have happened?'

'That's what I've been asking myself since you left.' D'albo raised his hands, feigning despair. 'Boyd must have had a hand in it, and to think that we gave that lad a second chance.' He flushed slightly as he invited Carty to sit.

'I must say, though, that we're all finding the story of what happened to you in Siberia rather incredible.'

'It's no story, Arthur. You can ask your friend Kosechenko!'

'Kosechenko's denying that he was even there. He told me that Lena Isotova had arranged your trip but it's all a little difficult to prove, now that she's dead.'

'Arthur, are you saying you *know* that she's dead or simply repeating what you have heard?'

D'albo looked unconcerned. 'It's a shame. She was a lovely girl and had the hots for you.'

'Is that relevant?'

'Of course! Sex and power, the whole world is like that, my boy, if you dig just below the surface.'

'It doesn't have to be. The greatest beauty and power lie in those things we cannot totally possess.'

'Very philosophical! What's happened to you, Scott? You seem to have lost that drive you once had, to be the best, the very best!' D'albo swigged down the remains of his glass and then poured another.

'Not really, Arthur. I've just seen another side to life, that's all.'

'Hmm, I'd like to hear about it over lunch sometime but right now I need to help those forensics get to the bottom of this mess. We'll see you back at Albion in a week's time.'

Fifty Eight

Time dragged as he sat in the garden that afternoon, his thoughts swirling with the leaves tossed against his feet in the light wind.

D'albo dropped too many hints. He knows I'm lying. It's going to be impossible to fulfil Hedditch's demands. But then *Basilides'* poignant words burnished again in his mind. " *Winning the game appears illusory – take great care!*"

While D'albo had made checkmate in the dream, it wasn't necessarily destiny. Carty took heart at the realisation that there would never again be the false comfort of his career to succour to. He had been transformed but with that rested the responsibility of being true to himself rather than to anyone else's expectations.

Inspired, he walked into the conservatory and glanced at his bookshelf. What he was seeking wasn't there. He then pulled open a drawer of his desk, rifling through various papers stuffed there by Diane, after having reviewed them in preparation for probate.

Underneath them sat the object, still wrapped in the brown paper bag.

Perhaps the I Ching might shed some light on all this, he thought, opening its distinctive cover.

Between the pages was a note from Nick.

Quieten your mind and hold your question, silently and sincerely for some time. Then, cast the coins six times.

He remembered watching Nick perform these simple instructions, regularly, one summer, in a mad quest to determine his future.

I wonder if it all came true for him?

He fumbled for three pennies in his coin pouch and composed himself, contemplating his question quietly.

How do I get out of this mess?

Soon the coins rang down, six times, on the bees-waxed oak table, the gathering place for his family's meals and on which his son had learnt to write and paint. Each time he noted down the number of heads or tails, as Nick had instructed and from which he could determine if it was either a yin or yang line. Then, with a gentle audible out-breath, he grasped the book, flicking through its pages to locate the hexagram he had just cast.

Number 29: Kan, - The Abysmal.

Its title raised a deep-seated insecurity which grew as he read the rest of the passage. Unfamiliar metaphors harked back to a time when conflict and war were more common and humanity was in closer contact with nature. The doorbell distracted him as he began to delve deeper, causing him to hesitate for a moment, fearful that it might be a journalist seeking an exclusive interview.

'Scott. Are you there?' Gordon Green's distinctive voice echoed from the other side of the door.

Carty briskly opened it, shielding his face from the onlookers' lenses.

'So, how did it go today?'

'As expected, come through,' he invited Green into the large conservatory.

'You've cast the I Ching, I see!' Green said, noticing the book lying open.

'Yes, God knows I need all the help I can get at the moment.'

'Danger,' Green murmured noting the scrawled down trigram. He knew the book by heart.

'What do you mean?' Carty shouted back as he filled the kettle.

'The hexagram, *Kan*, it represents danger. Its image depicts water gushing through a deep ravine and its message means to go with the flow and act in accordance with the situation in order to emerge intact.'

'By listening to the unconscious?' Carty shrugged, placing some empty cups on the table.

'Yes, water is a symbol of the unconscious.' Green smiled.

How ironic! The latent power of water again.

'So no easy and quick solution to my situation then?'

'Doubtful! Did D'albo behave himself today?'

'You wouldn't believe it. He held his own mini-press conference?'

'Ha! The arrogant bastard, still as self-absorbed as ever!'

Carty sighed, gazing out onto the overgrown lawn, the memory of the chess dream stirring again. 'By the way Gordon, who is *Basilides*?'

Green's brow furrowed. 'Why do you ask that?'

'It's the name of the hooded figure of my dreams.'

Green scratched at his grey locks, the synchronicity with his own dream defied belief. 'Well, as my memory serves me, *Basilides* was an Alexandrian scholar from the second century AD. He was a Gnostic, a seeker of truth and considered a heretic by the early Church,' he added, animatedly pulling a pen from his jacket. He then briefly moved over to the desk to pluck a sheet of A4 paper from the printer.

'An alchemist perhaps?' Carty jibed.

'Perhaps, but his appearance in your dreams is quite remarkable!'

'And why's that?'

'Because he also appeared in mine just days before you returned.'

'You're joking!'

'Not at all: he showed me that you were still alive.'

Carty brows arched. 'I'm amazed.'

'Don't be. The unconscious can be a good friend. I think you now understand that,' he said as he began to write. Carty smiled and filled a teapot with steaming water. Just months before, he would have openly refuted such a comment.

Green then turned the paper around and fixed him with an odd look. He wanted Carty to read what he had just written.

IT'S IMPORTANT THAT YOU DON'T ASK ANY QUESTIONS. JUST KEEP TALKING, ACT NATURALLY AND FOLLOW MY INSTRUCTIONS. OKAY?

Carty's expression spoke of confusion as he glanced up.

'Is that okay?' Green quizzed.

He nodded at the instruction.

'How are Diane and James?' Green resumed as he scrawled again on the sheet.

Carty played along. 'James is fine but quite confused about everything.'

'Where are they living?'

'At my mother-in-law's place.' His buoyant mood turned sullen. 'Gordon, did you know that Diane was seeing Nick?'

'I guessed that it might have been the case but I couldn't be certain. Nick and I haven't spoken much since you disappeared.'

Green pushed the sheet in front of him again.

CHANGE YOUR CLOTHES, PUT ON SOMETHING THAT HAS BEEN WASHED AND LEAVE YOUR MOBILE TELEPHONE HERE. WE'RE GOING OUT IN MY CAR.

Carty scanned his friend, his expression begging an answer. Green grinned then clicked open the cap to his sterling-silver lighter and with one swift movement set the page alight. He then held it out of the open window until it had been consumed.

'So where are you taking me?' Carty quizzed as they pulled out through the gates and past two photographers, rapidly snapping at them.

'Ever been to the Ironmonger Row Baths?' Green murmured back.

'No.' He had heard of the hot rooms but had never visited.

'Well, that's where we're going!'

'We are. Why?'

'You'll see.' Green's play-acting hinted of paranoia.

Stripped bare, their waists wrapped with short white towels, they strode into the spacious hot room. Despite his age, Green's musculature was well toned, suggesting that he had a physical regime of some kind.

'Well, Scott,' Green hummed as they sat on the plastic garden chairs. 'Finally we can speak freely without fear of being overheard. There are no mobile phones or bugs in here!' His face displayed relief. The baths had few visitors that afternoon and smacked of the bohemian.

Carty scoped the bare, white-tiled room and its other occupant, an elderly man, fully stretched out on the wooden slatted tops in the stifling heat.

'On second thoughts the steam room may be a better place to talk.' Green headed out, pulling back the cheap, plastic shower curtain covering the entrance.

The room lived up to its name: a solitary light peered through a shroud of hot mist that hung over the raised marble plinths running around its walls. It stirred the picture again of Boris' *banya*, the place where Carty had first learnt of Lubimov's machine.

'No one in here,' Green resounded as he laid down his towel, his profile momentarily muffled by the swirling vapour. 'Sorry that we had to go through that routine at the house but any part of your clothing may have been bugged, unless of course it had just been washed.'

'And the mobile phone?' Carty added.

'It can be switched on remotely to listen to your conversations as well as giving away your exact location. You may want to consider buying a pay-as-you-go SIM chip and changing it regularly. It will allow you the freedom to speak without our *friends* listening in or knowing exactly where you are.'

'Aren't you acting just a little paranoid, Gordon?'

'When it comes to intrusion into personal liberties, yes, I am a bit paranoid. Don't you remember what Hedditch said about being monitored?' he gestured with open arms.

'I do and while we're talking of Hedditch, is there any way I can avoid this straightjacket he's put me into?'

'Possibly, I'm working on it.' Green cocked his head. 'Anyway, we're here for a reason, to talk openly. Do you want to tell me what *really* happened in Siberia?'

Carty had known this was coming and had already considered the implications of what he might divulge.

'Almost all of what I told Hedditch was true.'

'Huh, well, he does suspect that you know more than you're saying.'

Carty sighed against the heat. 'Look, Gordon, Lena Isotova really was shot dead by assassins.'

'And the story about your attempted assassination and the coma?'

'Boilerplate! It's all true. I was drowning in Baikal and then...' he stalled as the terror of that moment surfaced again, the dense atmosphere a perfect backdrop on which the vision of that night could play itself out.

'The maiden, my anima, saved me from certain death.'

'How?' Green enquired gently, wiping his forehead.

'I hallucinated that she dragged me down into a violent vortex, a whirlpool that disappeared way beneath me into a blinding light.' His eyes dropped. 'As we entered its centre, everything became calm. Then she spoke to me: "*the essence of all starts here,*"' he murmured.

Green remained quiet, understanding that his friend had just described a near-death experience.

'It is the last thing I can remember of the attack.'

'But you survived!'

'Yes, a local man pulled me into his fishing boat and as I slipped into a state of hypothermia, he used his shamanic skills to keep me alive. When I emerged from the coma, I found myself in the hospital bed of a remote institute.'

Carty quickly recounted how he had been the subject of an acupuncture experiment.

'Laser acupuncture!' Green reiterated, cynically.

'That's right. It prevented my muscles from atrophying and kept my vital functions energised.'

'Sounds incredible!' He stood. 'Shall we take a plunge?'

They stepped out into the cool foyer. In front of them lay a small rectangular pool, which was filled by the continual running of an oversized Daliesque tap at its far end.

Green hung his towel and stepped straight in up to his waist, his breath audibly taken by the tantalising cold. Carty gingerly followed him in.

'That's enough for me. I'll see you back in the steam room!' Green uttered after a minute or so, dragging himself back up the steps.

'Fine.' Carty remained in the cooling water considering just how much more of the truth he could tell the older man.

Not overunity. Not the machine, he'll never believe me.

The steam had cleared slightly when he returned to catch Green sitting in a full lotus position, seeming to hover in the opaque atmosphere. It was obvious that the older man maintained his physique through yoga.

'I'm still amazed that you survived the coma,' Green chimed with a hint of sarcasm.

'Gordon, I'm not lying to you. The Institute's director had developed the laser techniques over many years, in an exchange programme with the Chinese.'

'But how did you communicate with him? Did he speak English?'

'Yes, he had learnt it at university. He had also read some of Jung's work,' Carty announced, keen to promote his own integrity. 'I left him your copy of *Psyche and Matter*. I hope you don't mind. I wanted to repay him for saving my life.'

'Ha, I knew that that book had chosen you for a reason.'

Carty ran a palm over his shimmering shoulders. 'It appears that his experimental work confirmed much of what the book was postulating.'

'Did it?'

'Possibly, he didn't say – but he had been forced to conduct PSI experiments at this institute during the Cold War.'

'PSI experiments!'

'You know about them?'

Green's brows knitted. 'It's well known that the Soviets had programmes investigating the paranormal.' Green's face turned grave. 'This is worrying, Scott. I suggest that you tell no one about it.'

'Believe me, I'm not going to,' he said. 'But that's only one part of the strange goings-on there.'

'There's more?'

'Yes, Boris, the man who pulled me from the lake, had the most incredible control over his body's energies. He was able to perform feats that I cannot explain and which certainly defy modern science.'

He briefly explained the Buryat's bare handed fire lighting and the levitation.

'He also taught me a system of breathing techniques and postures to enhance my *Qi*,' he added, 'and after some practice, I recovered more rapidly than he or I had expected.'

Green's constant bobbing head acknowledged the information. His yoga practice had the equivalent in *pranayama* – its arcane breathing techniques. He beamed with admiration.

'Well Scott, you have certainly changed from that sceptical man you used to be.'

'I guess I'm now *New* Carty!'

'*New* Carty?' Green echoed in bafflement.

Carty grinned benignly. 'It's something that came to me in a dream in which I met Tycho Brahe. He left me with a clue which was an anagram of his name.'

'You *do* know who Tycho Brahe was?' Green quizzed.

'An astronomer?'

'Much more than that, he was an alchemist, a follower of Paracelsus, the so-called *Christ* of medicine.' Green wiped his arms with his hands and then violently shook them, ricocheting beads of sweat off the walls. 'As a young man Brahe was forced by his uncle to practice law and it wasn't until mid-life that he settled into his love of astronomy and, secretly, alchemy. His work was continued by Kepler, who went on to define the laws of planetary motion.'

'Well I am certainly a changed man after my experiences.'

'And is there anything more you want to tell me?' Green asked, his mellow voice, strangely distorted by the audible hiss of steam filling the chamber.

'Boris was aware that I was being tracked down by a group of bounty hunters, so he hid me in the *taiga* to draw them out and then turned the tables on them. I narrowly escaped another assassination attempt.' He flinched in a somatic response to the memories.

So Jack's source was correct! Green grinned.

'Scott, you understand that you've lied to Hedditch, don't you?'

'No, I've simply been economic with the some of the facts because I knew that the truth wouldn't be believed.'

The blanket of scalding vapour swathed their bodies. Carty took a slow breath and stilled his mind as Green's face and body became a vague outline.

A pair of eyes formed from two small eddies of steam and then slowly a woman's face emerged, smiling. 'Tell him!'

'Are you all right?' Green registered his friend's vacant gaze. As a seasoned sauna visitor he knew that, for some, the heat caused dizziness and left them below par. He had no inkling that Carty had already been challenged by the extremes of a Siberian *banya*.

'Thanks, I'm fine,' Carty smiled. 'Lubimov...' he paused, conscious that he had unwittingly revealed the name. '...the director, had developed a solar heat-pump, that generated electricity from both light and heat.'

'That's interesting.'

'Its combined efficiencies were far greater than should have been possible, which he claimed was down to the alloy they were manufactured from.'

Green let out a loud sigh, smiling. 'It's not so strange. I read a scientific article recently about how the US Military had developed a flexible, plastic solar-collector technology, encapsulating metal nano-spirals which, it also claimed, were super-efficient.'

Carty laughed, reminiscing over his initial reaction to the enormous output registered on Lubimov's meters. Now home, though, he found it difficult to accept that back in that cavern, lay the answer to the world's energy needs and climate change.

'Gordon.' His bright eyes shone with a muted fear. 'There was something else. A phenomenon which defies explanation,' he murmured leaning forward, hesitant in unburdening the information as the image of the machine mentally churned once again.

'Have you ever heard of *overunity?*'

Green's frame rose as his expression registered surprise. 'Yes, but that's the stuff of science-fiction,' he denounced.

'But it's not,' Carty murmured. 'It's never been openly demonstrated or academically proven. Researchers ran into a brick wall in the 1980s with cold fusion and in the late 1990s, the *Times* ran an article postulating the possibilities of tapping the almost limitless energy inside a vacuum...but there's never been a tangible breakthrough.' His blue eyes stared back through the steam conveying a truth, a truth he would rather forget. 'Gordon, I witnessed an *overunity* machine – a contraption that imploded water at intense velocities, releasing such abundant amounts of energy that it powered itself!'

Green's gaze hardened. 'Tell me, Scott, was the name *Schauberger* ever mentioned?'

Carty looked agog. 'How did you know that?'

'An American entrepreneur presented a similar technology to me some years ago, but it seemed to work by the implosion of spiralling air, not water. He was seeking finance to build an industrial version to provide emission-free power. Being the head of alternative investments at a large merchant bank, I was already funding a number of solar power stations in Europe and looking for new ventures. So I raised it at a senior management committee meeting, thinking that an incredible opportunity existed to transform energy production and make money at the same time.' He dropped his head, pausing. 'The man never responded to my calls and then suddenly, I was manoeuvred out of my job.'

Carty shook his head slowly in a show of empathy. Finally, he understood why Green's reputation had been rubbished.

'But let me get this straight – you saw an operating version of Schauberger's trout engine?'

'Yes, yes I did.'

'Are you sure?' Green challenged.

'Absolutely! But it only exhibits *overunity* at specific locations on the planet's surface.'

'Really?'

'Apparently, at node-points, where the Schumann Resonance – the standing vibration of the atmosphere – is unaffected by man-made frequencies. Baikal's unique location, a vast body of pristine water over a mile deep in places, provides a perfect node.'

'I am aware of the Schumann Resonance. It has the same frequency as the alpha rhythms of the mammalian brain and influences all life processes on this planet.'

Large beads of sweat had formed on their skins and while the heat was becoming unbearable. Green was too intrigued to leave.

'What did it look like, this contraption?'

'Like a large metallic egg about a cubic metre in volume, fixed within a cradle to prevent it from levitating.'

'Levitating?' Unbridled excitement straightened Green's posture. 'That's incredible, unbelievable. And you're sure it demonstrated *overunity*?'

'Not 100 per cent, but clearly it was not a conventional technology. I was told that it was not demonstrating perpetual motion and will gradually stop in 20 years or so.' Carty drew in a breath. He wasn't quite ready to disclose the machine's other secret – the transmutation – just yet.

The overwhelming environment and information drove them out to the plunge pool again.

'Gordon, I need you to swear to me that you will not discuss this information with anyone, particularly Hedditch!'

'You have my word.' Green heaved a sighed. 'Unlimited power in Siberia directly threatens Russia's own lucrative oil and gas industry, let alone the international energy markets. This knowledge could endanger both our lives, Scott. Remember the hexagram you just cast – *Kan* – Danger? Anyway, I don't believe the collective psyche is ready yet to handle a world in which energy is completely free.'

'Maybe not, but the machine truly epitomises the hope for mankind, when it's ready to abandon its borders and disputes.'

'My God, you are transformed! Only months ago you were a hardened capital markets originator, hell-bent on shaping a brave new world through emissions trading.'

'I haven't completely abandoned that yet,' he retorted, defensively.

Green remained motionless, mulling the impact of Carty's story as the pool sapped the heat from their bodies. He chuckled. 'You know, it's ironic, but a much more conventional method of switching the world to limitless clean energy was proposed back in the seventies.'

'Was it?'

'Yes. It was called the Hydrogen Economy.'

'Ah, I did read about that,' Carty nonchalantly remarked. 'But the costs of producing hydrogen, let alone its storage and transport were then, and still are now, too cost restrictive.'

'Honestly, Scott, you've just admitted to witnessing a machine that can solve the world's energy problems and yet you still come out with these bullshit statements! What is required to kick-start the hydrogen revolution is the same scale of funding and academic drive that established the civil nuclear industry in the UK, after the Second World War. By comparison, hydrogen is cheaper and safer to produce and doesn't have the hazardous waste issues. It can also be stored until needed.

'In nickel hydride rechargeable batteries, I suppose. They're already part of our everyday lives.'

'Better to use fuel cells which are more efficient and, by using renewables, hydrogen can be produced from water, locally, where energy is needed. Granted, there will be some technical hurdles to overcome such as distribution and new pipeline materials.'

'And I suppose that investment would probably be many factors less than decommissioning old atomic power stations and building new ones.'

'Now you're talking!' Green cried as he climbed the steps out of the water. 'Hydrogen is the first and simplest of all the elements, the archetype of the *one*, the *yang*, the *beginning*. Ironically, when it burns it combines with oxygen to form water, the feminine or *yin*, which nurtures all of life. This can then be recycled to produce more hydrogen.' He threw a towel to the younger man.

Carty tied it around himself and followed him towards the hot room.

The older man smiled timidly. 'I must admit that I was a little rash in attacking your emissions business when we first met.'

'Really?'

'The world works in strange ways and the Kyoto Protocol's financial mechanisms, fragile as they may be, are important achievements. Without them, there wouldn't have been any unified action taken at all, to stem climate change.

Yes, but all that will be for nothing, if a massive solar flare engulfs the Earth.

The morbid thought quickly vanished with the sudden appearance of a lone figure, withered by the continual exposure to the heat. Old John's skill in imperceptibly slinking silently around the various hot rooms was uncanny.

'Time for your massage, Mr Green,' he announced in a local vernacular, self-conscious that he was interrupting. 'And do you two gentlemen want a cup of tea afterwards?' he croaked. Green, being a regular client, often had one to round off the visit.

'That would be nice, John. We will be out in a few minutes.'

As the man left, Green stepped into the sauna.

'Scott,' he said pausing for a moment, his face carrying a hint of disquiet.

'What?'

'Did Lena Isotova know about the machine?'

Carty shook his head. 'If she did, she didn't let on to me.'

Fifty Nine

The dawn air was unusually crisp for late August, rousing Carty, as he stood calmly on the lawn. Slowly and imperceptibly he straightened his spine and raised the back of his neck, willing relaxation into all parts of his being while waiting for an inner acknowledgment. Then, he took an inward breath, visualising it as a bright, energetic light, moving from his centre of gravity down to his tailbone and then up the spine causing that same electromagnetic glow he had experienced in the *taiga*. The *zhan zhuang* was not lost to him yet. Boris had recognised in him the natural, latent ability to control and focus his inner energy.

And here I am, practising this ancient art in a back garden in London!

He now understood that in its stillness, a paradoxical nexus could emerge, a *temenos* in which he could converse with his unconscious world of images and messages. In this state, the implications of Arthur D'albo's actions, or reporting to the intelligence services, had little meaning or relevance.

The subtle waft of roses, still in bloom, lifted his spirits and diverted his focus. His limbs tingled as he gently shook them for some time before quietly assuming the guard posture of *Baguazhang*.

Swiftly, he paced, sliding his feet around a wide circle, shifting his weight from one deeply bent leg on to the other while twisting his torso, to accentuate the pulsating flow of *Qi* out into his palms. He sensed that this combined spiralling and centring technique enhanced his own gravity: using the same vortex phenomena Ivan Yegorovich had harnessed with his machine.

Profuse sweating halted him, three quarters of an hour later and quietly exhausted, he rested his back against a mature laburnum, mentally collecting the energy back to the centre. Time, it appeared, had indiscernibly slowed down, allowing his thoughts to wander randomly and soon he was flicking back to Baikal's huge surface which would soon freeze over, locking in its secrets for another long Siberian winter. He could now only hope that Boris and Lubimov were safe and that his own escape would divert attention away from *Sphinx*. As for Yulia, her future might lay in the balance: the body that they had disposed of on the Turksib must have been found and the murder traced to her, yet she had still been willing to risk her freedom to help him.

Perhaps Boris will hide her in the taiga, just like Ivan Yegorovich.

The thought milled uncomfortably as a large hydrangea bush in the flower beds across the lawn, caught his eye. It had swayed unusually in the absence of any wind and scanning the ground, his sharpened focus caught a boot-tip, looming below its lower branches. He froze, inaudibly exhaling and slinking back against the trunk.

There were hushed mumblings before a figure emerged, crouching down low, followed rapidly by another, their faces partially obscured in the upturned collars of black fatigue jackets. Carty's stillness rendered him invisible as they skulked with their backs to him.

They took off, running at almost crawling height to reach the French windows before pausing to pull out their Glock pistols. Then they vanished inside.

For a moment he was confused. Hedditch had clearly told him that he would be under surveillance but evidently these visitors had more sinister plans. Numbed, his mind toyed with fear before his instincts kicked in. Sinking down, he quickly traced their footprints over the wet grass and slipped noiselessly into the house. For some seconds he hovered, his rationale overrun with the concern for the security of Diane and James. The only way he would be forced to give himself up would be if their lives were under threat.

But then I will also end up dead like Mark Boyd, in a mock suicide.

The unmistakable thud of footsteps down the staircase removed any luxury of time for strategy. He instinctively squatted down under the oak table and reminded himself that he had recently faced death in the *taiga*. He couldn't live in constant fear. This had to stop here and now.

As the intruders lumped past, he dived forward behind the second, driving an elbow up between his legs. The first turned immediately and automatically reacted, letting off a muffled shot. Carty had instinctively held the intruder in the path of the pointed gun and the shot had clipped the wrong man.

'Who are you working for?' Carty yelled.

The gun fired off a round and his human shield fell limp. *He deliberately killed his own man!*

Instantly the French window shattered with a shot, winging the gunman and dropping him. A second bullet burst his head before he hit the floor and then the tell-tale dot of a laser sighted rifle crisscrossed the room. Carty instantly slunk down between the two dead men, wrestling to control his rapid breathing. He panned the wall, watching and waiting for the dot to pick him out.

'Mr Carty!' a voice sounded seconds later.

Is this a game? Carty asked himself, play-acting dead as two strangers rushed into the room from outside.

'Shit!' One of them cried out and leant down to feel for a pulse but as he did Carty grabbed and locked the wrist, simultaneously swiping the pistol away and placing it to the man's temple.

'Don't move!' he articulated coldly, registering the shock in the stranger's eyes. 'And tell your friend to drop his weapon.' Carty pulled the man to his knees and swung around to sit behind him, squelching in his blood-soaked clothes. The other slowly followed the instructions, placing his rifle on the ground.

'Now lie down!' Carty barked. 'How many more of you are there?'

'None! We're the two-man unit designated to protect you.'

'You didn't do a very good job, did you? Who's your controller?' Carty tested, prodding the pistol barrel into the man's skull.

He winced. 'I can't tell you that.'

'All right then, we'll soon find out if you're telling the truth.' He reached up onto the table for his mobile.

Sixty

Monday 15th August 2005, Albion's Offices.

'Hi, Davina!' Carty casually announced to his former assistant as he stood in the doorway.

'Scott!' She beamed, racing forward to hug him, not quite able to believe he was alive until she had confirmed it with a touch. Carty noticed her tears and blushed.

'It's okay, Davina. I'm safe and sound but we've got some work to do to show the lovely men from the SFO that I'm not a criminal!' He joked sarcastically in the way he had always done with her.

'Where's that stick of rock then?' Don fired out, walking up to him and holding up a palm for a high-five. Carty chuckled, recalling the quip Don made just before he left for Kazakhstan. It seemed as if an aeon had passed.

'Good to see you, too, Don. How's the financial modelling coming on?'

'Sorry, Scott, orders from D'albo, no more emissions options!'

He shrugged and looked about. Nothing much had changed except that the team was a quarter of its former contingent. They congregated around him, amazed that he was actually among them again.

A quick scan of his former desk showed a mass of disordered papers and yellow sealing tape across his drawers and he guessed that the hard drive of his computer had already been imaged and pored over by the forensics.

What have I walked back into? His heart sank at the thought of the immensity of the task ahead.

Davina's telephone rang.

'Talk of the devil! It's Arthur,' she shouted over to him. 'He wants to see you and those SFO auditors in his office now,' she announced, pointing outside. Carty's eyes rolled skyward before turning to note the two grey-suited men. They showed a distinct lack of understanding in their manner as they sat in the glass-walled waiting room.

'They've been here for more than an hour.'

This isn't going to be easy.

D'albo, he knew, had no authority over these men or the investigation, but he evidently still wanted to demonstrate his power over his staff.

'I heard you were attacked in your own home, Scott. Is everything all right?' D'albo blurted unsentimentally as they entered the executive suite. Carty simply nodded back avoiding eye contact. D'albo read the body language.

'Good! Then let me introduce all the parties to each other. We have officers Miles and Hussey from the SFO.' He pointed them out casually. 'Mike Davidson is from Davidson, Trollope and Skinner, the independent forensic auditors, and across the table is Tom Jordak, President of Albion's security division.' Jordak swivelled in his chair, draping an arm casually over its back as he acknowledged the comment. Carty stared at him coolly, understanding that this was the fix-it man focused on limiting the damage to Albion's credibility and pointing the fraud squarely back at Carty.

'Tom is going to lead the forensic investigation.'

Davidson smouldered as he shook hands with Jordak, clearly unhappy with the arrangement.

Carty sensed the disquiet. 'Isn't that a little contrived, Arthur? I'm not sure if Tom understands the complex futures and options we were running.'

Jordak took the bait, his eyes narrowing as he flicked a glance at D'albo.

'Scott, I don't think we care for your comments. Tom has many years' experience and has already studied all of the positions you were running.'

'Whatever you say, Arthur. But we wouldn't want any reason to doubt the conclusions reached, would we?'

D'albo leered. 'Gentlemen, if you don't mind I would like to have a few words with Mr Carty alone. After all, he's still an employee of Albion.' The subtle war of words had got under his skin.

'So!' D'albo's bastardised American accent caused Carty's flesh to crawl as the man slammed the door behind the visitors. 'What do you think you're playing at, Scott? This is my show and even if you think you may be innocent until proven guilty, while I'm still in charge it's the opposite.'

'Thanks, Arthur, I'll remember that when I am asked in court about the cash you asked me to give to Kosechenko.' His blue eyes drilled back. At last he had come to terms with his father complex. There was no hook by which D'albo could emasculate him anymore.

'I don't know anything about a briefcase of cash, Scott. Are you trying to hide something; your guilt perhaps?' Sour-faced, D'albo postured in an attempt to intimidate, fearful that their conversation was being monitored.

Carty couldn't resist grinning as he articulated his words. 'But I didn't say *briefcase*, Arthur!'

D'albo feigned calm but his eyes blazed with anger. 'After all that I've done for you, this is how you repay me. You would be nowhere without my support and guidance over all these years.'

'But I *am* nowhere, Arthur. Everything has gone: my family, my career, my reputation, but I feel a damn sight more comfortable with that than with having to work in your shadow.'

'You better get out then. Only God can help you now. You're as guilty as hell!'

'Then I have God as my witness and time will tell who the guilty party is.' Carty steeled himself as he rose and turned to the door to leave.

'And don't think you got away with this. You're never going to be a free man,' D'albo shouted after him.

Carty should have felt jubilation at intellectually overcoming his mentor but he couldn't exorcise the sense of threat that the man's comment carried.

I'm going to have to find another way to extract myself from this situation, he reasoned. It had become clear he could never smooth talk D'albo to gain information about what he already knew was happening in the Irkutsk Oblast.

Mike Davidson lost no time that morning in revealing his timetable for the various issues he wanted to discuss and in quizzing Carty on specific aspects of the client accounts and how they worked. Davidson and the SFO officers voiced their concern over Carty's apparent unfamiliarity with the lack of due diligence requested by Albion's back office.

Jordak played on the more worrying issue: the damning evidence of Carty's signature on key documentation. These two factors had allowed a British Virgin Islands company to carry out trades on behalf of CentraniySib and in doing so, to embezzle funds without any alarms being raised, until it was too late.

'Gentlemen. I am leaving promptly at 5:00 this afternoon, if that is satisfactory with you?' Carty announced, glancing at the *Komandirski* as they broke for lunch. He had worn it that day for good luck. Davidson looked at the SFO men and then nodded his agreement but Jordak blanked him.

Carty aimed for the water dispenser where Davina was hovering. She looked up at him and smiled warmly.

'How are Diane and James taking all this?'

'James is great; he's getting used to me again. But Diane can't accept that I am back. I think our marriage is over.'

'I am very sorry to hear that, Scott.'

'So am I, Davina.'

'Do you think this fraud will be the end of Albion?' Her eyes searched his.

Dear Davina, he thought, *loyal as they come, just as long as her salary is being paid.*

'Probably for the derivatives desk. I suggest that you look for another job after the SFO has finished here.'

She shook her head in mild despair. 'Well, now you're back at least D'albo can take a holiday,' she cynically rebounded.

'I doubt it. The forensics will want to interview him again.'

'Well, they'll have to do it when he gets back!'

'Gets back from where?'

'He leaving for Head Office today.'

'What, Idaho? That's odd! He said nothing to me this morning.'

'Well, he's away for two weeks, three days of which will be holiday in the Caribbean. Apparently he's left Jordak in charge of the investigation.' She tilted her head in the direction of the interview room.

Carty was only partly paying attention as he mulled a thought. D'albo had boasted to Carty years before that because he was born in Switzerland to American parents, he was not domiciled in England for tax purposes. Any funds he earned offshore were not taxed in the UK.

Is that why Hedditch can't touch him?

The afternoon session revealed a far more aggressive approach from the forensics. They were firing hard questions at Carty, raised by analysis of client statements and records, indirectly accusing him of negligence in his duties. His earlier attack on D'albo now looked petulant. Hedditch could only protect Carty to a certain point and had done so by disclosing what knowledge the agency had of D'albo's involvement with the fraud. This still left Carty unsafe from being indirectly attached to any prosecution that Jordak was angling to make stick.

The SFO officers then demanded several fresh sets of Carty's signature to be analysed with those on the documents. He found the experience humiliating.

'When do you think the lab results will be back?' he probed.

'A few days, or perhaps a week at the latest.'

'It shouldn't affect our programme should it?' Jordak uttered indignantly.

Carty rolled his eyes at the officer. If only he had not been so arrogant in thinking he was *above* the checking of documentation on his trades, and so trusting of others, then perhaps things would have turned out differently.

Sixty One

'Can you get a couple of hours off this afternoon? There's someone I would like you to meet,' Green asked him hurriedly in a call early the next morning.

'Just as long as it's not a Jungian analyst,' Carty wisecracked. He used levity to help lighten his stress but Green blanked it.

'I see. Then let's meet at 2:30 on the corner of Walbrook and Bank, in the City,' Green instructed.

'Sounds good, I'll text you before if I have any problems getting away.'

It was 2:26 when Carty left the tube exit beside the Mansion House and walked the ten metres to where they agreed to meet. He kicked around watching the suits pound past. *What's the hurry?* He thought. Baikal had given him a peculiar point of reference to this bustling city, a sense of freedom, as well as a measure by which to gauge his own sanity.

A toot from a taxi pulling up across the junction, on Queen Victoria Street caught his attention.

'Get in!' Green shouted from the dropped passenger window. Carty sprinted the five metres or so to join his friend.

He felt a considerable comfort in being in the man's presence again.

'How's the investigation coming along?' Green enquired as the cab zoomed down Cannon Street. 'Is D'albo still being evasive?'

Carty shrugged. 'It's early days yet but I've been completely naïve. D'albo used my aloofness to play both sides beautifully. There are reams of trade confirmations, all with a fraudulent version of my signature on them!'

The cab took the slip road down onto the Embankment.

'He certainly took advantage of your blind side, but thankfully you listened to your intuition in time,' Green murmured, slipping forward to bang on the cabby's window as it neared Westminster Bridge.

'Pull over please. We're getting out!'

Striding into the middle of the street, Green immediately flagged down the next taxi.

'What are you doing?' Carty was confused.

'Never mind, get in!' he boomed.

'Turn back towards Blackfriars, please. I'll give you directions as we go,' he instructed, tumbling back into the seat as the vehicle swung out, across the wide road.

For a few minutes, Carty said nothing. Green had the driver bear off to the left and down a little-used side street, dropping below ground level before resurfacing some 60 metres further on.

'This will do, thanks!' he commanded, and the cab came to an abrupt stop. He leapt out and passed over a five pound note. 'Keep the change!'

Intrigued, Carty followed Green's rapid pace for some metres along a slim pavement and down narrow, worn steps, before stopping in front of a black door, heavily glossed and set back into the grey Victorian stonework. Green glanced quickly around and then rang the doorbell.

A demure, middle-aged woman answered, recognising Green and without question invited them both into a small waiting room.

'Please take a seat, gentlemen.' She wandered away. Green remained standing but Carty sat on an immaculately upholstered Queen Anne chair and took in the period paintings of semi-famous statesmen, adorning each wall. An overpowering scent of pot-pourri and the subdued tick from an ancient mantle clock kept the place from evading the present altogether.

Moments later she reappeared, quietly ushering them through into an oak-panelled corridor

'You know the way, Mr Green,' she instructed in her impeccable English.

Green invited Carty up an ancient staircase and at the top, knocked loudly once, before entering.

Natural sunlight filled a room that could not have been more dissimilar to downstairs: stripped pine floors, Barcelona chairs, and a contemporary desk over which a figure hovered, his hair greased tightly back.

'Hello, Gordon!'

'Scott, meet Jack,' Green announced.

No surname? Carty smiled hesitantly, holding out a hand. 'Scott Carty.'

'It's a pleasure to meet you, Scott,' Jack reciprocated and motioned to the chairs. 'Is tea satisfactory?' he asked, already reaching for a spotless sterling-silver cover.

'Hmm, unblended Assam, delightful aroma don't you think?' Jack murmured, pouring ceremoniously. Serious conversation was clearly not something he permitted before he had served his guests. It was a custom by which Jack had fostered the relationships of his well-established career.

'Now then, Scott, I hear you've had a bit of an adventure.' His restrained grin accompanied the passing of a bone china cup and saucer to his guest.

'You could say that!'

'And I'm sorry to hear that your minders weren't more attentive when you were paid a visit the other day.'

'Well, I'm still alive so I shouldn't complain.'

'Yes,' Jack rebuffed the sarcasm, his eyes now focused on pouring for himself. 'And how is the forensic work coming along?'

'It's tedious,' Carty shot a worried glance at Green.

'I must apologise, Jack,' Green interjected, recognising his younger friend's dilemma. 'I haven't yet told Scott who you are and why he can be totally open with you.'

He then turned to address Carty. 'Jack is a very senior member of the civil service and has full knowledge of your predicament and, of course, what Arthur D'albo has been up to. He is also a very old friend of mine.'

Carty nodded, understanding that Jack was probably responsible for ensuring ministers of State were well informed on matters of intelligence. He then continued, more relaxed.

'D'albo is currently at Albion's Head Office in the US...'

'...then on a brief vacation in the British Virgin Islands,' Jack interrupted. 'Yes, we know all about his travel plans, Scott. But what is the SFO doing with regard to his ghastly fraud?'

'The investigators are implying that I have been negligent in my duties and that I'm likely to be implicated in any litigation brought by CentralniySib, Albion or the Crown Prosecution Services.'

'I see their point.'

'Well, I don't. I'm not going to argue my case just yet, but I will when the time comes. D'albo is behind this fraud and the forged documentation. I just can't prove it.'

'We know.'

'Then surely you have evidence that the SFO can use to get me off the hook?'

'We can't do that, Scott. It will immediately alert D'albo and his friends to the on-going surveillance operations, causing them to cease their communications. That would then leave us totally in the dark about who, and what, is really behind this nuclear dumping operation.'

'But Hedditch is forcing me to do all the dirty work and yet he's not able to give me any assurances about proving my innocence.'

Jack adjusted his glasses. 'That's because the information regarding the fraud may have been obtained through sources that render them inadmissible in court.'

'Illegal eavesdropping?' Carty inferred.

'Look, on the face of it, the only crime D'albo appears to have committed so far is misrepresentation: claiming to act in an unofficial capacity for the UK government with various interested parties.'

'So it would be easier to take him down on charges of committing fraud?'

'Yes, but we want to ensure that we have all the information on the dumping business first, before we throw the book at him. D'albo had a number of Albion's back office staff moved around to facilitate his scam – a fact which, when challenged by the SFO, he claimed was a security measure to prevent fraud. He's extremely difficult to pin down.'

'Don't I know it,' he muttered, peevishly. 'The SFO have taken samples of my signature for a handwriting match. There's a 90 per cent chance that the results will show they're mine.'

'So, room for doubt!' Jack smiled coldly back, allowing Carty to take a short sweep of the two men. Jack appeared to be unhelpful but Green had brought Carty here for a reason. A hunch loomed. Jack wouldn't want to risk Carty opening up in court and implying that there was evidence withheld which could prove him innocent.

What the hell; I don't have anything to lose!

'I want to cut a deal!' he blurted.

'A deal!' Green reverberated.

Jack pulled back. 'Scott, unfortunately, in this instance we can't make deals,' he stated calmly.

'You might, if I told you that I had accidentally discovered why D'albo's friends were moving all that spent nuclear waste into the Irkutsk Oblast.'

The Whitehall man's beady eyes stared unblinking as he stroked his chin in a manner reminiscent of Edward G.

Robinson in *The Cincinnati Kid.* 'That would be very interesting,' he said casually.

Carty sensed the bluff. 'Well, if you want to hear more I have some conditions. If not, then I walk out of here and carry on assisting the SFO. If I am implicated as a defendant or as a negligent party in D'albo's fraud, then I cannot give any guarantees as to what representations I might need to make to protect my freedom. I may be forced to divulge all that I know, first to my MP under parliamentary privileges, and then in court.'

'Careful, Scott,' Green blurted. 'I invited you here as a friend, not to make threats!'

'Gentlemen.' Jack's forthright tone called for calm. 'Just what are your conditions, Scott?'

Carty eyed him nervously for some seconds. 'Firstly, Jordak, the Albion auditor, needs to be removed from the investigation. He's bent and will try to incriminate me by any method, fair or foul.' He sought acknowledgment from both men, but their silence remained pregnant.

'Second, I need to have some hard evidence demonstrating that D'albo is the architect of this fraud. And thirdly, I want your assurance that my family will be given protection for a very long time after all this dies down.' He scanned them as he spoke. 'The information I have is so sensitive that many people have been brutally murdered just because they were suspected of knowing about it, including the Americans and Lena Isotova. It's also the reason why there have been several attempts made on my life.'

'I am not certain I can give you all those assurances,' Jack articulated.

'I am pretty damn sure that a man of your standing can!' Carty bullied his host. 'They're not issues of national security and we both want D'albo behind bars.' His animated words rang with a brutal honesty.

Jack slid back in his chair and gently drummed his fingertips in front of his lowered eyelids. Seconds passed as he deliberated, weighing up the requests and the options open to him. Slowly his eyes opened fully to stare intently back at Carty.

'All right, Scott, let's suppose I can. I would need some guarantees from you in return.'

'Which are?'

'That you never speak of what you know – including the conversations today and those with Hedditch – to anyone. If you do, then you'll understand that we will not think very highly of it. I was contemplating having you formally sign the Official Secrets Act, but I am not sure that it would legally stand since it's your prior knowledge that is the issue here.'

'Jack, Gordon is a witness to these conversations. You are good friends so I will honour that friendship and give you my word.' He pushed out his hand in a gesture that forced the issue. Jack grasped it firmly, searching Carty's face as he did. He was curious for the story to unfold.

Carty sipped the tea and then began. 'It's simple, really. The Russians – I'm not sure if it's the State or one of the new oligarch-owned industries – have developed a technology that transmutes radioactive waste into harmless products.'

Jack's expression sat somewhere between incredulity and annoyance. He shuffled in his seat. Green simply returned a sublime smile. *Cheeky shit, outplaying us both like this!* he thought, having intuitively sensed that there was more to Carty's story on first hearing it.

'I know how it sounds,' Carty urged. 'It shouldn't be possible, although it is within the realms of quantum physics. It's modern day alchemy!'

'I see,' Jack sighed, 'And just how did you come by this information?'

'I began to suspect that the Americans were covering up the real objectives behind their visit to Baikal, having decided that they were too well informed about the nuclear industry!'

'And that's it?' Jack probed, unimpressed. Carty's eyes dropped.

'No. Lena Isotova had discovered that her boss, Kosechenko, was managing the dumping operation. She also had strong suspicions that D'albo was connected with it.'

'But did she have proof of any of this?'

'No, nothing tangible.'

'So how do you even know if this technology exists, let alone that it transmutes radioactive waste?'

'After I recovered, I was introduced to the elderly scientist who had spent his life developing it. He and his team were removed from their positions shortly after the collapse of the Soviet Union, and then, one by one, they mysteriously died. Guessing that this might also be his fate, he staged his own death and vanished into the Siberian forest.'

'More tea?' Jack asked, pouring without waiting for a response. 'The biscuits are also very good.' He offered a plate.

Carty resumed. 'The technology was decommissioned and assembled elsewhere in the region.'

'Now why in heaven's name would this man tell a complete stranger about an incredible technology such as this? And more importantly, why would you believe him?'

'It does seem implausible but he accepted that there was no other reason for me to be in Siberia, believing it was my destiny, after escaping near death, to learn his secret. He also understood that the outside world will someday need this technology.'

Green's eyes narrowed as he nervously scanned Carty's

Don't worry, Gordon, I'm not about to mention overunity to Jack.

'Your account sounds totally unconvincing,' Jack commented dismissively. 'But I will speak to the right people to obtain a technical assessment of what you have just told me.'

'I don't think you'll have much luck with that.'

'Why?'

'Because the physics we're talking about borders on conspiracy theory!'

'Scott, I assure you, I have my methods of finding out.'

'Well, I would like to know when you do.'

'You're not going to!' His tone was adamant. 'Gordon, any comments?'

Green swept his unfolding quiff aside. 'I'm stunned! If this technology exists and becomes mainstream, it would be the much awaited panacea for the disposal of nuclear waste.' He paused, his eyes heavy with a new worry, 'and that would then create an impetus for hundreds of new nuclear reactors to be constructed.'

'Why do you say that?' Jack asked.

'Because of Jevons' Paradox.'

'Jevons' Paradox?' Carty echoed.

'Yes. In the 1860s, Jevons proposed a theory based on the rapid technological advancements in burning coal. He predicted that with increased efficiencies, less of it would be consumed.'

'That makes sense.'

'But, it wasn't the case. Because of the improved economics, there was a greater incentive to consume more coal.'

Jack grinned. 'Dear Gordon, always full of useful information!' He picked up his cup, resting its saucer on his crossed legs. 'Perhaps, though, it's not such a bad thing. An increase in the use of nuclear power will reduce greenhouse gas emissions and climate change.'

'Hardly!' Green blurted, 'and it would also increase the risks of contamination to the environment through leakages, not to mention the possibility of another *Chernobyl* event.'

'But Gordon, that's not really relevant to Scott's predicament, is it?'

Carty pulled forward. 'Look you have to understand that this technology is totally unconventional. The Russians have found a unique way to exploit it covertly, by converting rich countries' waste under the pretence of storing it. It's highly lucrative. That's why anyone who learns about it disappears,' he expounded convincingly.

'What about D'albo, do you think he knows about it and how it's being used?' Jack posed.

'Unlikely. I think he is simply the go-between.'

'Well, we know what D'albo's incentive is for brokering the deal with the Japanese. Your story, though, does explain why they aren't receiving any reprocessed MOX fuel in return, and why both the Chinese and Americans are scrambling to find out what's going on in the Irkutsk region.'

'The Chinese!' Carty blurted.

'Yes, sorry, didn't I say that earlier?' The wily civil servant's trap hadn't worked. Jack drained his cup and then stood. 'Now, we have overrun a little and I must leave you. I have a rather important meeting relating to this and don't want to be late.' He turned his prominent nose towards Carty. 'Scott, thank you for coming here today, I doubt if we will meet again so I want to wish you luck.'

'And my assurances?' Carty fired back, anxiously.

'Keep your eyes open!' Jack's own eyes seemed obtusely magnified behind his lenses.

'I take it that means we have a deal.'

'Scott, I gave you my word. I trust you will keep yours!' He pulled on a dark blue mackintosh.

'Gordon, lovely to see you again and regards to the family!' He grasped his friend's hand. 'And gentlemen, if you don't mind, please have some more tea. Maria will show you out in ten minutes.'

He doesn't want to be seen leaving the building with us. The thought skittered as Carty scanned Green's face.

Sixty Two

Two days later.

Stepping out of his home, he was taken by an unexpected feeling of disappointment in the absence of the media. They had quickly lost interest in his story but the presence of an armed minder and an unmarked police car, kept his focus from slipping.

His mobile rang.

'Scott.' Diane's tone was shrill. 'I've just been asked to file an affidavit confirming that I have not handled or laundered any funds for you or for Mark Boyd!' Her strain was palpable. He had known this was coming.

'Why don't you come over later and we can talk it through,' he soothed her.

'After I've put James to bed.'

'Morning, Davina,' he shouted, noticing Davidson waiting alone, beyond the glass panelled room. 'Where's Jordak?' he asked.

'Head Office.' She stifled a grin.

'Is he meeting D'albo there?'

'I've no idea!'

Has Jack come through on his part of the deal? He took heart and stepped in to meet the forensics.

The clunk of the front door closing woke him abruptly as he dozed on the sofa, later that evening. His reflexes span him off on to the floor in a panic, conscious that someone may be attempting to harm him again.

'Scott!' Diane's voice called out, dispelling his fears.

'Why didn't you ring the doorbell?'

'Why should I? This is still my house, remember? Anyway your guard outside actually let me in!' She glared back at him. 'And here, you may want to read this!' Surly, she tossed a copy of the affidavit on the sofa. Carty picked it up and followed her through into the kitchen, watching her fall back into her former self as she routinely filled the kettle.

He remained quiet and she naturally assumed he was reading the affidavit but, sensing something else, she spun about to catch him scribbling down a note. He pushed it across the table into her view.

WE ARE PROBABLY BEING LISTENED TO.

She gazed at him calmly and took the pencil.

I NEED TO TALK TO YOU.

He nodded, raising a finger to his mouth and scribbled back.

NOT HERE, UPSTAIRS IN OUR BEDROOM.

The house had recently been swept for both bugs and micro-cameras. None had been found but he wasn't taking any chances: a device could have been easily planted at any time since.

Nina Simone's *I put a spell on you* washed through the background and with it Diane's cheeks flushed as memories of their lovemaking to its tones, flooded back. He grinned, gently tugging at her arm to pull her into the en-suite bathroom.

'So what did you want to tell me?' he asked, his mouth close to her ear as the shower pounded away in the cubicle, drowning out their voices to any eavesdropper. He expected something about the affidavit. She took a breath and settled on the edge of the bath.

'I met Davina yesterday for dinner. We took a cab and drove around for 30 minutes to avoid being followed, ending up at that back-street Thai café near where she lives. We went there once if you remember?'

He shook his head, impatiently.

'Anyway, Davina has found something that turns the allegations against you on their head.'

'Really! What?'

'She remembered finding a fax confirmation just after you had gone missing. It had slipped off the machine and down behind the office furniture. She felt it might be important.'

Carty's eyes widened. 'And is it?'

'Just a little! It's an automatic confirmation showing that a fax had been successfully transmitted as well as the date, time and number of pages sent. It also shows the dialled fax number.'

'Is it by any chance, a number in the British Virgin Islands?' Carty quizzed.

'Yes. Davina double-checked the dialling code – 001 284 – but how did you know that?'

'A wild guess. What date was it sent?'

'On the 16 June, days before you left for Kazakhstan.' Her face grew tense with expectation.

'What are not you telling me?'

'Part of the fax's content is also visible. There's a bank account number in Panama and the handwriting is D'albo's, Davina's sure of it.'

Carty flinched. 'Do you have a copy?'

'It's in my bag on the bed.'

'Then you must let me look at it.'

'Wait.' She held his arm, her eyes giving away her excitement. 'There's another document, which Davina cannot explain. It just appeared in one of her letter trays overnight.'

Jack's doing? He toyed with the thought as Diane quickly left to retrieve the two documents from her Hermes handbag. He smiled serenely as he watched, wondering just how long Nick Hall could maintain her taste in expensive accessories.

She handed him the papers, smiling. A weird combination of anticipation and fear bristled his being as he scanned the first page.

'It's D'albo's handwriting, I'm sure of it!' He confirmed, staring back at her. Then he gazed at the other sheet.

Sell all WTI calls on Monday.

It was an instruction to close-out all the crude-oil options. Just how many, though, he had only just started to uncover with the forensics, earlier that week. It was now evident just how much Jack's people had on D'albo.

'Was this one sent to the BVI as well?' he asked.

'Yes, you can see the number dialled on the top edge of the page. It was sent on Sunday 26th June at 11.17 pm. Who goes to the office and sends faxes on a Sunday night? It definitely wasn't you, you'd already disappeared!'

Carty hung onto her words but then his cool reasoning threw up a doubt.

'Using Davina's fax machine to send anonymous closing instructions doesn't prove it was D'albo.'

'Come on, Scott, his handwriting is all over it even if he didn't actually send it.'

She's right. It was damning evidence.

'Davina has made several copies and is holding the originals off-site. She's doing nothing until I have spoken to you.'

Slowly they then began to chuckle, like nervous teenagers, as the water thundered away, filling the room with steam. It seemed a fitting synchronicity with those conversations in the Ironmonger Row Baths, which ultimately led to his portentous meeting with Jack.

The smooth vocals were ebbing as they stepped back out into the bedroom holding hands. He fanned the papers in front of his face.

How can I deliver these to the SFO without suspicion?

'I have something else for you, Scott.' Her eyes leaked a tear. He froze, his rekindled feelings smothered as she handed him the Decree Nisi.

He slumped down on the bed and pored over it while she sat, touching him tenderly on the knee. It stated that the divorce was due to irreconcilable differences and the accompanying solicitor's letter shaped the conditions. He would keep the house in Hampstead and she would take the holiday home in Dorset and an agreed sum of money. Both would maintain James' education.

Carty couldn't complain; she could have already sold everything, presuming he was dead. His head sank to her shoulder. They remained motionless for some time until she lifted his chin.

'It is for the best you know.' She bravely wiped her wet, stained cheeks.

'So is it Nick then?'

'Yes. I want to be with him.'

'Does James know?'

'No. Perhaps you will explain it to him.'

'Yeah.' He stared back, his lids now heavy over his blue eyes.

Appreciating that she wanted his signature there and then, he complied and handed the papers back to her, believing that at the last minute she might reject them. She didn't.

As the front door clicked shut behind her, the impact of the revelations hit him. It was a strange coincidence that she had helped him in his quest for freedom, through the pursuit of her own.

Sixty Three

He rose early, drawn to the hanging chair in the conservatory, wrestling with a nervous impatience as he stretched his gaze out over the overgrown shrubbery. The import of the documents' contents and the possibility that they could ultimately buy him his freedom, had kept him awake for most of the night. The sun's early rays lit up the threaded veins of gold in the Baikal quartz and he knew that he needed to seek Green's advice.

'Hi, Gordon, are you free today?'

'Possibly, for a short while.' Green's answer was unusually nonchalant. 'We could meet at the same time and place as before,' referring to their recent convoluted taxi journey in the City.

There was an air of frustrated expectation about Carty as he sat with Davidson later that morning, the documents latent in his small leather portfolio case.

I need to be careful. Their premature discovery will look like I'm planting them, he contemplated, anxious that he was so near to escaping D'albo's clutches. *But am I?* The man would still probably maintain that Carty had colluded with Boyd and Lena in perpetrating the fraud.

He dove out at the appointed time and hailed a taxi, knowing that he would be followed. It slowed at the traffic lights near Bank station just as Gordon Green stepped out into the autumnal sunshine.

'Whitechapel High Street,' Green instructed the driver as he got in.

'Which end, gov?' the driver barked back.

'I'll tell you when we get there.' He slid the window shut.

'So, how are you, Scott?' he uttered, replying to his younger friend's stare with an inquisitive smile. Carty wasted no time in pulling open his case.

'Take a look at these!' He pushed the copies into Green's hands.

It took Gordon Green minutes to decipher their contents, before dropping them down on his lap, his brow flexing with the weight of the obvious question.

'How did you obtain these?'

'Can that wait until the next cab?'

'Naturally. Cabby, stop here, please!'

He passed a note through the window and tugged Carty's arm. They smoothly stepped out onto Bishopsgate and automatically flagged down another taxi.

'Take us to the Strand, please.'

He turned worriedly to Carty as they sat. 'Scott. Just what have you been up to?'

'A little investigative work: Davina found this fax confirmation some time ago but she has no idea where the other one came from.' He handed it back to the older man.

'Did she openly discuss these with you?'

'No, she passed them to a friend.'

'I see.'

'I've hardly slept, thinking about them.'

Green bobbed his head in feint acknowledgement as he scanned the document again.

'What is this telephone code?'

'British Virgin Islands.'

'And it's D'albo's handwriting I suppose?'

Carty smiled.

'Ha ha!' His guffaw caused the driver to shake his head. Hailing him in the middle of the road had not met with approval.

'It's Jack's doing,' Green muttered, grinning. 'But there's just one problem.'

'I think I know what that is.'

'When the SFO was called in, everything in your department was either documented or confiscated. If you produce these now and they are not mirrored in its records, then you will be accused of fabricating them.'

'I know. That's why Davina has to state that they were all found behind the office furniture.'

'Would she swear to that?'

'I'm not sure, but we're playing a massive game of poker here. If she does, the SFO cannot ignore them. It will be forced to investigate D'albo's links with this Panamanian bank account.'

'They don't need D'albo any longer!' Green murmured. 'Jack's just kept this whole process on slow-burn until you gave him that information.'

'Let's just hope Davina will do it.'

'Does she know?'

'Not yet.' Carty grinned expectantly.

'Oh, I understand. You want me to ensure that she does?'

'Could you?'

'Not directly, but I will think of a way.'

'Thanks, Gordon.'

Green put a hand reassuringly on his friend's arm. 'That was a pretty sharp stunt you pulled on Jack and I, the other day.'

'I had no choice.'

'Hmm, the implications of transmuting waste are huge and too much to contemplate right now. We'll speak again soon.' Green indicated to the driver to pull up.

'By the way, I saw Nick recently. He's a shadow of his former self.'

Carty shrugged. 'I don't know what to say, Gordon.'

Even after Nick Hall's unscrupulous behaviour, compassion still simmered for his old friend.

Sixty Four

Davina's stride quickened in thrilled anticipation of seeing the look of shock on the forensics' faces as they read the pages she was about to hand them.

Carty faltered in mid dialogue with Davidson as he noticed her approach, recognising the intent in her expression.

Had Green managed to reach her over the weekend?

'Mr Davidson,' she interrupted without knocking, her well-practised subservience allowing her to penetrate even the most senior of meetings.

'I found these documents,' she continued briefly flashing them. 'I think they are important.'

'Sorry, Davina but we're rather busy.' His tone was dismissive but the interest of one of the SFO officer's was pricked.

'Are they relevant to the investigation?' the man probed.

'They might be!' She leant forward, her blouse barely restraining her generous breasts as she slid the sheets across the matte surface.

He glanced over them for a minute before passing them to Davidson.

'Scott, have you seen these documents before?' Although attempting nonchalance Davidson's disbelief was transparent. Davina dipped her head to avoid eye contact. Carty, though, caught her for a split second before responding. 'I can't answer that until I've read them!' he jibed.

The SFO man passed the pages to him as Davidson swung back around to face her.

'Well, Davina, perhaps you can tell us again exactly how you came by these?'

'She doesn't need to answer that without her solicitor being present,' Carty gesticulated. 'And these look like *prima facie* evidence to me. The SFO needs to act on them.' His statement was aimed at the two officers. There were empty seconds before the more senior of them took control.

'Okay, Scott, you may as well leave for the day while we cross-check these with the document audit taken from your office. Davina, please remain here. I am sure there will be some questions that you can answer without a solicitor.'

'Then I should also stay,' Carty demanded, shooting a glance at her. She cockily placed a hand on her hip as if reinforcing her boss' statement. The officer hesitated momentarily.

'We can do this pleasantly, Scott, or...'

'I want copies of those faxes,' Carty uttered in mock capitulation before standing.

Davidson remained silent still poring over the discovery, clearly ruffled.

Carty was beside himself as he strode down the escalator experiencing mixed feelings of both elation and surprise as he began to realise just how seriously Jack must have taken his threats.

Nearing its base he caught sight of two men sauntering in the front lobby, their odd stares projecting an air of menace. Carty's nerves triggered.

'Can I help you?' he shouted out boldly, touching down on the polished concourse as one of the strangers peeled away to speak with the receptionist, preventing her from calling Security.

'Mr Carty, we're here to escort you home.' The other pulled aside a chequered sports jacket to reveal his ID.

'That's a good one. Last time I was offered a lift, I almost croaked! Anyway, my ride is over there.' He pointed at his despondent minder who had been relegated to a chair, overruled by these spooks.

'Your *ride* is aware of who we are.'

'I'm sorry but don't you understand the word *no*!' he shouted as fear rippled across his skin. The other man had moved back alongside to grab Carty's upper arm and reinforce the point. But at the moment of contact, Carty had simultaneously turned, leaving his arm empty and the man sprawling down on his palms. The first then moved in, clutching at Carty's lapels but he was immediately dispatched, yelping, as the sharp edge of Carty's shoe leather scraped down his shin. Carty then delivered a double-handed push, tumbling the man heavily over his grounded colleague.

'That's quite enough, gentlemen!'

Carty swivelled around to catch the familiar figure of Hedditch pacing towards him from the rotating glass doors.

'Scott. Do we really need to go through all this?' he asked, waving aside the two agents as they pulled each other up.

'Sorry, Hedditch, but I don't really trust strange men offering lifts. Anyway, what do you want? I thought we would never meet again.'

'So did I, but something has come up. Please follow me to the car.'

'I understand that you have negotiated a deal,' Hedditch laconically uttered, trying to conceal his contempt as they sat in the luxury of the Mercedes sedan.

'Perhaps I might have, but why are you picking me up now?'

'Orders.'

'Orders?'

'Yes. I don't know why but you're to have your bail lifted and be released from the investigation. There will be more evidence emerging in the next few weeks which will clear you of the fraud.'

'Released?' Carty's bluff was palpable.

'That's what I said. You'll need to go through procedures with the SFO and there will be a trial in due course. No doubt you'll be a witness too.'

Carty briefly mulled over the statement. 'Come off it, Hedditch, you just don't need my help monitoring D'albo anymore, do you?'

The evening was filled with a mixed sense of jubilation and anticlimax: Carty now had time on his hands but no one with whom to celebrate. Gordon Green was out of town and Diane was not answering her phone. He toyed with the thought of calling Sally. He had ignored her voice messages during the first week after his return and now remembered why: they had nothing in common at all.

As he sat musing over the extraordinary speed at which events had unfolded, an unseasonal mist rolled in from the Heath across his lawn. With it came the haunting recollection of Boris in kneeled ritual on Baikal's swathed beach, his voice resounding again somewhere in the ether – "*If the right man has the wrong means, the wrong means work in the right way.*" The words now rang with a sense of truth. The strange sequence of happenings had beggared belief but they had earned Carty his freedom.

Sixty Five

He arrived for work as usual the next day. Davidson and the forensics had been replaced by an ebullient looking man, who introduced himself as Giles, the SFO inspector now in charge of the case.

'Mr Carty, I understand that you are aware that some documents were discovered yesterday by Davina Nichols, your assistant.'

'That's right. I was allowed a glance but I haven't had the opportunity to analyse them in any detail yet!'

'Well,' he pulled them from an open manila envelope. 'Please would you do so now?'

A few minutes followed as Carty read them through again. Giles monitored him for the slightest *tell.*

'As I thought, they implicate D'albo, don't they?' Carty feigned ignorance.

'Yes, it would appear that they do.'

'And they support my alibi.'

'We never fully suspected that you were a guilty party.'

'Yeah,' he murmured.

Giles shrugged. 'But we would like to know how they suddenly appeared.'

'Hasn't Davina explained that to you already?'

'She has, but her explanation defies belief.'

'You don't believe her!'

Giles flushed. 'Surely you must know how these documents came into existence, Mr Carty.'

'No, no idea at all! I would appreciate copies though, to show my solicitor.'

'That might not be necessary.'

'Why?'

'We will be speaking with Albion's legal counsel to recommend that your bail be lifted and that you be removed as a suspect from this investigation.'

Despite Hedditch's tip-off the day before, his heart raced. The words were sweet music.

'All the same though, I would prefer to call my own counsel in to look over these documents, just for good order.'

'Of course, that's your right,' Giles retorted. 'And we would be keen for you to remain on call, to help wrap up the forensic investigations.'

'Just as long as Albion is still paying me!'

'That's Arthur D'albo's call.'

'Yeah, he has a lot of explaining to do when he returns from the USA.'

'I am afraid that will be my privilege, not yours.' Giles obviously sensed that the case's mysteries were about to unravel and relished the kudos in bringing the investigation to a successful conclusion.

Sixty Six

Three days later.

He couldn't have guessed that Green's promise of another trip to the Ironmonger Row baths would have followed so soon, but events had taken on a life of their own.

'Well, Scott,' Green hummed as they sat in the now familiar confines of the tiled hot room. 'Jack hasn't called me since we met with him, which leaves me to suspect that he took your information extremely seriously.'

'And he's kept his side of the bargain. Without those documents appearing, I would still be fighting Jordak.'

'That maybe the case, but it's a long way from being over yet, and you still need to be vigilant. Both CentralniySib and Albion will want D'albo's scalp and he will try to pull you down with him, or have his friends take you out of the game altogether!' Green's large face reflected an uncommon seriousness.

'What can I do?'

'All that can be done is being done, but you're still going to be caught up in this legal wrangle for a while.'

After some time they switched to the refreshing chill of the plunge pool.

'By the way, I have just been awarded a project by the London Mayor's office,' Green proudly announced, 'to consult on new social housing developments. We're considering micro-generation as part of the energy supply.'

'Micro-generation?' Carty probed, semi-interestedly.

'Yes, it's a novel twist on the household boiler: using the hot gases usually vented away, to drive a small turbine and produce electricity, which is fed straight into the grid.'

'I see. Two forms of energy are produced from the same unit of burnt gas.'

'That's right. It's simple, cost-effective and reduces emissions enormously. The idea is to produce affordable, energy-efficient houses.'

'It's a shame that I don't have the designs for Lubimov's solar-heat pumps,' Carty blurted.

'It is,' Green grinned, 'but I believe micro-generation could play a big part in mitigating the energy shortages Britain will face as North Sea gas dwindles and the country becomes beholden to foreign supplies.'

'And I guess that may just kick start the hydrogen economy and a behavioural change towards energy use and the environment, on every level.'

'Ultimately, nature is, and will always be, the true leveller of humanity. It simply gives without discrimination so that life can flourish.'

'I believe that's what originally drove me to develop the complex emissions derivatives.'

'That's refreshing. I'm wondering, though, if you would be interested in working with us. Your background and expertise would be a real asset to my small team, that is, unless, you want to go back to being an energy trader?'

'Can I think about it?'

'Of course.'

They wandered off into the steam room.

'You know, Gordon,' he swivelled to seek out his friends worn features. 'There's something I didn't tell you about what happened in Siberia.

Green's eyes widened into two shining buttons in the dense vapour. 'You've held something else back from last time we were in here?'

'I didn't think you would understand.'

'Try me!'

'It's to do with solar flares.'

'What about them?'

'Well, they follow an 11 year cycle of maximum and minimum intensity. The Russians have scientific data confirming that the flares are increasing dramatically, in both number and power, since the last peak year in 2001.' Carty shook his head. 'It also appears that the earth's magnetic shield has considerably weakened over the same period.'

'I think I know where you're going with this – a convergence of all these factors causing a *perfect* solar storm, threatening civilisation as we know it.'

'Yes. The Russians I met believe that the machine will be needed at such a time. It might be the only window of opportunity for change.'

Green's head swayed. 'I'm not convinced.'

'You're not?'

'No, not if you consider the *Rainmaker* story. It was because of the villagers' inability to accept their own apathy that an imbalance – the drought – occurred, forcing them to call in the old Taoist. Similarly, humanity needs to wake up and realise that in our drive for control over nature, we have unwittingly created a sublime monster that has the real power.' He drew a short breath in the stifling heat. 'And climate change may be in the zeitgeist at present but the constant desire for newness, satiated by the unsustainable production of needless *stuff* is just as big a threat to the environment. If, like the villagers, we don't reign in this reckless behaviour, a scenario will occur naturally, which will be beyond the capacity of any Taoist mystic or a super-technology to rectify,' Green uttered resignedly. 'But I suppose that it's always been the alchemist's predicament.'

'Which is?'

'The supreme task of redeeming the spirit trapped in matter. A rethink of how global funding invested into a new generation of efficient clean-technologies – like the nano-tech solar and hydrogen – will help turn a corner into a completely new but fairly conventional, energy revolution. The machine, for all its altruism, is not the answer. That an *overunity* technology exists at all is almost unbelievable but it simply must remain that, an enigma, until our human psyche has matured enough to use it wisely.'

"Only when the psychology is a match for the technology." – Lubimov's same message!

'But when do you think that will be?'

'Another 50 years, possibly more, so I urge you not to ever let on to anyone what you have seen.' His expression was nothing short of solemnity.

I wonder if Nick has told him about his Tesla magnets

In all the madness of his sudden return, he had selectively excluded his friend's brilliance from his thoughts.

Nick had known about overunity all along and, like Lubimov, quietly wanted my confirmation without being openly discredited.

Sixty Seven

Within days, a court hearing had lifted Carty's bail. The media had also rediscovered him and everyone was begging for exclusivity on his story.

He took a day's leave of absence before returning to Albion to collect his effects and calm his decimated team. As he stepped out of the lift he met Cynthia who, contrary to her usual contemptuous nature, raised a broad smile and showed him through to D'albo's office.

Document files were laid out across the floor in an orderly fashion and as Carty entered, Giles was striding around between them deep in thought.

'I have a lot more questions we need to ask Arthur D'albo then I previously thought,' Giles scratched his head.

'Like what?'

'Let's just say he was too cunning to have left any obvious evidence but we now have a much greater grasp of the fraud and a better idea of those who assisted him.'

'Who are they?' Carty persisted.

'All I can say is that a former junior minister of Her Majesty's government may be linked to these shenanigans.'

'Really! When was he in office?'

'Did I say *he*?'

'How long has it taken you to find this out?'

'A matter of days, but it seems the intelligence services have known about this for a much longer time.'

Jack again! He now realised just how deeply involved the agencies were.

'But who sent those faxes?'

'It wasn't D'albo. We've been checking camera footage coinciding with the date and time that they were sent.'

'You must have found something?'

'Only the night staff and cleaners had access to the building. It transpires that one of them, a young woman, quit recently. We're organising a nationwide search for her.'

'What about D'albo?' Aren't you going to call him in for questioning?'

'He's due back in a few days. We will wait until then.'

'And if he doesn't return?'

'That needn't concern you but suffice it to say that we are prepared, should he choose not to return.' Giles' look was fraught. 'Anyway, I need to be getting on.' They shook hands. 'I trust we can count on your help going forward?' His grasp lasted slightly longer than it should have done and Carty suspected he knew much more about this whole affair.

Sixty Eight

The muffled tone of his pocketed mobile barely woke him.

It came again.

Scrambling out of bed, it rang off before he could reach it.

It was 3:33, he noted, as the landline rang.

'Yes.' His answer grated with fatigue.

'I'm sorry to wake you but I've only just heard.' It was Green.

'Heard what?'

'Arthur D'albo...he's dead.'

Shock swallowed Carty for some seconds.

'He had a heart attack while riding a horse today. He broke his neck in the fall.'

'How could that have happened?'

'I'm not sure Scott, but it's late. Let's speak tomorrow.'

Carty slumped back, struggling with the news, confused, and yet also angry at being robbed of the opportunity to question D'albo's treachery in court. The dream of the chess game loomed again. D'albo had won with checkmate, but in life it seemed he had lost.

He woke late to the clamour of the media presence outside the perimeter wall of his Hampstead home. Green had already left several other messages as well as was one from Giles advising him that a car would collect him at 11:00 and that Scotland Yard detectives wished to interview him.

'Gordon, what the hell is going on? There's a press mob outside my house wanting answers!'

'News travels fast.'

'I'm going to need David Foreman again today.'

'I'll make sure he's with you at the interview. I wouldn't worry too much, though. It should only be routine.'

He gulped a coffee, slinking out of sight in an attempt to avoid the possibility of being photographed.

Has D'albo been killed or was it an accident?

The man, in his early 50s, was not unfit despite penchants for a regular cigar and a bottle of Jack Daniels. An overtly alpha-male behaviour combined with the increased stress, though, could have triggered a heart attack. Only a post-mortem would tell but the coincidence of the fraud turning against D'albo was telling. D'albo had slipped up with his Russian paymasters and the value and secrecy of the dumping business meant that no loose ends – like Carty's reappearance – could be tolerated.

The climate at the office was morose.

'CentralniySib's management have been formally advised,' Giles briefed him, 'and Albion's board wants to prevent a hostile litigation from a client whose business is potentially worth millions.'

'I guess we'll never find out how he forged those signatures,' Carty responded.

'We will in time, Scott. What I can tell you is that the girl sending the faxes has been located in Tampa, Florida. She obtained a green card to work and study there through her sponsor – Arthur D'albo. My colleagues have flown out today to interview her.'

'Poor soul! How did he get her to do that?'

'She comes from a single parent family and had dropped out of school. It transpires that D'albo had known her mother years before. We're not ruling out the possibility that she might be his illegitimate daughter.'

'Unbelievable,' Carty murmured, yet nothing now surprised him about his former mentor.

'I'm sorry, Scott, but as a matter of routine I need to ask you some further questions.'

'You do?'

'Yes. Can you tell me anything you might know about the circumstances of D'albo's death?'

'Nothing, Gordon Green told me early this morning. The news was shocking.'

'I'm sure it was. It's very convenient though.'

'Convenient?'

'For you.'

'What are you implying?'

'Let me put it this way. It's rather a strange coincidence that a number of people associated with you – Mark Boyd, Elena Isotova and now Arthur D'albo, are all dead!'

'If you have any suspicions that I am responsible for their deaths then why don't you charge me?'

'I don't work on suspicions, only on evidence. Surely you know something more about all this, something that you're not telling us.'

'No, I don't.'

'Well, I'm going to have caution you anyway. And while you're not a suspect we're will need to hold your passport until the investigation has been wrapped up.'

Carty wandered back to his office under a cloud, surveying what was for him, the end of an era. His mobile rang.

'How did it go this morning?' Green asked.

'Pretty rough, everyone is in shock. I am amazed that D'albo was so loved!'

'His face and yours are plastered across the news channels every 30 minutes so now it's your chance to force the game. You should insist that you're given a measured interview in front of the cameras waiting outside. Speak with Giles; it's the opportunity to tell the world that you've been completely cleared of suspicion.'

'What should I say about D'albo?'

'You'll need to check with Foreman. Just keep it minimal.'

By 3 o'clock the conference was underway and by quarter past it was over. In it, Albion's spokesman only wished to publicise the events of the day by stating that Arthur D'albo had died tragically and accidentally. Events, though, had come to light revealing that he was involved in activities to defraud both Albion and its clients of an estimated 150 million dollars, via an offshore company. He reiterated that all charges against Scott Carty had been lifted and that he would play a role in fully evaluating the fraud and the manner of its perpetration. Carty briefly spoke, explaining his sadness at the whole affair.

Sixty Nine

29th December 2005.

The Halcyon Days had always been a quiet time for Scott Carty, to rest and reflect on the year gone by and to galvanise his resolutions for the one ahead. This time around, though, he had only one: to shake free of the litigation, which was still dragging on.

In wrapping up the forensic work, he had satisfactorily uncovered how D'albo's options scam was used and in doing so, had exonerated himself. But questions about the man's egregious behaviour continued to haunt his logic.

What could have driven D'albo to so contemptuously risk the lives of others and ultimately, his own? Was he so bitter with his life?

It seemed that the man had been ruthlessly pursuing wealth at any price and as Carty churned over the possible reasons why, Boris' smiling face emerged somewhere outside of his field of focus. He was gripped again by the extraordinary occurrences at Baikal – the Earth's *Blue Eye* – a testament to the unknown powers that nature quietly possessed. One day his son would know what had really transpired there.

A deep concern for Lubimov's well-being now troubled him as did a gnawing sadness that had been with him every day since waking from the coma: the loss of Lena. Her soft, gap-toothed smile and grace of being, haunted him in those quiet moments, stewing over the 'what if' scenarios, had she lived. But she hadn't. The feelings she had awoken in him, though, had forged the courage to face what was missing in his relationship with Diane. It was essentially the fear of locked away emotions dragging him out of his depth, out of control.

In the months since his return he could only remember the scattered remnants of disrupted dreams. It seemed that *Basilides* and the maiden had deserted him.

"Does everything have to make sense?"

Remembering those words again, prompted a recollection. *The Wings of Desire!* He grinned broadly as he recalled Wim Wenders' movie masterpiece. Perhaps, as in the film, the apparition, a fallen angel gifted with a superior knowledge of mankind's fate, had supremely tested Carty's character through a process of self-learning.

Maybe this whole adventure had been just that, a test.

Now with the prospect of the fraud evaporating he would turn his mind to collating those scraps of paper upon which he had religiously recorded his dreams during his time away. Green had been the catalyst in persuading him to see the value of their symbolic messages rather than just dismissing them as an obscure flicker in the brain. And he would never have forged a friendship with Green, if it had not been for his friend Nick Hall who had sublimely seeped the possibilities of another world, into conversations, over the years. But in pushing carbon emissions in a quixotic rally to save the planet, Carty was ripe for an awakening. He just hadn't expected the life-changing events and their shocking insight in to what humanity might soon be facing: the *rational irrationality* of the modern world meeting, head on, the sustainable limits of the environment before being laid to rest by the collective psyche. The choice of how that might come about or even be mitigated was a responsibility that lay with every human being.

Green's unexpected call pulled Carty from his meditations.

'Scott, where have you been? I've tried to reach you several times over Christmas. You haven't returned my calls!'

'I'm sorry, Gordon, I was with James for a few days,' he responded apathetically. In truth he had not celebrated with anyone, in spite of the many invitations.

'Why don't you come over this afternoon?' Green's tone carried an undercurrent of excitement. 'We're having some drinks and there's someone coming who I think you would enjoy meeting.'

'Who's that, Gordon?' His curiosity was roused.

'Just come over. Consider it an excuse for an early New Year's celebration.'

'All right, I accept. Smart casual?'

'Yes. See you at four.'

He hadn't been to Green's house since that evening the previous summer, the evening in which the older man had initiated a doubting Carty into the world of the dream.

As before, Joey met him at the door before quickly running off to play with his friends.

'When is Joey back at school?' he asked Joanna as she took his jacket.

'He starts next week. I suppose James does as well?'

'That's right.'

She smiled kindly and ushered him through into the living room. Carty liked the comfortable warmth of being in her presence.

'Ah, Scott!' Green thundered. A throng of busily chatting guests hung around.

'You already know Jack,' he indicated with his throw away etiquette. Carty wheeled about and caught the Whitehall man's distinguished features and gel-plastered hair.

'Of course I do!' Carty smiled generously as he courteously threw out a hand to grip Jack's.

'How are you, Scott?' Jack asked in his polished diplomatic manner.

Is this who Green wants me to meet again? he asked himself.

Carty liked how straightforward Jack was in the face of the kind of knowledge that would bend most mortals towards drink or drugs. More importantly he was thankful that the man had, in part, secured his freedom.

'I am well thanks, and trying to get used to life after Albion.'

'Glad to hear it.'

Green passed an empty glass to Carty and poured Sancerre.

'There, let's drink to our brave friend. Not only did he survive the onslaught of his dreams and the trials of deepest Russia, but also the most despicable attempt to ruin his name and liberty.'

'Here, here!' Jack echoed, raising his glass to gently tap Carty's.

'Thank you,' Carty acknowledged. 'Without your help, though, I believe I would probably be either in a prison cell or dead!'

'Very dramatic, Scott, but you can be sure that a close watch is being kept on you and your family,' he whispered. 'We would however like you to speak with some government technologists, about that business that D'albo was involved in.'

Is that why Green invited me, so that Jack could discreetly tell me this?

'Any further conspiracy stories about D'albo's death?' Carty casually flirted in response.

'Whatever I think, Scott is inconsequential. D'albo had a lot of powerful friends and also, I suppose, a lot of powerful enemies. As far as I am concerned he had a heart attack and fell off a horse, and that's probably all you should concern yourself with.' His eyes were unswerving. 'Anyway, the important thing is that natural justice has been served.'

'Yes, and man's justice is to follow in a court of law.'

'I think you can safely assume that there will be no charges against you.'

'Can you influence the courts too, Jack?' Carty cocked his head as the man's expression turned po-faced.

'I know you consider my role to be above the law, Scott, but I work to protect any threat to it. It's the only chance we have to preserve the rights of the common man. My comment merely reflected that standpoint...we cannot have an innocent man being framed, can we!' He winked and took a slug of wine.

His job comes first, Carty mused, tapping his glass to Jack's again with a sense of gratitude despite a creeping suspicion that the man might be playing him.

'Scott, come through to the morning room, I have a something I want to show you.' Green insisted. Carty held his friend's expectant expression.

'Is it anything I should know about first?'

'After you,' Green replied.

As they ambled into the room still talking, Carty caught Joanna standing with Joey, in his peripheral vision and turned to meet her beaming back at him ecstatically. He was confused for a moment and then his mind froze with a sudden realisation. Standing beside her was a thin, shapely young woman, her blonde hair partly covering a face he immediately recognised. Her lips parted to a smile, revealing those unmistakable gapped teeth. He stared at her across the small space in disbelief.

'Scott!' she cried out, moving to him.

'Lena?!' he sang, cradling her cheeks in his palms and brushing her lips with his. Then he pulled back and gazed at her. 'I don't understand. How did you get here?' he stammered.

'Please don't ask me.' She threw her arms around his torso and lay her head on his chest, weeping. He held her close, taking in her same distinctive smell; everything else seemed to melt away.

'Well, my boy, this is the person I wanted you to meet!' Green announced. Joanna gently stepped up and took both of their hands, kissing their cheeks in turn. Then she gently held her husband's arm and led him out.

Carty wrestled to hold his emotions as tears welled up in his eyes. They were alone together again. What happened that last night at the Baikal camp was etched in his mind forever: he could still hear the echoes of her piercing shriek silenced by the gunshot and wondered how she had escaped the assassin's bullet. Lena squeezed his hand tightly, as if reading his thoughts. A grin slipped across his lips. These were questions for another time, another place.

Locked in an ecstatic embrace they kissed.

'Why don't you both come through and join us,' Green said, leaning in discreetly some 30 minutes later. 'Most of the guests have gone now.'

'Lena is free to stay in the UK under asylum,' Jack cheerfully announced gently putting a hand on Lena's shoulder. His familiarity with her didn't appear out of place. 'She escaped into China on the Trans-Mongolian railway,' he said, as if he was recounting a great story of adventure, 'and was in hiding for a while before approaching the British Embassy in Beijing.'

Of course! It was now obvious. The Whitehall man had given something away about the Chinese that day he left them behind in his office.

'Lena was able to tell us how you had arrived in Russia from Kazakhstan and about the attempts on both of your lives at Baikal.'

Carty smiled nervously, concerned at how much she might have known or said about her grandfather's technology.

Did she bargain this chip away to gain her freedom?

What he hadn't fathomed was that it was her confessions – not Carty's calculated threats – that had prompted Jack to provide the fax evidence against D'albo.

'She's safe here in England, but we're keeping watch just in case. I do believe that you two have a lot of catching up to do.'

'Thank you, Jack,' Carty said quietly.

An hour passed by in a mild haze of mulled wine and savouries before Carty announced he was taking Lena home. Joanna hugged them both.

'By the way, Gordon,' he caught the older man's gaze, as he contemplated the comment he was about to make. 'I've thought it over and I'm going to take you up on your offer.'

'My offer?'

'That social housing programme you mentioned – the micro-generation project.'

'Splendid!'

'Thank you for everything, Gordon.'

'No thanks necessary, Scott.' Green patted his shoulder.

Jack shook Carty's hand firmly. 'If you are going to be working with Gordon, there's a wind farm project that the Chinese have asked the UK government to assist in developing. I'm sure that you could offer your expertise in carbon credits.' Jack was a diverse man, well in tune with details that would cause others to lose interest. 'I will put you and Gordon in touch with them shortly.'

Seventy

As the low light of afternoon faded into evening, he found himself stifling so many burning questions thinking of how their lives would now be, together. Entranced by Lena's presence, he was at a loss to understand the feelings now engulfing him. Basilides had brought her back to him as he had promised.

I guess I must have proved myself worthy after all.

They embraced, water cascading over their naked bodies as the en-suite slowly filled with steam. He stroked her milky skin, savouring every moment.

'We have to be careful what we say. The house might be bugged,' he whispered, squeezing her close.

'Hmm, that was usual in the old Soviet Union.' She grinned, staring into his blue eyes.

'I saw you at *Sphinx*.'

'How?' His eyes widened in surprise.

'It was just after I recovered. Oleg Matissevich saved my life.'

'And mine too!'

'But you recovered faster,' she smiled. 'I was only able to leave my bed after you had gone into the *taiga*.'

'I don't understand! Why didn't Boris or Lubimov tell me you were alive?'

She shrugged. 'Lubimov told me that it was far too dangerous and that you would soon be leaving. He felt that you would insist on staying if you knew I was alive.'

That Lubimov – he's one hell of a player!

'And all this time I've blamed myself for your death, for making you reveal that Kosechenko was dumping that waste.'

'You didn't make me do it. I had to tell you.' She closed her eyes.

He held her head in his hands, brushing away the sodden strands of hair.

'I met your grandfather.'

'*Deda Vanya?*' she replied, her eyes shooting open again in shock at the comment.

Carty contemplated expanding on the conversations he had had on Baikal's shores with the master of *overunity* but decided against it. Whether she knew of the existence of the machine and its history was of no consequence at this moment.

'He's a remarkable man.'

'He was betrayed by a new Russia. I have a feeling that I will never see him again.' Her head dropped.

'And what's happened to *Sphinx*, to Lubimov and Boris?'

'I have no idea but Boris is a wild spirit, a man of the *taiga*, and Lubimov is needed for his ground-breaking work.'

'The laser acupuncture?'

'Of course.'

He searched her eyes. *Does she know more than she's saying?*

Seventy One

A castle's crenulated battlements stood out, just above the tree line. Carty knew he had been searching for it but the reason why had escaped him.

Soon he reached a clearing in the forest and found Boris sitting on the ground, littered with sycamore pods spiralling down from above. The Buryat caught one on an open palm and looked up, smiling.

'I've been waiting for you,' he uttered. 'And it seems he has, too.' He lifted a finger, pointing to the familiar outline of Basilides standing across the moat, accompanied by the maiden, resplendent in a white gown.

As his words trailed, Carty felt transported by some unnatural force across a drawbridge, alongside the two figures. They seemed pleased that he had arrived and together they turned to enter a long, arched tunnel. Carty was drawn along inexplicably in their wake, emerging out into the castle's grounds. There, they paused momentarily to take in the breath-taking view – a vast courtyard over 100 metres square, fringed by poplar and a perimeter stone wall. At its centre, an ornate round lake was squared by four life-size statuettes of Greco-Roman gods and babbling water sprang from the mouth of a huge, stone-carved fish.

Children's laughter distracted him and looking out he was amazed to see his son James and a young girl, throwing a ball to each other. The sun was bright and he felt tempted to swim.

'One must know before one can enter,' Basilides uttered. Carty turned to catch the figure's glistening blue eyes and the woman's smile conveying a deep sense of peace.

She took Basildes' hand to lead him away, up to the lake's plinth wall and then, together, they stepped out onto the water as it simultaneously rose up to consume them in a vortex.

Carty blinked and in that moment found himself alone in the forest, once more.

Lena, the woman he had grown to love, was lying serenely in his arms and a young crescent moon hung in the sky as he gently slipped away to record the dream. Its message was profound and he had an intuition to consult the *I Ching* once more.

Rolling the three worn coin, six times, he produced the hexagram.

Number 24 – The Return.

The passages resonated quietly with him and as he closed the book his instincts told him that things were now safe for them both.

Epilogue

Late July 2006.

The case was heard in the High Court in June. Carty had appeared as a material witness but his testimony seemed secondary, following the episode of two of the Albion directors and Duncan Watts *singing* in court. Each had attempted to divert blame onto the deceased D'albo, but their stories collapsed under cross-examination and they were charged with obtaining pecuniary advantage by deception, embezzlement and perverting the course of justice. Each received lengthy prison sentences.

The charges against the ex-minister were acquitted. His involvement had simply been the introduction of D'albo to various Japanese businessmen, receiving the appropriate introduction fees into an off-shore account. A separate case of tax evasion was to ensue and no doubt Jack's people would watch him in the future.

The young woman who had sent the faxes was, as Giles had suspected, D'albo's errant daughter, feeding a drug habit.

The media were then quick to give Carty's story coverage in Sunday supplements after his resignation from Albion, despite a tempting offer from its board to take on a senior position. He had chosen instead to focus on Green's projects and his dream-work.

In divorcing Diane he believed he had reached closure. She had saved his life through her actions, which could only have been born out of her love for him. It was a sobering lesson in devotion. They had agreed that James would visit him every second weekend and he decided to sell the house in Hampstead preferring to leave its memories behind. The urge to live with Lena had been pressing for too long.

Some days after moving in to their new home, and unpacking her possessions, Lena ceremonially produced a large plastic envelope that she had brought back from *Sphinx*. It contained papers that Lubimov wanted Carty to have but hadn't dared risk handing to him in case he was captured on the return journey. Lena was the safer option. She had held these back until the trial was over and the timing more auspicious. Moving in together was that moment.

The papers, written in Russian, contained detailed diagrams of Lubimov's hybrid heat-pumps and divulged the details of the photo-sensitive alloy used in their manufacture. She confessed that these had been confiscated by the Chinese and had no doubt been copied before being returned to her. Jack had also seen them.

So what if the Chinese have them, Carty thought. If there were one nation able to produce Lubimov's solar heat pumps, en-masse, at commercially competitive prices, it would be China, striving to solve its own environmental problems as it steamrollered into the consumer world.

Another document showed a graph. Its title, written in English, intrigued him:

"A correlation between solar flares and energy intensity."

It indicated the anomalies that Ivan Yegorovich had revealed to him and it seemed that Lubimov must have produced the data in collaboration with the older man. The upward trend line had been extrapolated forward beyond 2012, predicting solar flares with bursts of energy veering off the scale of any previously recorded data.

'Can I keep these documents locked away?' he asked, ruefully.

'They're yours!' She grinned back from where she knelt on the floor, her hands still deep in a cardboard box.

'What's in there?' He ventured as he looked inside it.

'These are my books from the apartment I shared with Tatiana,' she uttered jubilantly. Her former flat-mate had packed them away after the place had been ransacked.

'They are my prized possessions...a collection of Russian classics given to me by Ivan Yegorovich!' She held up one of the exquisitely, bound tomes. Gold Cyrillic letters sat embossed within its red leather dusk jacket. 'They were sent by my parents when I moved to London but I've never had the chance to read them, I was always too busy.'

She jumped up onto the sofa and, sitting in Carty's arms, tenderly fingered through *Crime and Punishment*. Soon, though, she was frowning at an opened page.

'What's a trout engine?' she proclaimed as she translated from the Russian.

Shocked by her words, he instantly lurched forward and grabbing the book from her, rapidly thumbed through it to find miniscule Cyrillic text and engineering diagrams of great detail, littering its pages. Then he stopped, his face drained as he came upon something he thought had simply been a figment of his imagination. There it was: a diagram of the *machine* in full technical wonder.

He fell quiet for some seconds, stunned and visibly emotionless, but taking it all in as if studying a complex options structure.

'What it is?' Her puzzlement confirmed that she was unaware of its true nature. This instruction manual had been sitting in London, for some years, unknown to Lena. It had been deliberately prepared at great cost by Ivan Yegorovich and passed on to her as a legacy, for safe keeping outside Russia. Fate now had Carty stumbling across the technology once more and its message was undeniable.

Gordon is wrong. The machine is needed!

And there was only one person with whom he could begin to discuss its possible construction. That person was Nick Hall.

Afterward

In May 2014, a few months after the first edition of Blue Eye went into print, I learnt from a NASA bulletin that a solar superstorm had narrowly missed the Earth during the summer of 2012. The news caused a chill to ripple up my spine, leaving me to reflect on the somewhat prophetic aspect of Blue Eye. Of course, it isn't a prophecy but the facts remain sobering.

On 23 July 2012, an enormous plasma cloud or "Coronal Mass Ejection" was spewed from the Sun, four times faster than a typical eruption. Analysis of the data has shown that the storm might have been stronger than the 1859 Carrington Event itself. It was a narrow escape. Had the eruption occurred just one week earlier, the blast would have directly impacted the Earth wreaking such chaos, that we would still be picking up the pieces more than two years on.

http://science.nasa.gov/science-news/science-at-nasa/2014/02may_superstorm/

http://www.youtube.com/watch?v=7ukQhycKOFw

Acknowledgements

My heartfelt thanks to my family who have been a source of inspiration and love, and have generously allowed me the time to complete this work, and to the late Graham Gordon-Horwood, kindred spirit, dream-worker and master of the *neijia*, who first fired my inspiration and to whom this novel is dedicated.

My appreciation to: Barbara, Josie, Daniella, Tibor, Merritt & Paula, Richard & Diana, Monica & Anthony, Justine, Clive, Claudia, Gaynor, Henriette, Emma, Cyrus, Nick, Birgitte, Melissa, Jazz, Stella and Coralie, for reading the successive drafts and giving me essential critical feedback.

Special thanks to: Dr Anthony Soyer, for his compassion and sage-like knowledge on matters of the body, mind and the spirit; David Guyatt, for his pragmatic state-of-the-world perspectives and his insights on Jungian dream-work; Richard Napper for sharing insights on the *neijia*; Sam Bourne, for her friendship and creative flair; Neil Fox for superb design advice and Wayne Dorrington for the inspired book cover; Birgitte Knaus for her indefatigable artistic spirit; Karen Scott for her spiritual support; Joel Simons, Olivier Post, Rodney Love, and Antoine Laurent for their respective editing brilliance; Sarah Juckes' guidance at Completely Novel and; Justin Solomon's *Byte the Book*, the friendliest forum in town.

Finally, eternal gratitude to Carl Gustav Jung, pioneer of the unconscious, and to the *neijia* masters: the Yang Family, Chen Pan Ling, Sun Lu Tang, Han Xing Yuen, Chu King Hung and many others, who, down the centuries, have preserved these arcane practices for the sake of future generations.

About Blue Eye

If you wish to know more about the issues behind *Blue Eye* and what lies in store for *Green Eye,* the next in the trilogy, please visit: http://www.blueyethebook.com

About the Author

Tracy Elner grew up in the London of the 1960s & 70s inspired by the natural world, conjuring, martial arts and some great friendships. In an international career spanning 25 years, he has been a material scientist and a commodities trader. During this time he visited some lesser-known parts of the world, including the former Soviet Union, as it stumbled into the world of the free-market. More recently, he consults to the renewables and emissions sector, using his real-world nous of business commerce and culture to help meaningful projects balance their expectations. He is also an ambassador of the Going Blue Foundation – the first global campaign to fight water pollution at source.

In his personal life, he finds himself most comfortable with conscious, creative people with whom he can enjoy the mutual sharing of knowledge. He has been practising and teaching the *neijia* healing arts for over thirty years and appeared on the TV programme *01 for London* in the 1990's, showing how they can be used to re-balance and energise daily life. He has also spent a similar number of years striving with dream-work for personal wholeness and wellbeing.

Blue Eye weaves his many unusual experiences into a modern day thriller concerning the global energy paradigm, sustainability, international business, love, and the journey of transformation for its hero, Scott Carty. It also raises some possibilities that defy this consensus scientific age. @blueeyethebook